MIDNIGHT
IN
EVERWOOD

M.A. Kuzniar spent six years living in Spain, teaching English and travelling the world, which inspired her children's series *The Ship of Shadows*. Now she lives in Nottingham with her husband, where she reads and writes as much as she can and bookstagrams @cosyreads.

MIDNIGHT
IN
EVERWOOD

M.A. Kuzniar

ONE PLACE. MANY STORIES

HQ
An imprint of HarperCollins*Publishers* Ltd
1 London Bridge Street
London SE1 9GF

www.harpercollins.co.uk

HarperCollins*Publishers*
1st Floor, Watermarque Building, Ringsend Road
Dublin 4, Ireland

This edition 2021

1

First published in Great Britain by
HQ, an imprint of HarperCollins*Publishers* Ltd 2021

HB ISBN: 9780008450663
TPB ISBN: 9780008450670
US HB ISBN: 9780008500405

MIX
Paper from
responsible sources
FSC™ C007454

This book is produced from independently certified FSC™ paper
to ensure responsible forest management.

For more information visit: www.harpercollins.co.uk/green

This book is set in 11.5/15.5 pt. Centaur

Printed and bound in Great Britain by
CPI Group (UK) Ltd, Croydon, CR0 4YY

For the sisters of my heart,
Chelsea Brothwood, Hannah Kuzniar and Christine Spoors

ACT ONE

Scene One

Marie looked very pale in the morning and was scarcely able to say a word. A hundred times she was going to tell her mother or Fritz what had happened, but she thought: 'No one will believe me, and I shall only be laughed at.'

—E.T.A. HOFFMANN, THE NUTCRACKER

Chapter One

Marietta Stelle's mother always said that nothing good came of a rainy day. However, it was a rainy day when the magic came, and once magic has entered your life, you stay in its glittering clutch forever.

A mysterious new neighbour – who Marietta would later come to learn went by the name of Dr Drosselmeier – heralded the arrival of magic and wonder in her life. Though he appeared to be but an ordinary man, enchantment clung to him. It dripped from his voice, seeped out from under his skin and whispered around his eyes.

Marietta was dipping in and out of pliés at her ballet barre when she happened to glance out her window and witness his entrance. A black town hat bobbed along the cobbled street below. The cloaked figure carried a single case, pausing to look up at the sprawling townhouse Marietta called home. He seemed to look straight through her, so Marietta took a step back from the window to study him from a more covert position: his face was clean-shaven, fair and younger than one would expect, considering the sweep of silver hair peeking out from beneath his hat. Creases burrowed into the skin at the corners of his eyes, marking him as a gentleman in his late thirties perhaps, and his irises were an intense frosted blue, lending him a bewitching stare.

The curtains of rain sheeting down Marietta's window failed to touch him and, after a momentary hesitation, he continued on his way. Rising up onto demi-pointe, her attention snared, Marietta watched him stride into the equally grand vacated townhouse opposite the Stelles'.

'We seem to have acquired a new neighbour,' Frederick announced later at dinner.

'Is that so?' their mother asked. She smoothed a hand over her honey-tinted coiffure, as if he were to make an appearance that instant. Ida Stelle's dark-blue eyes were a mirror of Marietta's, only hers were accompanied by a delicate nose and pinched chin beneath her lighter hair rather than the firm jaw, aquiline nose and raven hair both Frederick and Marietta had inherited from their father.

'A former doctor,' Frederick continued, 'turned inventor, so I hear. No family to speak of. He must possess a sizeable inheritance to have purchased the entire townhouse for him alone, though I failed to recognise his name. It was rather an unusual one; Drosselmeier.'

'No doubt he's of German heritage,' their father said, shaking a starched napkin out and draping it across his knees. 'How curious, it has been quite some time since we've had a new acquaintance on this street. We shall have him dine with us one evening to take his measure ourselves. An inventor, you say? In which direction do his talents lie? Telephones? Electricity? Is the next Marconi in our midst?'

Frederick gave a polite cough. 'In children's playthings, I believe. Toys and such.'

Theodore set his sherry glass down harder than was warranted. A few drops bloodied the ivory tablecloth. He harrumphed, the tips of his ears pinkening.

Marietta met Frederick's eyes. Theodore Stelle was not

a man persuaded of the merit or delights in creative pursuits. Marietta clenched her soup spoon, the familiar argument wearing deeper grooves into her patience each time it reared up.

'I shall extend an invitation,' Ida said, scanning the dining room, eager at any excuse to entertain a guest in their fine house. Her gaze took in the emerald and cream striped wallpaper, the large mahogany table and chairs, polished floorboards and huge arrangements of hothouse roses spilling over crystal vases, perfuming the room with the faint odour of decay. 'I have yet to hear mention of him among my acquaintances; I shall ensure ours will be the first dinner he attends.' She frowned at a petal that showed signs of spoiling.

Theodore gave a disapproving sniff. 'Are you certain that's wise? Perhaps he has yet to be mentioned for good reason.'

'Yes, I too am dubious on his trade selection. However, we mustn't let that discourage us,' Ida said. 'He's invested in a superlative address, which suggests he comes from good stock—' her eyes flicked to Marietta and back to her husband '—or a sizeable inheritance. This bears further investigation.'

Marietta glanced down at the table setting, growing hot beneath her Paquin dress in palest periwinkle. The voluptuous sleeves – edged in whisper-thin black lace that had so drawn her to the couturier's creation on her last visit to Rue de la Paix – now itched unbearably under her mother's matchmaking insinuations. Ida had been eviscerating a fortune on gowns at the House of Worth whilst Marietta had stolen away next door. She'd admired the delicately embroidered roses tumbling down the silky dress before purchasing it and absconding on a walk as her mother continued shopping. The afternoon free from her mother had been as happy as the blossoms that had floated through the streets of Paris that spring and she had a sudden, sharp longing for that halcyon day.

A flick of colour pulled her from the macaron-sweet memory, incongruous amongst the porcelain plates and silverware. A smear of gouache licked up Frederick's wrist, a flare of burnt sienna. She flashed him a look and he tugged his charcoal jacket sleeve down to hide the offending stain.

'Tell me, Frederick, what have you been occupying yourself with of late?' Theodore beckoned for his glass to be refilled. A footman obliged him and he studied Frederick over the Madeira.

'Much of the usual, I'm afraid, Father. My studies leave me very little time to devote to anything else.'

Frederick's lies were as sweet as the sherry Marietta sipped. She regarded the smile Frederick had pasted on as he deftly handled their father's inquiries. Only Marietta knew of the canvases stacked in Geoffrey's room – Frederick's closest friend and, as Marietta had learnt after being taken into her brother's confidence, his secret beau.

Frederick's experimentation with the new Fauvism movement translated to wilder brushwork and stronger pigmentation than she'd seen him paint with before. 'The likes of Matisse and Derain are sending the Parisian art world into an uproar,' Frederick had explained to Marietta some weeks earlier. 'When Louis Vauxcelles saw their paintings in the Salon d'Automne last year, he declared them "les fauves", wild beasts of colour and brilliance and life. Mark my words, art cannot die; art is the future and it is as tightly intertwined with my own lifeblood as ballet is with yours.'

To their parents' knowledge, Theodore had stamped out Frederick's passion for painting before his voice had broken, diverting his path onto law school. Frederick was now a post-graduate student, following in their father's footsteps and eventually bound to join Theodore in presiding over the courts of Nottingham. It was Theodore's position as a high court judge that had led to his being bestowed the courtesy title of Baron, a too-appealing prospect for the young Ida, who was a woman of means but craved the delicious satisfaction of her sisters addressing her as The Right Honourable. The match had suited the equally socially ambitious Theodore and the pair had been manoeuvring themselves upwards ever since. Having children proved to be another asset which they could use to aid them in this endeavour.

Marietta pointed her toes beneath the table, considering whether she ought to have the dressmaker adjust her dress so she might dance in it. The blush roses were the exact shade of her pointe shoes.

Theodore turned to her. 'And how have you been spending your days?'

Her daydream melted away, leaving her with the dregs of reality. 'I—' Her thoughts were slow, sticky as caramel.

'The usual agenda of shopping and luncheons.' Frederick came to her aid, raising his eyes to the heavens.

Marietta smiled at him and he inclined his head. The extra ballet practices that had been consuming her time remained an unspoken truth.

'That reminds me, your mother has informed me that you failed remarkably in sustaining Lord Compton's attention over afternoon tea last week, despite her efforts in contriving a meeting between you.'

Marietta's royal cheddar soup – already cold having been served room temperature so as not to necessitate the unseemly blowing upon it to cool it – turned thick and cloying in her throat. She sipped her sherry in an effort to settle her mood. When she spoke, it was in a more assured tone. 'Charles Compton is an utter bore and thoroughly ill-natured.' In fact, he had spent the entirety of their afternoon in the brand-new Ritz expounding on the chestnut thoroughbred he was having shipped from Argentina. Marietta had learnt far more than she had ever desired on the subject of polo ponies and had scarcely uttered more than a word. Though she had observed that his unfortunate macrodontia lent him a certain resemblance to his beloved thoroughbred. Grounds for marriage, it was not. By contrast, Ida had spent a pleasurable few hours drinking in the duchess's scrutiny of their dining companions and the Palm Court décor, redolent in soft apricot, panelled mirrors reflecting the sparkling chandeliers a thousand-fold.

Theodore's nostrils flared. 'Might I remind you that Lord Compton is the Marquess of Northampton. The next time you choose to insult a peer of the realm, you ought to recall that I have been more than generous in allowing you to host your upcoming performance in our ballroom. It is high time you demonstrated a little gratitude. I have invited Lord Compton and several other suitors to our Christmas Ball in the hopes that they shall find your dancing an attractive quality in a prospective wife. Perhaps this will even hasten a betrothal.'

Marietta regarded her father coolly over her crystal glass.

'Darling, it is most unbecoming to be unmarried at your age,' Ida added. 'When I was twenty, I had been married for three years.' She paused. 'Perhaps Lord Compton shall give you a second chance.'

Frederick cleared his throat before she could respond. 'Father, what are your thoughts on this new battleship? They say the HMS Dreadnought will revolutionise our navy.'

The soup course was cleared away and the next course brought in, the footmen fading into the background, ever-present shadows. Marietta tuned out the politicking between her father and brother, grateful for Frederick's interception of the conversation before she had spoken out of turn. Conversing with her father was a tactical art not unlike a game of chess; it necessitated clear strategy and focus.

She laid her silver fork down, the aroma of thick pastry and gravy clotting her stomach. Gazing out the window, she imagined the candle perched against the dark glass as a star to be wished upon. When she danced, she was a conjurer, writing spells with the whirls and arcs of her body. Her dancing was hers and hers alone, not for the enticement of any man, nor for her father to wield as a weapon against her. When she danced, she flew on gossamer wings that lifted her away from the dragging weight of her family's expectations. Enticed her with a glimpse of an alternate path to the one she was obligated to tread. When she danced, she had a voice. And nothing was more fearsome than a silent future.

Chapter Two

Though the hour had yet to descend into evening, the late November afternoon was ink-dark and thick with gloom. Streetlamps shone through the rain, a line of beacons that the horses followed, whisking Marietta to her ballet class in the Stelle family carriage. Thunder rolled through distant skies and cafés blazed with light and the promise of warmth as passers-by rushed inside.

Beside Marietta, Miss Worthers pursed her lips. 'Such terrible weather in which to be gallivanting about the city. Still, we might as well use our time wisely. Shall we go over the approved talking points for your next conversation with Lord Compton? Your mother has already drawn up a list.'

Marietta turned her attention to the carriage window. 'I would rather not.' They were passing through Old Market Square, which was bustling with preparations for the annual Christmas market, large crates unboxed to reveal glimpses of gingerbread and glass baubles. Marietta hoped the rain would freeze into snow in time for its grand opening. She heard Miss Worther's disproving sniff and awaited the inevitable diatribe. Her former governess turned paid companion was under the employ of her father and she had no doubt the beady-eyed woman was reporting back a log of her activities until she was safely married off. In the meantime, Marietta was forced to endure her suffocating presence like a second corset.

'I implore you to consider the consequences of your actions,' Miss Worthers chided. 'It is most unbecoming at your age to demonstrate such disagreeability.'

'I am beginning to suspect that the term *unbecoming* is used whenever one is met with a difference in opinion,' Marietta said wryly. Before her chaperone could voice another criticism, before the horses had halted, Marietta opened the carriage door and jumped down. Ducking under the brim of her hat, she lifted her high-waisted skirt up over her laced boots, and dashed in through the door marking the entrance to the ballet studio. She felt Miss Worther's stare score her back. When the carriage clattered up a narrow side street to lie in wait for her class to finish, Marietta sighed in relief as she hurried up a steep flight of stairs and into the safety of the dressing room, where she slipped into her softer dancing dress and ballet slippers.

Marietta was the first one in the studio. Warming up, she eased into lower and deeper stretches, cajoling her muscles after the damp and cold that had permeated her bones. Water ran in rivulets down the large windows on each side of the studio. It was perched atop the building, up another steep flight of stairs, an eyrie overlooking Goose Gate. The studio was a blank canvas. Pale wooden floors and mirrored walls waiting to be painted in music and life. Two long barres were fixed beneath the windows on each side and a small worn piano was set next to the door.

Inside the townhouse, Marietta's feelings were tightly corseted, but here that corset had been shucked off and she had escaped any watchful eyes. She leapt across the studio in a series of grand jetés, luxuriating in her freedom. As she performed a series of tight spins, twirling down the centre of the studio, her frustrations floated away as she felt the weight of expectation vanish until there was nothing but her and her dancing. She whipped a leg up high behind her in a penché, the vertical split a triumphant finish. But she was no longer alone.

Her ballet mistress glided into the studio, her spine as straight and unyielding as the starched collars returned from the Stelle launderer, despite the antique silver-plated cane she used. Olga Belinskaya had been born in St Petersburg in the early nineteenth century and was a former Imperial ballerina at the Maryinsky Theatre. She oozed glamour and refinement in a pastel chiffon gown, each step, each movement considered and elegant. Few lines dared creep across her classic Slavic features, her green eyes sharp and framed with false eyelashes, her silver hair pinned in a bun, shrouded by an emerald silk scarf.

'*Pozhaluysta*,' she said, sweeping a hand out. Marietta caught a flash of the sapphire cocktail ring rumoured to have been gifted to her by one of the tsarevnas after an exquisite performance of the pas de deux in the second act of *Giselle* had brought the young princess to tears. 'Continue.'

'I have finished.' Marietta swept a hand over her forehead. 'I wouldn't wish to intrude on class time.' She might be The Honourable Marietta Stelle, but in this studio Olga was of higher rank.

Olga struck the floor with her cane. 'You are in my studio, *devushka*; it is in my purview to decide when the class begins. Show me the Rose Adagio.'

Marietta swallowed her protests; Olga was authoritarian in her teaching, and if anyone disobeyed, the following class would hold an empty space at the barre. She stepped into the allegro entrance. One of the most technically challenging pieces in ballet and pinnacle of the role of Aurora she had been cast in for their upcoming performance of Tchaikovsky's *The Sleeping Beauty*, she was unused to performing it as a solitary adaptation, striking high balances en pointe.

'Pay attention to the shape of your arms; remember, dancing is in the details. Register the music and respond accordingly.'

There was no music playing but as Marietta spun slowly in place, keeping the arch of her back taut, she imagined the sweet strains swelling and spilling out into the studio. Ballet was the golden key to a world of her own, one which she never desired to leave. She pirouetted, lost within that world, spinning out into a high arabesque, when she became aware that the door was cluttered with onlookers; the rest of the class had arrived.

Olga ignored them. 'Your balance must be poised and assured. Tilt your face up,' she snapped with another thud of the cane. She stepped closer, until Marietta was enveloped in the heady scent of Jicky, her trademark perfume; a swirl of lavender and vanilla with an animalistic heart that felt overwhelmingly intimate. 'Feel the movement, it must be as ephemeral and fleeting as a wing taking flight.' She raised Marietta's chin with her cane. Marietta wobbled, struggling to maintain her balance on a single pointe. 'Ballet resides in your bones; it courses through your blood. For a dancer, it is the very essence of our identity, stripped down to its rawest, most intrinsic parts; you cannot leave it behind any more than you could forsake your own soul. Feel it. Feel the exquisite pain that comes from the purest form of love, for that is what it means to dance ballet.'

Olga walked away. Marietta was dimly aware of her calling for the others to enter and the studio filling with regimented lines of dancers. The air was thick with glances towards her and curious whispers. She took her place at the barre, Olga's voice still echoing through her.

An uncomfortable prickling gave way to a seeping awareness.

She could not sleepwalk through a life of luncheons and dinners and a marriage that would pin her in place, a butterfly with steel pins puncturing its wings, preserved and beautiful in its glass cage though its heart beat no longer.

She needed to set herself free.

Chapter Three

The following week was fleeting and stormy. Rain churned the skies over Nottingham, darkening their evenings and thickening the mood within the townhouse. It seemed the more Marietta tried to hold onto her final days of dancing, the faster they slipped away from her. The dark clouds pressed down on her as rehearsals for the Christmas performance of *The Sleeping Beauty* grew in intensity, punctuated by discussions and decisions over the dancers' futures, and the frivolous gossip on Drosselmeier that seemed to be voiced wherever Marietta went. As she stretched at the barre between rehearsals, the conversation of two of her acquaintances fluttered over her.

'Mother's cabled to Paris for a sylph dress for my Company audition. I do hope it arrives in time. I shall be most vexed if I have to perform without it; evoking the tone of *La Sylphide* is paramount,' Victoria said, pinning her chestnut hair into a glossy bun and dousing herself with a liberal cloud of La Rose Jacqueminot. She let out a theatrical sigh. 'I do wish my father could write a ballet to showcase my talents; Marie Taglioni was unspeakably lucky.'

Harriet, who was as matter-of-fact as Victoria was inclined to sweeping romanticisms, replied, 'Someone once informed me that a pair of her pointe shoes were purchased for a sack of rubles by a group of obsessed balletomanes that had them cooked and served with a sauce for dinner.'

Victoria wrinkled her nose. 'How perfectly ghastly.'

Marietta idly wondered what sauce they had selected.

'Though you ought to be dancing to your strengths, not appealing to your vanity or romantic fascinations after one too many attempts at ensnaring the latest prospects in town.'

'You make me sound like a common street girl!' Victoria laughed a note too high.

Harriet's smile was saccharine. 'Perhaps if you stopped pursuing the elusive Dr Drosselmeier, your variation would be perfect by now. I mean, really, you have yet to even meet the man.'

'I hear no one has had the good fortune to host him yet, though half of society have already started to plan their weddings,' Victoria grumbled. 'He's the most eligible bachelor we've seen in quite some time.'

'I heard he came to possess a fortune under mysterious circumstances and that's why the man is so secretive.'

Victoria sighed. 'Perhaps I had better refocus my energy on my variation.'

'That would be wise. What have you decided to perform for the panel?'

With a belated start, Marietta realised she was being drawn into the conversation. 'I shall not be auditioning,' she said with a smile as pinched as her mood. 'My family have quite forbidden it.' It had long been ordained that she was to relinquish her dancing and be married at the age of twenty-one, which she would turn on the eve of the new year.

'Why? Auditioning for the Company is more than a great privilege; it's an honour.' Victoria's hazel eyes gleamed in earnest as she slid deeper into her stretch. Marietta could count the freckles that clambered across the bridge of her nose, plastered over with pale powder in a failed effort to paint them out of existence. 'Their ballet dancers tour in the finest theatres, perform for the most distinguished of audiences, dance in Paris and Vienna and St Petersburg.'

'Though it's different for society women, isn't it?' Harriet's brown eyes held a touch of contempt. As a black woman, her life was contorted with challenges and obstacles that Marietta knew she could never understand. Marietta had been given every opportunity and privilege but Harriet, though she was a ward of Victoria's uncle, had had to fight to earn her place at the same ballet studio. Marietta's mother had done nothing to help relations after she had made it clear that she cared not for Marietta's 'frivolous dancer friends', discouraging social invitations between the women. Victoria, Harriet and Madame Belinskaya were never extended an invite for luncheons at the town house nor afternoon tea in the city, and consequently Marietta often found herself on the periphery, longing to be one of their close companions.

Marietta inclined her head. 'I am obliged to fulfil my familial expectations.' The words lodged themselves inside her heart like barbs. She schooled her face not to reveal her inner turmoil.

Victoria pursed her lips. 'Why can you not perform both? I'm a society woman and I'm not about to let a few old-fashioned-minded relics dictate what I can and cannot do with my life.'

Harriet scoffed. 'But your mother is a militant suffragette and most decidedly not a baroness.'

Victoria sent a scathing look in her direction and Marietta concealed a smile. She could never quite discern whether the two women were the most intimate of friends or the shrewdest of rivals, camouflaged as confidantes.

Though it disquieted her to admit it to herself, she carried a deep and unrelenting envy of them both. Victoria possessed an impeccable turnout as if she'd been born with her hips positioned at right-angles, and Harriet's leaps and jumps seemed to rewrite the laws of gravity. The three of them had commenced their dancing careers at a tender age and had since witnessed each other's victories and disappointments alike. Marietta could still recall the tartness of the lemon soufflé she'd eaten that day as the taste had lingered during that pivotal first step into the world of ballet.

She'd stood beside Harriet and Victoria, three young girls in pristine white dresses, filled with childish dreams and fancies, as Madame Belinskaya had prodded their legs with her cane, terrifying each of them before proclaiming, 'Khorosho – good.' Classes had begun that same day. Victoria and Harriet were already steadfast friends, having been raised as cousins, leaving Marietta on the periphery. An awkward child, at first she had preferred the relative solitude. Lately she was beginning to wonder if she should have ingratiated herself with them more. Her entire life was sliding towards an inevitable future, unless she chose to derail it, and she found herself short of allies.

Now, Harriet's deep-set eyes bored into Marietta's. 'Chasing after your dreams is a peculiar kind of suffering; it is not for the weak-hearted or cowardly-minded. It requires deep strength and endless determination.'

Marietta took a sharp inhale. 'I am perfectly aware of what it would take, thank you.' Determination raged through her like a fire, licking her nerves, her sinews. A plan was beginning to fashion itself in her mind; a way in which she could foresee snapping out of the *mind-forg'd manacles.*

'Feet in fifth, we shall begin with pliés,' Madame Belinskaya called out with the trademark thud of her cane, the floor at the front of the class pockmarked from her passionate outbursts. A simple melody was coaxed out of the weary piano by the equally weary Vassily, their resident pianist, who was as grey as Madame Belinskaya was illustrious. In a rustle of silks, the ballet dancers fell in line. Marietta held her chin high. Though it seemed easier to acquiesce to her parents' wishes, she knew if she did so, it would haunt her for the rest of her days. And Marietta Stelle was neither weak-hearted nor cowardly.

When Marietta returned from rehearsal, she was greeted by the tittle-tattle emanating from her mother's private drawing room during afternoon tea with her closest circle of confidantes and fellow traders in gossip.

'Young, too, to possess a full head of silver hair, though I do suppose it lends him a certain gravitas,' Adelaide, Geoffrey's mother, had mused as Marietta had wandered past the door.

'I've heard the poor soul is recently widowed,' Vivian, Ida's cousin, said with an affected sigh.

'Well, I heard that he has never married but has returned to England to secure an advantageous match. Apparently the doctor possesses a grand fortune.'

'No doubt he shall be seeking a wife to manage both the town house and his debut into society,' Ida said with a careful air of insouciance that caused Marietta to pause in the carpeted hallway. 'I have already extended the invitation for him to dine with us.'

Marietta frowned at the nearby Tiffany Favrile lamp, brought over on the steamer after a visit to New York.

'You must tell all. It has been quite some years since Edgar passed; perhaps Drosselmeier would consider me,' Vivian said between clinks of the bone china teacups. 'I hear he's rather handsome.'

Adelaide let out a peal of laughter. 'Oh, Vivian, you do tickle me sometimes.'

'Yes, quite,' Ida agreed. 'My cousin is most humorous.'

Marietta's smile was a secret shared with the William Morris honeysuckle wallpaper alone. She turned back downstairs to the ballroom, leaving her mother to the seething thoughts that had undercut her tone.

She could practically taste the curiosity rippling through her mother, deep and insatiable. She sympathised with the man, for Nottingham was rife with rumours of him and it seemed every direction she turned she found herself confronted with talk of him. And, although Marietta would not admit it to anyone, she was becoming intrigued by this mysterious new arrival.

Chapter Four

It wasn't until two days later that the Stelle family made the acquaintance of high society's latest obsession: Dr Drosselmeier.

When Marietta returned home from rehearsals that evening, she entered her bedroom to discover a new dress hung on her triptych screen, pre-selected by her mother to wear for dinner, signalling that they were to entertain company. It was blush rose chiffon, pinned in at the waist by means of a diamond brooch, and long-sleeved, with delicate ruffles frothing down the bodice. Marietta let the pearl-speckled lace sleeves trail through her fingers. They were as translucent and delicate as if they had been crafted from moonbeams. Ballet was poetry in motion and Marietta lived to lose herself in dance, but returning home to find this was a jarring reminder of the life she was expected to lead.

'My dressmaker in Mayfair assured me that the ruffles will aid in disguising your lack of assets,' Ida said, appearing behind her in a whirl of rose water and satin.

Ballet had lent Marietta a willowy figure, the endless pliés and battements resulting in hard muscle tone, slim hips and a flat chest, all of which were terribly unfashionable. Ida pursed her lips, scrutinising the ballet dress Marietta was still wearing; simple and diaphanous enough to allow the wearer to leap through the air. 'Must you wear that unseemly ensemble about the house? It is most improper.' The first time Marietta had worn it, Ida had practically had a fit of the vapours.

'Is there a reason for this excessive primping?' Marietta eyed the lustrous shine of Ida's gown. In deep cobalt, it evoked memories of sun-dappled water from summers spent luxuriating on the French Riviera, where both the days and skies seemed to stretch out endlessly. Scattered with sequins and embroidered with jet beads, it was more ornate than the ones she tended to don for family alone, accompanied by silk gloves and a double string of pearls.

'Dr Drosselmeier has graciously accepted our invitation and is dining with us this evening,' Ida answered as Marietta disappeared behind the large triptych screen. Painted in dark rose, it dominated a corner of her bedroom, although it was a room of generous proportions. Roses clambered across a wallpaper of silver firs, dark wooden floors lay underneath, softened with ivory carpets, and a set of bay windows overlooked the frosted street. The thick fabric of the curtains from one window sashayed across the wall to meet the next, creating the perfect concealment for the barre Frederick had built her some five years ago. Marietta exchanged the white ballet dress she'd been rehearsing Aurora's springing steps in for a chemise and S-shaped corset that would cajole some curves into existence.

'We're to be the very first to host the good doctor,' Ida continued proudly. 'As I understand it, he is quite the mystery. Young to have forsaken medicine for an unusually frivolous pursuit, and he possesses such a grand fortune for a family no one has heard mention of before.'

As Marietta emerged from behind the screen, Ida said, 'You may be dismissed, Sally.'

Marietta's lady's maid – a quiet, mousy woman in her late twenties with wide-set eyes that regarded the world in much the same manner as an injured squirrel might – bobbed a quick curtsy and scurried out. 'If you'll allow me, dear.' Ida grasped the laces of Marietta's corset.

'Really, Mother, I am perfectly capable of managing myself. You do terrify poor Sally,' Marietta said to no avail. She heard her mother's shake of her head in a tinkling of diamond and jet earrings.

'You are far too negligent with your own ministrations. And that girl is too twitchy and eager to please for my liking. I have taken note of the dinners she has allowed you to attend improperly dressed.' She pulled on the lacings, forcing Marietta's hips to thrust forward, her back to arch and her chest to form the pouter pigeon front.

'That will be sufficient.' Marietta's words rushed out in a single breath as Ida ignored her plea and further tightened the lacings before tying them, securing Marietta in her coutil, batiste and sateen confinement. 'I had been given to understand that the new style of corsetry did not impair lung function,' she said drily.

Ida ignored this comment, too. 'When Dr Drosselmeier joins us, I expect you to play the gracious hostess befitting of your rank. You are not beautiful, Marietta; no prospective Wordsworths shall ever wax lyrical on your allure. However, beauty fades and grace may last a lifetime. Tonight, I expect you to be charming. There will be not a mention of politics, dance or other scandalous subjects you have been known to pollute our discourse with. Nor any tiresome quarrelling with your father. Why you seem so determined to challenge him, I shall never understand.' She paused to survey her daughter, whose cheeks were blooming with pent-up frustration. 'Though you do possess a darling rosiness tonight, dear. How fortuitous that it complements the shade of your dress.'

While Ida summoned Sally, Marietta glanced in her cheval mirror. She wondered if their dinner guest disliked the theatricality of high society with its litany of social conventions as much as she did.

A toymaker, she thought to herself. *How ... refreshing*. At least he should prove to be more interesting than her litany of suitors who introduced one tiresome line of conversation after another. No doubt they were the first to host him due to their status as one of the richest families in the city, and certainly the most influential, thanks to her mother's efforts in social elevation. She sighed at the thought of Victoria's inevitable interrogation when she discovered the fact and wondered if Drosselmeier was aware of the effect he'd had upon the mothers in the upper classes. The rumours she'd heard fluttered around her thoughts and she was irritated to find herself rather curious after all. She straightened up when Sally re-entered the room to assist in dressing her. Her new gown fell in soft folds to her white Moroccan leather shoes, daintily heeled with three little straps.

'We ought to do something about her hair, Sally.' Ida examined Marietta's sable hair, tumbling down one shoulder in a lazy twisted plait, a hand coming to rest on her own elaborate pompadour.

Sally's eyes swivelled between them as if she were a spectator at Wimbledon. At least she had been ousted before Ida had revealed the direction her intentions towards Drosselmeier lay; the last thing Marietta desired was to be made the object of household gossip. Her patience frayed like a scrap of lace. 'Have you seen Father lately?'

Ida plucked a silver brush from Marietta's dressing table. 'Not since he declined to accompany me to my luncheon. Why do you ask?'

Marietta adopted an air of studied nonchalance. 'I wondered if you knew that he has company tonight.'

Ida paled beneath the rouge she'd never admit to wearing. 'Surely not, tonight of all nights.'

Marietta fastened a pearl stud in her ear. 'I'm afraid I didn't see with whom he was talking; I merely heard voices in the library when Jarvis took a tray of Bollinger in.'

Ida thrust the hairbrush at Marietta and swept out of the room. Adding the second earring and picking up a compact, Marietta met Sally's eyes in the mirror. She flashed a grin at her lady's maid as she dabbed a touch of powder on her nose.

'Very crafty, miss,' Sally said, holding open a box of silk gloves.

'Why thank you, Sally,' Marietta said, selecting a pair in the creamiest ivory. Ida would fail to find her father's alleged company downstairs, but Marietta would have staked money on the odds that she'd find something else to criticise instead.

Sally left the room, leaving the door open. Through it, Marietta heard the butler announce the arrival of Dr Drosselmeier.

Chapter Five

So it was, on a grey evening, that the Stelle family finally made the acquaintance of the much-gossiped-about Drosselmeier.

Marietta entered the drawing room just as Jarvis, their butler, announced dinner in his sonorous voice, such was her habit in order to avoid the litany of niceties in which she would otherwise be forced to engage.

Ida shot her an admonishing look, though she was careful not to crease her powdered face, which lessened its effect somewhat.

Marietta strolled in and plucked a glass of Veuve Clicquot proffered by the nearest valet. Her father had failed to notice her untimely arrival, being mid-discussion with Dr Drosselmeier on the new prime minister, Henry Campbell-Bannerman, and his landslide victory for the Liberals early this year. Marietta secretly approved of his social reform plans but Theodore was concerned they would give all the power to the trade unions and frequently espoused his dislike of the man. Drosselmeier's back was turned to Marietta, the fabric of his ink-black dinner jacket glossy under the light of the sparkling electric chandelier, his matching trousers cuffed to display black and white striped ankle boots, as jaunty as Frederick's sartorial selections.

'Shall we adjourn to the dining room?' Theodore's voice cut through their conversation. Drosselmeier inclined his head, turning towards the door. 'Ah, Marietta, at long last you've materialised.' The crystal glass in Theodore's hand was already emptied to its dregs, accounting for his joviality. 'Dr Drosselmeier, if you'll allow me to introduce my daughter, The Honourable Marietta Stelle.'

Drosselmeier turned to Marietta, his gaze falling on her. 'I am charmed to make your acquaintance,' he said with an old-fashioned, slight bow.

'Likewise,' Marietta said, offering her hand. He clasped her fingers gently. He was taller and more handsome than she had remembered from her initial glimpse, which explained the rife gossip. His eyes were a pale frosted blue and she found herself unable to stop looking at them. There was something uncanny in their depths that ensnared her attention. Before she could place it, an unrecognisable emotion swept across his face and his eyes turned to shallow pools, casting her out of the ancient heart of a glacier she had been lost in. Marietta blinked, breaking their shared gaze, only to discover that he had retained her hand. She withdrew it with a polite smile to hide the flush creeping beneath the bodice of her dress. If Cicero was correct that the eyes interpreted the mind then she wondered at the thoughts whispering through his. Her intrigue deepened.

'Dr Drosselmeier has kindly bestowed one of his inventions upon us,' Ida said, gesturing at a carriage clock perched on an end table, beneath a large painting of a cherubic younger Frederick.

Painted in slate grey with white panelling, the drawing room was a large space sprinkled with chesterfields and stuffed chairs, long windows, hothouse lilacs and a Steinway. A mahogany cabinet stretched up one wall, displaying the finest Stelle mementos: a handful of Frederick's old toy soldiers, taken fresh from the box and forbidden to be played with; Marietta's porcelain doll in her silk gown and ringlets that she'd loved and named Clara from afar with her hands pressed against the glass; the staged photographs of her and Frederick, uniform in their painted-on expressions, emotions tidied away as if they'd never existed. There was a space next to the one in which Frederick held his undergraduate degree, awaiting Marietta's wedding photograph. She averted her eyes from it as she wandered over to the clock.

'A fine piece it is at that, mighty clever,' Theodore said, holding out his glass to the nearest valet. It was refilled in a hurry. 'I maintain my opinion; there is a fortune to be made in selling these.'

Marietta studied the clock. She had yet to place why her father had shifted viewpoints; was he merely being cordial after pre-dinner drinks with Drosselmeier or was there something she was missing? It was a finely wrought construction in black walnut yet simple, a spiralling vine of roses carved into the wood its sole ornamentation.

'If you'll allow me—' Drosselmeier reached from behind her '—it requires a turning of the hands.' He wound them round the clock face until they were positioned at four o'clock then stepped back and waited with his hands clasped behind his back. A hidden pair of doors sprang open on the carriage clock and a toy soldier marched out. His little arms and legs moved on the mechanism that looped around and saw him salute them with a click of his boot heels before he marched back inside.

Marietta smiled. 'What a delightful invention.' She ran her hands over its surface, feeling for the seams of the doors, but the wood was smooth and flat.

'I say, show her what happens at midnight,' Frederick said, sitting on the edge of the nearest settee to gain a second look.

'Why, whatever happens at midnight? Now I simply must know.' Marietta glanced up at Drosselmeier in time to meet his smile. On the other side of the room, where her parents looked on, she couldn't help noticing Ida murmur discreetly to Theodore.

'Only the most magical things happen at midnight. When mortal folk are dreaming, safe in their beds, it is then that the sprites and goblins creep out and the air crackles with wild magic.' He wound the hands to the witching hour.

Marietta shivered. Outside the window, a blanched moon had swum up the sky, and now and then it peered milkily at them between cloud wisps. An owl hooted, a branch tapped against the window and the candles glowed like fallen stars. A glimmer of something a little like belief slid into her heart. When the clock struck midnight, a series of tiny hatches opened, revealing a collection of little fairies, twelve in all, arising in puffs of lilac tulle and silver glitter. They flew up and down on mechanised rose stems, descending in as magical a manner as they'd appeared, leaving not a speck of glitter behind them.

'What a charming creation,' Marietta said. 'Why, it's every bit as magical as the fairy tales I read as a child. My father is entirely correct, you do possess an extraordinary talent.'

'Come along,' Theodore called back to them as he escorted Ida into dinner, his cheeks ruddy above his silk tie, navy to accentuate his wife's dress.

'Though you are far too kind, your compliment has warmed me. May I accompany you to dinner?' Drosselmeier offered his arm.

Marietta acquiesced. She smiled and took it. His jacket sleeve was silky, scented with peppermint and secrets. She rested her fingertips atop it.

During the course of the previous day, Ida had overseen the household staff preparing the dining room until it gleamed, determined for it to be showcased at its best. The mahogany table and chairs shone with polish and a faint honeyed scent. Large crystal vases brimmed with roses and white stocks in a confection of pastel peach and cream, and the wooden floors were softened by the Persian carpet, which had been cleaned for the occasion. The electric lights had been switched off in favour of the softer glow afforded by candlelight. Tapered candles in silver holders punctuated the table settings. Other candles were capped with shades, melting the light into twinkling shadows.

Marietta found herself seated beside Frederick, on the opposite side to Dr Drosselmeier, with her parents at opposing ends of the table. His gaze brushed against her as they took their places and Marietta glanced down to hide her rising colour. She busied herself with unbuttoning her long ivory gloves at the thumbs and peeling back the silken material over her wrists.

'You appear to be settling into Nottingham rather nicely from what I gather. Tell me, how are you finding our fine city?' Theodore asked while his glass was filled with sherry in accompaniment to the soup course.

Drosselmeier shook out his napkin. 'I must confess, my enjoyment of it took me entirely by surprise. Most of society are in the belief that only the grand cities of London, Paris and New York are worth bothering with but I have found that Nottingham holds a certain charm of its own.'

His words were smooth and deliberate. Marietta swept a spoon across her soup; leek and potato with swirls of cream and fried croutons, quietly taking his measure herself.

'We're full of charm,' Frederick said drily. 'What was it that had you set your sights on Nottingham? I believe you mentioned you used to be a doctor?'

'That's correct. In fact, I owned a private practice in London some years ago.'

'A practice of your own is an impressive feat for a man of your age.' Ida's dark-blue eyes sparkled in the candlelight, her delight at his accomplishment obvious, her smile as effective an accessory as the pearls strung around her neck.

'That is most kind of you. Though I must confess, I found it all rather tiresome.' Drosselmeier twizzled his soup spoon in his long fingers. The silver sparked and Marietta glanced up at it. Between the flashes she caught a glimpse of a glass swan, floating along a mirrored lake. A vision of ice and stars and the cold, dark spaces between them that were wont to pinch her thoughts with terror if she dwelled too long upon them. She frowned and it shattered.

'I soon grew tired of the monotony and escaped London for a while, fortunately so, as it was then that I discovered my raison d'être in my current profession.'

As Drosselmeier continued, Marietta turned her attention back onto her soup, ignoring the anxious moth-wing flutters of her heart. She must have been imagining things.

'In crafting your own inventions?' Theodore finished his soup and proceeded to drain his glass.

Marietta sensed with sibling intuition that Frederick was attempting to hook her attention. Drosselmeier's smile poured across his features like honey. The slow, languorous smile of a person who believes they hold the secrets of the world. Marietta was curious what he would say next.

'I prefer to think of it as spreading a little magic,' he said, and, with a flourish, he shook out his serviette onto the tablecloth. When he whisked it away, Marietta pressed her fingers to her mouth. A small glass swan was sitting there. Delicate and gossamer-fine with a luminosity to it that played with the qualities of light and reflection.

'Oh, how utterly delightful!' she said, charmed yet bewildered.

Drosselmeier inclined his head with a small smile. 'Consider it a small gift.' He presented it to her.

Ida's smile cut wider.

Marietta turned the glass swan in the candlelight, admiring its delicacy. 'You flatter me, Dr Drosselmeier. I do possess an avid appreciation for swans; they are just the most exquisite creatures. Rarely do we witness such refined elegance in nature. I'm most delighted with your gift.' She wondered if she'd been dreaming when she'd seen the vision. It was warm in the dining room and the windows had clouded with steam.

'You are most welcome,' Drosselmeier said softly. 'Swans make for a beautiful model, though you must know they are as vicious as they are elegant. Nature is a cruel mistress and often brutal.'

Marietta looked up, curious at his words. 'I fear it is all too common that beauty is laced with a darker edge,' she said, and Drosselmeier's eyes locked onto hers, darkening with intrigue. She sensed that he was a kindred spirit, governed by an alternate set of laws to the majority of their class. 'Perhaps it is our own misunder-standing of nature that leads to us finding it cruel and brutal. For the swans, it is simply life,' she finished.

Frederick plucked the glass swan from her hand and examined it, turning it this way and that. 'Its design is marvellous, almost reminiscent of Bernini's Apollo and Daphne through the stretch of the swan's neck and the fluidity that's evoked, though instead of transmuting stone to silk, you've played with the effect of light by using glass as your medium.'

Marietta nudged Frederick's foot beneath the table. He gathered his senses, replaced the swan before her and cleared his throat.

As the soup course was taken away, replaced with the fish course and fresh glasses of white wine that Jarvis had pre-selected and run by Theodore for his approval, Marietta found her attention flit back to Drosselmeier, between the efficient bustling of the footmen serving their dinner à la Russe. The ivory candle shades illuminated his silvered hair and shadows skittered across his classic features as the footmen filtered back to their stations.

'Your son is extremely cultured,' he commented to Theodore, whose expression turned rigid.

'Where did you reside before your arrival in Nottingham?' Marietta asked before her father could respond.

'After I had made the decision to depart London, I embarked on a pilgrimage to study my craft.'

Marietta paused in selecting the proper silverware. 'Would you care to tell us more? If I didn't know better, Dr Drosselmeier, I would say you were being evasive.' Her smile was teasing.

Ida sighed. 'Marietta dear, would you kindly desist in interrogating the poor doctor.'

Theodore swilled his wine, unable to quash his spark of interest; Marietta suspected he was every bit as curious as she.

'That's quite all right. I am afraid I have been caught; I was being vague,' Drosselmeier said. He raised his eyebrows at Marietta's poorly concealed amusement at the fact. 'As much as it pains me, I cannot share the whereabouts; it's a trade secret and one that I am compelled to guard closely.'

'How intriguing.' Frederick grinned. 'There's nothing like a few choice secrets to retain an air of mystery.'

Drosselmeier's eyes didn't leave Marietta. 'Though I am at liberty to entertain you with the wonders I have witnessed in my travels. Of sitting atop a pyramid, witnessing an apricot and honey sunrise flooding the desert. Of ancient sea-battered ruins and cities buried deep within jungles. Of the icy wasteland of the vast northern tundra, where reindeer roam, the moon shivers and the Northern Lights enchant the skies.'

Marietta felt the stirrings of envy. It seemed having Drosselmeier as a regular guest would prove interesting indeed.

'It appears you are a well-travelled man—' Theodore cleared his throat '—though I am not so unworldly myself. You must join me for cigars after dinner and we shall exchange stories. I purchase only the finest; I share a supplier with King Edward, I'll have you know,' he added in an aside.

With the entrée of vol-au-vents came more champagne. Marietta declined both, listening to her father conduct the conversation as if they comprised an orchestra.

'I was remiss not to mention earlier what a fine cabinet I spotted in your drawing room,' Drosselmeier said as the remove was served. Pie in a burgundy sauce, potatoes sliced fine enough to render them translucent and a heap of fresh vegetables. Marietta cut dainty mouthfuls, stifled between the heavy richness of dinner and the unrelenting heat emanating from the flickering wicks.

Ida bestowed a beatific smile upon him. 'You are far too generous with your compliments, Dr Drosselmeier.'

'Perhaps you might allow me to craft you an addition for it?'

'Why, I couldn't possibly accept—' Ida began.

'It would be my pleasure,' Dr Drosselmeier said.

Ida's smile was laced with greed. 'Well, if you insist then we would be most appreciative. Your inventions are simply marvellous; I have never seen anything quite like them before.'

Marietta had no doubt that shortly everyone would be clamouring for a Drosselmeier creation. A nugget of magic in their own homes, an enchantment to kindle their imaginations, warm them with nostalgic thoughts of days long past, of fairy tales and toys and playtime come to life. The man himself was charming, too, and Marietta was pleased to find that she had enjoyed his company. It had been some time since the Stelles had had a dinner guest she had not found insufferable and, what was more, she was not the only member of the Stelle family enamoured with the stories he had spun.

Drosselmeier appeared the perfect guest.

Chapter Six

When evening tipped into night and the witching hour fell upon the Stelle townhouse, all was as silent as the stars etched in the skies. Marietta wandered down a hallway on the top floor. It was a world of deep burgundy carpet and oil paintings of notable Stelles throughout the ages. Though the rest of the house had since been redecorated in lighter pastels and florals, the hallway leading to the old nursery had been left languishing in the Victorian era. Marietta found Frederick warming himself before the fire in what was now the siblings' drawing room. His spotted necktie was undone, his black jacket shed. He spoke without turning. 'I haven't seen Mother this excited since the Cambers' son expressed an interest in stealing you away. I almost feel sorry for Drosselmeier.'

Marietta clicked the door shut harder than she'd intended. The rosy glow of the pale wallpaper and the crackling fire made the room cosy despite the dated furniture and ragged carpets. It was the only room in the townhouse into which their parents didn't venture and the two of them had spent many an hour together in this solace. It had been where Frederick had stood before her with his beau, Geoffrey, and unburdened himself of his secret. Where they stole away for entire evenings, Marietta pirouetting through the night as Frederick sketched, their confidences burrowing deeper and more heartfelt as they neared the bottom of the champagne bottle.

Frederick turned to survey her. 'Is there something bothering you?'

'I had forgotten about Philip until now.' She rubbed a temple as the memory of their awkward chaperoned luncheon last month came searing back.

Frederick grinned. 'Was he the one who monologued about hunting at his family's estate in Scotland, or the one who drooled when he ate?'

Marietta rubbed her temple harder. 'I'm sure that he didn't intend to drool. Perhaps he has some unfortunate affliction.'

Frederick gave a sharp laugh. 'I wouldn't pay him a second thought. According to Geoffrey, Philip happens to be pursuing a handful of women in London, who are conveniently located closer to the Cambers' Great House. I'm sure he'll prove to be as short-lived as the rest of your suitors. Wasn't it Henry Davenshire that proclaimed you "cold and unfeeling"?'

'He was an utter bore.' Marietta sighed. 'Why is it that some men feel the need to insult women if we dare not be enthralled by them and their inconsequential pursuits?'

'Pay them no heed, you are far more talented and generally splendid than the lot of them. So, what did you make of Drosselmeier?'

'An interesting man indeed. Most talented; I'm sure everyone will be clamouring for one of his pieces once word spreads.'

'Devilishly handsome, too.' Frederick gave Marietta a pointed look.

She pursed her lips. 'I would be interested to speak more with him but that is the limit of my feelings on the matter.' She patted her hair.

'I do adore you, Ets, but you ought to be forbidden from styling your own hair. At the very least to save poor Sally from Mother's criticism.' Frederick strode over and began fiddling with it. 'After dinner was a resounding success, I'm afraid Drosselmeier shall be

Mother's new target for her relentless matchmaking and undoubtedly a most frequent guest. Even Father seemed impressed with the man. Is that what's preoccupying you? Your frown lines have been deepening by the minute since you stepped through the door.'

Marietta realised he was right: as much as she had attempted to twist out of her fate, if she kept walking this path, it was inevitable. Her tentative plans hardened like a caramel glaze. 'Frederick, I have decided to audition for the Nottingham Ballet Company.'

Her brother sighed. 'No good will come of this, Ets. Father explicitly ordered you to stop dancing come the new year. Once his mind is set on something, it cannot be altered. And since he covers the cost of your classes, not to mention your dresses, costumes and ballet slippers ... Well, I just don't see how it could be possible. And I won't always be here to protect you from him.'

'You forget I'm no longer a child, Frederick; I do not require your protection. Besides which, I have quite made up my mind.'

Frederick repositioned her before the gilt mirror above the mantelpiece. Her raven hair had been reconfigured into an elegant low twist. She met his eyes in the mirror, the grey to her deep blue; if you blended them together like paint, they would forge the colour of storm clouds and misted seas. 'Wouldn't you have preferred to follow your dreams?' she asked quietly, dipping into territory they avoided discussing.

His hands slackened on her shoulders. 'It's dangerous to dream, Marietta. It will fill your head with tales sweet as sugarplums, until reality is nothing but disappointment.'

Marietta sank onto the petal-blue chesterfield basking opposite the fire. They had picked it out together, the room's one concession to modern aesthetics. 'I disagree. Dreams hold power, and when one truly believes in them, it feels as if there isn't anything on this earth you might not achieve.'

Frederick frowned. 'Do not go against Father.' His voice was deep with warning. 'An easy life married to someone like Drosselmeier in a grand house is not something to battle against. If you were caught disregarding his orders, you cannot comprehend what the consequences would be.'

'I would have thought that you of all people would understand that nothing about that would be easy.' Marietta regretted the impetuous words the instant they'd burst from her lips but she could no more bite them back than she could stop the rain hammering down the window.

Frederick took several beats to respond. An uneasy silence neither of them were accustomed to settled between them. She was all too aware how unusual it was that her brother was her closest friend and entrusted keeper of her secrets, but that had been their way since they were children.

It traced back to the moment Marietta had decided she would pen a letter to Pierina Legnani, prima ballerina assoluta, whom the young Marietta had just witnessed perform an astonishing thirty-two consecutive fouettés en tournant during her tour of *Cinderella* in London. Pierina's dancing had brought resolution to her heart; she too would dance. In selecting the creamiest sheaf of paper on which to inform the ballerina of how much her performance had moved Marietta – set beside a pretty specimen of heliotrope pilfered from the garden – she had picked up her father's most treasured fountain pen and placed it on the paper with enthusiasm. To her horror, the nib had shattered upon the page. Ten-year-old Frederick had borne the blame and punishment in her place. Her memories were still stained bloody with the crack of Theodore's letter opener splitting open her brother's knuckles.

'Frederick—' she began.

'Our situations are entirely different; you cannot pretend to know how I—' He stopped and cleared his throat roughly. 'You are unaware of your own privilege, Marietta.'

She pressed his hand. 'I do know that. I am sorry. Truly, I am. I'm a hateful creature and you are free to despise me!'

Frederick sat beside her. He patted her knee. 'I could never despise you.'

'I'm not afraid, Frederick. Being disinherited doesn't give me sleepless nights. I would prefer it to being married off against my wishes. Even a man like Drosselmeier holds no attraction for me; am I to spend the rest of my days serving and smiling at him as I become a shadow of my former self? I could not bear such a thing.' Marietta kept her voice hushed; the townhouse was crawling with spies, gossip the currency of choice. Frederick's discomfort deepened. He fiddled with his necktie. 'Frederick?' Marietta sharpened her voice.

'I don't suppose you remember Lucy Fatherdale?' he asked. 'We picnicked with her and Geoffrey last spring on the banks of the Trent.'

Marietta recalled the air had been scented with blossoms and grass and the ginger beer the men had drunk after rowing along the river. She had flung her hat onto the blanket, its ribbons trailing like a collapsed rainbow, and basked in the sunlight. Lucy, a pretty, petite blonde, had laughed and dashed her own sunhat aside, declaring, 'I doubt a few freckles will much change the course of events now!'

'Of course I remember her. Geoffrey's betrothed,' she said now, pretending not to notice Frederick's hand tighten on his knee. This was the other subject which they did not broach. Though Marietta knew of their true relationship, to everyone else, Geoffrey was merely an associate and friend of Frederick's. They had met while studying for the same degree but Geoffrey had recently done what was expected of him and become engaged. Even though the siblings were close, this was one matter Marietta did not know how to ask her brother about and disliked to pry. 'What of her?'

'Well, Geoffrey informed me that her older cousin, Lola Castleton, eloped with a man she'd fallen wildly in love with: an acrobat with a travelling circus, if you can imagine that. It was all a rather torrid affair. Her family were incensed and mounted an effort to retrieve her at once. They hunted the pair down until they were discovered in a seedy bolthole just below the Scottish border. Her beau was beaten and left bloody. As I hear it, he'd be lucky to walk again, much less perform with a troupe.'

'And Lola?' Marietta whispered.

'They were too late; She had already lost her reputation. Her father was incandescent with rage and had her committed.'

Marietta's blood chilled. 'Surely you are not suggesting that our father would—' She could not finish the thought.

'I do not pretend to know what he would or wouldn't do.' Frederick's whisper was pierced with anger. 'Though I do know our father and he is not a man that would allow his authority to be questioned.' He ran a finger over the scar that ran in a deep groove across the knuckles of his right hand. 'You've witnessed plenty of his tempers for yourself. Do not cross him.'

Marietta's heart fluttered anxiously. She had been holding onto the thought of auditioning, guarding it, polishing it bright with wishing and hoping and longing until it gleamed like a pearl. Now that pearl felt lost in some fathomless ocean she didn't know how to traverse.

Frederick stood. 'At least you shall be performing your Christmas ballet here. I'm still making inquiries into a suitable constructor for your set. The budget, or lack thereof, is proving to be a challenge but give me a little longer and I'm confident we'll have someone. I can take photographs on my Sanderson for you as a keepsake if you'd like?'

'Oh, I would treasure that. Thank you, Frederick,' Marietta said quietly.

She sat there long after Frederick had sauntered out. She stared at the moon, almost swept from the sky by the curtain of rain, yet refusing to relinquish its position; the brightest spark in the night. Taking heart from this, she crossed the room to their old writing desk and penned a letter, requesting an audition. She could not be a puppet in her own story; she must at least see if there might be another way for her. Then she sought out Sally.

'See to it that this makes the post at first light.' She handed the letter over.

Sally nodded and tucked it into her apron. 'Right you are, miss.'

That night, Marietta dreamt of moons and pearls and wishes that shone harder and fiercer than all else.

Chapter Seven

In the week that followed, Drosselmeier brought light to their evenings as November drew to a close.

On the following Tuesday, he brought a box wrapped in brown paper. Inside, there were rows of tin soldiers, nestled into the velvet lining. Frederick couldn't resist setting them up in the name of nostalgia and they had marched around, all shiny black boots and vacant polished faces, until Jarvis announced dinner. The soldiers now stood in the cabinet, staring out at everyone as if they were plotting an invasion.

On Wednesday, he joined them for afternoon tea and gifted Theodore an elaborate chess set with chequered squares that slid across to send unwitting opponents' pieces plummeting to their end. It had already been the battleground of several matchings of wits between Theodore and Frederick. Marietta was tempted to indulge in a game herself but with the tension crescendoing between her and her father, she demurred at his challenge.

On Thursday he had sent Ida her promised piece for the cabinet: a pair of silver candlesticks that hummed with his mechanisms, sending gold-winged bees flying around the petals that held lilac candles in place. When the candles were lit, the entire family dreamt of distant summers and the townhouse was perfumed with orange blossom and apricot tartlets.

On Friday, there was another dinner, where Marietta was presented with a music box that opened to reveal a waltzing princess. A creature of cloud wisps and the pale blue of starling eggs, with a gown that frothed about her legs in as many layers as a mille-feuille. If one sang a short tune to her, a secret compartment for one's most treasured jewels snapped open and Marietta was rather delighted by it.

The whole family had been enchanted by Drosselmeier as if he had bewitched them, yet each time Marietta exclaimed over his marvellous inventions, mechanised toys and pretty trinkets, she was unable to stop imagining the consequences that might arise from their shared dinners, seeing herself sealed in a specimen box with a label that read, simply, *uxorem*, her identity reduced to a single word.

Wife.

✻

After a gruelling rehearsal of the Rose Adagio, where she had spent an inordinate period of time balanced on a single pointe, maintaining her position as she rested a hand on Aurora's suitors, one at a time, Marietta's toes were blistered and bloodied and she desired nothing more than to submerge herself in hot water. When she returned to her room, Sally handed her a thick envelope. An inky stamp over the seal betrayed its origins.

'I thought it best to give this directly to you, miss,' Sally whispered, her eyes flitting from one wall to another, as if they were watching her.

'You thought right; thank you, Sally. Now, I would be most appreciative if you could draw me a bath.' Marietta waited until her lady's maid had scurried into the adjoining bathroom to open the envelope. Her fingers trembled and the paper sliced into her knuckle. A bead of blood fled down the writing, leaving a scarlet shadow.

You have been successful in requesting an audience with The Nottingham Ballet Company. Your audition will be held on the first of December, at four o'clock. Please arrive in a prompt fashion.

Marietta closed her eyes, relief and vexation intermingling, needling her mood into a spiky, querulous creature. It hadn't escaped her that she was improving at the challenging variation. Enough for it to make a formidable audition performance. Yet, although she had secured herself an audition, with Miss Mary Worthers glued to her affairs, she was no closer to being able to attend it. She committed the letter to memory before feeding it to the fire, watching the words flame with all the brilliance of a jar of sweets. All too soon, they flaked to ash. She could almost taste the lingering smoke and imagined her own melancholia carried the same bitter tang. She instructed Sally to shake half a jar of pink bath salts into her clawfoot tub and was on the verge of disrobing when Frederick knocked at her door, announcing his presence.

She sighed. 'Can this wait? I'm having a bath drawn.'

'What a delight you are tonight,' he said, strolling in and settling himself on her chaise longue, one berry-red shoe resting on a pin-striped knee. He slung a matching pin-striped elbow onto her favourite cushion; hand-stitched black velvet and antique silk with a lace border. Frederick had purchased it for her during a stroll through the Lace Market during the May he had become enamoured with the notion of incorporating lacework into his paintings. They'd wandered arm in arm through the oldest part of Nottingham, now the epicentre of the world's lace industry, perusing the showrooms and lingering over cream cakes in the corner of a bakery. How distant that day seemed to Marietta now. That very evening, Theodore had summoned her to his study to inform her that after she had seen the year out, she would not be continuing with her dance studio. 'Prancing about the stage is a pastime for children; it is not befitting of a woman in her twenties,' he had told her with the finality of death. And Marietta had grieved.

'Thank you, Sally; that will be all.' Marietta turned to her brother. 'I was under the impression that you were staying late at the courthouse today.'

Frederick kneaded his forehead with a knuckle. 'Father was being particularly pompous; listening to him gave me the most frightful headache. I slipped out early for a drink with Geoffrey. I know, I have not a shadow of doubt I'll regret it bitterly later—' he pulled a face, warding off Marietta's interjection ' —but it did lead me to a rather serendipitous encounter.'

'Is this tale going to be as long as your beloved *Paradise Lost*?' Marietta crossed her arms over her cream silk robe, her hair in two curtains down to her waist. 'I have yet to eat and my toes are bleeding.'

Frederick eyed her feet, clad in satin slippers, warily. 'Take a seat, I have a feeling you'll be wanting to hear this.' His shoe tapped against his knee, measuring the beat to which his enthusiasm marched. 'You asked me some time ago if I knew of anyone who might be willing to construct a set for your Christmas production.'

Marietta sat on her window seat. It was cold beneath her silk and she shivered with anticipation. 'Am I to understand that you've found someone?'

'Not only did I find someone, I have found someone who will craft the most exquisite, wondrous set you've ever dreamt of.' Frederick spread his hands like a magician's reveal.

Her irritableness melted away. 'Are you serious, Freddie?'

'When have I ever been less than serious?' He winked. 'Now you shall have the finest stage in all of England for your swan song. And I have been given assurance that it will even possess …' he paused for effect '… moving parts!'

'Oh, do you mean to tell me what I think you're implying?' Marietta clapped her hands together in delight. 'However did you persuade Drosselmeier to take on such a task?'

'It seems my years of studying the fine art of persuasion were not wasted after all.' Frederick grinned. 'Drosselmeier is eager to reach new customers ahead of opening his latest venture. And everybody who's anybody in this city will be attending our Christmas Ball; I merely pointed out what a brilliant opportunity it would be for him to advertise. He readily agreed and is prepared to engineer it at cost to himself. He's a dammed fine inventor, I'm certain you shall have the finest of all sets.'

'It sounds wonderful. Madame Belinskaya might finally crack a smile upon hearing the news,' Marietta said and Frederick snorted.

'I have already accepted the deal on your behalf; now go and relax.' He nodded towards the steam gathering in the bathroom; a rose- and bergamot-scented storm. 'I'll have a plate sent up for you.'

When he took his leave, Marietta disrobed in her white bathroom, peeling back the thin bandages on her feet. The floorboards were cold and she stepped into her claw-footed tub with a hiss and a sting. She lay back, melting into the bathtub. The water settled around her in a delicious moment, easing the winter that had seeped into her joints. Closing her eyes, she breathed in the perfumed aroma, allowing her thoughts to drift unmoored. They floated out of her control, onto the Rose Adagio and the forbidden audition. Trying to tug them in one coherent direction, planning how she might attend, failed. The memory of her previous conversation with Frederick unhinged her concentration. As did the knowledge that there were institutions for ladies of a certain mindset. She was at an impasse. How could she battle against the limitations on her freedom if doing so would bear a steeper cost? Her mood disintegrated.

Later, she ate alone from a silver tray. Cheese tart with butter-rich pastry, a crystal dish of ratafia trifle, orange segments. Her silk sheets welcomed her but sleep slipped further and further away as her worries clamoured louder than the call of her dreams.

The performance drew closer and her future was held tighter than ever in her parents' grasp.

Unless she could find a way to audition.

Chapter Eight

Upon awakening the following morning, Marietta felt an insatiable urge to be idle. It was a Sunday and there were no ballet classes or rehearsals to absorb her time. Nor was there any luncheon or afternoon tea she was promised to attend. She slipped a white cotton tulle peignoir over her night chemise and stretched, luxuriating in the time unspooling out before her. She breakfasted long after her parents and brother before donning her woollen winter coat and stepping out into the gardens.

Wide stone steps led down onto the frost-encrusted lawn that swept out before her. The sky was gunmetal-grey, the trees skeletons, the remnants of the rose and wisteria garden rendering the landscape bleak. A spectral fog drifted by. In the distance, the manicured lawns fell away to the most expensive view in Nottingham: the castle. Though castle was a generous term, Marietta mused, stepping onto the lawn, as it better resembled an ornate mansion perched on Castle Rock, the original edifice having been destroyed hundreds of years prior. The frosted grass crisped beneath her buttery kidskin boots, buckled at her ankles, and a solitary thrush's song fluted out. Marietta paused to search out the bird when an accompanying crunch sounded.

Drosselmeier's voice was arresting in the haunting expanse. 'At once a voice arose among the bleak twigs overhead in a full-hearted evensong of joy illimited.'

'I would not have placed you as an admirer of Thomas Hardy,' Marietta said. 'You do not strike me as a man enamoured with Romanticism.' At last she spotted the black-spattered cream breast of the songbird. It granted them a final tune before spreading its wings and vanishing into the silvered air. Marietta turned to Drosselmeier.

'Is that so?' He smiled but offered no opinion. 'Forgive me for imposing myself upon you. You cut such a romantic figure wandering through the mist before the castle that I felt quite compelled to join you.'

His black gloves were clasped behind his back, a Chesterfield coat in charcoal tweed with a velvet collar keeping out the worst of the chill, his top hat a hasty addition, the fact betrayed by his dislodged hair.

'You are most welcome to accompany me,' Marietta said, glancing back at the house. It loomed at their backs, a commanding presence in Georgian stone and columns. She half-expected to see Miss Worthers peering from one of the uppermost windows, as if her chaperone could sense Marietta was in the company of a suitor alone.

'I have been given to understand that I am to devise a set for your rendition of *The Sleeping Beauty* at your annual Christmas Ball.' Drosselmeier paid close attention to Marietta as they walked through the gardens. She shifted away as he continued to speak. 'I confess, I am very much looking forward to attending.'

Marietta smiled. 'You are too kind. I myself am eager for my first glimpse of your set; I'm sure it will be nothing short of wondrous.' Each year the Stelle's Christmas Ball was the talk of the city but this was the first year Marietta's ballet studio had been invited to perform. As it was her final year of dancing, it was customary to perform on a stage in the theatre but Theodore had swiftly put an end to that notion. Marietta had persuaded him it would be more appropriate to dance at their ball and, in a rare moment of sentimentality, he had concurred.

Drosselmeier's frosted eyes lingered on her face. Marietta shifted their path onto a trajectory that circled back towards the house. She glanced up at the clouds haunting the sky above. 'Such unfortunate weather we have been suffering through lately,' she said, attempting to shift their conversation, puzzled by the change in his demeanour.

Drosselmeier stepped up onto the stone mezzanine outside the morning room. He towered above her. A light wind tossed up Marietta's hair, left free and trailing down her back in a moment of rebellion. Drosselmeier tracked it. His slender fingers opened and closed. 'And yet my set will pale in comparison to you,' he said, his voice silkier.

Marietta's smile was tight. 'I hope it will be a performance worthy of your praise,' she said by rote, her manners grafted on her down to the marrow.

Drosselmeier's answering smile was slow, his eyes never leaving her face. Marietta could almost feel his attention; a tangible beast with an overpowering appetite. His voice pitched lower. 'I must tell you, your earlier surmise was quite incorrect. I have long found myself fascinated with Romanticism. One of its influences arose from my homeland, after all; *Sturm und Drang*.' He took her hand, holding it between his.

Marietta had been about to sidle past him to gain entry into the house but his hands gave her pause. Her breath caught in her throat and disappointment scudded through her at the thought, sudden and unbidden, that he might be on the verge of a proposal. 'Forgive me, my German isn't up to the same standard as my French. Storm and ambition, was that?'

Drosselmeier stepped nearer. 'Very close. Though *drive* would be a better fit. I'm a driven man, Miss Stelle. What I covet, I find a way to possess.'

'How fortuitous for you. Now if you'll be so kind as to excuse me, I have a pressing matter to attend to.' Marietta forced a pretty smile. The gardens suddenly felt too large and empty, the house too silent. There were staff in every room; why had none passed the windows and given her reason to demur?

Drosselmeier retained a hold on her hand. 'I was hoping I might steal a moment more of your time.'

She glanced up at him, searching for a polite refusal, one which wouldn't cause offence, when a prickling awareness took root in her. One that whispered of something unnatural, something uncanny. She froze, staring at his irises, storming around his pupils, at the shadow-twitch of a mouse tail whipping back inside his coat pocket. It was as if he had been wearing a mask since that first dinner and now it had unfurled once more. Long enough to afford her a glimpse of something *else* beneath. Her senses flared; a shiver darted down her spine. 'What are you?' she whispered without thinking.

Drosselmeier started and dropped her hand. His mask of careful pleasance snapped back in place. The sudden motion reclaimed Marietta's senses and she shook her head. 'Forgive me, I am quite fatigued from rehearsals,' she said with a light laugh, smoothing the edges of the conversation back together, even as her heart still beat sparrow-quick in her chest.

'There is nothing to forgive,' Drosselmeier said smoothly. 'I shall enjoy watching the result of your diligence. Watching you.' His hand lingered against the small of her back under the pretence of guiding her back to the house. Her discomfort deepened as she felt him wind a lock of her hair around his finger.

✿

Marietta walked upstairs to the drawing room she shared with Frederick. The memory of Drosselmeier's touch swam inside her, slippery as jelly sweets. Upon opening the door, Frederick and Geoffrey's conversation startled to a close.

'My apologies, it wasn't my intention to intrude.' Marietta made to leave.

'Nonsense, there's no need to leave on our account,' Frederick said, pouring brandy from a decanter into two glasses and handing one to Geoffrey, who was surveying Marietta.

'I am certain you would rather enjoy your privacy,' Marietta said, knowing that for the two of them, these moments alone were scarcer than they would like.

'Are you quite all right?' Geoffrey inquired. 'You look rather out of sorts; perhaps you had better rest a moment.' With a head full of dark curls, golden-brown skin, sharp cheekbones and full lips, it was no wonder Geoffrey had commanded the attention of many ladies before he had become engaged. A brocaded gold waistcoat over his white shirt and scarlet necktie did nothing to dispel his attractiveness and Victoria had been among those that were greatly disappointed to learn that he was now betrothed. It amused Frederick to keep a tally.

Marietta sat herself in a wing-backed chair. The emerald velvet was worn but her French cashmere plum tea dress was thick and soft, her legs cosseted by a frothery of petticoats. 'I was waylaid in my walk in the gardens by Dr Drosselmeier,' she said, glancing up at Frederick. 'He gave me a most peculiar feeling. And now I cannot help but wonder who he is and where he came from. Why has he refused to speak on anything that occurred before his arrival in Nottingham?'

Frederick frowned. He leant against the mantelpiece, his brandy alchemised to golden silk by the fire flickering in the grate.

'How diverting; it has been some time since we've had a decent scandal to gossip over,' Geoffrey said, his gaze soft against Frederick. He reached for the decanter on the walnut side table and poured himself a second snifter. 'Tell us precisely what occurred and spare no details.'

Marietta relayed the events in the garden back to them. She flushed upon describing how Drosselmeier had caught her hand, trapping her in the conversation. How he had touched her without invitation. The jelly sweets squirmed inside her and she pressed her fingers to her lips.

Frederick rubbed the growing crease between his eyebrows. 'Seriously, Marietta, you are allowing your imagination to descend into fantasy. Perhaps the man simply values his privacy, which he is well entitled to. He doesn't owe us an inventory of his personal history; neither does that make him a nefarious character simply for failing to provide one.'

'I'm telling you, Frederick, there is something about him. As if he is the proverbial wolf clad in sheepskin. I can feel the wrongness gnawing at my bones.'

'Do you recall when the nanny read us fairy tales before we were put to bed?' Frederick asked.

Marietta gave him a puzzled look. 'Yes, what of it?' Their nanny had been an affectionate older woman with the most beautiful book of bedtime fairy tales. Stories of fairies and elves, water nymphs and sprites, painting the dawn with violet petal-brushes, skimming over rivers on the backs of moths, dancing in the final wink of starlight. Marietta's dreams had been swollen with longing and she'd embarked on boundless quests to uncover the creatures' magical world, convinced there was a hidden glittering layer of enchantment buried beneath the dull veneer of everyday life.

Frederick laughed. 'You became so infatuated with the notion of discovering those elusive fairies at the bottom of our garden that you tore all your hems and dirtied your finest satin slippers searching until Father put a stop to the bedtime stories.'

'He sat me down and informed me that the stories were eating away my logic,' Marietta remembered aloud. 'It wasn't until sometime later that I came to the realisation that he hadn't meant literally. All those years I had been imagining the fairy tales nibbling at my mind like a parasite, feasting on old memories and facts as if there was only so much room inside my head.' She smiled wryly.

'You do have a tendency to let your imagination roam wild,' Frederick said in a gentler tone. 'But Drosselmeier is a decent and clever man; you have no reason to think ill of him.' He loosened his emerald necktie and sat beside Geoffrey, who rested a hand on his leg. Both men were at ease in Marietta's company since she had learnt of their relationship and it gladdened her to see evidence of this.

Marietta turned her attention to her brother's beau. 'And you, Geoffrey? Do you share Frederick's opinion?'

'Sorry, old girl, I do. It sounds rather as if the doctor was trying to muster up the courage for a proposal.'

Frederick held his arms out, a showman seeking recognition. Marietta gave him a cold stare. 'Do you remember teaching me how to play chess?'

Frederick grinned. 'Of course. I still maintain I was an excellent teacher; to this day you play like a woman possessed.'

'Only once I had mastered the strategy of the game. As I sat behind the board for the first time, aware of the myriad pieces and moves at play, you instructed me to follow my instincts. It was the wisest counsel you've ever imparted to me.'

'With such games, yes. You are prone to overthinking. Yet in the ways of men, you are painfully naïve.'

The betrayal bit deep. 'In that case, I shall leave you to your libations,' Marietta said, standing.

'If he truly intended anything nefarious, I would be the first to spring to your defence, Ets,' Frederick said, a little gentler. 'To me it merely sounds as if the man has taken an interest in you. Spare him a little compassion; it is not always easy to be bold on matters of the heart.'

Chapter Nine

'I don't suppose you've seen Miss Worthers this afternoon, Sally?'

'You just missed her, miss. She had the carriage take her into town for a spot of shopping.'

Marietta went downstairs. Frederick stood in the hall, fiddling with the silver cufflinks his valet had fixed in his sleeves.

'Frederick, I don't suppose you would escort me to ballet? Miss Worthers seems to have forgotten her obligation and I fear I'm going to be terribly late.'

'Sorry, Ets. You've caught me on my way out to reconvene with Geoffrey for a spot of billiards at the club. Why don't you ask Mother?'

Marietta gave him a look. 'Are you deliberately being insufferable? You know how Mother feels about ballet. Besides, she's calling on a friend.' She had yet to forgive Frederick for calling her *painfully naïve* a few days earlier.

Frederick shrugged. 'It looks as if you'll have to give this one a miss then.' A footman cloaked him in his winter coat and he hurried down the steps and onto the porch that swept out before the townhouse, where the family chauffeur was waiting for him with the automobile. The same one Marietta had specifically requested. She took a deep breath, suppressing her irritation, half-frozen on the front step. Though it was early, winter had already seized the afternoon, transmuting it to deepest dusk. The sky was stained like wine, the edges of clouds tinged with purpling scarlet.

Jarvis shut the front door behind her to keep the heat in. Carlton, the chauffeur, started the engine and the motor trundled past her. Frederick stuck his head out and gave her a jaunty wave as he was driven past. Resentment stole into Marietta's mood. She couldn't afford to miss an entire rehearsal, not when she had been cast in the principal role. A role which she needed to perfect for her upcoming audition. If only her father didn't possess such ridiculously out-dated views. Her eyes fell on the automobile displayed further back in the drive.

Theodore's Rolls-Royce 10 H.P. With twin cylinders and a massive horsepower of ten, the Rolls-Royce was his prized possession, one which not even the chauffeur, had he been here, was permitted to drive. That pleasure was reserved for Theodore alone. Marietta slid her gaze back onto the house behind her. The curtains were drawn against the early night, its inhabitants either otherwise engaged or occupied outside the slumbering townhouse.

Pulling on her leather gloves, Marietta strode towards the Rolls, her breath pluming. After a moment's consideration, she began the process of starting the engine. When it hummed to life, she slid into the driver's seat, stunning herself with her own audacity.

Despite being a behemoth, the white automobile handled lightly and with precision. Marietta grinned, stroking the wheel as it purred and preened beneath her touch. It was faster and smoother than the old Rover in which she'd learnt to drive. Her plait whipped over her shoulder as she drove out of the wrought-iron gates and through the estate with no one any the wiser. 'Thank you, Freddie,' she murmured.

It had been two years since she'd insisted on him instructing her how to drive an automobile in secret, much against their father's wishes. The day had dawned clear and bright with the snap of autumn in the crisp fallen leaves. Marietta's hair had flown out behind her as she'd accelerated down the roads hidden behind their country estate, hitting over twenty miles per hour, the countryside flaming with the rich colour of a fox's tail.

Now, she chugged past an assortment of stately homes, past the castle and through the city centre as night sighed and settled in. The dome of the town hall was a shadowed husk, the last of the lamplighters trailed past ancient spired churches and modern department stores, their streetlights sputtering to life. And everything dripped with festivity. Carols leaked from church doors, chestnuts roasted on carts and children pressed their faces against toyshop windows. Tomorrow would bring December. Marietta cast her gaze over the streets, her sudden freedom wild and heady. A woman, dressed in evening silks, looked askance at her as she drove past. 'How very scandalous of me!' Marietta called out, giddy with her own daring.

✿

'*The Sleeping Beauty* is the first true ballet *russe.*' Madame Belinskaya prowled along the front of the class. She wore a single egg-shaped emerald strung on a pendant, swinging heavy and pendulum-like over her heliotrope chiffon dress. A delicate tracery of diamonds cobwebbed over it and Marietta had already overhead several speculations on the priceless jewel's history. Now and then, the soft thud of Madame's cane adjusting legs, arms, hips and backs interrupted her oration. Marietta swept her right leg out in a circular motion, brushing the floor with her toes, moving in synchronisation with the class as they executed rond de jambes at the barre. 'When you dance ballet, you are dancing through history and into art. It is steeped in culture and so you must understand what has led you to this point, where the dance has been and what it has represented. Within *The Sleeping Beauty*, we witness the departure of ballet from Paris and discover the shape the Russian Court has held since Peter the Great, its rules and forms as intricate as the inside of a Fabergé egg. An entire world contained within its jewelled shell.' Her hand fluttered to her emerald pendant and Marietta wondered at its origins once more.

Madame Belinskaya had repeated this particular speech many times during rehearsals, and with each repetition, Marietta felt the words burrow deeper into her soul. Some nights she dreamt that she was a tiny porcelain doll, dancing inside a Fabergé egg. In those dreams she danced to music so ancient it no longer carried a name, her heart blazing hot and star-bright. The morning coffee sipped from her Sèvres cup tasted bitter after those dreams, her days were duller, the skies greyer and drowned in clouds.

Madame Belinskaya's cane slammed into the floorboards. 'Grand battements, ladies.'

The dancers faced the mirrors as one, assumed fifth position with their feet, their arms gliding out to the side, and swept their right legs up high in front of them. In front of Marietta, Harriet whipped her leg up at a dizzying height. Marietta strove to reach higher and higher until her leg strained its protest. She glanced at the windows but the darkness was too absolute to discern anything beyond the department store where she'd left the car before racing over to the studio at an inelegant speed.

'Victoria,' Madame Belinskaya called out, 'show us the Bluebird variation once more.'

'I dearly wish we possessed male dancers among our ranks,'

Victoria said, her plaintive sigh as affected as many of the mannerisms of the upper classes. 'I long to perform the coda as Princess Florine without having to wrangle all these pas de deux as solo pieces. Imagine if we had a troupe of *tramagnini* to lift us, how we would soar. Then I should feel as if I were flying across the stage.'

'This is not the seventies, nor are you a prima at La Scala,' Harriet said as Victoria walked past. 'Stay focused, there are men at the Company.' She laughed. 'I'm certain you'll have your wings soon enough.'

Victoria gave her a coquettish smile and assumed her starting position, prepared to flutter into life as a bluebird.

Something deep inside Marietta's stomach twisted. She had been permitted to attend classes once it had been ascertained that Madame Belinskaya adopted a strict female-only policy. Harriet's light interjections served as a reminder that her parents would never allow her to set foot on the stage in a man's arms. Yet how could she strive for greatness, aspiring to be recognised for her talent alongside the likes of Anna Pavlova, if she allowed her skills to perish in the studio. A flash of a thought, of that doll dancing within a jewelled egg, dusty and time-forgotten. She shuddered and turned her attention back to Victoria's winged footwork, her legs beating hummingbird-heart-fast. A knot of anxiety nestled within Marietta as she watched a myriad of brilliant talent spill across the studio in the progression of the rehearsal. She couldn't help fretting that, even if she risked it all, she might never rank among the Company after all. Each of her competitors was as ravenous for that spark of hope as she. They were a thousand untold stories and she was not the sole dancer with dagger-sharp aspirations.

Upon the drive home after class, her anxiety bloomed into a potent cloud of dread. As she rolled up the driveway, the automobile lights fell on Carlton, pacing outside. Frederick must have returned before her then. His expression melted into relief as she came to a stop. She exited the Rolls and strode towards him, the cold snap in the air evident from his pink extremities. 'I'd rather you wouldn't speak of my little outing to anyone, Carlton,' she said smoothly.

The relief fell from his face. His bushy eyebrows clenched together. 'The master expects a full record of my comings and goings, miss.'

'Perhaps you could omit this one, just this once.' Marietta dipped a gloved hand into the folds of her dress to retrieve a couple of crowns.

'Alright, miss,' the chauffeur said, taking the coins and darting a furtive look round the drive before giving her a curt nod and taking his leave.

Still, Marietta's anxiety lingered as she stole back into the house and her bedroom. Sally promptly appeared to dress her in a Turkish-blue gown with soft sleeves draping off her shoulders and pearl beading forging a nacreous trim around the neckline. Long pearl necklaces tumbled down her bodice and soft elbow-length gloves in rich cream drew the ensemble together. Sally arranged her hair in a gentle wave over one shoulder, pinning it back with a sapphire comb. 'You look lovely, miss,' she told her, handing over dangling silver and pearl earrings, one at a time. 'Now you'd best be quick, your father wants a word with you before dinner.'

Marietta's hand stilled. 'Did he happen to mention in regards to what?'

'Sorry, miss.' Sally shook her head, meeting Marietta's eyes in the mirror. 'He's awaiting you in the library.' She twisted her apron in her fingers. Marietta gave her a tight smile before making her way downstairs. Trailing her gloved fingers down the polished bannister, she kept her poise in place like a shield.

The library carried the scent of port and crisped, old pages. Mahogany bookcases lined the walls like soldiers, leather armchairs in verdant greens were grouped together around a low table on which perched a decanter of vintage red wine, Drosselmeier's chessboard and a humidor. Glass-fronted cases in the low-lit edges of the room displayed valuable snuff boxes, a historic gavel Theodore had won at auction, rare editions of Dickens's books and aged maps of their country estate, curling at the edges. Ferns clustered in one corner, a misplaced jungle. The fire was lit, shadows whirligigged on the crimson wallpaper and danced along the Anatolian carpet that a worn lion skin mooched on. When Marietta had been a child, she had ridden the lifeless creature, the carpet transforming into the topography of the African plains in her mind's eye.

It had been Theodore that had exhorted the values of an excellent education. 'Aristotle once said that "the energy of the mind is the essence of life",' he had told a young, beribboned Marietta. 'See to it that yours does not perish.' The words had been accompanied by a copy of *Great Expectations*, which Marietta had not appreciated the irony of until later.

Marietta stepped over the lion's jaws, its glass eyes dull, and took the liberty of seating herself opposite her father, who was reading a newspaper.

'This very evening I was informed by my household staff that my own daughter has become a thief.'

'I merely borrowed the automobile, a necessity in order to—'

Theodore slammed his newspaper down. Marietta flinched, lowering her eyes. Headlines screamed out at her from the crisp paper he had his valet iron for him so as not to deposit ink upon his digits.

***Arrested suffragettes on hunger strike! New line of
the London Underground opened today! Workmen's
Compensation Act passed!***

'And that you bribed the chauffeur, no less. I am appalled by the
behaviour you have so wantonly displayed today. Several of your
mother's acquaintances have sent word of your shocking carousing
through the centre of Nottingham. She is quite mortified. I suppose
your blasted brother instructed you in driving an automobile. I shall
be having a word with him.'

Marietta retained her silence.

'I cannot begin to comprehend the thoughts passing through your
head. You displayed an utter disregard for both your own reputation and
ours, not to mention attempting to handle such a machine by yourself.
If your actions were not so thoughtless and infuriating, I might be
impressed. You possess a sharp mind and not a little of my own penchant
for strategising. You'll make someone a fine head of household.'

He was becoming distracted. Marietta knew she ought to maintain
her silence; retorts were sticky and invited further vexation, feeding
the flames of argument. But her skin prickled, his opinions rankling.
She raised her head and met his eyes. 'I am worth more than that.'

Theodore held up a finger, a warning she remembered well from
her adolescent days. 'Do not test me. I am already severely disappointed in your actions today.'

Marietta's flames of indignation ignited. 'Women attend universities now,' she said. 'Some of us may own property, train as doctors,
and one day in the near future, we shall attain the vote, too. For *all*
women, no matter their class or skin colour. Your attitude is outdated.
A relic better befitting your collection than seeing the light of day.'
She gestured at the glass cases.

Theodore's forehead mapped his consternation. Clouds gathering before a storm. When he spoke, his voice was iron. 'No daughter of mine will address me in this manner, do I make myself clear? I shall not tolerate such brazenness.'

Marietta stood. 'You forget yourself, Father; I am no longer a child.' She walked out of the library in a slow, measured manner. Only once she had shut the heavy door behind herself did she close her eyes, breathing deeply for a spell.

That evening, Marietta rang her bell and ordered a pot of coffee. It arrived with a slice of Victoria sponge, clouded with cream, and her favourite Sèvres cup, hand-painted in gold and Prussian blue. She sat on her bed-silks and poured cup after cup, thinking deep into the night by the light of a single candle. A plan began to form. If she engineered herself to be in the city centre at the opportune moment, she saw no reason why she could not evade Miss Worther's close attention and attend her audition. She crossed the room to her dressing table and opened her jewellery box. She might not be a woman with an independent purse, but she was a woman of means. She ran a finger through the diamonds glittering back at her, contemplating their worth.

From her window, the gas lamps illuminated the street. A bank of clouds clustered on the horizon. When Marietta glanced up at them, for a moment she fancied she'd been transported to some faraway land with mountain ranges looming in the distance with great frosted peaks. Madame Belinskaya had told stories of such sights in continental Europe, where she had toured, dancing on stages across their grand cities. Marietta's longing and ambition rent through her, fierce enough to tear the world in two. She pledged a silent vow to herself: that the plans she had forged over coffee and candlelight would be worth the risk.

Chapter Ten

Nottingham welcomed Christmas in style. The day December arrived, the winter market opened, spilling out from Old Town Square in twinkling lights and festive cheer. It was the kind of event that enticed old and young, rich and poor alike, out from their homes into the cold. The air was scented with iced gingerbread, sugarplums and mulled wine. The spectacle crawled all the way from Long Row and Cheapside, culminating in the centre of the square, where a gigantic Norse fir tree glimmered in strands of electric lights.

'Two hours ought to do nicely. Thank you, Jameson,' Marietta said, gesturing at the vast façade of the Griffin and Spalding department store that rose six generous storeys above her and Miss Worthers.

'Right you are, miss.' He doffed his hat and swung back onto his seat, his black and white livery blending with the carriage paint.

She watched the coffee-coloured pair of horses weaving around the Christmas market that was bustling under the dingy winter sunset. She steadied her nerves for the lies she was about to spin, sweet as sugar. The hour of her audition grew closer. She held onto her beaded reticule, the Italian silk-lined bag weighted down with her pointe shoes and ballet dress tightly rolled and fitted inside.

'I am still failing to understand why it was so imperative we shopped today.' Miss Worther's words were accompanied with a disapproving sniff. Her beetle-eyes scoured the square. 'The city is frightfully busy this time of year.'

'I think it rather magical.' Marietta feigned a look of delight. 'Why, that vendor is selling the most darling boxes of marzipan. I simply must purchase one for Frederick's Christmas stocking.'

Miss Worthers cast a doubtful look at the tangle of stalls and melee of crowds. Vendors shouted their wares, the crowds pressed in and smoke chugged up from the roasting carts. 'I am not certain it is the proper place—'

'Nonsense,' Marietta said firmly, banking on her companion's reticence. 'Why don't you collect your orders and I shall meet you in the tearoom shortly. There really is no need for both of us to venture into this madness.'

Miss Worthers patted the faded roses on her deep fuchsia hat. 'I must admit, the temperatures are rather frigid for my liking. Perhaps a spot of tea shall set me to rights.'

'Be sure to take your time,' Marietta said. 'I may indulge in a short wander to peruse what other wares might sweeten up the Christmas stockings.' She fled into the glittering chaos before Miss Worthers could brook an objection. After pausing behind a stall, Marietta glanced back to see her companion vanish into the Griffin and Spalding foyer with the rest of the smart winter-coated and hatted bustle. Her pinch of guilt was washed away by a wave of empowerment; today, her future rested in her own hands. She then broke into a clipped pace in the opposite direction.

Cutting up Market Street and crossing onto Upper Parliament Street, she let a precious few seconds drizzle by as she gazed at the proud edifice shining before her. The Theatre Royal. The portico stared back at her in all its elegance, its six Corinthian columns holding up the weight of culture in the city. Marietta squared her shoulders and marched in. She was escorted to the back of the theatre by a prim woman who glanced at the rich cloth her coat was cut from in confusion. Ignoring her, Marietta claimed an empty dressing room for herself and changed out of her mauve velvet dress. Between its thickness and the winter coat she had worn, she had absconded a corset without notice. A fact she was grateful for, as no one was there to aid her in its removal. The chatter and gossip of other auditioning dancers filtered through the thin walls and Marietta felt the first nip of nerves.

Before the clocks could strike four, she was waiting in the wings, dipping her pointe shoes in rosin to ensure a better purchase on the stage. The woman who preluded her danced like a dream. Her limbs stroked the air as she coaxed an ethereal gracefulness from her final pirouettes, a bird taking flight. The judges passed no remark other than a desultory, 'Thank you, we shall inform you of our decision in due time,' and the woman nodded, walking across the stage and past Marietta, her neck and arms glistening with sweat, snapping her out of the illusion.

'Miss Marietta Stelle.'

She walked onto the stage. Four tiers of empty seats stared back at her, heavy with expectation. She was framed by a tall column at each side, curtains draped above, electric chandeliers bright and hot on her face. Three judges were to witness her dancing. The tight, haughty expressions they wore did nothing to dispel Marietta's nerves. Two women, imperious enough to rival even Madame Belinskaya, and a man whose attire suggested he had just stepped from Bond Street. He raised a monocle to one eye and peered at her through it. 'A segment from the Rose Adagio, performed as a solo variation. My, that is an ambitious piece. I do hope your decision to adapt Marius Petipa's choreography into a solo piece was a worthy one.' He snapped his fingers at the partial orchestra, who began to play.

Marietta's nerves swelled into a thing with teeth and claws. It left her stricken with a sudden paralysis, depositing her half a beat behind the music pouring into the theatre. Yet this was it. The single chance she had been waiting and hoping and fighting for. The world slipped away until there was nothing but Marietta and the stage she stood on. And so she danced, giving life to Aurora, lending the princess a voice.

No longer was the young princess promenaded by each of her four suitors, one prince giving way to the next in a ceaseless tide. No, Marietta forged her story anew as she pirouetted, unfurling her own free will onto the stage in a string of unsupported arabesques and attitudes. Soaring further into the dance, the music softened into a delicate touch that she fluttered along to, pursued by the strong, rising brass at the climax, the pinnacle towards which Marietta had been striving; that high, solitary arabesque en pointe. The moment crept closer and closer until it arrived in a grand swoop of music that set her soul alight with yearning. Elevating her leg high behind her, her supporting leg lifting her skyward, arms reaching out, Marietta held the position, her face tilted up towards the judges and an imaginary audience.

And there, sat at the very back in the previously empty seats cloistered in the shadows, was Drosselmeier. Yet there was no hiding his silver hair, gleaming like a beacon. Even from this distance, Marietta could see his gaze was locked on her. *How had he known?* She lost her concentration. For a precious second, Marietta wobbled. Fighting to hold her balance, she regained the precarious position. Then, as the music reached its conclusion, she pirouetted, spinning out of control as if her legs had run away with themselves. Her balance slipped and she fell out of the pirouette, attempting to disguise it with an impromptu glissade; gliding across the stage as the music ended. She tore her glance away from Drosselmeier, onto the judges. They looked glazed over and she was unsure if they'd noticed or were too fatigued with the long day of auditions to pay close attention. Either way, Drosselmeier's distraction had wrenched away the wish she had danced her heart out for; that through ballet she might take flight. A gossamer-winged creature on a silver wind, light and free.

She let out a soft gasp. The tiers of seats were empty once more. Perhaps she had conjured his presence, her own imagination seeping poison into her head. No. There within the very recesses of the theatre, a door swung closed. Her throat thickened with fear. For what purpose had he decided to witness her audition, and worse, how had he come to know of the event? Even though Frederick had been quick to dismiss it, she had suspected that there was something peculiar about the man after their walk in the gardens; yet this seemed more ominous still.

One of the women cleared her throat. 'Thank you, we shall inform you of our decision in due time,' she said with no intonation, just as she had to the previous dancer.

Choking back the despair that threatened to suffocate her, Marietta inclined her head and exited the stage. She laced herself back into her velvet dress, topped it with her mulberry winter hat and matching coat and ventured back out into the bustling streets. Every second breath, she tossed a glance back over her shoulder, making certain that among the top-hatted gentlemen on the street, none were Drosselmeier. The gloaming was fast upon her and she had scarce enough time for her second matter of the day.

In her hurry, she almost collided with Victoria, strolling down the street in a claret tea gown and matching coat, arm in arm with Harriet, in cinnamon silk and a fur-trimmed cream coat.

'Marietta?' Victoria's brow puckered. 'Whatever were you doing in the theatre?' With a quick dart of her eyes to either side of the street, she stepped closer and whispered, 'Are you auditioning?'

Marietta inwardly sighed. The chances of colliding with anyone she knew were scarce, yet with a single comment she would be undone. 'It was a passing whim. A mistake,' she said, glancing at Harriet. 'I would be grateful if you did not mention this to anyone.'

'Oh, we would never,' Victoria exclaimed. 'Though I am sure it was not a mistake.'

Harriet said nothing yet her gaze was knowing.

Marietta wondered how things might have been different if the two women were confidantes. Perhaps their trust and kinship would have cushioned her life, their conversations brightened her days. She had a sudden pang for what could have been and never was.

'Do enjoy your outing together. I'm afraid I must dash; Miss Worthers is awaiting me in the tearoom.' Marietta smiled and made her exit.

Unlike other ladies of her class that had inhaled Edith Wharton's novel as if it were a salubrious offering from the gossip columns, Marietta had regarded it as a cautionary tale. Torn between pity for the trapped Lily Bart and frustration at the woman's conniving and self-sabotaging ways, she was resolved never to become such a dependent, grasping creature. Hence her current position, standing beneath a faded sign that read *Pawnbrokers*. She steeled herself against the mild humiliation sure to incur and strode in, her pocket heavy with shame and a Cartier diamond brooch. She was less naïve than some might suspect and if she were to be independent and go against her parents' wishes, she knew that would require more than simple determination; she needed funds. Though a small voice now whispered in her head that she'd never need to use them after how badly her audition had gone.

'I'll give you twenty pounds for it,' the man at the counter said, laying down his magnifying glass. He might have been Theodore's age but possessed such a weathered and ruddy face, Marietta couldn't be sure. Life had not bestowed kindness upon him. The store was dark, lit with gas lamps that were in want of a good cleaning. A gin bottle rested on the counter. Blue Ruin. It flavoured the man's sour breath.

'I shall accept nothing less than fifty pounds,' Marietta said.

The man grunted. 'It's not worth more than thirty and I'm sure to have problems selling it. None of my customers will want such fancy fripperies, I can tell you that.'

The shelves were filled with mere trinkets and the plainer accessories of life, it was true, but Marietta had already caught a glimpse of a gold pocket watch chain drooping out from a drawer the other side of the counter, and behind that, a padlocked back room. She arched an eyebrow at the man. 'Forty-five before I take my custom elsewhere. Do not make the mistake of taking me for a fool.'

'Forty.'

Marietta reached for the Cartier brooch. Set in platinum, two diamond-studded bows enwrapped a diamond flower of such delicacy it could have been crafted from Chantilly lace. It winked at her in the dim light and Marietta looked away. It had been gifted her by her father upon the event of her eighteenth birthday.

'Forty-five pounds it is,' the man said hurriedly. He scowled at her as she watched him count the notes out. She gave him her sweetest smile and hastened out the shop.

Marietta hurried inside Griffin and Spalding, marched past the glass bottles of perfume, through the copious displays of hats and gloves and up to the tearoom. Not a trace remained of Miss Worthers. She returned to the foyer. Through the glass doors, she spotted the black and white Stelle carriage. The town hall clock struck six, booming out across the square. When Marietta turned to peer back inside the department store, she spotted an irate Miss Worthers, puffing her way. 'You have been gone for two hours, I have been beside myself with worry.'

'I do apologise. I'm afraid I have no excuse for my untimely behaviour other than I became quite swept up with all the festive happenings and couldn't help myself exploring just a moment longer. The time seemed to run away from me.' She offered a diffident smile. 'You do know best of all how I adore Christmas,' she added, hoping her former governess would remember her childish excitement at the season with fondness. Also prepared for the other eventuality, Marietta pulled a velvet box from her bag, careful not to disturb the underlying pointe shoes. 'When I realised my error in judgement, I purchased these for you as an apology.' She handed over the box of violet creams.

Miss Worther's expression softened like melted chocolate. 'Well, I suppose there was no harm done. Come, Marietta, we had better return to the house so you may ready for dinner. I believe your mother has once again requested the pleasure of Dr Drosselmeier's company for this evening.'

Marietta's heart sank. After her terrible audition, the very last thing she felt like was playing Drosselmeier's betrothed-to-be.

'I'm afraid the excitement of the day and how dreadfully busy the market was has given me the most frightful headache. I think I shall have to excuse myself and dine alone in my room as I couldn't possibly face the good doctor this evening.'

Chapter Eleven

With only a few days until Christmas, preparations were well underway for the annual Stelle Christmas Ball. Scents of spiced gingerbread biscuits and mulled wine were in the air, and evergreen boughs dripped in red velvet bows, bedecking the entire townhouse. Marietta's performance was quickly approaching, leaving her flitting between rehearsals, attempting to evade Drosselmeier at the dinners he kept attending, and the whirl of social engagements that snowed down on her as Christmas neared.

Still, she took pains to await the postal delivery each day, prepared to steal away the envelope she was awaiting from the Company before it attracted the attention of one of the valets in her father's pocket. Though after the way her audition had concluded, it was likely a futile gesture. To her knowledge, Drosselmeier had not since spoken of that day. She knew he was not what he seemed but she too could bide her time – as Frederick had instructed her with chess, the long game was pivotal and necessitated patience. Waiting and watching, as the ground hardened with frost and the moon and the sun twirled their ancient dance across the skies, for his mask to slip once more.

With just two nights remaining before Christmas, rehearsals had ceased. Marietta endured teas and drinks and dinners with her family, who found inventive ways to seat her beside Drosselmeier at every occasion. He had become an ever-present spectre. Forcing them together further was his latest creation: *The Sleeping Beauty* set for the Stelle Christmas Ball. Large and mysterious packages were carted over from his townhouse each day. 'For what purpose have you had them wrapped?' Marietta had inquired the previous week.

'Perhaps I wish to surprise you,' he had said with a secret gleam, as if he knew of the thoughts she harboured. The suspicion festering within her. Strange occurrences seemed to happen around him and though Marietta grasped to explain them, she could not. And the more she considered them, the more they evaded her logic and trickled from her memories until she struggled to recall them at all.

'And what if I happen to dislike surprises?'

His answer had been a slow smile before vanishing into the ballroom, shutting the doors behind him. Out of curiosity, Marietta had peered through the crack between the doors. As a child, vexed at her exclusion from some glittering ball or other, she had spied upon them, delighted by each flash of crystal chandeliers, lit by a thousand candles, each sparkling gown that waltzed past. Yet instead of a glimpse into Drosselmeier's machinations, there had been nothing, instead a void black as a moonless night.

Pressing two fingers against the ache in her temples, Marietta now wandered down to the ballroom to check the progress of the set. Madame Belinskaya was most displeased they had not had the opportunity for a full dress rehearsal upon it and she was to send word to the ballet mistress of its completion post haste.

The doors were locked. Through them she discerned the sound of tinkering with tools, metallic clangs and voices. Drosselmeier's deep tones pitched against her father's imperious intonations.

'It is the invariable tragedy of life that it is never as long as one would wish it. I do not grow younger, despite my best efforts,' Drosselmeier said, eliciting a chuckle from Theodore before he continued, 'and I oft find myself in need of companionship. Someone with whom to languish before the hearth on the harshest winter nights. To gift me with an heir with whom I might share my knowledge, my legacy.'

'It could be argued, and undoubtedly has in some circles, that I am guilty of over-indulging my daughter. She has had every advantage with books, her education and those dance classes that so consume her. As a result, she is an entitled, wilful creature.'

Drosselmeier laughed. 'I confess I have noticed her pertinacious manner, yet I am certain that I could tame her, if you would do me the honour.'

Marietta caught her breath before it spiralled free.

'Do not be so quick to declare your confidence. Marietta is not to be underestimated; her intelligence is fierce enough to outsmart a sphinx. Though you yourself are quite the Renaissance man. Your courtship shall prove to be an interesting affair indeed.'

'Of that I have no doubts.' The men laughed.

Exhausted by her quickening despair, Marietta leant against the door. Frederick had been right after all; she was painfully naïve when it came to the ways of men. Her father and Drosselmeier were engaged in a different game altogether, one which she had not allowed for.

'I am delighted in your interest, Dr Drosselmeier. Come, let us discuss matters further over a glass of my finest Armagnac.'

Marietta exited before she was seen. Her chest clenched tight and tighter. Her father and Drosselmeier were biting away at her life, hungry and relentless. It wouldn't be long until they had devoured it entirely.

Ida was engrossed in the latest issue of *Tatler* in her personal drawing room when Marietta called on her. The room was a pâtissier's delight in pastels; hand-painted lemon wallpaper, wing-backed chairs plush in cream and mint. Light and soft and rose-scented.

Marietta entered like an ice storm. 'May I speak with you a moment, Mother?'

Ida turned the page. 'Yes, dear. What troubles you this fair morning?'

Marietta selected the chair opposite her mother. 'I have come to seek your counsel. By chance, I have overheard a matter which concerns me deeply.'

'It isn't becoming to listen at doors.'

Marietta waited. She rearranged the folds of her periwinkle tea gown, trimmed with cobalt satin ribbon and yoke frill.

Ida set her magazine aside. 'I suppose the harm has already been committed. What have you unwittingly discovered?'

'I have reason to believe that Dr Drosselmeier is seeking Father's permission in—'

Ida pressed a hand to her chest, cosseted in an embroidered garnet tea gown. A soft gasp fluttered from her. 'Do my ears deceive me? Could the good Dr Drosselmeier possibly be petitioning your father for your hand in marriage?'

'I believe that to be the case.'

Ida's cheeks bloomed with pleasure. 'Oh Marietta, darling, what a fortuitous twist of events. Indeed, the fates have smiled down on us this morn. It seems we shall have a wedding to make preparations for.'

For a second, Marietta wished she had been built to a different model. Most women seemed to delight in engaging in discussions of weddings and children. What did it suggest about her that this was not her desire; was she lacking some intrinsic part of what it meant to be a woman? Was she broken, destined to either submit to a life that bent against the wild winds of her own ambition, or to be cast out adrift and alone?

Marietta spoke her next words quietly, knowing the instant they had tipped from her tongue, Ida's smile would sour. It had been some time since she had seen her mother display such genuineness. 'I do not wish to marry him, Mother.'

Ida's brows drew together in the vaguest semblance of a frown. Once, she had smiled freely, only frowning whenever life conspired to displease her. Once, her emotions had tumbled across her face with abandon. That was before the fine lines had started their creep over her features. They dug in like sharp-fingered goblins and gnawed at her youthfulness, encouraging Ida to close her face off to the world. Witnessing this, Marietta felt she almost understood the lengths Countess Báthory had resorted to in her battle for youth. As reading the *Aeneid* would have her believe, the descent to the underworld was easy.

'I possess no desire to marry Drosselmeier,' Marietta repeated. 'I confess I am not enamoured with the man and to spend a lifetime with him would be unthinkable for me.'

'Darling.' Ida reached for Marietta's hands, holding them in her own. It brought a lump to Marietta's throat as the days when she had been dressed as a doll and paraded about Nottingham, hand in hand with her mother, came to life. Ida's blue eyes shone as if she too was remembering those days. 'There is no need to be frightened, Marietta. I understand your reservations but, remember, women do not marry for love. I certainly did not. And yet I have had many happy years with your father and taken great pride in being a dutiful wife.'

The lump in Marietta's throat swelled. 'Did you ever wish you had chosen differently? Been free to choose who your heart dictated?'

'I did not,' Ida said firmly. 'Your father was the best prospect and I did what was expected of me. Besides, romantic matches are oft an ill-fated affair.' She softened. 'Drosselmeier is a good and kind man and he will take considerable care of you. Of this I have no doubt. I have nurtured an inclination that he thought affectionately towards you since that very first dinner when we made his acquaintance and I am certain that you shall make a most charming bride for him. Perhaps a summer wedding so that we might sail to the continent this spring. I believe a wedding dress from Rue de la Paix is in order, and a trousseau of Italian silks, too … ' She retreated into her own daydreams, unaware of Marietta.

Marietta did not see the silks and laces that her mother dreamt of. She saw her pointe shoes packed away in a box, where they would languish until dust shrouded both her shoes and her delusions of freedom. Her sadness fractured, filling her with ragged ice. 'You have failed to understand me,' she said, the ice leaching into her words, turning them frozen and brittle. 'I will refuse his hand. I do not trust Drosselmeier. There is something disconcerting about him and I no longer feel safe when I am in his presence.'

Ida's laugh was light and musical. It suited the delicate freshness of her drawing room. 'Do not be so innocent, darling; such is the way of men. They tend to assert an overbearing dominance over women; it reminds them of their ancestors who rode across the kingdom in armour, protectors of the land and all fair women who resided there. A trifle foolish, perhaps, but harmless enough. You shall soon become accustomed to it; there is no need for such dramatics. And once you are wed, I can teach you the ways in which you may shape their behaviour to your own benefit.'

Marietta released her mother's hands. With such opinions Ida would never understand. Little wonder that Frederick could not be his honest self in her presence. She shuddered to think how her mother would react if she knew the true state of affairs between him and Geoffrey. 'I think not. If you will not trust my word then has it not occurred to you that I may wish to pursue avenues other than marriage? My life ought to be mine to do with what I wish.'

Ida pinched the bridge of her nose with two delicate fingers. 'Upon reflection, do you not find your behaviour deeply selfish?' When she glanced at Marietta, the steel in her gaze was hard and unyielding. 'Your father and I have provided everything you could have wished for since the day you were born. You are not free from obligation. You shall repay us and fulfil your debt to society by accepting Drosselmeier's proposal, once offered. I shall not hear otherwise on the matter. I will forgive your words today as I understand the news was unexpected, but I anticipate after time to reflect you will come to your senses. This is the path you are on, Marietta. The next time we speak, I expect you to understand this and be graceful about your position in life.' She stood up, smoothing down her dress and composure in one. 'And when you marry, you shall wear a smile as lovely as your wedding dress.'

Long after she exited the room, Marietta remained, frozen with worry as her life marched out of her control.

Upon awakening the following morning, Marietta found a velvet box beneath her pillow. She set her coffee cup aside to open it. Inside, she was surprised to find the same Cartier brooch she had pawned but a few days earlier. A thick notecard held an insignia of a mouse, stamped in a swirling design that incorporated the initial 'D'. She pressed her trembling fingers to her mouth. She had thought no one had seen her inside the pawnbrokers; how had Drosselmeier known of the brooch? Perhaps he had followed her from the theatre. Ripples of unease furrowed through her. Her suspicions were further substantiated, yet it appeared Drosselmeier was becoming bolder, and she worried what he intended next.

The door clicked open and Sally entered. 'Your diamond brooch. I had wondered if you'd misplaced it. Is everything all right, miss? You've gone awfully pale.'

'I too thought it had been misplaced. Was this not returned to you?'

Sally shook her head, her mouth opening as she spoke. Marietta failed to hear a single word above the roaring horror in her head.

Drosselmeier had entered her bedroom while she slept.

Chapter Twelve

In a rare spell of fortune, when Marietta entered the dining room for Christmas Eve dinner, she managed to source a seat beside Frederick. Having no family to speak of, Drosselmeier had been invited to join them and sat opposite. Marietta felt him watching her, his frosted eyes sinking ever deeper into her skin. A gaze with hooks and shadows.

As per custom, they dined on courses of minced pies, roasted nuts, roast goose stuffed with chestnuts, served with gooseberry and bread sauces, followed by fruitcake and plum pudding, flaming with brandy. And all the while, Drosselmeier watched Marietta. She started concealing her joy, burrowing it into that place where her life was tethered, its only witness the blood roaring through her veins, the wind-rush of her breathing. When she was a girl, Christmas Eve had been her favourite day of the entire year. The traditions of feasting and exchanging gifts beside the Christmas tree in the evening filled her with sparkling delight. Marietta clenched her spoon and smiled brighter, suddenly determined not to allow Drosselmeier to dull that delight.

When the feast came to a close, Marietta followed her mother to the drawing room, to retire for coffee and await the men. A large deep-green Christmas tree sparkled in the centre, lit with candles and festooned with glass baubles, golden bells and sugarplums, with red ribbons laced around it. Presents wrapped in silver paper were heaped underneath. Ida played carols at the Steinway while Marietta sang *O Christmas Tree* and *The Twelve Days of Christmas* until even she, at long last, felt the festivities of the season penetrate her mental chainmail. Tomorrow, at long last, she would take to the stage as Aurora. After that, the future stretched wider with possibilities than it had in an age.

Drosselmeier was the first to join them, his arms filled with berry-red and green crackers. Ida pulled one with him, squealing when it burst in a shower of sparks and a loud bang. A paper twist of roasted nuts and a wind-up toy mouse fell into her lap. Her laughter ringing out, she wound it up and they all watched it scurry around the base of the Christmas tree, squeaking and swishing its tail as it went.

'Would you care to pull one with me?' Drosselmeier offered Marietta a striped green and gold cracker. Not trusting herself to voice the emotions sending her stomach pitching, a sea in a winter's storm, she grasped the end and tugged. Drosselmeier pulled back, his long fingers tight around his end. The cracker failed to succumb to their efforts.

Marietta gave him an impassive look. 'You are mistaken if you believe that in allowing me to win you shall wend your way into my affections.'

Something unfettered ran across Drosselmeier's face. 'Perhaps it is not necessary for me to win your affection. Marriage is predominantly an economic agreement after all. Affection oft follows later.'

Marietta stiffened with anger. She doubted any man should ever possess her love, not while she remained her own greatest devotee. She did not voice the thought aloud, not under the surreptitious glances her mother was casting at her and Drosselmeier, heavy with

81

curiosity and touched with a knowing compassion. This was likely to be her final Christmas with her family with what was to come and she did not care to tarnish it. She wrenched the cracker from Drosselmeier while he was awaiting her response. It exploded in a spurt of golden confetti, raining sugarplums and hazelnuts. A small nutcracker accompanied them. Painted in the livery of a toy soldier, he wore shiny gold buttons on a red, double-breasted military coat, and navy trousers tucked into glossy black boots. She slid it into her dress pocket without a word.

'Am I correct in assuming that you've heard of my intentions towards you?' Drosselmeier's gaze dipped to encompass her ivory satin gown, encrusted with midnight beading and vintage blush lace. His breath was hot against her bare collarbone and she inched away a little to reclaim her own space. Yet he moved with her, closing the gap between them, his thigh pressing against her gown.

'Do my eyes deceive me? Have you started without waiting for us?' Frederick exclaimed upon entering the drawing room with Theodore. His spotted necktie was undone, and the scent of cigar smoke clung to him.

'Why, of course not; you are just in time for the presents,' Marietta said, diverting the energy of the room. Drosselmeier shifted away from her and their intimate conversation shattered.

'Brilliant.' Frederick clapped Theodore on the back. Jarvis poured glasses of hot mulled wine as the presents were given out.

Marietta's gifts were well received. A Burberry driving cap for Theodore, an elegant writing set adorned with lilies for Ida and a gold fountain pen for Frederick. His proper present was a box of paints, wrapped and sitting on his bed, to be discovered later. Marietta opened boxes of chocolates, a lace-trimmed picture hat from Paris, a bottle of Après L'Ondée by Guerlain that conjured the scent of orange blossom and violet basking in vanilla sunshine, and a delicate pearl comb from Ida, studded with shining blue glass.

'Allow me to draw your attention onto my gift,' Drosselmeier said, approaching her once more. He plucked a present in shining silver paper from the air with a flourish and handed it to her. It tinkled with the motion. Tiny bells and a sprig of holly were affixed to the satin ribbon. A paper tag inscribed her name alongside the swooping outline of a mouse incorporating Drosselmeier's initial that she recognised from her returned Cartier brooch.

Her hands trembled at its sight. 'You are most kind,' she said stiffly. She dug her nails into the ribbon to untie the tight bow and loosen the thick paper. Inside was a box. Stamped with golden lettering that read *Drosselmeier's Enchanting Creations*. The little wooden lid slid open to reveal a glass globe sitting in the velvet lining. Upon lifting it out, she discovered it was a large, ornate snow globe, set on a bronze base with thick glass. She shook it, setting the snow a-whirling over the beautiful scene inside, crafted down to delicate minutiae. A heartbeat later, she realised some of the details were moving, as if miniature dolls were living inside the creation. An eerie echo of her own dreams of dancing within a Fabergé egg.

Frederick's face loomed over it. 'Ah, Paris.' He peered into it. 'What marvellous attention to detail; why there are even little boats chugging along the Seine.'

Marietta frowned and shook the snow globe once more. The feathered flurries settled over the same scape she'd been previously admiring. St Petersburg. The Mariinsky Theatre. And tiny figures waltzing before the famous eggshell-blue and white building in all their finery. Where Madame Belinskaya had once prowled the stage. Where Tchaikovsky's *The Sleeping Beauty* had first been performed some sixteen years ago. It was Marietta's deepest heart-wish to visit. She watched the last snowflakes fall onto the fir tree nestled beside the theatre. 'How can it be possible for us to see different scenes within the same snow globe?' she asked Drosselmeier, quite forgetting herself in her wonder. It failed to surprise her that Frederick had been entertained with the promise of Paris. Her brother desired nothing more than to decamp to L'Hotel on the Sixth Arrondissement and wander his beloved Oscar Wilde's haunts by day, painting by night.

Drosselmeier sat beside her, taking the snow globe in his hands and shaking it. 'Ah, this is no ordinary snow globe. It holds a certain charm of its own. What you see within it is a reflection of your deepest self, nothing but the desires it pains you to harbour.' His voice slunk lower. 'It haunts you, does it not? The depth to which you feel, which you want. I can taste the longing pouring through your veins, calling out across the worlds.' He brushed a lock of hair from her shoulders. His touch grazed her with ice. Froze the words on her tongue.

'Drosselmeier, you simply must grace us with your company and let us in on your secrets,' Theodore called from across the room, watching something Frederick had set up on the floor that moved in little mechanised jerks and whirs.

'Yes, do come and share your magic,' Frederick added.

Ida clapped her hands together. 'Why, it is enchanting!'

Drosselmeier handed the snow globe back to Marietta. Her immobility shattered as she looked within its glass, searching out his secrets. Yet the snow had already shifted, obscuring whatever dark dreams of his had played through the globe. 'Now that would be divulging too many of my secrets,' he whispered as he walked away.

The Christmas party promised to stretch deep into the night but Marietta's armour had cracked. A thin trail of despair bled through the fissure. She soaked in it until she could bear it no longer and slipped away.

In her bedroom, she abandoned her gown and corset, unpeeling the straitlaced version of herself she had been all evening. Exchanging them for a softer ballet dress, the bodice white and fitted, the skirt ephemeral and gauzy, and white satin pointe shoes. Tying the ribbons around her ankles tended to soothe her, grounding her thoughts in the present, in the lustrous sheen of satin as it slipped through her fingers. Tonight, nothing calmed her wild heartbeat. She needed to dance, to feel like herself. And not a small part of her desired to ruin Drosselmeier's surprise and see her set for the first time. It was not his place to withhold it from her. She loosened her hair from its pompadour, letting it fly down her back in a burst of raven feathers, and walked downstairs. Taking care to tread softly, Marietta made her way past the library and dining room, where the footmen were clearing evidence of the feast, and entered the double doors of the ballroom.

She switched the lights on. The series of chandeliers flickered to life, illuminating the room. Tables coated in starched white table-cloths like fallen snow, surrounded by plush chairs, were dotted around. A space was carved out for dancing in the centre. The panelled walls, oil paintings and thick drapes over the eastern windows bore evergreen garlands. Sprigs of mistletoe and intermingling wreaths of holly and ivy formed the centrepieces. The front of the ballroom had been raised by means of a wooden platform into a stage. Crimson velvet curtains hung over it, obscuring the set from view. A pair of Christmas trees framed it, drizzled with ribbons and tiny glass baubles, ready to sparkle and bask in the candles that would alight on their branches.

Marietta closed the doors behind her and crossed the ballroom in a spark of defiance and delicious anticipation. She ascended the steps. The velvet curtains were thick and heavy, falling behind her with a swish as they enclosed her on stage. A secret world only she could enter.

Chapter Thirteen

The ballet set was a frosted night. Fir trees glistened under the bright starlight, twinkling with electric lights. A tower hulked in the corner, brooding and sinister, and in the centre, a palace sprawled out, its twisting spires piercing the night sky. There were no doors to enter the palace. In their place, a large grandfather clock counted the hours, the gatekeeper of time and doorways both.

Half-hearing the opening strains to the Rose Adagio – the scene scored into her memory, echoing with her almost-fall – Marietta rose en pointe in a series of fluttering steps across the painted snow-white stage. She traced one pointed foot up her other leg in a développé, reaching her knee before stretching it out and up, her weight balanced on one pointe. Though she twisted her body into unfeasible shapes through ballet, she never felt as relaxed or as free as when she surrendered herself to the dance. Marietta smiled as she closed the position, pirouetted and repeated it, twirling across the stage and into an arabesque, her heart beating as if it might take flight. If only she could have danced in such a manner during her audition. The grandfather clock ticked with each perambulation of its hands about the clock face. Marietta's thoughts fouettéd through her mind, turning faster and faster, each one sparking a new whirl before the previous had expired. Her life had taken a crooked turn as if it were a pirouette destined to crumble.

Something behind her clicked.

Marietta looked about herself but she was alone. The sound appeared to have originated from the palace. It was painted in the pale pink of the peonies that bloomed in the Arboretum in May, with lily-white towers. Small mechanised figures had now materialised in backlit windows, affording a glimpse inside. Two young princes in livery similar to that of Drosselmeier's toy soldiers were sword fighting. A queen sat beside a king, both waving from their thrones. And high above them all, sequestered in the tallest tower, was the oldest story of all. A princess. A vision of beauty clad in her lovely gown, whirling before her mirror. Again and again she turned, spinning a dark fairy tale, trapped within the mechanism. Inside a prison of silk and satin and gauze. When Marietta peered closer, she saw golden mice embroidered on the princess's dress, ballet slippers on her feet. A facsimile of her own Cartier brooch pinned above her heart.

Marietta stormed back onto the stage.

She did not notice the hours deepening into night or the hands sweeping round the grandfather clock. She lost herself in her dancing, spinning and turning until her vision blurred, determined to execute a perfect string of fouettés, her frustration a swelling tide spilling out into her leaps across the stage, propelling her further and higher, the invisible orchestra swallowing her pain until she felt fierce once more and a new feeling bubbled to the surface. Rage.

Her lips curved into a new shape of smile; a promise.

Then came an unmistakeable sound further back in the ballroom and her smile faltered. It appeared she was no longer alone. She flung open a velvet curtain, revealing Drosselmeier standing there.

She stepped back in astonishment. 'Dr Drosselmeier. You quite startled me. I had not thought we would still have guests at this hour.'

'My apologies.' His frosted eyes trailed down her thin dress.

'I had hoped to secure a moment alone with you tonight before you absconded.'

'And what matter could be so imperative that you wished to discuss it tonight?' she asked, with a sharpness to her tone that would not have been there several weeks prior.

Drosselmeier stepped closer. 'Dear Marietta, I believe you already know the matter of which I speak. Would you do me the honour of becoming my wife?' He reached for her hand.

Dazed, Marietta allowed him. 'I am greatly honoured by your request yet I am afraid I must decline.'

Silence fell between them. His grasp on her hand tightened as she tried in vain to withdraw it, her face becoming hotter as her unease grew.

Drosselmeier's stare hollowed her out. 'As I have already told you, what I covet, I find a way to possess. And you, Marietta, I have coveted for quite some time.'

Marietta's thoughts tumbled and spun. 'Why, whatever for? I am not a beautiful woman; there are others far lovelier than I. Far kinder, far more caring and far richer, too. I urge you to turn your attentions elsewhere.'

'Ah, but you are a creature as driven as myself. I can see the ambition, the longing, the wanting in your blood. I hear it singing to me. It was you that has summoned my attention, Miss Stelle. I am quite under your spell.' He spoke in a sonorous voice, deep as wild magic. His words were a violent promise.

Marietta stepped back, pulling her hand from his. 'Do not transfer the blame upon me, I refuse to have anything to do with it. You know very well I did nothing to lead your thoughts in such a direction.'

'Are you playing games with me?' he murmured. 'For I must confess, that is a delicious thought.' He moved closer to her, his hands coming to rest lightly on her shoulders.

Marietta was suddenly afraid. 'Do not dare to presume you may touch me in this manner.' She pushed his hands off her. He let them trail down her arms, holding her tighter in his grasp.

He bent his head to her neck and inhaled. 'Is that a hint of anger I detect? It perfumes your blood like an aged wine.'

Horror sliced through Marietta. She fought to maintain control over her senses so that her voice wouldn't tremble and betray her fear. 'I demand you release me at once.'

He removed his hands. Marietta strode on shaking legs towards the stage exit, her pointe shoes clacking.

'I shall not accept your refusal,' Drosselmeier called after her.

She stopped. 'I assure you that I shall never be your betrothed. My mind is set on the matter and no amount of following me through the city or entering my bedroom by night shall alter it. You are behaving in the manner of a petulant child who lusts after a toy he cannot have. That is the sole reason you cannot accept my disinclination to wed you; you are ensnared by the hunter's thrill.'

Something in Drosselmeier's eyes shifted and she knew her words had met their mark. His gaze turned colder, wilder, his smile a weapon. 'Perhaps. Yet it is the strongest women who taste the sweetest when they are broken.'

'You shall never break me.'

The clock struck midnight.

As the hands slotted into place, the first chime sounded. Deep and melodic at once, it was not unlike the way in which Drosselmeier's voice crept into your senses. He gestured at the grandfather clock. 'Please, be my guest. I did not invite you into the ballroom tonight, it was your doing alone to venture here. Now that my surprise has already been spoilt, why not stay and watch.'

With the second chime, the clock began shuddering. Marietta took a step back. 'I do not think that a wise idea.' She wondered if he had lost his mind. Drosselmeier slid a hand into his jacket pocket and retrieved a small object. He held it up. It was a key.

On the third chime, the centre panel of the grandfather clock opened.

Marietta's fear took wing. Her heart fluttering in her chest, she ran down the centre of the ballroom to the double doors. They were locked. She screamed through the gap where they joined; the doors were paper-thin and there were a number of staff in proximity at all times. Surely at least one of the footmen would hear.

The fourth chime sounded.

Drosselmeier's laugh was as unfeeling as a killing frost. He jumped down from the stage and walked towards her, amusement stalking the lines round his eyes. 'Do give me a little credit. As you have already learnt, I have far more cunning than your average suitor. I shall not be as easily persuaded to turn my attentions elsewhere. Not now this has become so very interesting. The more frightened you become, the greater my appetite grows. I shall make you mine, *meine kleine Tänzerin.*'

Marietta's gaze fell to the opacity between the doors. She peered through the keyhole and into blackness. When she pounded her hands on the doors, it sounded muffled.

The fifth chime.

She ran back to the stage in an attempt to distance herself from Drosselmeier's advances. He continued his slow walk after her. Marietta's fear burrowed under her skin, quickening her breath. At once she knew what it was to be prey, the rabbit's terror of the fox, the fundamental knowledge of what it feels to be crushed within those jaws evident in its frantic eyes. So too did she see the women that had fled this path before her, an unending current from the belittled, trapped and underestimated to the broken and tormented. She backed away from him until she was pressed against the grandfather clock. A whirl of cold air seemed to emanate from it. 'I beg of you, release me,' she whispered as Drosselmeier set foot on the stage.

The sixth chime.

Drosselmeier's answering smile permitted her a glimpse beneath his mask. She could not comprehend what she saw there yet it sent her out of her mind with fear. Panic dribbled down her logic.

'I will make you regret denying me.,' he whispered. 'After a little time to think on how foolish your refusal is, you shall beg me to reconsider.'

Marietta climbed into the grandfather clock. She clicked the panel shut behind her and held onto it with her fingernails. Her breaths came hard and fast against the wood as she closed her eyes, waiting for Drosselmeier to rip the panel open. She felt the seventh, then the eighth chimes resonate through the clock and yet still she waited. She had heard tales of the things some men liked to inflict upon unwilling women and she could think of no other reason why Drosselmeier would have locked her inside the ballroom with him.

The ninth chime. The air was colder inside the clock, icing her arm. On the tenth chime, Marietta discovered a tiny crack in the wood. She peered out, holding her breath. Drosselmeier had vanished. Bracing herself for his sudden reappearance, she tested the panel with a gentle touch. It failed to open from the inside. She had trapped herself inside a virtual coffin.

Recalling Drosselmeier's carriage clock she suffered a panicked notion that perhaps the clock only opened on the stroke of midnight and she would be left imprisoned within it until Christmas was over. Without a sound, she reached back, feeling for the back of the clock. Once she was certain Drosselmeier had exited the room, she was sure she could find a weaker point in the construction to force her way out. She stretched her arm back, further and further, yet there was no back to the clock. The eleventh chime rang out.

She stepped away from the panel to investigate, mindful that Drosselmeier might at this very moment be walking towards her in the darkness, aware of a second entrance to the clock. She went deeper. The air froze around her.

The twelfth and final chime struck.

Her teeth chattered and her fear bit deeper; the cold must be another of Drosselmeier's tricks. With each step, she lowered her pointe shows softly onto the wood, determined not to call attention to her location. Until her shoe crunched down on something and she stilled. The darkness had shifted from the opacity of confinement and loss of hope to a dark jewel that glimmered with the promise of distant starlight. Her eyes adjusted to the darkness, revealing a white glow.

She was standing in snow.

And surrounding her, as far as the eye could see, were white-topped fir trees.

ACT ONE

Scene Two

If Marie no longer dared to mention her adventures, she was still besieged by memories of the Kingdom of Sweets; and when she reflected on them, she could see everything clearly, as if she were once again in the Christmas Forest, or on the River of Attar of Roses, or in the City of Candied Fruits. And so, instead of playing as she used to with her playthings, she would sit very quiet and still, lost in thought, and everybody called her 'the little dreamer'.

——ALEXANDRE DUMAS, THE STORY OF A NUTCRACKER

Chapter Fourteen

The snow was crisp and firm, forging a path of granulated sugar. Marietta wandered deeper into the enchantment. It was heavy with the scent of forest, snow and marzipan. Emerald fir trees towered up, brushing against the midnight patchwork of constellations. When she had last considered the night sky in Nottingham, Orion had been hunting through it, Perseus triumphed over his defeat of Medusa and the charioteer Auriga blazed by. A canvas of Greek mythology, the stories familiar old friends. Here, the stars were a language she did not speak. Pivoting in place, her breaths grew ragged, her thoughts tangled with wonder. 'How can this be?' she whispered aloud, uncertain and deeply suspicious of Drosselmeier's involvement with it. Drosselmeier. The mere thought of his name lanced her with panic. She could not return to that locked ballroom. Far better to hide for a short while until the danger had passed. Even as the cold settled onto her skin and her breath turned to frozen wisps.

A sweet melody, reminiscent of Chopin's most beloved nocturne, trickled out from behind the wall of firs to her east. Entranced by its rising and falling notes, Marietta followed the path of the music to a glistening, icy bend of river, lit by glowing globes of ice. Children and adults alike skated along, clad in fur-lined capes and velvet trousers, conversation and laughter spilling from them. Marietta studied the scene. She had been considering whether she'd delved into an elaborate invention of Drosselmeier's, yet here were people. This could not be his creation. He must have led her to some strange point of entry, trapping her elsewhere until she acquiesced to his demands. Fear prickled down her spine as the curtains were whisked away and Marietta realised what she had been denying for weeks: Drosselmeier possessed strange and powerful gifts. Perhaps it was the confrontation with the physical proof of another world or perhaps it was that Marietta had recovered a long-forgotten sense here, but being in this place reinstated her old, childhood belief in magic.

And Drosselmeier had been wielding enchantments from her first glimpse of his entry to Nottingham; she had just lacked the belief to recognise it.

A small child, chubby with youth and rosy-cheeked, waved at her. After a brief hesitation, Marietta waved back. With a glance over her shoulder, Marietta approached the ice. The music emanated from two men with twirled beards and fluffy hats playing peculiar stringed instruments. They were situated on the other side of the looping river bend. As she neared the ice, she discerned that the river swept around a large town.

She saw wooden chalets, their sloping roofs dusted with snow, and taller constructions with swirling, whipped-cream peaks. A town square was crammed with little wooden huts, arranged in concentric circles through which more people bustled around a market. Beside that was the beginnings of a great frozen lake. A tall, sheer bridge crossed it at a vertiginous point, extending to a palace that belonged in a pâtisserie window. The palace and lake were wrapped in a cloak of sheer ice-cliffs, draped with waterfalls frozen mid-fall, glimmering under the starlight like Marietta's sequinned Worth cape back home. Everything was edged with the encroaching fir trees.

A rustle sounded from the forest. Marietta stepped onto the ice with a shiver, desperate to lose herself within people and the twisting paths that drew to mind a Bavarian fairy tale of a town. Grappling for purchase in her satin shoes, she affected a gliding motion across the ice until she'd navigated her way over the river and back onto the snow of the opposite bank. When they were younger, they used to spend Christmas on their country estate up north, where Marietta would pester Frederick until he'd take her skating on their frozen lake. There, the ice had been rough and the wind harsh, filled with teeth and distant bird cries. Here, the ice was smooth and the skaters accomplished, their skates thin and light as wings.

A path presented itself. Pastel pink and lilac cobblestones. Marietta followed it into the town. As she passed the chalets, she discovered they weren't wooden after all but frozen gingerbread. Icicles clustered along their slanted eaves. Other little dwellings were circular with the striped red and white of candy canes. She paused and grazed a wondering hand over the cobblestones, smiling with delight when she smelt marzipan. The path soon widened, pouring into the central circular market. Here, the air itself was sugared. Sweet and soft, like inhaling a wisp of lost cloud.

Small gingerbread huts perched on the marzipan cobblestones, with iced roofs and windows through which wondrous items and confectionery were being sold. Marietta wandered by, her heart full of that childlike wonder that leads young ones to await Father Christmas's sleigh and stockings filled with sweets and toys by that nocturnal visitor, garbed in green. She wished she had never lost her belief in magic. Never set it aside when she grew older and it was no longer charming for her to still hold such beliefs. Perhaps then she might have trusted her instincts.

One hut offered molten chocolate in peppermint bowls; another, pale-pink sugar mice that squeaked once tasted; yet another, working gingerbread trains that chugged along candy cane tracks. And then there were the huts that whispered of grander shades of magic. The ones which sold keys in an assortment of shapes and sizes, vowing entry to the world of your choice. Silvered sleigh bells promised to ring the instant someone fell in love with you. Snow globes that revealed the viewer's heart-dreams like a window cut into their souls. Marietta frowned and stole closer to examine one when a voice sent her thoughts spiralling.

A woman was leaning her elbows on the window of her hut, watching Marietta. She was almost concealed from sight by a plethora of dangling snow boots and a counter stacked with tiny peppermint fir trees, dipped in chocolate dark as night. She spoke in a curious tongue that Marietta was glad to find she could understand once she'd puzzled through the nuances of her accent.

'From whence did you originate?'

Marietta hesitated.

The woman laughed, dissolving her eyes into a sea of crinkled parchment. 'Alas, do not fret. We greet plenty of wanderers each moontide.' She had the tiniest button of a nose, yet despite her easy laugh, her eyes remained cold.

Marietta kept a firm hand on her wits. 'Might I inquire as to where I am?'

'Why, you have discovered the delights of Everwood, of course. A land of ice and sugar, enchanted beyond measure. From which door did you seek entry?'

'Do you mean to inform me that there are more worlds than mine and yours?' Marietta's mind whirred and ticked faster at the very notion.

The woman gave another hearty laugh. 'There are many more than you or I could even guess at. Some are miniscule, entire universes in a space the size of a teacup. Others are grander than you could imagine. Though you must never forget, you yourself change to suit each one. The moment you stepped into Everwood, you were granted the ability to speak and understand our tongue. Other changes bear lasting consequences. My son once found himself made of wood in a land of puppets. He took haste to leave that one.' Her eyes glazed over as she peered into her own memory. 'Though his left knee still bears a stiff creak on a frozen day.'

Marietta's head was set a-whirling, as if she'd been spinning in fouettés. 'Oh dear,' she managed.

'Though in Everwood we're well used to wanderers, of course. Lost souls have a habit of finding themselves here. It is always a little overwhelming at first, but my best advice to you would be to *leave*.'

Marietta was certain she had misheard. 'I beg your pardon?'

The woman shrugged. 'It's a fine idea to have a taste of another world, a morsel to remember in future years when you've silvered and the stars are calling for you, but unfamiliar dangers cut the deepest.' The smile melted from her face, her grey, lined eyes haggard in its absence. She nodded at the palace towering above the town, her voice whisper-soft. 'I suggest you leave before you attract their attention.'

Marietta looked at the palace. Its peak punctured the star-speckled sky.

The woman retreated into her tangle of wares before reappearing with a pair of boots. She set them down on the gingerbread counter. The colour of fresh white wool, they were equipped with thick soles. 'You have such strange shoes in your world.' She cast a look at Marietta's pointe shoes. 'Mighty pretty but once the snow has invited itself onto your flesh, it won't be long before you find yourself suffering from ice fever.'

Marietta resisted the urge to wrap her arms about herself. It was all she could do to keep her teeth from clattering together. She held her chin high and met the woman's eyes. 'They are perfectly lovely. Though I regret I'm not carrying any currency with me.' Shame engulfed her in a sticky burst.

'Your kind never do.' The woman's voice sharpened. 'I would be happy to exchange them for the trinket adorning your hair.' She pointed at the pearl comb Marietta still wore.

Marietta closed her fingers around it, considering. Her toes had grown numb in the bitter conditions and she feared frostbite. Yet the comb was laced with cultured Akoya pearls and worth far more than the trade the woman had offered. 'I'm afraid this is rather dear to me as it was a gift from my mother,' she hedged.

The woman softened. 'How about that then?' She nodded at the satin sash looping Marietta's waist. 'Or if you exchange those—' she pointed at Marietta's gold earrings '—I shall add this into the bargain.' She bent beneath the counter and emerged with a cape in richest emerald, trimmed with gold. It looked thick and warm and Marietta felt the cold more keenly at the sight of it.

'Very well.' Marietta unfastened her earrings.

The woman seized them at once, her eyes agleam. 'There's always a pretty price to be fetched for a wanderer's wares. That manner of crossing holds a magic all of its own.' She slid the snow boots over to Marietta.

Sliding off her pointe shoes and the padding ensconcing her toes was a delicious relief. The snow boots were lined with a thick fluffy material that Marietta held no words for, as comfortable as treading upon the softest carpet. After fastening the cape round her shoulders, the chill lessened. She tied the ribbons of her ballet shoes together, draped them round her neck and thanked the woman.

She flapped a hand at Marietta. 'Yes, yes, much obliged I'm sure. Now you must leave at once. The frozen sugar palace might look a delight to set your mouth a-watering but unspeakable cruelties have poisoned those candied halls.'

Marietta glanced once more at the distant palace. 'Is it truly made of frozen sugar?'

'Yes. Made by the Grand Confectioner himself. It's a mastery of craft all confectioners in Sugar Alley aspire to. And cold enough to strip the skin from your bones.'

Marietta heeded her words and traced her path back. She had dwelt long enough in this peculiar place; Drosselmeier must have returned to the Christmas celebrations by now. Once Frederick heard of his unwanted advances, she hoped he would be cast from the townhouse. Still, she had a twinge of regret that she couldn't stay and discover more of this enchanting place. Her walk slowed as she absorbed the scenes around her. Pillowy rolls baked in the shape of snowmen, the aroma reminiscent of bakeries she'd patronised in Paris. Snowflakes fashioned into jewellery, velvet mittens scented with vanilla. A vat of popcorn emitting curlicues of caramelised steam as the seller shovelled it into twists of paper. A large stall, grander than all, sold nothing but small glass vials of shimmering blue-green. Its sign advertised them as melting enchantments. As Marietta passed by, the sellers closed their gabled windows to the protests of the long queue outside.

When she took a wrong turn and found herself confronted with a stable, she halted. Miniature reindeer cavorted about, fluffy with stubby legs and antlers strung with tiny golden bells that jangled sweetly. Their formed antlers marked them as full grown yet they reached just the height of Marietta's knee. She smiled before tearing herself away to cross the frozen river.

The lights and bustle of the town receded. Marietta trudged through the snow slower and slower, the cold permeating her bones. The fir trees closed behind her, enfolding her in their silence once more. Her fear of Drosselmeier fluttered anew, alongside a fresh worry; being preoccupied with fleeing him, she had failed to look back to take note of what the entrance to this world had looked like and she very much doubted she would happen to find the grandfather clock on a mound of snow to mark it. What if Drosselmeier's plan was more nefarious than she had accounted for and she was destined to be trapped in this world? Her confusion settled deeper; she could not understand why he had sent her into such a delightful town.

She walked and walked until she was certain she had been walking further than she remembered. Worry edged into panic, needling her with its barbs. In each direction she turned, she faced giant firs and heaps of glittering snow. Nothing distinctive marked her path, no music or light could be gleaned from any which way she faced. It was all endless, silent forest. And once she had turned, she found she couldn't recall the initial direction she had been headed for. It was possible she had twisted her route and was none the wiser. Perhaps Drosselmeier had never intended her to reach the darling town. Perhaps he only knew of this forest.

Her breath a feathered plume, she buried her hands in the pockets of her cape. Something crinkled against her fingertips. Marietta frowned and pulled it out. It was a note, written on a scrap of parchment and wrapped around a small sachet. It proclaimed itself as:

Shrinking dust.
Apply a fingertip's worth to shrink
any part of yourself you desire.

Marietta thought of the woman's tiny nose and wondered if she'd added it on purpose. She shook the thought away; with a woman driving such a hard bargain as she, it was sure to simply have been forgotten in the pocket. She tucked the sachet into her dress pocket, sank her hands into the velvety depths of her cloak, and continued her slow, trudging progress through this frostbitten world.

Staring up at the unrecognisable stars, she noticed they were brighter and more numerous than the constellations on Earth. The realisation struck her with the force of confronting something bigger than a mortal mind could comprehend, that of being immersed in a world other than hers. She kept walking, deeper into the silence. She grew colder and colder and colder.

Suddenly, a whisper curled her senses with fear.

Chapter Fifteen

Marietta grasped her pointe shoes; the box inside them was hard and would suffice as a make-shift weapon. She turned to see ... nothing. Perhaps she had imagined it, a trick of the cold or a symptom of overexposure.

A second whisper hissed through the air.

'Show yourself,' she demanded.

It fell silent. Marietta began to feel most peculiar. As if she was being watched. Not trusting whatever strange creature might be stalking her through the forest, Marietta ran. The star-dappled snow lit her way through the firs. Yet each tree she passed seemed to darken with shadows. She slowed, watching them closely. The forest was filled with wild and twisting shadows. The air around her felt tighter, as if she had inhaled one and now it ensnared her lungs, grasping tendrils wrapping around her, suffocating her from within. She whirled around, breathing harder. And yet, the more she stared at them, the harder they were to discern. They were an ephemeral substance, nothing but wisps of smoke dragged together with malice cobwebbed across them.

Marietta fled. Her lungs heaving, her throat closing with panic, she ran towards where she approximated the town ought to be. But the sweet melody that had first entranced her had vanished long ago and all that lay before her were firs and snow and stars. She ran deeper into the forest. A stray branch lashed out, slicing her arm, and she cried out.

Branches drooped under the weight of the snow blanketing the forest. Once, Madame Belinskaya had told stories of the stretch of ice that comprised Siberia, wild and vast, and Marietta had shivered to hear them. Now she found herself venturing further into this land, she couldn't help imagining how one could lose themselves in a place such as this.

She forced herself to run faster, her breath tearing from her lungs. Her cut was a long scarlet thread from which droplets beaded down onto the snow. Her fairy tale had become *Hansel and Gretel*, cut from a darker cloth. When she glanced back, she saw her blood freezing in place like tiny rubies. A dark mist was stalking her, following the blood trail. Marietta let out a quiet sob no one would hear and ran on, weaving between the gigantic firs, despairing of her pursuing fate. It became harder to breathe and eventually she slowed.

Shadow pooled at her feet and the air was suddenly awash with whispers. Harsh and guttural, they were in no language she might discern yet they spoke of her darkest fears and stole her breath with their creeping fingers. Her chest squeezed tighter than an over-laced corset. She inched backward until she felt herself pressed against a fir. Its rough trunk scratched, the entire forest craving a bite of her flesh. 'What are you?'

The whispers thickened until a thousand voices filled her head, pressing against her skull, choking her with fear and doubt, and all the while the forest grew darker and darker until even the stars were a memory. She stumbled and reached her palm out, arresting her fall on a tree. It was wracked with vibrations. A distant trembling shook the forest. Something was moving towards her. The reverberations grew louder and nearer before she placed the sound; hooves pounding into the snow.

The shadows soared at her like a great-winged bat and wrapped their wings of darkness around her, close and suffocating. Marietta's vision shuttered and she fell into the snow. With great effort, she reopened her eyes, watching the tendrils snaking around her. Her thoughts were crystallised as old honey, her breaths slow and shallow as if she were drowning in a sticky sea of it.

In a spray of snow and a deep grunting, a large sleigh appeared, rushing through the firs. Two moose pulled it, crowned with widespread antlers. Filigreed silver runners swirled up into ornate mice that fronted the sleigh, staring through the forest with hunters' eyes. Glossy obsidian sides were hung with lanterns that flickered with an icy glow and four soldiers sat within, on garnet-cushioned benches. The one at the forefront spotted Marietta in the snow and gave a sharp pull on the reins, halting the pair of moose.

The darkness having receded a little at their presence, Marietta rose to her feet. Tendrils of shadow clung to her feet, coiling up her legs.

A soldier exited the sleigh. He was dressed in the same fashion as the others; a double-breasted garnet jacket, adorned with gold buttons and epaulettes, and cream breeches tucked into black boots. Tall, with broad shoulders and sculpted features, he regarded her seriously. He appeared as if he had been painted from one palette; his irises were butterscotch, his face golden and capped with bronze hair. He reminded Marietta of the bronzes she'd studied in Athens when her father had taken her and Frederick in the name of education. She swayed on her feet, unsure for a moment if she was walking those buttery sunshine streets once more, but no; that soft glow was silvered starlight. It had returned. Yet still the darkness clung to her, its whispers softer, scuttling into her ears alone, her breaths catching in her throat.

Before she could speak, the soldier unsheathed a silver sword, cutting through the air, a whisper's-width from Marietta's arm. She gasped and looked down. The sword was agleam with the light of a thousand stars. It cut through the shadows like smoke and severed their hold on Marietta. She filled her lungs with relief, holding an unsteady hand to her chest.

The shadows crept away and misted out of sight.

The soldier considered Marietta. She met his eyes, her head echoing with warnings.

'The forest is no place for wanderers. You are fortunate you merely encountered the Shadows,' he said at last, sheathing his sword. 'I am Captain Legat, leader of the King's Army, and I shall grant you our assistance if you'll accompany us.' He failed to voice it as a question. Stepping back into the sleigh, he took up the reins once more. The moose pawed the snow in impatience.

Another soldier hopped from the sleigh and offered her his hand. Marietta hesitated. The captain glanced back at her. 'My offer shall not stand for much longer.'

Marietta stiffened at his tone. 'I'm merely contemplating whether or not to trust you.'

The soldier offering his hand smiled. 'Listen. Do you hear that?'

Other than the soldiers and moose, the forest was silent. Marietta looked at him in confusion. His smile turned wicked. 'In Everwood, we say when the forest sings with life, you may bide your time for its attentions reside elsewhere. It is when the forest falls silent that it has turned its eye on you.'

She looked back. The trees devoured the horizon, their silence becoming ever more ominous the longer she considered it. There was not a branch sighing in the breeze, no suggestion of birdsong, nor the soft patter of shifting snow.

Marietta gave her hand.

He helped her up into the front of the sleigh, beside Captain Legat, who had first come to her aid. 'Will you take me back to my world?' she asked him.

'We are returning to the palace,' he said, snapping the reins and sending the moose charging back through the forest, the sleigh soaring through the snow after them.

Chapter Sixteen

Outside the sleigh, snow-coated firs rushed by at a rapid rate, infinite as the stars. Marietta took a deep, steadying breath.

'The Shadows are terrifying. They bring out your inner darkness, prey on your hiddenmost weaknesses and fears,' one of the soldiers said, leaning forwards. Marietta shivered. 'Though you're most fortunate you didn't meet with worse. If you'll allow me, I need to inspect your arm.' He held a thick white cloth. 'My name is Fin,' he added softly as if it would help her trust him. Strangely, it did.

Marietta held out her bloodied arm. She took the opportunity to study the three soldiers sitting shoulder to shoulder in the back of the sleigh. Fin appeared of a similar age to herself, with curly black hair, warm brown skin and high cheekbones. The other two were a handful of years older and facsimiles of each other with blond hair and steely eyes in a paler, rosy face. Brothers, perhaps. The younger of which had been the one to help her into the sleigh.

'These injuries are superficial. Pass me some snow, will you?' Fin asked the brothers beside him.

The third soldier scooped up a handful of snow and passed it forward. His hand was missing its two smallest fingers. His eyes were sharp, evaluating, and Marietta determined never to underestimate him.

Fin gently cleaned Marietta's arm before binding with a cloth. Her skin tingled beneath it like a sherbet lemon on her tongue.

'And you mean to tell me there are worse things lurking in this forest?' She turned her gaze back to the watchful trees. Ever present, ever silent.

Fin met her eyes. 'Yes. It is wise not to attract undue attention in these parts. Those worse things? They glom onto blood trails and will hunt you to the stars and back for a taste. The Shadows are unsettling and can melt your wits, but they cannot touch you.' When he removed the cloth, Marietta was startled to find her lacerated skin had knitted together, already the pale pink of new flesh. 'Thank you,' she said, running her fingers over it. The commonplace utilisation of magic made Marietta's brain itch as she failed to apply logic to the phenomenon. Witnessing enchantments in this vein was far from the old beliefs of cunning folk or an infatuation with parlour magic.

'I wouldn't thank him,' the younger brother said. 'Fin isn't being chivalrous; he's far more interested in preserving his own hide.'

Fin stood up and flung the bloodied cloth far from the sleigh. 'Can I not be both?' he asked. His voice was cut through with a seam of compassion that his gentle working hands had also conveyed.

'I'm Claren,' the younger brother said, ignoring Fin as he continued to appraise Marietta. 'This is my brother, Danyon.'

The sharp-eyed Danyon gave her a smart nod. Marietta inclined her head, noticing that Danyon's hair was cut shorter, his uniform neater than his brother's.

'Pleased to make your acquaintance,' Marietta said. Their accents were deep and harsh, the cadence of their voices taking some time to become accustomed to. 'You may call me Marietta.' A howl pierced the silent forest. Wild and guttural and close. The soldier sat beside Marietta urged the moose to gallop faster, the tableau of trees whipping by. 'How does the town survive living alongside such a dangerous forest?' she asked.

'You'll find that it takes more than a few beasts to threaten Everwood. Not with the King's Army defending it.' Claren grinned at her.

Marietta couldn't help considering that he would have enjoyed Frederick's company and the sudden thought jolted her; she ought to find a way back home. She had dwelled in this world with its enchantments and dangers longer than originally intended and was disconcerted to discover her awareness of time had become muddled. Perhaps she ought to secure passage back soon. Phantom eyes burnt Marietta's back, her fear of Drosselmeier an ever-present shadow reminiscent of the *abonné* lurking in Degas's *L'Étoile*. She tossed a smile over her shoulder at Claren, scanning the dark expanse of trees at his back.

'Now is not the time to charm a wanderer,' Danyon told his younger brother before turning to Marietta. 'The river marks the boundary of Everwood. There are wards in place to guard against the threats of the Endless Forest.'

'Everwood is your town? I had been led to believe it was the name of this world.' Marietta ignored the blush crawling over her neck. She was all too aware of her unchaperoned position among the four men, though their lack of response to the situation indicated their social values were as differing as the worlds they inhabited. A small smile flitted over her lips at the thought of Miss Worther's expression if she could see Marietta now.

Danyon shook his head. 'No, our world is Celesta. Everwood resides in the frozen east, Mistpoint in the flowered fields and cruel tides of the south, and Crackatuck in the green-valleyed west. The Thieves Road connects the three kingdoms, cutting through the forest and climes, though it isn't warded.'

'And all manner of dastardly bandits roam it,' Claren added, his smile tipping higher on one side. 'Brave or foolish enough to take their chances on the open, unwarded road. Though Everwood isn't always as protected as Danyon would have you believe.' He winked at Fin. 'Remember when the Grand Confectioner lost his mind on snowberry crèmes and the enchantment slipped, allowing an intruder to rampage the palace?' Claren and Fin laughed.

'Have you quite finished divulging palace secrets to a wanderer?' the butterscotch-eyed soldier asked, his voice crisp as snow.

Marietta stole a look at him. His focus was on the moose he guided between fir trees, an immense ice gate crystallising before them. He radiated strength and quiet power, a knife in the dark. If Danyon was not to be underestimated, then Captain Legat was to be avoided altogether.

'Sorry, captain,' Claren and Fin said, snapping to attention.

'She ought to know a little of our world if she's to accompany us to the palace,' Danyon said. His jacket bore similar gold epaulettes to the captain's, more ornate than Claren and Fin's. Marietta failed to understand the embroidered pattern of swirls that marked them. Though she was well versed in the strategy of warfare through her meandering studies from the Greco-Persian Wars to the Warring States, she held not a scrap of interest in the pomp and trivialities that accompanied such battles. But she did observe that the captain's held a tiny embroidered mouse holding a golden sword.

The captain's knuckles paled around the reins. 'She ought to be returning whence she came,' he muttered under his breath.

Marietta's own misgivings at heading towards the palace melted away into defiance at his attitude, which seemed an echo of her father's. 'Well, I do apologise for my most unwelcome presence, but it isn't as though I intended to linger in your world, or indeed enter it in the first place,' she said stiffly.

'You wanderers never do, yet still you seem to drift about our town like aimless snowflakes until your fate calls for you,' he said.

Marietta turned her curiosity on him. 'Whatever do you mean?'

Fin cleared his throat. 'You are not the first wanderer we've rescued from the Endless Forest. Everwood oft seems to be a beacon for those that have lost their star's shining path.'

'The Grand Confectioner seems to welcome them, though I cannot think why he should,' the captain said. Marietta didn't know how to respond. After a silence thick as clotted cream, the captain spoke again, over his shoulder. 'Someone pass her that blanket.'

Fin handed it forward. 'Don't mind Captain Legat; his head whirls with concerns the rest of us couldn't see through a snowstorm.'

She wrapped the blanket around her shoulders. Matching the sleigh's rich garnet, it was lined with soft white fur and warmed her chilled flesh at once.

The sleigh hurtled through the ice gate and onto a marzipan-cobbled path, frozen and slippery enough to grant them passage. A soft sigh escaped Marietta's lips in a puff of sugared air.

A delicate ice bridge arched over the lake she'd glimpsed earlier, extending to the frozen mountain the palace topped. Ice cliffs encircled it, the waterfalls suspended in time, sparkling in sapphire and opal and moonshine. The palace was a meringue, piped impossibly high. It held no windows, instead the walls glowed and shimmered with light. Blush pink, pearl and mauve, layers of creamy pastels swirling up and up and up, to the peak, gleaming the same hue as Degas's *Blue Dancers* in the distance.

'What a beautiful sight,' Marietta breathed. 'I cannot comprehend how it was constructed from sugar alone.'

'All sugar and frozen solid, too. The Grand Confectioner designed it himself.' Claren draped his arms over the back of the front bench, gazing up at it with Marietta.

'Who is the Grand Confectioner?' The term seemed self-explanatory yet the god-like reverence afforded him gave Marietta pause.

Legat coughed under a white-gloved hand.

Marietta slid a look to the captain. 'If you do not wish me to educate myself on your world, why are you escorting me to the palace?'

'I'm not.' Legat's clipped tones severed her argument. The huffing moose approached the beginning incline of the ice bridge.

Marietta caught the puzzlement that swept across Fin's face before he appropriated the same soldier's mask Captain Legat wore. Danyon passed no remark. Claren, his uniform as lapsed as his attitude, was sole in his protestations. 'The ball will be in full enchantment at this hour. Think how beguiling a sight that would be for her!'

'I have not a granule of doubt she will survive missing it,' Legat said. 'Once I've had the moose stabled, I shall send a guard to escort you to your door, wanderer.'

They slid onto the ice bridge, fine as spun sugar. It looked as if it would shatter beneath the weight of the moose and the grand sleigh hurtling across it. Marietta gripped the blanket, pulling it tighter around herself to ward off the glacial breeze. To either side, the view swept down to the snow-coated valleys below, gigantic firs reduced to doll-sized proportions. The sheer plummet was dizzying and Marietta tore her eyes away. 'I'm failing to understand for what purpose you brought me to the palace if you're having me escorted directly back to the forest?' she asked. His motives confused her, though the confirmation she hadn't been an unwitting volunteer in her own kidnapping sent her darker thoughts scuttling away.

'You were in immediate danger; I removed you from the situation.

I am the Captain of the King's Army, I do possess more important tasks than cavorting about the forest searching for a wanderer's door,' he said wryly. His expression was calm and measured. It rankled Marietta.

They soared over the final stretch of the ice bridge. The palace doors loomed, a lattice of silverwork set into the thick-walled sugar. Legat called a command to the moose and they banked right, swerving round the thin loop of a path wrapped around the palace, a precipitous drop on one side, the ice cliffs towering above them. Marietta suffered a swoop of vertigo and clamped a hand down on the side of the sleigh. A low doorway materialised and they plummeted into it, skidding to a stop.

They had halted in a low-ceilinged, vast area. The floor was glossed in obsidian, impervious to the moose shifting on their hooves. When Marietta glanced down, it reflected her intrigue back at her, along with her bedraggled appearance. A doll with ripped seams. She smoothed her hair and looked about. On one side, a low, wide rectangle was cut from the wall, forming the entrance. Snow fluttered through it. Opposite, a huge decorative door was mounted in a wall of frozen sugar, glimmering in the glowing ice lanterns dangling from the rocky ceiling. She ascertained it led to the palace and her intrigue deepened. Though the market woman had warned her from it she harboured a desire to glimpse it for herself. The child that resided within her — the one that had clasped a clothbound volume of fairy tales to her chest as if the stories themselves might warm her with their magic — would never forgive her otherwise. Either side of the great expanse of space, heaving with sleighs and bustling, liveried footmen, were doors. On the left, the doors were large wooden squares, with little latches and windows, through which moose poked their heads out, surveying the scene. On the right, the doors were waist-height, striped in jaunty red and white, and swung open and shut. Miniature reindeer frolicked in and out of their own accord, approaching the footmen to be fussed before darting away and back into their little stables.

Three footmen approached their sleigh and the soldiers hopped out. Marietta followed suit. In an inverse of the soldiers' uniforms, the footmen wore white jackets over garnet breeches, tucked into high black boots. Tiny mice were engraved on their silver buttons. They reminded Marietta of something but when she cast her mind back, she found her recollections of her own world hazy, as if she was peering into an antique looking glass that mottled her memories.

Moving seamlessly, the footmen unharnessed and stabled the moose, pushing the sleigh into a line that another team of footmen were de-icing. The sleighs were an assortment of sizes and colours like bonbons in a sweetshop. Marietta's eye was drawn to a behemoth in holly-green and gold that sat an additional layer of passengers stacked above the first like the larger horse-drawn omnibuses that served Nottingham, and a narrow sleigh with long, curved runners protruding before it.

'There is always a bevy of guests visiting the palace,' Danyon explained, noting her interest. 'King Gelum is well known for his extravagant balls and they're always well attended.' He nodded at the narrow sleigh. 'The one-person sleighs are owned by guests residing within Everwood. Smaller sleighs are pulled by a team of reindeer. The larger sleighs are long distance and require moose, in addition to the ones the King's Army use for patrolling the forest, like ours.' He indicated the sleigh they had just departed and Marietta frowned at the mice fronting it; something felt familiar about them.

Then Claren appeared at his side and Marietta lost her thought-wisp. She could better differentiate between them now. Claren's mussed hair and slight slouch looked as if someone had made a copy of Danyon and smudged it, rendering his outlines less crisp, less professional.

The captain pulled a timepiece from his jacket. It was gold and featured more dials and hands than Marietta had seen on a clock before. 'I must appraise the king of our findings.' Legat snapped the timepiece shut and returned it to his pocket. His gaze rested on Marietta's, hardened gold. 'On no account are you to leave the stables before I have returned to secure you an escort. That's an order.'

Marietta levelled a stare at him. 'I am not one of the soldiers in your retinue, captain. You cannot direct your orders onto me.'

'In this palace, this kingdom, you fall under my command, wanderer. Danyon, I require your accompaniment. Claren and Fin, your guard duty in the throne room has commenced.' Legat marched away, leaving Marietta stewing in her own broil of indignation and contempt. Two footmen scurried to open the ornate door, its width greater than a Steinway, the metallic lattice glittering as Legat and Danyon strode through. Marietta was flashed a glimpse of a dusky corridor beyond before the door clanged shut.

'Frightfully pompous, isn't he?' Claren grinned at her. 'Shall we defy him and take a peek inside?'

Marietta turned to him. 'Why are you so keen to tempt me inside the palace? What stake do you hold in this quest?'

Claren's voice slid into a more seductive note and despite herself, Marietta's desire to witness the wonders she imagined within the palace grew. 'I would wager you'll never see a more magical sight in the remainder of your days.' He raised his eyebrows. 'Besides, perhaps I'm secretly yearning you'll grant me a dance.'

Fin groaned. 'Must you always behave in such a terrible manner?

The captain will have you stripped of your rank if you continue to flout his rule.'

She had a sudden, visceral memory of her nanny reading the Brothers Grimm story *The Shoes that were Danced to Pieces* and drifting off into dreams of enchanted castles and dancing until dawn wrested the sky from the moon. Upon confessing her secret wish to be one of the princesses, nanny had chided her, reminding her that, 'A little magic may sound like a wonderful adventure but disobeying your father is not the path to follow.' Marietta was so very weary of men that behaved like generals in the war of life. She turned to Claren. 'Escort me to the ball.'

Fin cleared his throat. 'Are you certain that's wise?'

Marietta was still watching Claren, awaiting his response.

His smile was slow. It sparked his steel-grey eyes. 'After you, wanderer.'

Chapter Seventeen

Marietta felt like Alice wandering down the rabbit hole as she entered the passageway the captain had disappeared into. Claren led the way, falling into a self-appointed role as tour guide, regaling her with morsels of information about Everwood, intensifying Marietta's cravings to nibble just a little more of its magic. 'In this world, we say Mistpoint looks to its past, Crackatuck to the future, but here in Everwood, we delight in enjoying the present.'

There was a flash of consternation on Fin's face at this. Claren remained ignorant to it and continued expounding on the hedonism of their kingdom until Marietta almost expected to enter a bacchanal. Fin fell back to amble at Marietta's side, her stride slower after switching back to pointe shoes. She'd left her boots and cape in a little mechanised cloakroom. She readjusted the pearl comb in her hair and smoothed down her ballet dress as they progressed through the dark and winding passageway. Here and there, a globe of ice glowed of its own accord, lighting their way. A trio of black and white birds with hooded eyes and curving bright-blue beaks filtered past, regarded them curiously before continuing to waddle on their way.

'What were those?' Marietta asked, understanding how Darwin might have felt disembarking the HMS Beagle on the Galapagos Islands. She hadn't seen the like of them or the miniature reindeer in her world and each time she thought those words to herself — *her world* or *this world* – her thoughts tipped on their side as she considered the machinations of the universe, wider and stranger than she'd known.

'They're frostpeckers,' Fin said. 'In some parts of Everwood, they're consumed as a delicacy but King Gelum is fond of the creatures and passed a declaration protecting them. He has since installed a colony of them within the throne room.'

'Curiouser and curiouser, cried Alice,' Marietta murmured to herself.

The hallway curved a final time. A pair of golden doors greeted them, bracketed by two footmen. Upon seeing Marietta and the soldiers approach, they each grasped a golden handle and opened the doors. Music and scent and life poured out of them.

And in that flash, the world spun, sugar-laced and poetic.

The throne room was larger than any ballroom. A grand staircase rose up one side, the frozen sugar walls glowed in pale violet and indigo hues and a central oval stood on a raised platform with golden cages sprinkled about. Thin chains were attached to their tops, and now and then, one ascended up to the ceiling. Or they might have, if there had been a ceiling. The centre of the palace was hollow. Multiple floors rippled up, connected by a single staircase which ran in a helter-skelter manner up around the edges. Marietta's stomach swirled at the height of the looping staircase, the sloping levels spiralling up around the carved-out space. If anyone slipped ... She shuddered, tucking the thought away.

The throne room was filled with people in glittering gowns and suits, dancing around the dusky edges, where little golden globes of ice were strung along the walls. Shadows clotted in the spaces between clusters of gossipers who reclined on satin cushions the size of settees. Beside the door, large, translucent igloos held benches carved from packed snow, lined with furs for people to sit and exchange confidences within, and towards the back of the room, on a high platform, stood the throne. A rich shade of crimson, its most distinguishing feature was the wall of stalactites and stalagmites that entwined to form its back. It was empty.

A few tiny streams cut through the palace, frozen thoroughfares that servers skated down, evading the frostpeckers. Other servers strolled round with trays of delicate petits fours, piped twirls of ice cream and frosted goblets filled with a creamy drink.

Marietta had stepped inside a fairy tale.

Ballgowns in every shade she could imagine, and some she couldn't, sparkled and fluttered. There were silks and satins, chiffon and tulle, intricately designed dresses in bewitching fashions she'd never thought to imagine, women in suits and men in gowns, and everyone's faces painted in an indulgence of colour. 'It's beautiful,' she whispered.

Claren seized two goblets from a passing server's tray and handed her one. 'A shame we hadn't staked a purse on our wager, I'm rather short of funds these days.'

Marietta sipped at hers. It was thick and sweet to taste with a hint of spice, and delicious beyond measure, like drinking molten starlight.

Claren toasted her. 'Snowberry crème. They're deliciously potent. Do have as many as you'd like,' he said, surveying her over his rim.

'Captain,' Fin said, snapping his heels together and saluting.

Taking another languorous sip, Marietta observed the sudden reappearance of Legat. Shadows crept beneath his eyes and the beginnings of stubble shaded his face. He was graver than when she'd last set eyes upon him. 'Come with me,' he said. 'I'm escorting you back at once. And I shall ensure that this time you follow my command.'

'Then I had better make this count,' Marietta said, enjoying the way his jaw tightened at her pronouncement. Somewhere between encountering this magical world and surviving the prospect of her own demise had left her exhilarated and uncaring. It was deeply liberating. A waltz was playing, dark and fast and intoxicating. It slunk into her bones, entwined itself with her senses. Marietta hungered for it, her skin itching to be swallowed in motion, wrapped in music as if it had been made for her and her alone. She downed the goblet and handed it back to Claren, who looked intrigued. Sweeping her arm out, she stepped out from their corner and into the moving tide of dancers.

'That is expressly what I had forbidden,' she heard the captain say.

Retaining a modicum of discretion, Marietta stayed flat on her feet, keeping her turns understated and demure, dancing balancés to the count of the waltz. Adding in little spins and moving into a seamless adagio when the music shifted, becoming slower and more urgent, coaxing a new rhythm from the dancers. Marietta's fluidity evoked the pattern of water, deep and endless and graceful, her steps light, her arms as feathery as a swan.

Floating past a woman her own age in the inky periphery, Marietta slowed, her attention stolen. The woman wore a plum-coloured dress with iridescent silvery stars stitched into the gauzy overlay. Knee-height, it flared out at her waist and spun up and around her Rubenesque figure as she danced. High-heeled shoes enlaced her ankles, and her short plum curls were arranged around a black headdress that spiked up like twigs, twinkling with diamonds. Her eyes were painted the same shade of plum as her hair and dress, her cheeks fuchsia-pink, her lips glossed in midnight. She was devastating. Yet her glance at Marietta spewed vitriol. Marietta stared back, unflinching. The woman's lips parted, a single word hissing off her tongue: *Leave.*

Marietta flinched. First the market woman, now this. For a place well used to wanderers venturing through, it was most unwelcoming. Perhaps that was why most ended up leaving. Yet the ball was charming and it had been some time since her heart had been this light. She danced on. She hadn't paid the captain and his infuriating orders any heed nor would she this woman either. But her focus had spooled away like smoke, obscuring her steps. She stumbled, leading the two men dancing together behind to collide with her. Their glares hot on her skin, she made her apologies. They tugged the mauve brocade of their matching jackets down and the first held his arm out to the second, who took it with an imperious stare in Marietta's direction before dancing off, their trousers comprised of ivory ribbons, billowing around them. Another couple whirled by, a woman in a whisper-thin gossamer dress that emitted a sweet vanilla scent like perfume unfurling from flower petals.

Amongst the glittering attendees of the ball, Marietta felt the dullest jewel. So, she rose up on en pointe for the first time, pirouetting back into the stream of dancers, the ballroom rushing around her, the music accelerating with her dancing, dipped into a penché with one leg high behind her, then spun in a tight succession of soutenu turns, spinning faster and faster, ignoring the other dancers pausing to watch. She twirled to a finish before gliding into an arabesque.

When she lowered her leg and caught her breath, she set eyes on the king. He was seated upon his throne, his gaze affixed to her. Fair, with onyx eyes and rich golden hair that swung down to his chin, he wore a crown of interwoven icicles studded with crystals. A long finger rested on his thin lips, one leg in tapered charcoal trousers crossed over the over. White pointed shoes and a black and white striped shirt beneath a woven silver waistcoat completed his monochrome attire. A tiny embroidered mouse scampered down his shirt sleeve and disappeared, appearing moments later on his trousers. Marietta blinked and it vanished.

The music slowed, elongating its notes into melodies that sugared the throne room. Marietta slid onto one of the icy thoroughfares, turning her steps slow and gliding. Her glance back at the soldiers threw up Claren's flirtatious grin and the map of creases spanning Fin's forehead.

The captain materialised at her side. His strides were long, maintaining pace with her. 'It's time to leave, wanderer,' he said. 'At once.'

The other guests had resumed their dancing, though they kept sidling looks at Marietta. She wished she could linger awhile in this dream of a ball. Let its magic seep under her skin. Yet, like a dream, its beauty was sweeter due to its transient nature. She was unsure how much time had passed and feared missing her performance as Aurora. With one last, longing look, she followed the captain.

The music jarred and broke. The other dancers slowed, searching out the cause; the musicians had ceased, their instruments swallowing their notes. A sudden wave of conversation from the cushioned alcoves and igloos was all at once audible before it too leached to silence. Even the servers retreated. The entire ball was suspended.

'What has happened?' Marietta asked the captain.

A rare emotion flitted over his expression before he schooled it back into place. 'It seems you have caught the king's attention.'

'Captain,' the king's voice boomed through the hallowed silence. 'For the love of all that is sweet, do tell us who you have there.'

Chapter Eighteen

The ballroom fell silent as Marietta stepped into the centre of the iced floor. She swept into a deep curtsy before the captain reached for her elbow, guiding her back into the crowd. 'No one of note, Your Majesty. She is but another townswoman,' he said.

The king smiled. 'Bring her to me.'

Marietta approached the throne. Now the music had halted, she was all too aware of the whispers misting around her as guests stepped away, carving a path free for her and the captain.

King Gelum descended the steps from the throne to stand before Marietta, evaluating her. He was shorter than he'd appeared from afar and seemed to emit the aroma of spiced cloves and mandarin zest. She met his eyes, and as she did so, she felt the worlds tremble around her. A quivering of the threads the fates had embroidered for her.

He held a slim, tapered hand out to her. She took it and the king twirled her in place, her dress swishing around her knees. He lowered his gaze to her feet, the hard onyx gemstones of his irises glittering in fascination. 'How lovely,' he murmured. 'Would you dance on your toes for me again?'

Stepping up onto the tip of her ballet slippers en pointe, Marietta took a few quick little bourrée steps backwards.

'Why how marvellous. How marvellous indeed.'

The captain cleared his throat. 'Your Majesty, she is but a local woman. I possess not a dusting of doubt that this is but some delightful novelty purchased from the Veil of Enchantments.'

King Gelum held up one long finger. His amusement was sharp-edged. 'Now, captain, we mustn't be greedy with the girl. You are as aware as I am that no one in Everwood, in this world, can dance in this manner, no matter the enchantments purchased. It is a wondrous sight indeed.' He tilted his head to one side, evaluating Marietta. 'How would you like to stay as an honoured guest in my palace?'

'I am most flattered by your invitation, however I am afraid I must decline. I have a prior obligation I must see to,' Marietta said. The upcoming performance of *The Sleeping Beauty* would see her light up the stage in the position of a prima ballerina and she could not pass on such a gift.

The king looked amused. 'I am not accustomed to refusals.'

'It was not my intention to offend—'

'You are strong-willed, I admire that.' The king's attention lingered on her. 'Imagine the sparkling balls and feasts where you would dance every night. Garbed by your own dressmaker, you would have a new gown for each performance you enchant us with.' He snapped his fingers and a man, dressed in candy-cane stripes and bearing a silver tray, appeared at his side. The king waved a hand at the tray. 'Would you care for one?'

Marietta selected a chocolate mouse with a cherry for a nose and sugar-whiskers. Temptation was a devious creature. It whispered in her ear, played to her vanities and slunk deep and deeper yet until it set her heart aflame with longing. For why did she care to return to her own world for a single performance when here she might dance as if she was one of the princesses in that old story, left with ragged shoes each morn and sleeping with a secret smile on her lips? The king admired her will. Perhaps she could be freer here, then. Frederick she would miss but she supposed she might visit him. Perhaps bring him back with her so he might learn of the delights of Everwood beside her. Or, if she truly did not care for life in the palace, she would just leave herself when the time came.

She felt rather than saw Captain Legat stiffen beside her.

Caught in a heady rush that showered her with glittering thoughts, Marietta smiled. 'I shall accept your most generous offer, King Gelum.'

'Oh wonderful, wonderful!' The king clapped his hands together with childish glee and Marietta's smile curved wider. 'I shall have you escorted to your suite.' He clicked his fingers and Legat stood to attention.

'Right away, Your Majesty.' He beckoned to Claren, who stepped forward at once.

'Thank you kindly,' Marietta said, allowing Claren to guide her away. When she glanced back, she noticed two guards, each suited in a livery of indigo and charcoal, stood in the shadows. Their features were shrouded with blank white masks, rendering them faceless and mute. 'Who are those?' she asked in an undertone.

'They're the Faceless Guards. Unlike the traditional soldiers that make up the official King's Army, protectors of Everwood, the Faceless Guards work only for the king. They're not trained as soldiers; they function purely as King Gelum's personal bodyguards. In fact, no one's ever seen their true faces,' Claren said, and she cast another wondering look back. She noticed Legat shifting his gaze from her, wearing a mask of his own, his golden hair tousled as if he'd run a hand through it. The spectacle struck up again, the servers skating out to offer petits fours and goblets as the musicians launched into a fast waltz.

Marietta and Claren set foot on the winding staircase. The stairs were lacquered in rich garnet and thick cream, alternating colours in candy cane stripes. Every few steps, they passed a door. Mulberry with pointed arches, set into the curving midnight wall. She wondered where they all led. A golden cage with three women clothed in matching sapphire suits winched past them, riding down to the throne room. They all turned to fix their opera glasses on Claren and Marietta with a flash of silver-painted lips and hair, a trio of fallen stars.

'It seems I shall be spending a little longer in your world after all,' Marietta said.

'So it does,' Claren said. Although his tone was polite, he was less chipper than he had been and Marietta considered that perhaps he was envious. After all, she was to be a guest of his king.

He didn't speak again and it wasn't long until they halted before a door. Two faceless guards stood to either side of it. 'Is this security really necessary?' she asked Claren.

He tugged his jacket collar. 'The king insists on it,' he said at last, holding the door open for her.

She took her leave of him and entered the suite, shutting the door.

A sigh caressed the air behind her.

Marietta spun to face the two women watching her – one of which was the woman she'd seen earlier, a confection in plum and midnight shades. 'I told you to leave,' she said, her voice smooth and rich as buttercream. A venom-laced edge lurked beneath it that better suited the contempt twisting her glossy black lips.

'Why did you?' Marietta asked, her irritation blossoming. 'I was not given to believe that I was not the sole occupant of this suite.'

'Well, it hardly matters now but this is no place for a wanderer,' the woman in plum said.

'What *were* you given to believe?' the other woman asked, distracting Marietta from that peculiar statement. She was tall and slim with dark-brown skin and hair, and eyes just as dark with emerald flecks. Gold dust was sprinkled across the bridge of her nose and cheeks, complementing the filigreed golden band across her forehead and the golden embroidery laced atop her fitted peach dress. A little chiffon cape shimmered over her ensemble. She walked over to Marietta, her golden painted lips curving into a tentative smile. 'Do come and seat yourself; let us get better acquainted.'

Marietta disregarded the other woman's scoff at this and allowed herself to be guided into the room.

On the far side, the frozen sugar of the palace exterior curved round the space, filling it with a gentle, opalescent light. To her right was an open archway, through which was a line of grand armoires and wide swathes of mirrors. Before her, the woman in plum was lounging on a thick carpet that spread out across the central circle of the room and on which were scattered plush cushions in jewel tones, each one larger than an armchair. Chaises longues in rich crimson and sultry indigos were perched here and there. At her left, gauzy ivory drapes hung from tall ceilings, the odd flutter revealing water and steam beyond them. It was all soft and peppermint-scented.

'I had been led to understand that if I were to dance for the king, I should possess my own suite.'

'Were you? Or did your own mind conjure that fact? King Gelum delights in turning our expectations against us,' the woman in plum told her, inspecting her nails.

Marietta sank down onto a periwinkle cushion. Disappointment fatigued her.

The other woman sat beside her. 'Do not trouble yourself, you will find us amenable to share quarters with. Even Dellara.' She sent the woman in plum a cautionary look.

Dellara leant forwards with a wicked smile. 'Speak for yourself. Tell us, what brought you here?'

'I came from another world,' Marietta said.

'That is painfully obvious.' Dellara scanned Marietta's hair and torn dress that still carried a spattering of blood. Her lip curled. 'Do tell us the details. As you can see, we are quite parched for entertainment in this suite.'

'I suffered an unfortunate interruption while dancing and fled inside a grandfather clock – a large timepiece,' Marietta added upon seeing the word lack register for them. 'I walked through the back of it and into this.' She gestured at the surrounding opulence. 'I have never known of the existence of other worlds. I never believed in magic, though I once longed for it. When I was forging my exit from your world, I found myself lost in the Endless Forest and was besieged by the shadows that lurk there. By happenstance, Captain Legat and his soldiers liberated me from their attack and brought me here.'

'She's one of them,' Dellara said in an aside to the golden woman.

Marietta frowned. 'Excuse me?'

'You've entered Everwood from one of the worlds where enchantments are confined to the rank of bedtime tales for milk-fed infants, where magic is but a story and everything is dull and straitlaced as a result,' Dellara said. 'Congratulations, wanderer, you've committed an extraordinary feat. Those worlds are rare, rarer still to find the doors within them.'

'You may call me Marietta,' she managed, processing those ramifications. Had Drosselmeier truly intended to dispatch her to this world? It seemed a strange kind of punishment, unless he had meant for her to perish in the Endless Forest. And if he had, how had he come to possess such a power?

'I am Pirlipata,' the woman dressed in gold said. 'And this is Dellara.' She rested a hand on the shoulder of the venomous woman in plum and black.

'You shall address her as Princess Pirlipata,' Dellara said.

Pirlipata gave Dellara a long look. 'No titles are necessary. Here we are now, one and the same.'

Marietta looked at the women in bemusement, wondering at their stories though her pride was wounded that she was not the king's sole guest. Still, dancing the nights away, one glittering ball at a time, was a dream she could not refuse. She was determined to impress the king so she might forge her own place here.

This close to Dellara, she noted her grey eyes. Deep and extraordinary. Shadows crept in the edges of her irises like smoke. Whatever Dellara was, she wasn't entirely human. Latching onto Marietta's sudden attention, Dellara grinned, revealing a mouthful of sharp, pointed teeth.

Pirlipata's forehead bore a delicate crease. 'Honestly, Dellara, the woman's just arrived.'

Marietta chose to ease her pointe shoes off at that moment.

Pirlipata picked one up to examine it. 'What curious shoes you have. Do you truly dance on your toes?'

'Yes, I've been ballet dancing since I was a child.' Marietta nestled her toes in the thick pile of the carpet. It submerged her feet up to her ankles.

'How remarkable. You are talented indeed, although I must say it sounds rather painful.'

'Sometimes it is, though I am comforted by the thought that I am creating something beautiful and perhaps a little pain is worth the joy it gives me.'

Like a predator, the notion of pain attracted Dellara's attention. 'Being a woman is a bloody business. Rest while you can. You shall be dancing every night now.'

'As I intend to. Dancing is all I long to do.'

Chapter Nineteen

The next morning, Marietta stood before the frozen sugar wall, mulling over the events of the past day. Its glow never hinted at an alteration in light and she found it hard to discern the hour. The portion that wrapped around their suite was a whorl of opalescent lavender, deepening into a coruscating mauve that swept down onto another floor. It was translucent, and as Marietta peered out of a paler, cherry-blossom-pink swirl, she stole a look at the frost-encrusted landscape outside. A swollen pearl of a moon stared back at her.

'I wouldn't if I were you.' Dellara's voice crept behind Marietta, from where she was ensconced in a heap of clothing; whisper-thin petticoats and velvet skirts, satin ballgowns and high-waisted striped trousers, silk slips and gauzy capes. Jeanne Paquin and Jean-Philippe Worth would have murdered for a glimpse at the sartorial treasure chest Dellara was poring over.

'I'm sorry?' Marietta touched the wall, curious if it ever melted. It was freezing to the touch and she withdrew her hand at once.

'It's an inadvertent rite of passage to lick the walls. Each year, some young one believes they'll be the exception and get a mouthful of sugar for their efforts. They never do. And I have no desire to drip-feed you water as you stand there with your tongue affixed to the wall.'

Marietta paid no heed to the condescension dripping from her tone. 'How does it remain frozen? Surely you have periods of sunlight in this land?'

'Winter is our true reigning king. It's long, dark and seemingly eternal. We won't see a glimpse of sun for several moontides now. Besides which, the walls are enchanted; they cannot melt.'

Marietta was bewitched; magic was ingrained into the very fabric of this world.

'The palace, the gingerbread chalets and huts in the town, the marzipan whirls of apartment suites and cobblestones, all of it is locked in an immutable state. Spellbound to remain frozen. If you attempted to eat any of it, you'd break your teeth. Even the moose are wise enough not to take a nibble.'

Marietta was vaguely insulted. 'I am certain I possess more intelligence than a moose,' she told Dellara, who shrugged and resumed examining her wardrobe.

Yet Marietta's curiosity danced on. 'How did they become enchanted? Who in your world holds such powers?' How did Drosselmeier connect to this strange and wild puzzle she'd been confronted with? How had he discovered the doors between worlds?

A faint sigh escaped from an ivory satin cape, edged in glistening peach feathers that fluttered as if teased by an errant breeze. 'The Grand Confectioner is the enchanter. We hold only small magics, often pretty and sometimes useful but insubstantial as a snowflake in comparison to true power.' Dellara's eyes shadowed. 'Once every few lifetimes, someone with such power walks these lands. The Grand Confectioner's identity and motivations are shadowed in secrecy. Legend has it he's an ancient sorcerer from another world that preferred ours. Celesta is a world of doors and magic, and he holds them all.'

'One of the soldiers happened to mention yesterday that the Grand Confectioner allowed the wards protecting Everwood to lapse after indulging in one too many libations.'

Dellara turned back to her cape. 'That's nothing but old palace hearsay. Nobody witnessed him intoxicated; only the empty glasses were glimpsed. And an intruder managed to enter and almost murder the king.' She gave the cape a nostalgic smile.

'All these worlds,' Marietta murmured to herself. 'Wondrous and terrifying to consider. "What immortal hand or eye ..."' She directed her gaze onto the other woman. 'Have you ever travelled to another?'

Dellara's patchwork of venomous words and smiles fell away as she met Marietta's eyes. Within them, she glimpsed something as ancient as starlight. 'Yes,' she said.

Marietta disliked to pry, despite the avalanche of fresh questions she now had. She had spent the equivalent of one night in this sugared world. They had slept on the oversized cushions and thick carpet the night before, the situation proving more intimate than Marietta was comfortable with. She had inquired as to the location of the beds, only to be met with Pirlipata's quizzical expression and the fast knowledge that this world didn't possess such a thing as beds. She had lain there, fatigued with the aftereffects of the day, deliberating on whether she had made the right choice. Until Pirlipata's gentle breaths and Dellara's soft snores had lulled her to sleep, giving in to the sweet release of unconsciousness.

Marietta directed her gaze back onto the world outside. Her absence must have been noted by now. Her gut twisted at the thought of Drosselmeier and what comment he would make to the constabulary. How cruel it was that her home would now forevermore be tainted with him. Once she had better navigated this world, she would find a way to send word to Frederick. Everwood was delicious, tempting as a box of the finest chocolates and more magical than a book of Grimms' tales and she longed to share it with him. 'I was wondering if perhaps I might explore the town this morning,' she said aloud to Dellara. 'I have a craving for more of those divine chocolates.'

Dellara laughed.

Marietta puzzled at this but her ruminations were forgotten with the arrival of a line of servers in festive uniforms, carrying a breakfast feast on silver trays. Marietta joined Pirlipata and Dellara, lounging on the cushions, and dined on snowman-shaped loaves, herbed butter, whorls of creamed cheese and sugared pastries, and bowls of glazed frostberries. She exchanged pleasantries with Pirlipata, who was a kinder soul, until her presence was requested by the king, leaving Marietta in the company of Dellara, who was equally unimpressed with the arrangement.

They drank cups of a pot of molten drinking chocolate, thick and creamy and layered with delicate spices, the chocolate rich as bottled poetry. Just as Marietta was debating a second cup, another server scurried in and placed a small box at her feet. It was filled with chocolates. Shaped like mice, each one held a different filling. Some were expected; berries and cream flavoured or caramel. Others were a fantasy she held no words for. 'How generous of the king,' Marietta said, offering them to Dellara.

She said nothing and Marietta excused herself to bathe.

The bathing pool was cut into the smooth stone floor on the other side of the gauzy drapes. Marietta shed her silk robe and descended the steps leading into its balmy water. Big enough to swim lengths in, one entire side bubbled like Hecate's cauldron, releasing large, toffee-scented bubbles. Another side featured a waterfall, spooling out from the rocky wall in a rush of warm water and peppermint-green mist. Marietta swam a languid length in the pool before lying back and watching the obsidian ceiling that shimmered in unfamiliar constellations until she felt as if she were swimming in starlight.

After, she donned her robe and sauntered over to the armoires to dress for the day, luxuriating in the languorous pace her new life afforded. She supposed she would meet with the dressmaker soon and intended to borrow something beforehand. Yet digging through the armoires, she struggled to source anything similar to the dresses and gowns she was accustomed to wearing. There was an overwhelming array of colours, textures and designs that would put a couturier's studio to shame, and the only corsets she uncovered seemed to be constructed as outerwear, which was most puzzling.

Dellara materialised behind her. 'Nothing take your fancy?'

Marietta opened another armoire and peered inside. A dress comprised of nothing but iridescent peacock feathers gave her a silky wave. 'I would not have thought my choice of wardrobe would be of the remotest interest to you.'

'You're entirely right; I'm buried under a veritable snowstorm of things to do today.' Dellara's voice was slow, indolent, her smile a deadly thing, better suited to creeping through forests, hunting across tundra. She waited. 'I am rather gifted when it comes to fashion, I'll have you know. If my life hadn't set me on this path then I could have risen to prominence in the Silk Quarter.'

Though masked in her disdain, Marietta heard the note of truth shining through her words. 'In that case, I concede.' She stepped aside, letting Dellara feast her attention on the armoires. After a cursory glance, Dellara stared at Marietta's face.

'Is this necessary?' Marietta asked coolly.

'You have a similar build to another woman who was here not too many years ago. Her clothes ought to suit you fine until the dressmaker pays you a visit.' Dellara tapped a magenta-polished nail on matching lips. 'You have a regal face,' she said; 'perhaps we can work with that.' She delved into the nearest armoire.

Marietta frowned. 'You're mistaken; queens are beautiful. I am not.'

Dellara looked back over her shoulder, the shadows darting round the edge of her irises thickening like smoke. 'No, *you're* mistaken. Queens are powerful.' With a flourish, she extracted a gunmetal-grey gown that skimmed along the collarbone and bared shoulders, with glittering silver thorns dripping from the belted waist. It came to a finish in knee-length, jagged flutters.

Marietta considered it. In Nottingham, she had dressed for ballet or for society. Function or etiquette. The gown Dellara was proposing was for her own enticement only. 'Will you and Pirlipata not mind lending me access to your wardrobe? I do apologise for intruding on your space; as I mentioned, I was unaware that this would be the situation.'

'Yes, I realise that.' Dellara gave her a searching look. 'I have my own armoire that's off limits to you.' A wisp of sadness tugged the corner of her lips down. 'And Pirlipata wears only gold.'

Marietta didn't wish to probe that sadness. Dellara busied herself with fishing through a drawer with fresh determination. 'Wear it with these,' she added, passing Marietta a pair of thin, light trousers in a rich sapphire shade before flopping back onto a chaise as if the whole experience had been greatly taxing.

Her mother would have been scandalised at the form-fitting trousers that clung to her hips. To Marietta, they were as liberating as her ballet dresses. She pirouetted on the polished lilac stone floor, her skirts flaring out, emitting a scent of winter jasmine and snow.

When Marietta's summons from the king came, she was prepared. Two faceless guards escorted her down the stairs. She marched ahead of them, down the candy-cane-striped steps, discomfited by their presence and their masked faces, blank as dolls. Perhaps the forest was more dangerous than anyone was letting on to necessitate them. Her view stretched to rows above and below, the central throne room the core of the palace. The single door was guarded by another pair of faceless guards. Next to it, remnants of a lost mosaic clung to the sugar wall.

Golden cage-lifts glided up and down, the glossy obsidian flooring now emptied from the grand ball she'd danced her way into the previous night, leaving the throne on prominent display. The king reclined there, outfitted in an icy blue creation beneath a shocking lime cape, shot through with gold. He was deep in conversation with the captain.

'Ah, here is my enchanting dancer from a distant land.' King Gelum broke off their exchange, absorbing Marietta's presence. The faceless guards were dismissed as she curtsied.

'Good afternoon, Your Majesty,' Marietta said.

A muscle twitched in the captain's jaw. She disregarded it as the king continued to speak.

'I shall be holding a banquet in a few days and I will require you to dance for my esteemed guests. Now, my little dancer, would you care to show me how you perform when the floor is yours alone?' He swept a hand out to encompass the empty throne room.

'Why certainly.' What a change it was to dance for someone appreciative.

King Gelum clicked his fingers and a couple of musicians sprang to play.

The music was slow and thick as honey. Marietta's dancing drizzled out of her in soft pliés, silky glissades that glided across the floor, and luxurious penchés, one hand grazing the floor as she dipped down, a single leg lifted high behind her. As she danced, she caught a faint glistening from the corner of her eye; the delicate lines of thorns were rippling. Her gown was enchanted. Marietta smiled, performing a slow revolution of her arabesque on demi-pointe. Her heart skipped as she broke into a string of pirouettes, her smile stretching wider across her face, the air tasting sweeter, her thoughts lighter than a soufflé.

The music slinked to a finish.

'Utterly delectable,' King Gelum declared.

Chapter Twenty

The following days took on a dream-like quality. Marietta rose late, feasted for breakfast and bathed. And every evening, she danced in the finest silks and gossamer gowns for the king, her spirits soaring with each leap she took across the throne room until she felt she might brush the stars. With each word of praise the king uttered, she shone brighter, danced harder. But tonight, she began to tire as her feet cramped and her chest grew tight. She glided to a halt in a chassé and performed her révérence – a curtsy to end the performance.

Captain Legat stood on the periphery, observing the scene. When she gravitated towards the carved snow-bench behind him, she noticed his eyes flick to the king, a flicker of concern dancing over his face.

'I did not give you my permission to cease,' King Gelum bellowed.

Marietta looked at him with a start. 'I am afraid I was tiring; I must rest for a moment to catch my breath.'

The king twirled his long fingers against his throne. His twining ice rings clinked against the arms. A clink for each minute trickling by that Marietta refused to look away from his hard gaze, refused to yield.

'You must keep dancing.' Captain Legat's whisper, deep and silken butterscotch, poured into Marietta's ear.

'I cannot. I require a break,' she said, suddenly distrusting the look in King Gelum's eyes.

'I have travelled throughout my own world and others and have yet to meet another woman as talented as the likes of you.' King Gelum's words purred at her.

'I am no more talented than a legion of women. We are all more capable than you know,' Marietta said, her concern growing.

'It does not bode well for you that you possess such an urge to challenge me. Though I must confess, I will enjoy it immensely.' The king's fingers stopped clacking against the throne and Marietta froze. She had not missed the violent promise in his words that echoed Drosselmeier's. King Gelum smiled. 'You shall dance for me now as your king commands'.

Before Marietta could protest, her legs suddenly jerked away from her. She found herself walking as if she were a marionette doll, an invisible hand pulling her up on strings until she was en pointe. She gasped. Whatever strange magic was at play it twisted itself around her like the ribbons on her ballet slippers, pulling her into odd contortions that mimicked dancing. With it came a memory. Of Drosselmeier watching her during her Company audition, of her legs spinning out of her control. The magic tugged her through the motions, disconnected and hyperextending until she cried out with pain. And yet still the music whirled on, the faceless guards watched, and she was forced to dance faster and faster.

She summoned the rage that had stormed through her like wildfire before the clock had struck midnight upon Drosselmeier's stage. She closed her eyes, resisting the magic. It was to no avail. She opened her eyes as her body danced wilder.

The rage settled deeper. Coiling within her, it contoured itself to nestle around her bones, becoming one with her. 'Please stop this enchantment,' Marietta beseeched him.

The king looked amused. 'Then you shall not stop until I command you.'

Marietta set aside the blistering pain in her feet and rose en pointe, not allowing the king the satisfaction of seeing her wince. The music grew louder. She pirouetted across the throne room on the horizonal axis. Each time she spun, she whipped her head around desperately searching for an exit, a means of escape. But the door was heavily guarded and she couldn't see any way out. She glanced down at her blush-pink pointe shoes only to see that they now bloomed crimson with blood.

'If you struggle against me, if you give King Gelum the opportunity to lay down his might, I cannot help you.' Captain Legat's whisper came fast, urgent as his arm scooped her up, taking all of her weight.

Gathering her last reserve of strength, Marietta arched back against him, lifting her arms above her head into the crown-like couronne. She felt the captain still as she pressed into him, heard his sharp intake of breath. After a pause, he reacted, firming his hands about her waist, before she could try to evade him.

Taking the moment to compose herself, to steady her growing anxiety, she stepped free of the captain and turned to address the king. 'It has been an honour to perform for you, but perhaps it would be best if I took my leave of you as it seems I am not suited to be a guest of the king after all. I really must be returning home.'

'Oh my little dancer, you are naïve. When you leave here it will be because I no longer possess the desire to see you dance. And your departure shall not take you through those doors.' He snapped his fingers and the magic seized hold of Marietta once more.

She was pulled up onto her toes, her limbs contorted into positions that ripped a scream from her lips. He continued speaking but

Marietta could scarcely hear past the pain that swelled and consumed her. 'I suggest you spend your time dwelling upon how better to entertain me rather than foolish notions of leaving the palace.'

Glistening snowflakes trickled down Marietta's dress in a river of melted pewter. Her tulle drooped. Still she danced on her toes, never once given a moment's respite.

King Gelum laughed. It was thin and high and cold, a shard of ice stabbing through Marietta. His glimmer of interest was colder. This was a king that revelled in pain like tyrannical monarchs of old. Marietta's heart beat harder, aware of her own vulnerability as she glanced around the grand room and saw it for the first time as it really was – a gilded cage. This close, his perfumed suit was overbearing, the clove-spiced mandarin bitter. An enchanted mouse ran across his jacket and dived beneath his collar. 'My palace is enchanted,' he said in a low, intimate voice. 'It recognises that you're mine. And it will keep you ensorcelled within it.' Slowly he feasted his eyes on her bloody ballet slippers. She fought not to flinch. 'Soon you shall learn your proper place, my little dancer.' In a whirl of his garish cape, he resumed his seat at the throne and summoned a server. A girl dressed in a striped red and white skirt held out a box of tiny cakes to him.

'Now for the question of your punishment,' he said, regarding the cakes.

'Do you not consider this sufficient punishment?' Captain Legat asked. 'I presume you wish for her to continue dancing.'

The king slowly bit into a cake; its chocolate casing splintered. 'She will dance when commanded, regardless of her punishment. A true artist soldiers through mere discomfort in the pursuit of their craft.'

Marietta's blood beaded onto the ice. 'I dance only for myself,' she whispered.

King Gelum frosted over.

Captain Legat stilled. He met her eyes and gave an imperceptible shake of his head.

'I dance for no one else. My dancing has always been and shall always be my own,' Marietta repeated, weak and unable to articulate her rage and passionate defiance. 'This is not dance, this is cruelty.' The magic spun her in place, a wicked parody of her words.

King Gelum's frosted exterior cracked. He bestowed a charming smile upon her. 'How quaint the world you hark from must be.' Marietta regarded him warily. 'Dance for yourself, you shall. Henceforth, I am withholding all sustenance from you until you have earnt your keep. Unless you wish to perish, you will perform for me.'

He released Marietta from her magical bonds. She sank onto the ice with a cry.

King Gelum strode from his throne. 'Take her away. I cannot bear the sight of her after her brazenness.'

Captain Legat knelt beside her. He offered a hand.

Marietta disregarded it. She rose to her feet, crying out for the second time as the pain threatened to overwhelm her. The captain quickly escorted her out of the throne room.

It wasn't until they were ascending the stairs that he spoke. 'I warned you not to set foot in the palace to begin with. Now, not only have you courted the attention of the king, but you've incited his wrath. If you had heeded my caution in the stables, you would already be safely returned to your own world by now.'

Marietta could scarcely think. Her legs were numb, her pointe shoes tattered and stained. 'Why are others always blamed in arousing a man's anger?' she asked quietly. 'You know nothing of me nor my life yet you make assumptions ascertained from the brief period in which you've known me. Well, Captain Legat, I hasten to inform you that you do not know me, nor is my return to my own world the simple matter you believe it to be.'

She glanced up after his silence had lasted several beats. He was frowning.

'Other than the obvious, why is your return not a simple matter?'

She had not expected an apology. Neither did she expect his response to rankle her, not when she remained in such pain, her feet growing numb and unfeeling, her prospects bleak and fearsome as an eternal night. 'I do not wish to discuss it. Besides which, I believe you'll find that you were the one who brought me to the palace.'

The captain now appeared equally rankled. It satisfied Marietta to see his mask splinter, his eyebrows ride high. 'Now who is being accusatory? You were the one who chose to enter the ball, who then resolved to dance, after I had expressively forbidden you from both.'

'I did not choose to be brought here, or indeed to this world,' Marietta said, continuing to climb the spiral staircase. She bit back a wince and he held his hand out to aid her. She did not take it.

Captain Legat withdrew his hand, his expression shuttering. 'Do not fear, the next time I happen to encounter you in a forest, I shall most certainly leave you at the mercy of the shadows.'

'One cannot help but ponder why you are now pretending to be chivalrous.' Marietta fixed him with an imperious stare. 'If you truly wished to warn me then why not help me now? Find a way in which I can escape.'

His face gave nothing away. 'I am afraid I cannot.'

'Then I have nothing more to say to you.' With that, Marietta attempted to march ahead of him. The pain overwhelmed her. The staircase twisted around her and darkness cloaked her in its velvet embrace.

Now and then, awareness pricked the darkness like a wink of

starlight. She was weightless, soaring up through the centre of the palace on wings. For a moment, she believed she had died until she felt the sway beneath her and realised she was being carried by the captain. She opened her eyes to protest as she felt a hand smooth her hair away but a tide of weakness swept over her and she faded once more.

Chapter Twenty-One

When Marietta next opened her eyes, she was recuperating on a chaise back in her suite. Dellara and Pirlipata were tending to her feet, wrapping them in snow-white bandages. Her pointe shoes had been cast off, reduced to scarlet rags. Her head whirled as she attempted to sit up.

'Do not move,' Pirlipata said kindly. 'You've suffered a great shock and must rest.'

Dellara evaluated her. 'Still under the impression you're dwelling in some wondrous story?'

Marietta groaned and sat up. 'Why did you not say something?'

'I instructed you to leave the moment I first laid eyes on you,' Dellara said.

'Perhaps you ought to have been more specific,' Marietta said. 'I had no way of knowing this lay in store.'

'We are not allowed to warn newcomers,' Pirlipata said. 'It is forbidden, punishable under the king's treason laws.'

Marietta surveyed her bandaged feet. 'Thank you,' she said quietly. No one was to blame for her current predicament, save herself. She had disregarded multiple warnings for petty vanity's sake and a craving for defiance and admiration as if she had been a girl once more, hoping for Madame Belinskaya to cast her in the principal role of *Coppélia*.

'Surely this is not the prison in which the king intended to incarcerate me?' she asked.

'You're not in the prison; those are carved out beneath the palace. You're one of King Gelum's *pets* now, no freer than the prisoners, but I'd rather lounge in this gilded cage than let sugar-rot lay siege to my bones in that dark pit,' Dellara said, reclining on a nearby cushion.

'I should have refused his offer to host me,' Marietta said bitterly. 'A gilded cage is still a cage.'

Pirlipata sat beside her. 'If you had refused, he would only have ordered his guards to seize you. Do not torture yourself with what-ifs.'

'I still do not understand why. For what purpose?'

Dellara leant forwards with a wicked smile. 'From what I witnessed in the throne room, you're to be his entertainment.'

Marietta's breath grew ragged with fear. She had escaped Drosselmeier's wicked grasping ways only to stumble into another terror.

'Dellara, must you frighten her so? The woman is pale as snow and ice cold.'

'My apologies,' Dellara said drily. 'I had meant your dancing. Rest your worries, the king couldn't bed us even if he wished to; the man is impotent.'

Marietta felt her cheeks bloom even as relief flooded her.

Dellara arched an eyebrow at her furious blush. 'Oh darling, if you keep that up, you won't survive long in this world. Though it has to be said some of the courtiers do enjoy laying siege to innocence.'

Marietta struggled to stand up. 'I cannot stay here, I cannot be his prisoner. I must find a way back to my own world.' Panic squeezed her chest tighter than a corset. 'How did the king force me to dance? I had not thought he held magic, too.'

Pirlipata held her back with a look of deep sadness.

Dellara stood up. 'Not all enchantments are delightful. Some are steeped in dark magic. Like this palace – there's no way out. It may as well be a fortress, with enchantment stacked upon enchantment forbidding your escape. King Gelum holds not a speck of his own magic but the palace is bidden to act on his every whim and desire. The sooner you accept your new life, the easier you will find it.' She picked up a blanket and spread it over Marietta. 'Now sleep. You must heal.'

Marietta heard hushed voices as she regained consciousness, and was unsure how long she had drifted in and out of sleep.

'You ought to try at the very least,' Dellara was urging Pirlipata. 'You cannot afford to lose hope; if your hopes are vanquished then he has defeated you.' She fell silent upon noticing Marietta's re-entry to the world of the living.

Marietta was wary at once. Their looks mirrored each other's suspicion. Pirlipata's was infused with sadness, Dellara's with fire. 'There is no need to confide in me,' Marietta said, finding a glass of water sat beside her and drinking deeply.

'We are due a visit from our dressmaker. On occasion, if she happens to be in a more pliable mood, she will deign to deliver a note for us,' Dellara said at last, speaking fast and hushed as a winter's gale. As if by forcing the words out quicker they would not be overheard by prying ears. 'I've been attempting to convince Pirlipata to send word to her family to inform them of her captivity.'

Marietta set her glass down. 'How can your family be unaware of your captivity?' she asked. 'Are you not a princess?'

Pirlipata lowered her eyes. 'They believe I have been wed to King Gelum.' She plucked at the sequins on her dress. They scurried away from her fingernails, a sparkling migration across the golden sheath she wore. 'He delights in the ruse he devised. It is why I am forbidden to dress in any shade other than gold, the traditional bridal colour in my home of Crackatuck. Gold for joy, for our magnificent sunsets that draw tourists from all corners of Celesta and beam from our oldest university's turrets. And when my parents sent letters, requesting a visit—' Her voice wisped away.

'He commands us to participate in the charade,' Dellara finished for her. 'She was forced to write a response blaming her newfound duties as Queen of Everwood for why she was unable to entertain them for a visit presently.'

'At first I defied him. I attempted to pass my mother an encoded message, signalling the true state of affairs in this palace, but King Gelum found out. He notices everything. It's a preternatural gift of his. And I am not the only one who has suffered at his hands.' Pirlipata swallowed, her voice cracking with emotion, and dread pooled in Marietta's stomach, unsure she was prepared to hear more. As she witnessed a look of sadness from Pirlipata towards Dellara, Marietta noticed for the first time silver scars filigreed across Dellara's arms and legs. They crept up beneath the fabric of her dress in a lattice of pain etched into her skin. Marietta was nauseous at the thought of what Dellara must have suffered to gain them. She chided herself for being so wrapped up in her own cloud of indulgence and childish fantasies during her first few days in the palace that she had been oblivious to the truth in front of her.

'You weren't to know,' Dellara told Pirlipata. 'My scars do not define me,' she added to Marietta. 'I am more than my body.'

Marietta's attention whirligigged. It halted on something Dellara had mentioned earlier. 'Why might the dressmaker not be inclined to aid you?'

'No one would wish to become the king's latest acquisition.' Dellara's refrain from contempt was palpable.

'We cannot fault her for that,' Pirlipata said.

'So it is possible she *might* aid us?' Marietta drew the thought out.

Dellara's refrain melted into incredulity. 'Are you snow-blind?'

'Of course,' Pirlipata told Marietta, placing a hand on Dellara's arm. 'Though I am not convinced I could ask that of her. If she were to be caught and bear the consequences of my actions, well, that is not a price I am willing to pay.'

'I understand. Though it signifies the presence of people within the palace who might be sympathetic to our plight—' Marietta forged ahead in a flurry of fresh ideas '—which means we might escape King Gelum's clutches. We merely need to seek out trustworthy allies to help us slip through the enchantments and—'

'No.' Sparks seeped from Dellara's fingertips. 'It's far too dangerous. Someone would inevitably betray us to secure the king's favour and his wrath would end us.'

Marietta spoke once more. 'Supposing the king—'

'King Gelum holds a veritable battalion of spies in his employ,' Dellara interrupted Marietta again. 'For this precise reason. He is known as the Great Betrayer and once you have sunk to those glacial depths, you expect others to betray you. It's too great a risk and the subsequent devastation would be untold. The king is a cruel man, Marietta, do not tempt him into unleashing that cruelty on you. Nothing is worth the loss of your life,' she said quietly. Shadows laced over the entirety of her irises, submerging her pupils.

It took effort for Marietta to subdue her reaction. 'What of your magic? I presume, like the king, you are in possession of certain abilities.' Pirlipata glanced away and Marietta hoped she hadn't committed an otherworldly faux-pas. Nevertheless, she stiffened her spine and marched on to her point. 'Are you capable of shattering the enchantments that keep us incarcerated in this palace?'

Dellara continued to stare at Marietta, her black eyes swirling. 'I possess some magic,' she said, 'though not sufficient to break the bounds of the Grand Confectioner's enchantments; those are cast deep, penetrating the very material this world is crafted from, and cannot be manipulated. It's impossible to find the like in the Veil of Enchantments, nor Sugar Alley. But I hold enough magic of my own to be capable.'

The dregs of Marietta's hopes rose, a sole star in a dark night.

'If my wand hadn't been taken from me,' Dellara finished. Her eyes faded to dusk.

'King Gelum has it hidden under lock and key in some forgotten crevice of the palace,' Pirlipata told Marietta, keeping a watchful eye on Dellara. 'That is how she came to be captured, the loss of her wand ensured her vulnerability.'

'Why did he wish to capture you?' Marietta asked, watching the shadows in Dellara's eyes recede.

She rolled them. 'He was threatened by my power.'

Marietta suffered a moment of respect for her. 'Forgive me for inquiring but I cannot help but be curious if I am to reside here with you both,' she said politely, covering her desire to learn the king's motivations. If he was to be her opponent then she must study him intimately. Learn his strengths, weaknesses. What he desired and feared, his secrets and shame. Not for nothing had she pored over Sun Tzu's words in her history lessons some years ago.

'Then I shall share my story with you,' Pirlipata said. 'It is long and painful and I shall only speak it once.'

'I would be honoured to hear it.' Marietta waited for her to begin.

'There has never been war in Celesta. We are unlike those great worlds that span vast continents and landmasses, where distant wars might never beat their drums upon your own shoreline. Celesta is a small world, its three kingdoms nestled close and much entwined. When tensions grow taut, they are resolved, not easily so, but to mount an attack would be to cut into ice only to have it shatter beneath you. It was during a diplomatic visit that King Gelum latched onto me. He believed that possessing me would lend him a certain cachet. A credibility to his role as king that was taken, not earnt.' Pirlipata's words grew rigid with anger. Hard and powerful and vengeful. 'When he declared that we were to be wed, he failed to take into account the possibility of my refusal. I was travelling home along the Thieves Road with my beloved cousin and favourite attendant when his soldiers ambushed us. They had been sent ahead to hide amongst the firs and bide their time. They seized us and slit our attendants' throats. Their bodies were left to the beasts in the forest, but the king ordered them reclaimed. He wanted me to witness his power. To fear him. I had to endure their decomposing bodies on display in the throne room as a warning to both me and anyone residing in the palace what we would invoke upon ourselves if one word of our fates was whispered to Crackatuck. I have remained here ever since. But I shall never be his. I am my own master, king and hero.' The golden sequins on her dress blazed in liquid sunshine, their beam transmuting Pirlipata from princess to goddess.

When they faded back to gold, Marietta retained the warm glow of their inspiration. 'Thank you for sharing,' she told Pirlipata. 'Ladies, I do believe it is time the three of us forged an alliance,' she said. 'I have heeded your words, Dellara, that nothing is worth the loss of our lives, yet is not living them here, entrapped in this palace, beholden to a cruel king, an equal loss? Do we not owe it to ourselves to reclaim our rightful positions, rulers of our own destinies? With our combined skillset, I am certain we have the means with which to shape the perfect plan to achieve this.' Dellara's scars and her own sharp pain gave Marietta pause but she was determined not to be too blinded by fear to fight for herself. She would not live out the remainder of her days locked in this suite, this palace. Everwood might be spun from sugar and enchantments but it was rotten to the core. 'What do you say?'

Dellara tilted her head to one side, considering. 'No.'

'No?' Marietta repeated. She'd mistaken their first, tentative confidences as the beginning tendrils of friendship, reaching out to include her in the bond between the two women. She hadn't known she'd even yearned for that until now. Dellara and Pirlipata were woven together in a friendship deep and elaborate, wrought over time and pain. Marietta couldn't pirouette in and be granted a small piece of that in days. She was just lonely and had been lonely for longer than she'd realised; dancing had filled her days and soul but it had cost her friendship.

'No,' Dellara said again. 'Oddly, I don't possess the slightest desire for you to have us all executed.' She sauntered off to an amethyst chaise longue perched beside the thick sugar wall, the backdrop a soft lilac glow framing her spiky midnight suit. She plucked a small bottle from a golden tray and began painting stars on her feet.

Marietta was affronted by the dismissal. She felt wild, ravaged by a fever dream of hope.

Pirlipata rested a hand on her arm. 'Try not to let her bother you; she always behaves in such a manner with new people. It takes time for Dellara to trust. And time is all you have now that you're in this palace.'

Chapter Twenty-Two

That evening, Marietta was forbidden to dine but forced to witness Dellara and Pirlipata's silent feast. Faceless guards flanked them, monitoring each twitch of their fingers, each look they traded. Marietta had attempted to remain in the bathing room, idling in the steam, but the guards had dragged her out to sit with them as dinner was served. It seemed King Gelum intended Marietta to become acquainted with hunger before she declined to dance for him again. Her stomach tilted at the creamy wild mushroom soup Pirlipata was eating, casting an apologetic glance at Marietta. At the chocolate hazelnut meringue tart Dellara was indulging in, maintaining shadowed eye contact with the guards. When the huge tray was cleared away, the scent of the feast lingered. Marietta could almost taste the chocolate. She drank a surplus of cool water directly from the tap, plying her stomach with water to forgive the lack of dinner. A headache mounted an attack with a vengeance and her wounded feet bit at her with fiery teeth. Eventually she struggled into a pale imitation of sleep, a thin veil draped over her consciousness.

Upon awakening, the punishment continued. Faceless guards stood over her, monitoring her as she envied the breakfast fruit, buttery golden pastries and pot of rich drinking chocolate that Dellara and Pirlipata shared. She considered bluffing the king, refusing to dance for him, wondering if he truly was prepared to lose his latest entertainment, but his summons never materialised.

'Food is always linked with power,' she overheard Pirlipata saying darkly. It prompted an unbidden memory of Victoria mentioning words to that effect when her suffragist mother had undertaken a hunger strike in prison. At the time Marietta had not paid it much heed, had been far too preoccupied with dancing Myrtha in their production of *Giselle*, devouring Victor Hugo's *Fantômes* as one of the original inspirations for the romantic ballet that had debuted in the Salle Le Peletier. Now she twinged with guilt as she watched lunch, and then her second missed dinner, pass her by like the ghost-maidens. It was a ghastly affair. Unthinkable that women should suffer so for their voice to be taken into account. Frederick had been right: she was not as well aware of her own privilege as she ought to have been.

In a bid for distraction, Marietta retreated to the bathing pool. Though she didn't bathe for fear of disturbing her bandages, it was cathartic to dip her fingers in the churning bubbles, the toffee-scented steam clouding around her. Pirlipata walked through the gauzy drapes and swam lengths in the pool. Afterward, she lay in the bubbles and spoke with ease to Marietta. On their families and friends and the passions that fuelled them. Marietta attempted to distil into words her love of ballet and the hold it had on her life, explaining, 'Sometimes I feel as if the desire to dance might consume me. It nestles deep in my bones, a compelling force. I dance until the world falls away and nothing else exists save myself, in that moment, all-encompassing and all too precious. The truth of it is that it is a part of me and to take it from me would mean cleaving me apart, condemning me to live a half-life.' She ought to have woven Aurora's tale upon the stage, the culmination of years spent under Madame Belinskaya's tutelage, instead of being lured into serving as entertainment for a cruel king. That loss cut deep.

Pirlipata had listened and understood before confiding in her that she missed climbing the rocks and mountains that ringed Crackatuck more than she missed her family. 'Though they are not aware of my captivity, they have never once questioned my wedding King Gelum in some secret ceremony they were not privy to, nor have they seemed concerned with my lack of contact since our correspondence about their intended visit.'

'One of the soldiers informed me that Crackatuck looks to the future,' Marietta mused.

'Yes. History is valued in Mistpoint, where they live their lives entwined with their islands of ancient weather-worn ruins, infused with their ancestors' memories. In Crackatuck, we look forward. Our universities are greatly admired as we have always prized knowledge and culture above all. And that,' Pirlipata added softly, 'will be King Gelum's eventual downfall.'

'How so?' Marietta listened closer.

Pirlipata spared a glance at the drapes, thin and bright as moon-light, susurrating in the steam. 'He fears culture and art and what it may wreak upon his rule. Crackatuck have always held the majority of Celesta's printing presses, yet the few that remained in Everwood were ordered to be destroyed. Books have been forbidden here since the king caught the first taste of rebellion stirring up his people.' The drapes fluttered open for a moment, affording a glimpse of the suite and the door opening. Pirlipata fell silent at once. A single server was escorted in by faceless guards, deposited a silver tray heaped with dishes and departed. The guards remained. Pirlipata did not speak on the matter again but Marietta's intrigue remained piqued.

Over the following days, Pirlipata and Dellara flitted in and out of the suite at the king's command, dripping in glamour, clad in enchanted gowns that set the air around them a-glittering, while Marietta languished in a bitter concoction of defiance and regret. Her thoughts became sticky-slow as if her head had been filled with treacle and moving began to necessitate a great effort. She was consumed with imagining biting into moist chocolate cakes, polishing off entire vats of thick, comforting casseroles, tureens of soup, delicate pies submerged in heavy sauces, and heaps of bread, fluffy and crusty all at once. When she closed her eyes to rest a moment, she dreamt of garden picnics with Frederick and their nanny, of the honey sandwiches and lemon tarts they'd gorged themselves on, filling their mouths with sunshine. When they were older, they'd continued the tradition; though Nanny had since departed the earth and they were far too old for such trivialities, they'd picnicked in the name of nostalgia, the bottle of Frederick's purloined vintage Taittinger their sole concession in adapting the menu.

Marietta opened her eyes one evening to Pirlipata peering at her with concern, gold threaded through her cloud of hair, golden butterflies dancing up the crescent moon-curve of her ears. 'We cannot miss tonight's frivolities but we shall find a way to bring you some sustenance,' she said and Marietta spent the length of the ball dreaming in flavours and textures. She was greeted some time later with an anguished Pirlipata bearing a welted cheek and Dellara's bloodied nose along with the news, 'I am so sorry, Marietta; we were searched at the door.'

Curiously, her hunger abated. Some dim, near-forgotten part of her was aware that her faculties were impaired, yet the urge to care was fleeting and, in one misted moment, lost. Time blurred, her tenuous grasp on days trickling away into sleep. She dreamt of wraiths of mist feasting on a forest. Of ice-flecked seas, of winters that devoured all. Of eyes that froze her skin until she became a creature of frost, her hair a spill of snowflakes, her heart encased in sugar-spun glass. In the distance, a wolf howled. Drosselmeier materialised to gaze down at her, reaching out to twine his fingers through her hair. She fled through her fogged memories, hunted by tooth and claw, mice dancing along at her feet; her heart beat too fiercely in its glass case and she shattered from the inside out. Waking with a start, she searched the corners of the suite for Drosselmeier.

'We must do something before we lose her, Dellara.'

'We should be thankful that the palace has its own supply of fresh water imported from Mistpoint. If we were in the town she wouldn't have lasted this long. I hear the courtiers' whispers that the mineral sickness spreads further.'

'A person cannot survive off water alone.'

'Then we'll redouble our efforts to sneak something in. I shan't let another one die.'

Marietta heard their urgent whispers as if from a great distance. She opened her eyes to plead with them not to risk themselves on her account, that she no longer hungered, wondering why their faces were unusually grave, why the words were shaped like icicles upon her tongue. Before she could force them out, a pair of faceless guards marched in and wrenched her up onto her feet.

The room blurred and her head roared. She heard a protest but it was quashed by a soldier's voice she did not recognise. 'She has been summoned. King's orders.'

Chapter Twenty-Three

Against her expectations, the soldier escorted Marietta further up the spiral, her head tipping back, the hollowed centre of the palace a dizzying prospect. They lapped around it and it loomed at Marietta until she felt its nothingness, its vacuity shift into something more tangible, gobbling up the heart of the palace and hungry for more, a beast that would devour everything in its midst.

They halted before another identical door. The soldier knocked. His fist sounded as hard as the bronze lion knocker mounted on the townhouse door and for a moment Marietta expected to hear Jarvis announce a guest for dinner. Though the voice that bid them enter was not his. The soldier threw Marietta onto a small wooden chair, the force with which he handled her sending her slipping off the side. Her body felt as insubstantial as a will o'the wisp, drifting over a sea of ice.

The door slammed shut. A pair of strong arms suddenly lifted her back onto the chair. A murmured, 'What have they done to you?'

Marietta forced herself to look at the man swimming into her vision. The captain. He seemed to be peering back at her in some concern. A hard rim brushed her lips and she tasted liquid, registering that it was hot and salty and satisfying. Her preservation flared to life and she began to gulp it.

'Pace yourself or you will bring it back up again,' the captain said.

She drank slowly. The mist encasing her brain receded. Captain Legat handed her a roll and she bit into it, groaning at the taste. It filled her, warming her from the inside. She glanced at their surroundings as she ate.

It appeared as though she was sitting in a log cabin. It could have been perched atop a mountain in the Swiss Alps for all its rustic idyll. The walls, low ceiling and floor were hewn planks of frozen gingerbread, a fire crackled before plump chairs and furs, and a large desk sprawled out across half the cabin's cosy interior. She was seated before the desk, the captain at her side, monitoring her. She looked at him and he stood, offering her a wry smile. 'Has it passed your examination?' He took the carved gingerbread chair behind his desk and passed her a fresh glass of water in an ice glass. Large lanterns were mounted on the walls, lending the space a flickering glow.

'Why have you summoned me?' Her voice felt harsh, alien to her after days of drifting in and out of consciousness, weak and silent.

He sighed, running his fingers roughly through his bronze hair and closing his eyes for a beat. 'I could not, in all good conscience, allow the king to starve you.'

Marietta met his eyes. They were warmer than the rest of his face, as if within them it was impossible to hide his emotions. She decided she admired his eyes; they were honest and kind. Aware that she'd been staring into them for longer than she ought, she lowered her gaze to the desk. There was an abundance of papers, fountain pens, a half-drunk cup of molten chocolate and wax seals stamped with sword-fighting mice. She frowned at the latter, the image resonating through the time-fogged looking glass of her memories.

The captain cleared his throat. 'When you leave, take care to appear as weakened as when you entered. I cannot afford to nurture suspicion.'

Marietta inclined her head. The cabin gave a sickening swirl. 'Of course.' She fought to her feet. Captain Legat rose from his chair to help with the endeavour. He spread a thin swathe of cloth over his desk, placing another few rolls along with several oat and nut biscuits upon it. 'Wrap this around your waist, your dress has grown loose enough to hide it,' he said, meeting her eyes. She nodded and he turned around. Her hunger a gnawing fiend, she failed to feel a sliver of embarrassment at hiking up her dress in the presence of a gentlemen. Though she did manage a smile at the thought of Ida's reaction to her situation, certain her mother would have decried her as a cigarette-smoking, scarlet crêpe de Chine-wearing fast girl.

'Thank you,' she said after she had finished. The captain turned round and surveyed her. He gave a curt nod then checked his timepiece. 'We can afford a little longer.' He motioned to the seat.

After a brief hesitation, Marietta sat.

'Can you manage any more?' he asked and she nodded. He slid a pot in her direction and she picked up the accompanying fork and ate the baked dish. He sat and sifted through his papers, marking the occasional note on them, and time drizzled by.

When next he glanced her way, she asked, 'Why?'

The quill in his hand stilled. Its feather glistened white as snow, soft as ermine. It could have been plucked from Victoria's Odette tutu; overlaid with swan feathers that fluttered as she channelled Anna Sobeshchanskaya, the original Odette at the Bolshoi. Though Victoria had delighted in informing them all that Anna had been replaced for the premiere after selling the expensive jewellery a government official had gifted her and marrying the dancer cast as Siegfried instead. Marietta had remarked how telling it was that Siegfried hadn't been recast for the offence.

'Why have you taken it upon yourself to aid me?' she repeated.

His eyebrows pinched together. 'As I told you, I could not in all good conscience allow you to stave.'

'So you said. Yet I cannot help but wonder where your true motivations lie. After all, you will not assist me in leaving this palace. I suppose, as captain of the King's Army, that's understandable. This, however—' she gestured at the half-emptied dish '—is not.'

The captain tapped his quill on the papers. Marietta slid her gaze onto them. An elegant penmanship curled over the pages. 'I have witnessed enough suffering for a lifetime,' he said, shuffling the papers out of her sight. In his abruptness, a ringlet of crimson ribbon unfurled from his interior jacket pocket.

'Careful, you're revealing your heart,' Marietta said wryly, gesturing at it.

He tucked it out of sight and rose to his feet. 'It is a mere token of affection and I do not care to discuss my personal life. Nor will you.' His tone was icy, his face frosted over. Those warm butterscotch eyes she had so admired cooled as he looked down at her.

'You had better leave now.'

Marietta felt her cheeks warm. 'Fine.' She stood, ignoring the tilt of the room.

'And do keep up the pretence,' the captain snapped as he strode towards the door.

Marietta clutched her arm, feigning an injury, and glared at him as she made to leave.

The captain reached the door before her and opened it with barely restrained force. 'Take her away,' he commanded of the soldier, shutting it without looking at her.

The soldier didn't search her. The pretext of being escorted to and from a punishment had fooled him into a false sense of security.

Once she had been tossed into her suite and the door locked behind her, Pirlipata and Dellara helped her onto a sapphire cushion.

Pirlipata's brow creased in delicate confusion upon Marietta's summarisation of events, while Dellara tapped a finger against her lips and gave her an evaluating stare. They secreted the food within the armoires, and that night Marietta felt the first stirrings of her appetite return. Dellara rationed the food out and she was glad of that when she was forbidden from joining them for meals the following day. The king still did not summon her. She was starting to realise the true extent of his cruelties and life in the palace.

Chapter Twenty-Four

Marietta was recuperating well but still stewing at Captain Legat's strange and sudden dismissal until several days later when she was taken into his study once more. She crossed her legs at the ankles, smoothing down her berry-red dress. A furred cape caressed her shoulders and Dellara had painted her lips in matching red. 'Are you toying with me, captain?'

He passed her a plate; toasted and thickly buttered garlic and herb rolls with a pot of something sweet and smoky reminiscent of soupe à l'oignon. A cluster of herbs with a single white flower floated on top. She picked it up and examined it. It reminded her of the daisies she'd once plaited into chains.

'Saltspray flowers,' the captain said, nodding at it. 'They hark from Mistpoint. It's said their petals carry the taste of the ocean. The stew is named for it. And no, I am not, to answer your previous question.'

Marietta rested the sprig on the side of her plate. 'Why am I here, captain?'

'I behaved poorly last time we met. Forgive me.'

Marietta paused, spoon in hand. 'Is that an apology?'

Captain Legat gave her a wry smile. 'I wouldn't grow accustomed to it.'

Marietta's smile surprised herself. She skimmed her spoon along the surface of the stew, soaking in its warmth as she ate. They sat in companionable silence until Marietta grew aware of the opportunity before her and commented, 'You seem young to have achieved the rank of captain to the King's Army.'

The captain leant back on his chair, surveying her. After a few moments, he replied, surprising her again. 'It was happenstance. I saved the king's life when I was a young soldier. He then took a particular interest in my career and I soon found myself accelerated through the ranks.'

'You must have made quite the impression,' Marietta said, slicing a roll in half. 'How ever did you save his life?'

He tapped his quill on his papers. 'It was during a routine perimeter check of the staircase when I heard it: a great howl that froze the blood in my veins. The screams followed shortly after. I had never heard anything like those sounds. Pain and fear and horror.' He closed his eyes for a beat. 'To this day I have never managed to discover why or how the wards collapsed that day, nor how an intruder made his way into the palace.' He met Marietta's eyes. 'The stories trivialise it, I cannot abide them. My soldiers were not there that day; they cannot understand how such an experience changes a person. Somehow I was the sole person left protecting the king. A boy, facing an armed intruder several times his size. The responsibility of the kingdom in his shaking hands.'

Marietta laid her spoon down. 'I cannot imagine what a harrowing experience it must have been for you as a young soldier.'

Captain Legat grimaced. 'I was badly injured. My arm was severely wounded and took considerable time to heal,' he said drily, rubbing his left shoulder as if the intruder still had its hooks in him. Marietta winced. He gestured at his sword, resting against the wall, its metalwork shimmering under the ice-lanterns. 'When my father assumed his place in the constellations, his sword, Starhunter, was left to me. It's forged from steel and ice and an ancient curse. Nothing else could have slain such an opponent.'

'Then you're a hero,' Marietta said softly.

The captain grimaced. 'I would not presume to call myself such a thing.'

Marietta half-smiled to herself. 'Heroes never do. Am I correct in assuming your father was a soldier before you?'

'Yes. Though in Everwood, since King Gelum took the throne, all boys are dispatched to the Military Quarter upon reaching seven years of age. The soldiers' code of conduct is ingrained in each of us.'

'Seven?' Marietta repeated. 'How very Spartan. Does King Gelum have need for such rigid enforcements in his land?' She toyed with the saltspray flower.

The captain watched her fingers dance over the petals. 'It's mandatory. The day you turn fourteen, you are permitted to leave in order to secure an apprenticeship in silks, sugars or enchantments, or join the King's Army. We believe every seven years the stars bestow a new gift upon us. Some families hold celebrations to mark the occasion. If I had been born under a different star, perhaps my fate would have twisted in another direction, but it was not to be.'

Marietta's fingers stilled on the flower. 'Where did your true passions lie?'

'Joining the King's Army is an elite prospect,' the captain said loyally. 'Only the finest are selected. If you prove worthy, nothing will match its pay.' He glanced at his sword then back at her. A sadness lingered in his voice. 'It is of no consequence discussing what might have been.'

'I understand more than you know,' Marietta said quietly.

'Your place might not be here in Everwood, but it is written in the stars that you will be a dancer,' the captain said.

Marietta frowned. 'How did you—'

His gaze rested on her, soft and knowing. 'I see it when you dance.'

Marietta smiled at him. He cleared his throat and pulled a paper-wrapped wedge from a desk drawer. 'These past few days I had business elsewhere. I passed by my mother's house on my return. She bakes the finest cakes in all of Sugar Alley. This one is my favourite; I saved you a slice.' Marietta noticed a tinge creeping across his throat with interest.

'Why ... thank you.'

'It was nothing,' the captain said gruffly, tipping it onto a plate and passing it to her. He took off his jacket, folding it neatly over the back of his chair, the gold buttons and epaulettes gleaming in the firelight. His shirt was rumpled beneath, the shadows under his eyes pronounced as he ploughed through a stack of correspondences marked with the king's signature seal.

She watched him drown in their contents, now and then punctuated with a rub of his temples. Rather than question him, Marietta ate the cake. White chocolate and snowberry, it was sweet and light and tasted of Christmas morning. When she returned to the suite, its taste lingered on her lips.

The following day, King Gelum summoned her down to the throne room.

'Well, my little dancer, have you learnt your lesson in obedience?'

Marietta nodded, too fatigued to resist the siren call of sustenance any longer. She began to dance.

Chapter Twenty-Five

'I can't stop thinking of the way your eyes danced when you last smiled at me,' Claren told Marietta the following week. He was escorting her back up the spiralling stairs after yet another performance. Her dress was an inky ripple of night, her hair flowed down her back, embedded with glittering icicles. Black satin pointe shoes were tied with ribbons around her calves. All she lacked were raven-dark feathers to cast her as Odile. Since she had buckled to his command, King Gelum had ordered a shoemaker over from the Silk Quarter to fit her with a rainbow of dancing shoes. The shoemaker had been fascinated by Marietta's pointe shoes and had performed an intricate study of them before forging his replicas. She had stretched and rehearsed Aurora's springing steps by habit, testing the new pairs were of sufficient quality. This had delighted both the shoemaker and Pirlipata, who formed her audience. Secretly, Marietta had been relieved her feet had healed while she had drifted in that fugue state, lack of food tipping her over the edge of life, darkness awaiting her below.

She gave Claren a cool look, freezing the smile on his face. Anger was an uncomfortable emotion. It nestled under her skin with sharp edges that bit. 'Perhaps once I am free of your king and this palace then I shall find it within me to smile once more.' The thread of gold stitching along her hem reared up, a wave of lost sunlight against the night of her dress.

Claren appeared sincere for once. 'I'm sorry, Marietta, truly.'

Marietta gestured down at King Gelum, resting upon his throne below, in a silver suit and a white furred cape. 'How can you bear serving such a man?'

Claren tugged his jacket, making it more dishevelled than it was prior to his adjustment. 'Being a member of the King's Army is a well-respected position and the pay is good. You have to understand—' he lowered his voice '—I had no idea this was going to happen. If I had, I would never have suggested . . .' He trailed off, looking at her with eyes of the bleakest winter's day; grey and miserable.

'At ease, soldier,' Marietta said wryly, her golden hem melting back into place. 'You are not the sole person to be held accountable for the events of that night. I too was reckless in my behaviour.' Reckless was one word for it; childish might be another. She was ashamed of how easily she had been seduced by a wondrous palace and pretty enchantments.

She didn't seek Claren's assistance; his naïvety on the king's nature and position amongst his ranks would only jeopardise her. Besides, what power did one individual hold to subvert the magic regulating the kings' commands? No, she required a greater plot. Marietta continued to think and Claren fell silent until she entered the suite, where he bid her goodbye and the guards locked the door with a golden key.

She stood and surveyed the suite. She had a sudden sympathy for Persephone descending into Hades' underworld; she too had drawn the lot of mists and darkness. For here she stood, imprisoned in the gilded cage she had fought her life to avoid.

Marietta found herself falling into a routine over the following weeks. Life cannot be suppressed indefinitely and so it began to take on a new rhythm. Pastimes were scarce in the opulent suite, confined to ornamenting themselves in enchanted creations and allowing Dellara to paint their faces, their skin the canvas of her creations, swimming lengths and languishing in the bathing pool, or conversing among themselves. It was the latter that Marietta was most invested in. Pirlipata and Dellara had proven themselves an infinite resource in their knowledge of the palace and Everwood, and Marietta was determined to unveil its secrets.

'I wish I had a book in which to lose myself,' she said, dipping a pastry into a glass of molten chocolate. From the corner of her eye, she caught the glance Pirlipata and Dellara exchanged.

Pirlipata was first to speak. 'I once was particularly fond of the tale of the first armoured princess, Ithye. She is the star I look to and I hope one day to be worthy of gaining a place amidst her constellation of protectors.'

Marietta thought back to her dinner with the captain and how he'd spoken of the stars. 'Why are the stars important to you? What is your relationship with them?'

'We believe that the spirits of our loved ones join the constellations when we pass from this world,' Dellara said. 'All the tales of our world are bound up in our stars. We're taught them from the day we're born and they're the last thought the day we die. Our fates are written in the stars.'

Pirlipata inclined her head. 'Each of us possess a starname, too. A secret name no one knows as long as we live, save those we choose to entwine our lives with forevermore. Our starnames become known once we have ascended into the skies. They are who we shall become in our final place, resting in the skies.'

'Who selects your starname?' Marietta asked.

'We do,' Dellara said. 'We are responsible for gifting ourselves with a name once we truly understand who we are. It's an empowering act, stepping into your own identity, forging a deeper empathy with yourself.'

'I like that,' Marietta said, wishing they had an equivalency in her world. Though Everwood had become her prison, she had seen how Claren was treated no differently for whom he chose to spend a night with. How Pirlipata wasn't judged on the basis of her skin colour. Yes, Everwood was her prison, but Frederick and Geoffrey and Harriet couldn't escape theirs, thanks to social convention. She set her half-eaten pastry down. The tray swam in melted chocolate and frozen cream. 'Do tell me more about these armoured princesses.'

'In Crackatuck, we have a long tradition of armoured princesses.' Pirlipata slid her golden cape down her shoulders, revealing her arms, as sculpted with muscle as the Farnese Hercules. 'The future belongs to us and so we must be willing and able to protect it, our swords and minds both sharpened blades. All rulers are educated at university and trained in the art of sword fighting. My armour was red. As fiery as the sunsets that ripple across our land and the last colour you see before the all-encompassing darkness.'

Marietta pictured Pirlipata encased in red, her dark hair around her head like a halo topping her armour. 'Where is it located presently?'

'King Gelum is in possession of it. When the day comes for me to reclaim it, he will pay for each day I have been without it. For each day I have been clothed in gold rather than red.'

Dellara's eyes darkened to a maw. 'Red for the blood we'll spill in the streets, red for the rebellion,' she chanted beneath her breath.

'So there is a rebellion,' Marietta said. 'Am I to retain a hope that they will set us free?'

The shadows whispered into Dellara's sclera. 'Being exposed for a member of the rebellion costs those brave individuals their lives in the bloodiest of executions. It is a habit of mine to hold an ear to the palace gossip, yet no one seems to be aware of either their true numbers nor where they are based. It's a rebellion mired in secrecy and fear and anger. I've heard tell that the sole sign of a rebeller is a curl of scarlet satin they carry secreted about their person.' She shrugged and reached for a pastry. 'I'm not certain whether there is any truth to that though.'

Marietta silently thought back to the red curl that had fallen from inside the captain's tunic which he'd passed off as a token of affection. She vowed to discover what he was hiding. Perhaps it could be the very thing that would help her escape this palace.

Chapter Twenty-Six

The king's party meandered their way into the heart of Everwood, where a large space was cleared beside the frozen lake. Sugar swans glided upon the ice, enchanted to serenade the spectators that stood in regimented rows. The soldiers of the King's Army maintained the perimeter as the Faceless Guards undertook surrounding and protecting the king himself. Marietta's heartbeat was as delicate as hoarfrost. She turned her gaze to the distant firs, signalling the boundary of the Endless Forest.

'Don't,' Captain Legat said softly.

Marietta bestowed on him her coolest look. Pirlipata and Dellara remained in their suite. To flee into the forest, residence of creeping shadows and wild horrors, while they remained imprisoned would be both reckless and unthinkable. When the king had proclaimed she would dance at his annual Festival of Light celebration in the centre of Everwood, Marietta had been struck by temptation, that she couldn't deny, but she was decided she would return to the palace. When she found a way out, it would not be by herself or for herself.

She walked at the captain's side. He was dressed in full livery, including a fur-lined hat, dark against his hair, and his sword at his hip. The king's most trusted soldier. Underneath her furred cape, Marietta wore a thousand glittering snowflakes, sewn together to form a gown as delicate as Chantilly lace, light as gossamer and the pale blue of a frosted morning. Her pointe shoes and cape were a fairy tale of Prussian blue. A single question burned the tip of her tongue but she would not ask it of the captain yet. She required a moment alone with him.

They followed King Gelum to an opulent throne, crafted from sugarplums. Bewitched sugar mice squeaked on servers' trays and a snowberry crème fountain had been erected beside him. A handful of well-attired guests dipped ice goblets into its stream and sipped, surveying the décor from their brioche tier of seating.

It was beautiful. And then Marietta looked deeper. On her welcome to the palace, she had been so overawed by the finery and indulgence that it had blinded her to the truth that lay like thorns beneath the snow. She would not make the same mistake again.

Her hoarfrost-heart splintered. The audience were clothed in ragged dresses, an insufficient barrier to the bitter temperature. Evidence of sickness was plain on many faces. As was their hatred and contempt for the king's party.

'Cease that at once,' Captain Legat said under his breath.

Marietta snapped round to glare at him. Her anger faded upon seeing him address a small child. The boy turned imploring eyes to the captain, his hands filled with water from a nearby fountain. He couldn't have been more than four or five years of age and was accompanied by an older sister.

'What on earth is the matter with you?' Marietta hissed at the captain. 'He's just playing.'

Captain Legat disregarded her. He slipped something from his pocket and handed it to the girl. 'Use these until they run out. Melt the snow from the Endless Forest, it's safer. Send an adult. Do not cross that boundary yourselves, do you understand me?'

She nodded and grabbed her little brother's hand, tugging him past a globe of lit-ice and away. As they flashed by the enchanted lantern, a hard lump formed in Marietta's throat. The girl's face was shot through with silver, her irises and hair half-leached of colour. 'What was wrong with her?' she asked quietly.

The captain was grave. 'The mineral sickness. Melting enchantments are overpriced and the townspeople poor. The water that runs through these public fountains is tantamount to poison.'

Marietta grasped his wrist. 'Why then was the boy attempting to drink from it?'

'Some feel they have no choice; to thirst is a terrible thing. And many children have not had the luxury of education these days.'

'Yet Everwood possesses riches surely? I've witnessed the king's many entertainments and tonight is no exception—' Marietta halted her thoughts as the captain stiffened. She let her fingers slip from his wrist.

'Not here,' he said shortly.

King Gelum's voice boomed out, announcing her performance.

Marietta stared at the captain. 'I cannot dance for these people,' she whispered. 'This is a travesty.'

Captain Legat turned his gaze on her. 'You can and you must. For if you do not then you shall suffer also.'

'There are *children* suffering.' She felt half-frozen with shock at witnessing the extent of the king's neglect. His cruelty cut deeper than she had known; he had been allowed to carve through his people with the might of the throne behind him. For there was no other governing force to hold him accountable.

Yet it seemed the captain no longer deigned to converse with her.

As the music began, Marietta danced in doll-like bourrée steps to a music-box melody, the atmosphere hardened like a caramel glaze.

Travelling on the diagonal, she performed a series of petit piqué battements, her legs whipping the air as if it was cream, her arms soft in port de bras. As she slowed into a glissade, a gliding transition, King Gelum pronounced, 'I declare the Festival of Light begun! Let us celebrate the darkest point of winter and recognise that our days of light are forthcoming.' He held his arms high.

The night erupted in illuminance. Swathes of ivory chiffon billowed overheard, sprinkled with light. Fir trees strung with glass baubles flickered alight. A luminescent powdered sugar-snow began to softly fall. Marietta drew her glissade out, slowing to watch an iridescent mouse run across the ink-black pool of the sky. She stretched out into an elongated arabesque.

A curl of scarlet dropped onto the ice.

Marietta held her arabesque.

The caramel glaze of tension shattered.

A lone scream of defiance, rage and desperation led the charge. King Gelum's military procession snapped to attention, barricading the king as the citizens of Everwood surged in his direction. A chant formed. *Red for the blood we'll spill in the streets, red for the rebellion.*

Marietta ran. Trapped between the king and the growing crowd, and clad in her shimmering gown of snowflakes, she was indistinguishable from the king's party of revellers. She threw a longing glance in the other direction, at that silent wall of firs in the distance that held her freedom, before dashing behind a gingerbread stand selling molten chocolate. Shouts and cries and clashes.

When she looked out, she saw a rally of townspeople taking on the soldiers as the captain drew his sword. She heard King Gelum instructing him to deal with the dissenters before the Faceless Guards marched the king back to his sleigh. She watched the captain rush about, issuing orders and organising the king's retinue of faceless guards to escort the king back to the palace. Then King Gelum's royal sleigh rushed away, its mouse-carved runners spraying snow in its hurry. Several sleighs of faceless guards followed, the air thick with the sound of moose hooves pounding the snow. Marietta's breath caught. The rebellion held a mighty task before them; the king's defence was near impenetrable.

'Allow me to return you to the sleigh.' Captain Legat appeared at her side as if he'd stepped out from the night itself.

'I had wondered why you had reacted in such a strong manner last week, when you unceremoniously bade me leave your study.' Marietta addressed her words forwards, watching the glimmer of the Festival of Light play out against the chaos in the streets. She felt the captain stiffen at her side. 'It failed to make any sense to me. At the time I dismissed it as my own confusion owing to my state of mind. Now, though, I understand.'

'Then perhaps you might enlighten me as to what you are referring to.'

Marietta turned to him. 'Red for the blood you'll spill in the streets, red for the rebellion you belong to.'

Captain Legat's fingers tightened on his sword hilt. His butter-scotch eyes hardened.

'Such an innocent thing, a curl of ribbon. Doubtless no one would consider it twice. One of the countries in my world once associated revolutionaries with a red Phrygian cap. Once it is uncovered it takes on more importance, of course. Becomes a powerful symbol.'

The captain gave a dry laugh. 'Someone has been filling your head with fantasies.'

'Indeed?' In an emboldened move, Marietta reached for the captain's jacket pocket.

He caught her hand in his and whisked them around. Her back cold against the frozen gingerbread wall, he released her hand.

'I saw the ribbon dropped onto the ice before the protest erupted,' she said a little breathlessly. 'You cannot pretend it means nothing. I *know*.'

He stood before her, close enough to keep her pressed against the gingerbread. 'I possess it as a ruse. As captain of the King's Army, it is in my purview to ascertain and deal with any threats to the king's rule.'

Marietta looked up at him. 'You're lying, Captain Legat.'

'And you have no idea what you are stumbling into, wanderer.' His voice was veined with anger. Yet it was the deepest pools of anger than ran with denial.

'Why do you insist on calling me by this moniker? You have never once addressed me with my name.'

The captain's face revealed nothing. 'Ought I to have? I do not know you, neither do we hold a friendship.'

Marietta's thoughts were a map of consternation. She surveyed the captain. Lifted an eyebrow. 'Are you in the habit of gifting your mother's cake to veritable strangers?'

'Are you under the delusion that I hold some degree of affection towards you? I can assure you that I do not.'

Marietta's laugh was hollow. The captain's gaze dipped to her mouth for a second. 'Nor would I desire you to,' she told him.

'Very well,' he said curtly. 'You may see yourself to the sleigh. I must attend to an urgent matter but another soldier shall escort you back.'

'Fine.' She turned on her heel and strode away.

The commotion had intensified. Under the bewitching night sky, unrest poured across the frozen lake. Marietta glanced back at the captain just in time to see him slip away. As she kept eyes on him, she watched him double back and alter his direction. She took a deep breath and followed him.

Chapter Twenty-Seven

Captain Legat's path circumnavigated the frozen lake. Marietta took care to keep from sight as he twined past a glass wall of a mountain and entered a narrow alley. It was a maze, constructed from sugar, between a pair of ice cliffs that teetered up to brush the stars. Studded with alcoves and delicate sugar-stairs, signs heralded all manner of sumptuous delicacies crafted within. Marietta's heart beat faster as she took it all in, illuminated by strings of tiny ice-lanterns above. Chocolate truffles imbued with the finest liquor that promised euphoria with a single bite. Petits fours laced with beautifying charms. Caramel buttercream birds granted with flight. This, then, was Sugar Alley.

Captain Legat removed his hat and ascended a staircase. Marietta glanced over her shoulder. At the opposing end of Sugar Alley, she thought she caught a swoop of silver hair yet no sooner had she fixed on it, it had already vanished. She shook any fearful contemplations from her head and followed the captain.

'You oughtn't to have risked yourself for such a foolhardy visit,' a woman said, the curves of her accent deep and caring.

'It was imperative I see you,' Captain Legat replied. 'The protest has erupted. I needed to ensure your safety.'

Marietta, on the other side of the door buried within a sugar wall, hesitated. It seemed she had inadvertently pursued the captain to a lovers' tryst. Her breath caught in her throat.

She turned to leave.

'You must take greater care. If the king knew of your role in the rebellion—'

Marietta paused. It seemed the captain's paramour knew his secrets. She attempted to listen closer but the sugar step crunched beneath her ballet slipper.

The door whipped open. The warm honeyed glow of the interior framed Captain Legat.

'Of all the foolhardiness—'

'I apologise,' Marietta said. 'I held no notion of what I was intruding upon.' She lowered her eyes.

After a harsh sigh, the captain pulled her inside and shut the door. 'You had better not speak a word of this to anyone, do I make myself understood?' His golden eyes shone hard with fury.

Marietta inclined her head. 'I shall be the height of discretion.'

'Allow me to introduce you to Robess.' The captain met Marietta's eyes. 'The leader of the rebellion.'

An older woman radiating authority, Robess scrutinised Marietta in much the same manner as Madame Belinskaya observed her turnout. She was tall and wore her silver hair pinned up in a bun, and was adorned in a matching silver jacquard suit. The quaint sugar-room felt too small for her all-consuming presence. Her steel gaze flicked to Captain Legat as she murmured, 'The wanderer?'

Marietta retained a check on her surprise. 'You have heard mention of me?'

'My son keeps me informed on all the occurrences at the palace,' Robess said.

Marietta's surprise deepened. She noted the sculpted cheekbones Captain Legat had inherited from his mother, the smooth sureness of their composure, their height.

'I shall leave you be,' Robess said, departing through a smaller second door. 'I imagine you possess much to discuss.' Her composure melted a little, revealing a mischievous twinkle.

Captain Legat cleared his throat but Marietta was too distracted to discern his mother's words. Her exit had afforded a glimpse of what lay through the second door: a printing press. With a sherbet's-fizz of realisation she knew she'd infiltrated the rebellion's headquarters.

'I knew you belonged to the rebellion,' she said quietly. 'Though I well understand why you did not share the fact with me.'

'Come, I shall escort you back to the palace. The king will be wanting to know where his dancer is.' He guided her to the door then hesitated.

'Then we shall concoct a story on how you rescued me from a band of dastardly rebellers.' She dropped her voice. 'Your secret is safe with me, captain.'

His eyes lingered on hers. 'Call me Legat.'

'After you have spent the past few moontides referring to me as a mere wanderer? I think I may prefer calling you captain,' she said with a flicker of a smile. An arched brow.

His answering smile set something deep within him aglow. It danced straight through her.

'Whatever strikes your desire, Marietta.'

An endless winter's night reigned over Everwood. King Gelum's envoy of sleighs had already poured across the ice bridge and back to the palace, leaving Marietta and the captain riding in a lone sleigh. The streets had emptied and Marietta felt as if they were the sole inhabitants of the world.

The paths were lit with globes of frozen ice that flickered with enchantments, lighting the way through the snow-coated valley.

When the marzipan-cobbled path curved, the captain followed it, driving a team of miniature reindeer that pulled the small sleigh. Marietta inhaled the scent of firs, snow and sugar, glancing up at the sky. It was silvered with stars. Which belonged to Pirlipata's armoured princesses? She hadn't thought to ask. She was unused to unfamiliar skies and so very far away from home.

'It must be difficult to be away from your mother in such dangerous times. You must wish you were closer so you might protect her,' Marietta said.

'I do. I look to her as if she were one of the great stars shining down on us, illuminating my path.' The captain's voice slunk lower, more honest. 'I spend every day compensating for my role in preventing the last orchestrated attack on King Gelum's rule. If I had not saved his life—'

'You were so young,' Marietta said softly. 'You could not have known.'

His look at her was pierced with anguish. 'Yet it led to his fear of an uprising. It was the moment in which he banned printing presses from Everwood, hoping a lack of education, of organisation, would thwart future rebellions. And it has worked thus far.'

Marietta's heart hurt for him. 'Until now. You will succeed this time, I know it.'

'And what of you? I'm curious to learn more about from where you hail.' Captain Legat glanced at her, his bronze hair gleaming in the light of the lantern suspended above the sleigh. Marietta's stomach twisted and she glanced down. 'Do you miss it?' he asked.

'There are aspects that I miss.' A series of unwanted images flashed through her mind's eye. Drosselmeier's chipped-ice stare, seeking her out across a dark theatre, his fingers creeping into her hair, his breath hot against her neck. 'I miss my ballet studio and my brother dearly.

And though your food and drinking chocolate are simply marvellous, I oft find myself desperate for a cup of coffee.'

The captain gave her a curious look. 'What kind of beverage is coffee? I have never heard mention of such a thing.'

Marietta laughed. 'It is a bitter, strong drink that people imbibe to render them more alert. Rather useful in the mornings, I find, though I have a habit of drowning it in milk and sugar to flavour it more to my liking.'

His smile was faint, fleeting. 'I do not pretend to understand how you are feeling.' He swallowed. 'If only I could turn this sleigh around. Return you to your world.' His face betrayed a stifled wildness. In that flash, Marietta saw him as somewhat akin to herself; a caged bird.

She laid a hand on his arm. 'I understand,' she said quietly. 'You have responsibilities here that necessitate you filling your obligations to the king. Lest you draw attention to others that need you more than I. Besides, my fate is now aligned with that of Pirlipata and Dellara; I could not forsake them now. You spoke honestly of your own unwitting role in circumnavigating an old uprising. Well, I too regret the mistakes I have made in the past. I was a selfish, vain creature, ignorant to the world around me. I still have much to learn but I am hopeful that I shall be wiser in the future. If I ever return home.'

'It's in the stars that you shall dance in your own world once more.' The captain laid a gloved hand atop hers. She felt its warmth, a beam of sunlight cutting through the harshest winter. 'Of that I have no doubt. Many wanderers, lost souls, find themselves in Everwood for a spell; most return home.' He hesitated then. 'Some time ago you informed me that you were far from safe in your own world. I must confess, I have often dwelled on that since. Is that what led you here?'

Once, Marietta would never have considered telling him her story.

She had kept herself locked away as tightly as she was in the frozen palace, hesitant to share even the smallest morsel of herself with others apart from Frederick. But Dellara and Pirlipata had shown her another path. One of companionship and finding strength in each other. So, she began to speak of Drosselmeier, the truth bleeding from her lips.

The captain's hand fell to his sword hilt. 'Do you wish me to—' He stopped and cleared his throat.

Marietta's hand still lingered on his arm. 'No. I will not have anyone else fight my battles for me. I shall seek a way to defeat him myself and it will taste all the sweeter for it. Besides, we come from different worlds, lest you forget.' Her smile was wry.

After a beat, Captain Legat inclined his head. 'You are more than capable of doing so. I understand it cannot have been easy to share that with me but I am honoured and grateful to have been taken into your confidence. In fact—' He handed her a battered notebook from his breast pocket. 'Since you are already in possession of my deepest secret,' he said roughly, 'what is one more?'

She took it curiously, made to open the cover when the captain shook his head. 'Do keep it hidden.'

She secreted it under her cloak.

As their sleigh rushed through the illuminated night and towards the frozen sugar palace, Marietta wished the world would still, just for a moment.

Chapter Twenty-Eight

'Where, perchance, has my dancer wandered off to?' King Gelum asked.

Marietta stiffened. Dread pooled in her stomach, heavy as clotted cream. She had been observing tonight's feast in the throne room alongside Dellara in an attempt to keep her eyes averted from Captain Legat's, whose gaze she kept inadvertently meeting. They had not conversed since the events that had transpired a few days ago, since their intimate sleigh ride back to the palace with his most dangerous secret in her possession. An inchoate awareness that she had penetrated his armour. And he hers.

King Gelum had accepted their tale of events yet was reluctant to allow her a moment's respite on each occasion she was within his presence. She ached to sit, her feet blistered and sore, her muscles tiring.

A trade delegation from another world had arrived less than an hour earlier, stepping directly into the throne room by means of tiny golden keys which cut an entrance through magic Marietta could not decipher. Dellara had informed her that they were rare and valuable beyond measure. The guests were now ensconced in a celebratory dinner that the king was presiding over. Seated on low cushions, they dined from the backs of silvery sugar swans, their backs heaped high with delicacies from Sugar Alley.

Marietta stepped forward. A woman in a raspberry-pink gown tittered and whispered to the man sat beside her. Marietta suppressed a smile at the golden birdcage perched atop her head, replete with miniature songbirds fluttering about her pinned curls. Bright yellow, each one was a ray of sunshine distilled into feathers and song.

King Gelum pointed to a stretch of opaque floor that ran alongside half of the diners. 'I command you dance for the Bellinnese.'

Despite a flicker of temptation at the notion of publicly refusing the king, Marietta acquiesced as the musicians picked up their instruments in a hurry and began to play. Closing her eyes, feeling the music unfurl, she danced. Attempted to conjure the vision of weightlessness that Anna Pavlova and all the greats of ballet conveyed. To transform into an ephemeral creature of silk and gossamer, carried by the wind. Yet, having been commanded to dance, she failed to summon the passion slumbering in her bones. Her ankle buckled during a pirouette and Marietta fell.

The Bellinnese fell silent. Several called short tunes to their birds, which returned to perch on fingers and curls of hair, their baleful eyes swivelling moons. Marietta chanced a glance at King Gelum. Though his expression maintained an immaculate calmness, his thin lips had paled and clamped together, conveying his distaste.

She rose to her feet, disregarding the sidled looks, the whispers unspooling behind hands, the concern on Pirlipata's face, seated at the king's side. The music floated on, clambering up to a sweet harmony. Yet as Marietta resumed her variation, she suffered the acute anxiety known to dancers; something was wrong. One of her ankles pinched, lending a jaggedness to her motions, turning them unwieldy. She sprang up into a restrained jump and it gave out. She toppled down onto one of the sugar swans. Its delicate neck snapped, its head falling and shattering like ice.

'You are making a spectacle of yourself,' the king hissed and someone trilled a laugh. King Gelum's eyes, limned with sapphire paint in a resemblance of birdwings, cut her a look brimming with promised pain. 'Get up.'

Marietta arose with great difficulty. A sigh of disgust rippled through the diners. She glanced down; the broken sugar swan had sliced her left calf. Blood trickled down her leg. Worse, when she stood on both feet, her right ankle was unsteady, unable to sustain her weight.

The king's lip recoiled. 'I order you to dance.'

'I cannot, I've turned my ankle,' Marietta whispered. When she raised her eyes, she caught Captain Legat's look. Caution scored through it.

The king's silver suit sparked with lightning, illuminating him in an incandescent bolt of fury, his voice a clap of thunder. 'I order you to *dance*.'

Marietta lifted her chin high and began to dance a series of slow balancés on flat feet, ignoring her protesting ankle. She was out of step with the music, a broken doll cast aside. The king tracked her. His eyes were hungry, straying to her bleeding leg. When he trailed a finger over his mouth, his tongue darting out to lick his lips, she swallowed back the bile creeping up the back of her throat. She wished she might dare to throw that shrinking powder on him that the market woman had gifted her. See him small and insignificant, able to quash with a simple step. Yet she feared his faceless guards would tear her limb from limb if she dared attempt it. She drew a ragged breath and danced through her pain.

'If you continue to force her to dance, you'll break her and she'll never dance again. Is that what you wish?' a smooth voice asked. Dellara appeared at Marietta's side, hands clamped on her hips, her eyes inked over. Her skirt was a tangle of fluttering scraps of material in a deep plum that echoed her hair.

'I do not recall summoning you, fairy,' the king said, shifting his attention back to Marietta.

'I don't recall needing to be summoned.'

The king whipped to his feet, another lightning bolt shooting down his suit, his rage a palpable force. The diners seated nearest him edged away, sending a flurry of birds whirling up in a cloud of sapphire feathers and shrill tunes. Marietta backed away, stumbling on her ankle. Several Bellinnese women opened the doors of their gilded birdcages and whistled for the birds' return.

'Pretty,' Dellara said to the lightning bolt. 'Though you must be aware what the gossipmongers spread around the palace about your overcompensation.' Her look was ripe with meaning.

King Gelum strolled over to her. He reached out, taking her face in one hand, wrenching it up, forcing her to meet his winged eyes. Fear cut through Marietta, rendering her immobile. A whisper passed between the king and Dellara, hushed as wings in the night. King Gelum's suit ignited in a blaze of glory as he released Dellara and exited the throne room by means of a small door cut into the wall behind the throne. A cotillion of faceless guards leapt forward and seized Dellara. Marietta clamped a hand over her mouth, swallowing a cry. Dellara was dragged through the door after the king, her small stature overpowered with a frightening show of force.

The Bellinnese gathered themselves and fled in a twittering. As the throne room roared with chaos, Pirlipata materialised before her. She seemed to sense in which direction her thoughts lay. 'There is nothing you hold in your power to help her now; interfering would merely cause you to share her fate and render her bravery futile. We must leave now.'

Marietta closed her eyes. A faint scream ricocheted from the hidden room. It ripped through her. 'This is too much to bear.'

'Bear it for Dellara; she will need us.' Pirlipata grasped Marietta's arm and supported her as they walked towards the staircase. The faceless guards allowed their departure, their heads slowly turning to watch their path as Marietta limped past. Another scream tore out and her step faltered.

Pirlipata held her steady.

Her focus had been too wavering to count the doors but Marietta knew they must be drawing closer to their suite; they were at the approximate height for it. As they continued to ascend, the frozen sugar peak glowed above, its pale frosted blue holding all the palace secrets within its whipped confection. Servers scurried past, steaming trays resting on their fingertips, their eyes gliding past Marietta and Pirlipata. Crafters plodded by, too immersed in deep discussion of sugar-work to pay attention to another victim of their king. Two women exchanged kisses and syrup-sweet promises in an open door before one stepped back inside, releasing the other to the night, her teal gown puddling behind as she swept past Marietta.

Once they reached the suite, their pair of guards locked them inside.

Marietta set to bandaging her leg as Pirlipata sank onto a cushion. Her golden sheath dress was tarnished.

'I am responsible,' Marietta said. 'If I had not fallen—'

'You must not allow yourself to think in such a manner. I understand well how you feel; Dellara has diverted many of my own punishments onto herself, yet she refuses to be dissuaded. No good shall come of torturing yourself with what might have been.'

Some hours later, a pair of faceless guards crashed through the door. Marietta and Pirlipata rose from their vigil. Dellara was a slumped figure, held between the guards. They threw her down on a chaise longue and marched out. Marietta suffered an overwhelming urge to claw the blank masks from their faces, to force them to confront the cruelties they were complicit in. When it occurred to her that she felt differently towards the captain, who was responsible for waging a secret rebellion yet refused to aid them lest it derail his grander mission at play, her rage swelled. How had she considered that a tolerable excuse? Why had he not saved Dellara? She rushed to Pirlipata's side. The princess had propped Dellara's head up on a small cushion and was smoothing the hair back from her pale brow.

'Where has he hurt her? We must stem the flow at once,' Marietta said, watching her purple-shaded gown bleed into murderous crimson.

'That is but her enchantment. Dellara's gowns always sense when she is feeling particularly wrathful.' Pirlipata rolled up one of Dellara's gauzy sleeves, revealing blistered, bloodied marks that carried the imprint of fine chains. Marietta hissed between her teeth.

Dellara's eyes snapped open. 'You.' She extended a midnight-painted nail at Marietta. Her fingers were dipped in the colours she'd painted before the feast; inky violets, deep sapphires and glossy blacks, as if she'd dragged them through the night sky.

'You should not have interceded on my behalf,' Marietta whispered, unable to tear her eyes from Dellara's wounds. 'There was no need for you to do that.'

'Couldn't bear losing another.' Dellara drifted out of consciousness.

Pirlipata ran into the bathing chamber and emerged with a heap of towels and a basin of fresh water. Marietta rolled up Dellara's sleeves and they bathed her wounds before administering soothing balms and wrapping them out of sight in clean bandages. Dellara moaned, her eyelids fluttering.

Marietta rested a hand against her forehead. 'She feels feverish.' She exchanged a look with Pirlipata, who frowned and soaked a towel in water, wrung it out and pressed it to Dellara's head.

'The shock must have tumbled her into an ice fever,' Pirlipata told her. 'We must keep her hydrated. In this instance, we are fortunate to remain within the palace with its plentiful supply of water. The ice fever shall prise a deathly toll from Everwood this winter with their deficit of melting charms or imported clean water.'

Marietta nodded, unable to forget the faces of children condemned to a slow death by way of the mineral sickness, families unable to afford the steep price of the ever-dwindling supply of melting charms, overtaxed to allow for King Gelum's endless balls and feasts even as they thirsted. With each glance at Dellara, guilt stained her.

Pirlipata pressed her hand. 'Take heart, Dellara is too fierce for a fever to end her. She'd be mortified at the very thought.' They shared a quiet smile and it occurred to Marietta that these women had become dear to her over the past few months she'd been imprisoned with them. She had never had the pleasure of female friendships. And now their fates were entwined, bound together with blood and pain, and a loyalty that ran deeper than either.

Chapter Twenty-Nine

Over the days that followed, Marietta and Pirlipata took turns tending to Dellara, who hadn't yet regained her lucidity. So accustomed to the woman's spiked words, it pained Marietta to see her tossing and turning, occasionally crying out, her voice soft and vulnerable. When a summons to the captain's study materialised, she marched into his cabin, overbrimming with feeling as if she belonged to the ranks of the Erinyes, those ancient Greek goddesses of retribution and vengeance.

'Dellara requires medicine. An ice fever has taken root after your king was allowed to maul her. With all the wondrous magic residing at your fingertips in this world, there must be something you can do for her.'

The captain stood from his desk. His jacket had been dispatched, his white shirt rumpled. His sleeves were rolled up, revealing sculpted golden forearms. 'Dellara is not human. She will not succumb to a mere fever.'

'Does it not bear considering that even if she does not perish, she is suffering?'

Captain Legat hesitated. 'Leave it with me. I shall see what I can do.'

'Good.' Marietta crossed her arms, anger still carousing through her veins. She refused to be derailed by the captain's less than polished state. 'Why did you not save her?'

'I wish that I could have. You know well I harbour nothing but distaste for the king but I am afraid that once he succumbs to that mindset, he cannot be roused from it until his wrath is spent.'

'Very well,' Marietta said. 'I am still awaiting to hear why you summoned me.'

He walked around his desk and pulled a chair out for her. 'Show me your leg.'

'I beg your pardon?'

His flicker of amusement only served to rile her further. 'I saw your injury. I was concerned you might be too consumed with caring for your friend to change your bandage,' he explained.

'I assure you, I am capable of executing more than one task,' Marietta said coolly, ignoring the chair. She had been resting her ankle and both it and her wound were healing fast.

The captain leant back against his desk, crossing his arms as he surveyed her. 'Have I offended you in some way?' he asked at last.

'Not at all. I merely find it difficult to reconcile myself with your kindness towards me.'

His eyes were locked on hers. 'And why is that?'

'How can you be so compassionate in one regard and yet utterly unconscionable in others? I understand you have other obligations and perhaps I am incorrect in this, perhaps running an underground rebellion is a far nobler cause than all others, but does it justify your callousness elsewhere?' Her words were soaring arrows. And each one hit their mark.

The muscles in his jaw worked. 'I—'

'And furthermore,' she plunged on, all the pain, fear and rage she kept locked inside bursting out like stardust, 'you took advantage of my being in a vulnerable situation to ... to make me feel things.'

Captain Legat looked taken aback.

'Sympathy,' Marietta said. 'I felt sorry for you. As if you were the victim in all this. As if your king was torturing you alongside us.'

The captain stepped towards her, her anger proving to be infectious. 'I may not be the king's plaything but do not make the mistake of thinking I do not care. I fed you when you were at risk of starvation.' His eyes burned. 'I am working day and night to ensure his reign of terror ends.'

'You can leave,' she hissed at him. 'Step outside the enchantments that encase the palace and retain me as his prisoner. Do not pretend to understand how it feels to be confined within these frozen sugar walls. Waking each morning into the same endless night. I feel as if I am losing my mind.'

'Once you have joined the King's Army, it is disloyal to leave. And disloyalty is treason. I am risking my life for the people of Everwood, for carrying everyone's freedom on my shoulders. I am sorry you are his prisoner, I truly am, but you do not have the liberty to proclaim your privileged existence is more perilous than the families I visit in Everwood. Their grief is deep. Bodies of children are left on the ice cliffs each night for the mountain vultures.'

His words hit Marietta with searing clarity but she could no more stop their argument than she could hold up the tides of the ocean. It ran between them, taking on a rhythm and wildness of its own. Nor could she elucidate why she felt such anger, burning inside her, why her breath hitched when she looked at him, why she longed to raise her voice and shout and lose her fingers in his tangle of hair. 'And yet you were the one to save his life.'

'An action I shall regret until the day I join the stars. Every time I am forced to watch you bleed and break at his command, I long to be in your place, to be the one to bear the brunt of his wrath,' he said fervently, breathing hard.

Marietta looked up at him. He was closer than she'd realised. He smelt of the forest, of fir trees and snow and a hint of smokiness, and his jawline bore the shading of burgeoning stubble. She wondered if he'd been up all night. She watched his throat bob up and down as he swallowed. 'Marietta, I want you to know, I—'

'Yes?' she whispered.

He looked at her for a long moment before shaking his head as if to dislodge whatever thought had taken root there. His timepiece sounded, shattering the fragile spell in which they had been locked. He looked as though he wanted to speak further and she was disappointed when he cleared his throat. 'You ought to leave before we attract attention.'

Marietta inclined her head and walked back to her suite in a daze that failed to abate when the guards locked her back inside and she took up the mantle in monitoring Dellara's condition. That night, there was a small vial of medicine perched alongside their dinner. The following morning, Dellara had regained her senses.

✧

'King Gelum has long since ruled with a frozen fist,' Dellara told Marietta, reclining on a chaise as she polished off a rich gingerbread cream cake. 'But he failed to both take into account what resided within his council room, and that I could possibly notice it.' Her eyes were shadowed storms.

Fairy, King Gelum had called her. If Dellara was truly a fairy, she was far from the kind that had flitted through Marietta's imagination as a child, dainty in petal dresses, sipping on nectar. No, she was cut from a different, fiercer mould. 'I am afraid to ask,' Marietta said after Dellara had devoured another slice.

'There's something about you.' Dellara drew the words out as if she was tasting them. 'You've captured his imagination. Stirred something up. There are drawings of dancers plastering his walls, parchments written imagining the specifications of your world and its possible locations. Drawings of you.'

Sickened, Marietta set her cup of molten chocolate down.

'It isn't safe for you here,' Dellara said. 'I've never seen the likes of his obsession with you.' She paused to drink two cups of chocolate in quick succession. 'Worse still, I managed to glimpse his desk. There were strategical maps of Crackatuck there. Reports on the number and skillsets of Crackatian fighters. Information pinpointing their whereabouts. It appears the unrest during the Festival of Light has been playing on the king's mind. I would wager he plans to dispel any further thought of an uprising with a show of strength. Inciting war ought to do the trick.'

Pirlipata sighed. 'There has not been war in Celesta for an age. Not since the peace-keeping accords were signed between our three lands.' She stared out at the sugar wall. 'My people are loyal and brave and intelligent but they do not possess the cruelty that King Gelum does. The majority are scholars. If he intends to invade, they must be warned, as must Mistpoint. I shall not let our world fall to a vindictive petty man who refuses to accept my rejection of him.'

'I had a feeling you might be so inclined,' Dellara said.

Marietta pressed Pirlipata's hand. 'What do you suggest we do?'

Dellara indulged in a languorous stretch. 'I believe you were right last moontide. There is no sense in waiting for either our impending doom or the rebellion to take hold. We shall have to engender our own escape.'

When the guards unlocked the door to allow a server through, they were greeted with the women conversing on which scent best complemented which shade of tulle. The server kept his eyes averted as per custom and sat a heavy silver tray down on a cushion before scurrying back out. Marietta eyed the tray, waiting for the guards to leave. She'd risen early by habit to stretch her limbs and perform barre exercises using the curved headrest of a chaise longue. As she had performed sets of relevés, small, ankle-strengthening rises, some hidden emotion had soared up within, deep and unavoidable, until she had poured it out into dance. Gentle at first, testing her weakened ankle, then stronger, fiercer. Frustration at Captain Legat, veined with anger and something else, something unidentifiable and entirely new. She danced in silence, her sole witness the cold moon-soaked land beyond the sugar wall. She had not eaten after, both she and Pirlipata choosing to pass their share onto the ravenous Dellara. Now the scent of souffléd root vegetables, crispy, brown-sugar-glazed slices of cheese, bowls of frostberries, spiced apple cake and whorls of pastry dripping with salted caramel sauce summoned she hunger.

The faceless guards scanned the room, paying no heed to Dellara's argument for vanilla-scented magenta against Marietta's sudden predilection for praline-scented pearl. She suffered a bite of fear that they might decide to search the armoire where she'd hidden Legat's notebook. But at last they retreated, locking the door once more. The talk turned fiercer, growing teeth and talons.

Diving into their dinner, Marietta now well accustomed to eating with her fingers from a shared tray, she and Pirlipata were reining in Dellara's bloodthirsty imagination.

'As I reiterated earlier,' Marietta said, 'the aim is to be discreet. The fewer witnessing our exit, the better. We must be intelligent, not cause carnage.'

Pirlipata looked nauseated. 'I am in agreement.'

Dellara took delicate nibbles out of a pastry, sprawled over the carpet beside Pirlipata clad in nothing but a furred cape. 'And if we're attacked?'

'Then we shall allow you to wreak your devastation upon them.' Marietta was unable to quell her simmering hope. Her ankle healed, Dellara back to her usual spirits, they were stronger than ever. There was nothing Marietta wouldn't do for these women and she knew they felt likewise. It reminded her of her bond with Frederick and how dearly she missed him, but they were bound together by blood and family. These women had chosen her.

Dellara's grin displayed her sharpened teeth.

'And you are certain we cannot obtain one of those golden keys?' Marietta asked.

'Too costly and rare,' Pirlipata sighed.

'Then according to what I have noted, there are three main problems to overcome,' Marietta said. Dellara, licking salted caramel sauce off her fingers, motioned for her to continue. 'First, there is the suite door. It is perennially locked and secured by a pair of faceless guards. Secondly, the staircase. As it is the main thoroughfare of the palace, we shall require a way to traverse it without being sighted. And finally, the door to the palace. Not only does the throne room reside before it, which is habitually filled with an assortment of soldiers and guests at any one time, the passageway is enchanted to return you to King Gelum.'

A silence fell. The barriers laid out before them, the impossibility of their task loomed. Yet Marietta refused to allow her hopes to diffuse. They had all suffered too greatly to not press on. She wished she could dispel the memory of Dellara's blood-soaked appearance and subsequent ice fever. Dellara had dismissed it, instructed them not to pay it a second thought. Yet there was the occasional tremble in her fingers and the sudden, vehement dedication to escaping. Both whispered of more than an impending invasion fuelling her desire to tear her way free. Marietta forced her attention back to the matter at hand. The silence deepened.

Pirlipata lanced through it. 'What about disguises?'

'I'm sorry?' Marietta asked.

'Why do we not don disguises to traverse the stairs? No one would toss us a second glance if they believed we were soldiers.'

'This king doesn't believe in female soldiers.' Dellara's tone turned venomous. 'He outlawed them.'

Pirlipata continued speaking before Dellara had the opportunity to descend into her darker thoughts. 'Servers, then. Or apprentice confectioners or pâtissiers perhaps.'

Marietta tapped a finger against the tray, considering. 'An excellent suggestion. Though where might we acquire the necessary clothing?' It was a small piece of a much larger puzzle but it necessitated solving one piece at a time before the grander picture was revealed.

Dellara's smile was caramel-slow. 'The captain.'

Marietta came back to the conversation with a start. 'Captain Legat?'

'Oh, that is an inspired idea,' Pirlipata said, selecting the ripest frostberries. Tiny gold rings stacked up her fingers twinkled in the glow from the frozen sugar wall.

'I disagree.' Marietta looked between them. 'It would mean cross-ing the king and he would never do that.' He wouldn't risk drawing any attention his way, not when he had invested everything in the rebellion. Her face warmed upon remembering his accusation of her privilege. Worse, she held no arguments against it. He had been right. And she would not pitch herself against the greater good of his actions for Everwood.

'I'm sure you could think of a way to surpass his loyalty to the king.' Dellara twirled her fingers above the tray, plucking a slice of spiced apple cake from it with slow deliberation. 'Use your imagination. He's attracted to you.'

Marietta felt a hot tinge creeping up her neckline. 'You are mistaken.'

'Not at all.' Pirlipata bit into a frostberry. 'Anyone can see that he favours you.'

Marietta fumbled for a response. She thought once more of her last visit. Of his eyes burning into hers, burnished in the lanternlight. Of how they'd darkened as her breath had hitched. *Marietta, I want you to know I . . .* What had he been on the verge of saying? Her blood warmed and she shook off the thought.

'You'll ask him,' Dellara said. 'Do flirt a little when you do though, hmm?' She gave Marietta a salacious look that sent any possible responses flying from her head. She grinned. 'I'm sure you'll enjoy that, too. Don't think we haven't seen the way you look at the good captain.'

Marietta drank some water. She ignored the sly smile Dellara sent in Pirlipata's direction. 'Would it not be wiser to consult one of the other soldiers I became acquainted with before entering the palace, Claren perhaps?'

'They're lower-ranked soldiers. I'm sure they're capable of charming a wanderer when they set their mind to it.' Dellara bit into her cake, taking care not to dislodge the fuchsia-pink gems affixed to her lips. 'But they'll be more tentative about calling notice to themselves. Besides which, Fin's too shy for such a task and Claren's too invested in his own frivolities.'

'Yet you do not believe that the captain of the King's Army would be concerned with getting caught?' Marietta pointed out.

'Not as a leader, no. He's accustomed to thinking for himself and he'd be better placed to formulate a plan and act upon it without having to concern himself with sneaking around behind his commanding officers' backs.'

Dellara's explanation poured out in a manner that Marietta found she couldn't refute. Perhaps she ought to consult the captain. After all, she was merely seeking a few purloined items of clothing, nothing more.

'Very well, I shall put the question to him,' Marietta said, ignoring the looks Pirlipata and Dellara were now trading. She wondered if he would invite her to his study again. Now she was healed and no longer starving, there was no excuse for them to dwell in each other's company. A fleeting sadness swept over her. She firmed her resolve against it; she still had his notebook in her possession. 'Then we shall move along the staircase in disguise. What might be the best manner to flee this suite?'

'We ought to work backwards,' Pirlipata said, digging out another handful of frostberries. Deep magenta with a frosted skin, they were plump and bursting with a sweet sticky juice. 'None of this is worth contemplating if we still do not have an inkling on how to leave the palace.'

'Isn't it obvious?' Dellara's voice drawled, painting her words in honeyed tones. Marietta and Pirlipata looked at her, waiting. 'We don't leave through the main door.'

'I was not aware there was an alternate exit to the palace,' Marietta said.

Pirlipata crinkled her forehead. 'If there is one, I am not aware of it either.'

'Neither of you are thinking outside the globe. We don't leave this palace. We leave this world,' Dellara said with a flourish.

Pirlipata's muddled expression cleared. 'Oh.'

Marietta's confusion didn't abate. She frowned. 'What am I missing?'

'All those doors running alongside the staircase?' Pirlipata turned to Marietta in an excited glaze. 'Where do you think they lead?'

'Tell me,' Marietta said, catching the spark of her enthusiasm.

Dellara leant forward, her gem-encrusted lips sparkling, lending her an eerie glow. 'They lead to different worlds.'

Chapter Thirty

Other worlds. A frisson fired through Marietta, raw with nerves and hope and the inconceivable knowledge that she was an insignificant speck in the universe that had swollen far greater than she could picture. Her one foray into another world had culminated in her capture but Dellara was dagger-sharp and if she believed this was a more likely escape route through the ensorcelled palace then Marietta was inclined to agree. 'How might we find our way back to this world? Or return me to mine?'

'There are doors located across the worlds,' Dellara said.

Pirlipata gave Marietta a reassuring smile. 'Do not fear, we shall not stop searching until we are able to return you to your home.'

'Or find you a better one,' Dellara added.

Pirlipata gave her a look, deep with meaning and the unique irritation that tended to run between siblings or the oldest of friends. 'That is far from helpful.'

Dellara flicked a shred of pastry off her dress. 'I was under the impression she wasn't enamoured with her own world. She only mentions it in passing and never seems happy to speak of it. And then there are the nights she's seized with nightmares.'

Marietta toyed with the crispy-coated slice of cheese she'd picked up. 'I was not aware I spoke in my sleep.'

'You don't,' Dellara said slowly. 'But I can taste your dreams. And the acrid tang of fear that bites the night when you suffer a nightmare.'

Marietta was well acquainted with those nightmares. It had been an indeterminable amount of time and yet Drosselmeier continued to haunt her, stalking through her imagination by night, that dark time when fears seem to creep closer under the silvered moon. Sometimes the boundaries of her consciousness grew thin and she thought she caught a glimpse of Drosselmeier within the palace. Yet time and magic were two grand forces at play and she was trapped between them, left distrusting what was real and what was fantasy. 'There are aspects I would prefer not to return to,' she said, setting the cheese down. 'Though that does not mean I would rather stay away. There are people I miss, a dream I cannot let fade from my sights. Things I am now prepared to confront.' Her awareness of her own body had been heightened through all she had endured. She knew now how it could fight and resist and wield power. Upon encountering Drosselmeier once more, she would not embody the subservient Edwardian lady he had so expertly manipulated. She would claw her way free of him.

'Good for you.' Dellara toasted her as if her apple cake were a saucer of Taittinger. 'You'll be far happier if you fight your demons.'

'Is that what happened to you?' Marietta asked, somewhat wary.

'Better. I slaughtered mine.' Dellara's answering grin sent shards of ice down Marietta's neck. 'And when I stood there, coated in their viscera and bone-flecks, I answered to no one.'

'King Gelum called you a fairy,' Marietta whispered.

'King Gelum is an incompetent fool. *Fairy* is what the Everwoodians call anyone who's shed their mortality, who's eschewed the boundaries of what it means to be human. Demon might be more accurate.' The shadows lurking round her irises crept a little closer, eager to have their stories told. But Dellara didn't divulge any more, not on how she came to acquire her wand nor on the magic that whispered against her skin. Marietta did not press her. Dellara was unfurling her secrets, bit by bit, her trust frost-brittle, and Marietta had no inclination to poke and prod and shatter it. Neither did she wish to say something that might cause offence, despite the fire and brimstone her imagination conjured at Dellara's confidence. After all, she was in another world and etymology differed here. She had witnessed Dellara offer herself as a sacrifice on her behalf and that was not an action her understanding of a demon would do.

'We ought to discuss how we shall leave this suite.' Pirlipata glanced at the door and the invisible guards beyond, measuring their lives with their keys.

'We shall cause a distraction,' Marietta said. She'd given this segment of the plan a great deal of thought. Though tackling two armed faceless guards by herself would have been an issue, now the women had banded together, she was assured they could overcome their iron-strong force. 'We shall draw them into the room, where a trap will lie in wait. Between us, we will disarm and silence them.'

Dellara examined her nails. Upon awakening from her fever she had been mortified at the state in which Marietta and Pirlipata had dared to allow her to convalesce in. Now she lounged in hand-painted silk pyjamas, doused in scent and decorated in all the shades of an aurora rippling through a wintry night. 'Not a problem.'

'Then, we have it? Our plan is complete?' Pirlipata looked between them.

'Other than procuring the disguises, yes, I believe we are ready.' Marietta bit into a pastry in private celebration. Its buttery crispness yielded to her, a river of salted caramel sauce melting over her tongue.

'Not quite,' Dellara said. 'I'm going to need my wand retrieved.'

Worry crept up Marietta's spine. 'You had led me to believe the king had hidden it in a secured location.'

'He has. Only I happen to know precisely where it is. In this palace, few things transpire without my knowledge.' Dellara stood up and began pacing to the frozen sugar wall and back. 'It's under the king's throne. There's a secret chamber buried beneath it. A single mechanism was crafted to open it and King Gelum retains it on his person at all times. No one else has ever descended to its depths.'

Pirlipata and Marietta watched her pace, a contained storm. 'It frightens me too much to inquire how you know that,' Pirlipata said at last.

'Are you certain you need it?' Marietta asked. 'Retrieving it would require elaborate measures I am not certain we are capable of, not to mention delay our departure departure.'

Dellara spun to face her. 'I refuse to leave this palace without it. I'm tired of living without my magic, of bearing a half-existence, condemned to fall prey to paltry fevers and the slow knit of my flesh back together.'

'I understand,' Marietta said quietly, feeling that she did.

'You do not and you could not, but I wouldn't expect that of you.' Dellara's temper simmered down. 'While we are there, we shall liberate Pirlipata's armour.' She gestured at Marietta's pointe shoes, resting in the corner. 'The King abuses what makes you special, turns it against you. For Pirlipata and I, he simply stripped us of our talents.'

'Then we shall fight to return them to you both,' Marietta said and Pirlipata's smile glowed.

'King Gelum is hosting a ball in two nights' time that the dress-maker shall be gowning us for.' Pirlipata exhaled. 'I have come to the decision that I shall pass her a note to my family. If we are to flee through the worlds then I cannot allow the chance to warn Crackatuck melt away.'

'You must not put those thoughts to paper,' Marietta said at once. 'Most likely the walls have eyes in this palace and someone shall read it. You do not want the king to invade sooner if it is found out.'

The emerald flecks in Pirlipata's eyes shone. 'I intend to write it in code. I was instructed in such protocols when I attended university. A story for another time,' she added upon recognising Marietta's interest.

Marietta nodded. 'Very well. King Gelum does seem inordinately fond of hosting balls,' she mused.

'They shall become far grander now,' Pirlipata told her. 'The deeper into winter we march, the more time eclipses between us and our memories of the sun, the more often and ornate the balls grow. King Gelum proclaims it is his royal duty to keep the good people of Everwood entertained, but the truth of the matter is that this king is given to decadence and cannot help himself spending an exorbitant price on festivities.'

A deluge of images of the poverty and thirst and mineral sickness in the overtaxed town snowed over Marietta. From an opulent townhouse to a decadent suite, she had never known hardship. Couldn't imagine the choice facing mothers her own age; to allow their children to thirst to death or condemn them to a slow battle with the mineral sickness. In another life she could picture herself on the frontlines of the rebellion, working side by side with Captain Legat and his mother. But this was not her world, nor her battle. When she returned to Nottingham, she was determined to open her eyes to the people around her. Lost in thoughts such as these, it took Marietta a moment to note Pirlipata's deliberate use of the pronoun. 'This king?' she echoed. 'Who was his predecessor?'

'Queen Altina Mus and King Elter Mus. They were a charming royal couple.' Pirlipata puffed out a sad sigh. 'Fair and just and much beloved by their subjects. Until Gelum Mus, a distant cousin of theirs, stepped in and overthrew them.'

'It was a veritable bloodbath,' Dellara said. 'And not the sort I approve of.'

'His treason was swift and vicious, proving it impossible for anyone to intercede, and his wave of cruelty in his first moontides on the throne – reinstating the ancient ice prison, introducing public executions – ensured that all of Everwood were too terrified to challenge him.' Pirlipata shook her head.

'How terrible,' Marietta said, the weight of their history pressing down on the room.

'It is. And if King Gelum wages war who knows what the conse-quences shall be for our peaceful little world? He is a merciless tyrant, reigning with ice and terror, and funnelling Everwood's resources into his prestigious military quarter and luxe balls. I do hope this rebellion does not freeze over like the last attempt.' Pirlipata winced. Marietta's heart filled with frost. 'I wonder who is leading the charge this time,' Pirlipata continued.

'Do you recall the previous king and queen?' Marietta asked Dellara, hoping the desperation she felt didn't infuse her words.

Dellara bowed her head. A strange light danced over her expres-sion, one which Marietta struggled to place. 'King Gelum murdered the entire court in an icy rage. Sugar-poisoned, they say. Now our Queen Altina shines brighter than ever, the biggest star in the sky, watching over us all.'

Marietta placed her expression then. It was hope. Trembling and soft and entirely unsuited to the horrors of the world but there nonetheless. Existing. Surviving.

'I have heard tales of the soldiers and the military quarter,' Marietta said, dancing over the knowledge that those stories had been relayed to her by the captain, ensconced in his lantern-lit gingerbread office, warm and spicy and intimate. Her face glowed. 'Though none of those loathsome faceless guards. Tell me, who are they? I presume King Gelum had them brought into the palace?'

Dellara's softness disappeared. 'We never used to have a contingent of them to supplement the soldiers; Everwood has always had a strong military tradition but soldiers are merely human and King Gelum won them over to his side with mutiny and threats. Now he forever distrusts them should they turn on him if someone decides to rise up against him. That day the armed intruder penetrated the palace's enchantments, the king found himself suspiciously short of protection. He grew harder on his soldiers over the years. Then the faceless guards happened to appear one day.'

Marietta's thoughts ran red with rebellion.

'I've heard rumours that they are no more human than I am myself,' Dellara added.

Marietta shuddered. 'That I find easy to believe.'

Their talk eventually passed onto other matters, lighter topics, keeping the cold darkness of the perpetual winter a little more at bay.

When Marietta awoke the following morning to yet another black sky, glittering with the weight of a thousand stars, something hard dug into her neck. She sat up. It was a small box, the label bearing the same line-drawing of a mouse she kept sighting all over Everwood. Only this one bore the king's signature seal. When she removed the lid, she found a nutcracker upon a velvet cushion inside. It was fashioned after the soldiers of the King's Army, down to the smart red tunic and detailing on the epaulettes. Then Marietta noticed the mouse-carved hilt of the Starhunter sword and the butterscotch eyes. Her blood ran cold, and the nutcracker fell from her hands. It had been sculpted in the likeness of Captain Legat.

Chapter Thirty-One

The next ball to be held in the palace was to take place later that night. Pirlipata had informed Marietta it was to be a themed black and gold ball as she ran through her barre exercises. After, she shed her ballet shoes and retired to the bathing room, sinking into the pool. If all marched along according to their design, the first cog of their escape plan would be manoeuvred into place. *I want you to know, I—* The lost words ghosted around Marietta's mind until a darker skein of thoughts unravelled. The nutcracker. Its uncanny resemblance to Captain Legat. The king was growing suspicious; now was the time to take greater care than ever. A headache nestled at the back of her head, creeping in with a noxious dread.

Closing her eyes, she sank down beneath the frothing water, the peppermint-tinted waterfall cascading onto her shoulders. With a deep breath, she dived underwater to swim a length. Water rippled past her outstretched fingers in shades of mint and seafoam and pale teal. When her headache skulked away, she slid the tattered notebook the captain had handed her from a nearby towel and settled down to read it. It had taken considerable resolve not to peek through its pages but she had desired to keep it private, and in the suite, privacy was a rarity. It was a little secret between her and Captain Legat, the knowledge of which thrilled her. She smiled at the neat swirl of handwriting in which he had penned a series of his innermost thoughts. Some were scarcely more than a single line: *Look to the stars*. Others were complete stories, spinning the origins of Everwood into something resembling a volume of Grimms' tales. One alluded to King Gelum's bloody usurping of the throne. Another seemed to refer to an upcoming event, where it would *snow scarlet ribbons and ice will melt to the people's will*.

Marietta tightened her hold on the book, careful not to let the steam curl its fragile pages, the heart laid rent upon it. The captain's feelings on the king ran deep and treasonous and, now, not only was she aware of his role in the rebellion, she held condemning evidence in her hands. Held Legat's trust in her hands. She had not realised that behind the disciplined soldier's face lay the soul of a poet, his thoughts buried treasure. Rather than speaking his mind, he had shown Marietta his most private thoughts which were writhing and raging, beautiful and melancholic. Upon reaching the final page, drowning in his words, unable to stop hearing his voice, smooth and deep caramel, her heart quickened its beat as she discovered a short note addressed to her. *Marietta*, it began, the curve of his quill soft over her name, *I wished to share my little ramblings with you as you have graced me with your art*. Not entertainment, nor a mere hobby, but art. It seemed the captain understood her more than she knew.

When she padded back to the main room in a fluffy robe, another woman was present in the suite, listening to Dellara, who was standing atop a small podium, listing detailed instructions. 'And I shall require pockets, deep ones, none of those flimsy shallow ones for decorative purposes. Tailor me something that could accommodate a dagger.'

'Is it wise to speak in such a manner?' Marietta asked Pirlipata in an aside.

Pirlipata's lips quirked. 'Ivana is well used to Dellara; she does not take her words to heart.'

Ivana was a severe woman twice the age of Marietta with thick eyebrows, sloped cheekbones and coal-black eyes. A lacing of frost was painted over her olive face, veiling her, the pattern continuing over her one-piece, paired with the highest-heeled shoes Marietta had ever seen. Her measuring tape around Dellara, she squinted at the measurements before moving on, memorising the stream of numbers. 'All done. Next.' She cracked the tape like a whip and it extended.

Pirlipata nudged Marietta and she stepped forward. The dressmaker eyed her. 'You're new,' she commented, her manner brisk as a starched collar.

Marietta stepped up onto the podium. 'I am.'

'Very well. Any preferences or needs to allow for?'

'Her dancing must be accommodated.' Pirlipata came to stand beside Marietta.

'You dance? I am greatly fond of watching dancers,' Ivana said, looping her tape around Marietta's waist. 'What kind of dancing do you perform? Salembe? Crackatian?' She paused her measuring to twist her wrist out in an embellished flick.

'No, I dance ballet, a particular type of classical dance from my world.'

Ivana, who was stretching her tape down Marietta's leg, paused to consider her. 'Then you do not originate from any world I have heard mention of before. How very curious.'

'I shall require the dress to be free about my legs as I lift them very high,' Marietta said, feeling a peculiar hollowness at the reminder of how removed she was from her home, her world.

'Yes, yes, no problem.' Ivana snapped her tape away and beckoned to Pirlipata. 'Your turn, Princess.'

Marietta stepped down and meandered over to Dellara. She

glanced at the farthest armoire. She had buried the nutcracker in its depths. She had mentioned it to the other women the previous night. They had advised caution but disregarded it as a serious threat, claiming the king was often prone to jealousy. But it weighed Marietta's soul down with fear and she kept thinking of it.

The dressmaker packed the tools of her trade away in an efficient manner and left without a word.

'I slipped her my note,' Pirlipata said at once. 'She took it, I was watching.'

'Good,' Dellara said. 'I suppose a conscience grows heavier the longer you drag it around.'

'How can she manage to sew three ballgowns in such a short timeframe? Surely that cannot be possible,' Marietta said. She had been longing for her own enchanted gown since she'd been locked in the palace and was a little bereft that she hadn't had a greater agency in the design process.

'She presides over a team of seamstresses that have spent moontides deep in their craft, preparing for the winter ball season,' Pirlipata said.

Dellara's smile was glazed. 'She's magical with her craft,' she said. 'The queen of the Silk Quarter. You'll see.'

Some hours later, Marietta scarcely recognised herself. A strapless golden bodice encased her like a second skin. Onyx silhouettes of fir trees glittered atop. The skirt was jet tulle, voluminous in its whispering mille-feuille layers. Black pointe shoes enveloped her feet, and when she peered in an armoire mirror, the Odile to her Odette looked back at her. Her eyes were darkened in smoky hues, her tinted eyebrows were branches from which tiny golden leaves trailed on vines down her cheekbones. She had painstakingly brushed her long hair with a butterscotch-scented oil that she realised as a blushing afterthought reminded her of the captain. It flowed down her back, entwined with golden swirls of silk that rippled when she danced.

'I declare you perfect. The captain will have a hard time keeping his eyes off you now,' Dellara said with satisfaction, examining Marietta's face and laying down her brushes. Marietta's cheeks warmed. 'Even better.' Dellara's grin spread wider. 'You look in need of a good ravishing.' She winked at Marietta's flushed face and pulled on a pair of black velvet boots that reached her thighs. Marietta averted her eyes, feeling as if she'd strayed into the unsavoury world of the Moulin Rouge. The feeling was not unfamiliar to her; during her stay in Everwood, she had already witnessed a lifetime's worth of debauchery within these frozen sugar walls. Dellara laughed. 'I knew it; you're from one of those worlds.'

Marietta's blush deepened as she gave Dellara a look of deep irritation. 'And which worlds might you be referring to?'

'The ones without any fun in them.' Dellara arched an eyebrow, the filigreed black lace around her eyes lending her a devious look.

Ignoring her, Marietta turned to Pirlipata and helped her arrange the silken folds of her long golden dress. It slunk down to the floor, the sparkling colour punctuated with tiny black storm clouds that floated up and down the satin, occasionally pausing to puff out spurts of inky raindrops. Pirlipata had inked a matching raindrop on one cheek before painting her lips and the tips of her dark hair in gold lacquer.

Dellara eyed Pirlipata's statement. 'If you're planning to get us all killed, I may as well enjoy myself tonight,' she continued beneath her breath.

Ivana made the final adjustments to Dellara's dress; a bauble of a gown in glistening, ruched golden satin. Strings of black gemstones wound round her neck and each arm, rendering her a dark, luminescent figure. 'A light dusting of sugar to finish.' Ivana approached Marietta, a golden pot in one hand revealing sparkling contents, a soft brush in her other hand.

'Do not sugar her.' Pirlipata's voice carried the strength of her missing armour. Marietta glanced up in surprise. The dressmaker's fingers twitched.

'Remember what we discussed.' Dellara's drawl was honey poured atop the significant look she gave Pirlipata. 'We need her to sparkle so she can charm the captain,' she whispered and Marietta frowned. 'Do continue.' Dellara waved a hand at Ivana. 'Sugar her.'

Pirlipata glared at Dellara, the air between them crackling with tension Marietta had never felt resonate through the bonds of their friendship before.

Ivana dipped the brush into the pot and applied the sugar to Marietta's bare shoulders, arms, neck and in a path down through her cleavage in a manner that Marietta considered most affronting, but the matter-of-fact dressmaker ignored her intake of breath and ploughed on. When she'd finished, she plucked her bag from the side table and left, her heels clacking. Every inch of Marietta glittered sweetly.

Dellara swept a shadowed paint over her lips and blotted them with tissue paper before meeting their eyes in the mirror. 'We've set our plan into motion. May the stars shine brightly over us. Executing the next part is in your dominion, Marietta. Do not disappoint us.'

The throne room sparkled like the inside of a champagne flute. Gold and black were the reigning colours. Tiny golden bows had been affixed round the frostpeckers' necks, initiating them into the colour scheme as they meandered around the iced streams and fountains. The igloos had been replaced with bubbles suspended on thin golden chains, large enough for a couple to steal away into. Shimmering icing had been poured atop them, rendering them private.

Marietta danced, her thousand-layered dress diaphanous as a Renaissance gown. As she danced, she observed the scene. Looking for the right opportunity. Servers wearing nothing but golden paint whirled around, their onyx slabs stacked with small gingerbread cakes, each topped with golden caramel buttercream and a tiny gingerbread man in a black bow tie that sang and spouted edible glitter. She spotted Fin and Danyon standing by the main door, deep in conversation, wearing black and gold livery. Then the back of Claren as he climbed up into one of the bubbles, pulling a woman in a black and gold striped suit in after him. The king, wearing a golden suit dusted with crushed golden jewels, danced with Pirlipata, whose serene smile failed to fool Marietta. Pirouetting, Marietta watched their faces blend into one brilliant melee. She had yet to glimpse the captain. It occurred to her that he may not attend; he surely held responsibilities that took precedence over a ball. Even so, she couldn't prevent herself from searching through the crowds for him. Her mission notwithstanding, the words he'd written echoed through her dreams at night. Some she'd committed to memory, familiar and soul-stained. *Look to the stars.*

'Any sightings of our good captain yet?' Dellara asked, sweeping by in a golden whorl of skirts and energy.

'I cannot see him anywhere,' Marietta said in an undertone.

Dellara pursed her lips. 'Give it time. Perhaps he'll appear later.'

'I have been dancing for what feels like hours, the night must be drawing to an end.' Marietta took a gingerbread cake from a passing server's slab, trying her best to disregard the flesh he displayed.

Dellara helped herself to two. 'Oh, you haven't seen anything yet. The king lives for hosting balls,' she whispered into Marietta's ear, twirling around to speak into her other ear. 'And he likes them best of all when they defy logic and run through the night. Things are about to get strange and wondrous.' She waltzed away, licking frosting off her fingers in a suggestive manner.

Marietta took a delicate bite of her cake, all too aware that both women were relying on her. She very much doubted she would be able to persuade the captain into aiding them and loathed the thought of asking him to put himself at risk for her. She surveyed the ball, idly dipping the gingerbread man into the swirl of frosting and eating it, glitter falling on her tongue in sweet bursts, smoky and creamy at once. The ball began to twinkle, brighter, golder than ever.

Tiny winged creatures darted in and out of her vision, teasing her senses with gossamer wings that brushed aside logic. Watching the ephemeral sight, she absentmindedly finished the cake, wondering where the captain was. Was he aware that King Gelum was scheming an invasion? He must be. She mustn't make the error of believing that his loyalties ran towards anything but the rebellion. No matter how much Dellara and Pirlipata attempted to convince her otherwise. No matter how she had secretly fizzed and fluttered at their mention of him, dwelling on how his eyes had darkened as he'd steadily returned her gaze, standing too close, as if any moment he might close the distance between them. She shook her head. Traitorous thoughts.

Captain Legat suddenly appeared at her side. Marietta cleared her throat, hoping her thoughts weren't painted on her face. He wore a suit tailored from wisps of night with a dark chocolate scent playing about his lapels. Gold paint ran up his cheekbones and through his bronze hair, flecked with black stars.

'You're not wearing your uniform.' Marietta looked up at him, the throne room still playing host to a myriad of odd illusions. Perhaps she had imbibed one too many snowberry crèmes, the alcohol turning her heady and introspective and tempted.

He leant past her to select a drink of his own, his hand brushing against hers. 'I am not working tonight.'

'I had thought you believed that a soldier ought never to be off duty?' Marietta blinked hard, attempting to ignore the constellations that had tumbled in from the night sky and become tangled in the ball.

The captain gave her a disconcerting look. 'Tonight I am.'

'Why are you regarding me in such a manner?' Marietta lifted a hand to check her golden leaves weren't dancing across her face. Her hand floated up of its own accord, her skin glittering with sugar. She watched a tiny pixie dance across it, plucking granules to stow in her petal-knapsack.

'Did you partake in the enchanted cakes, by any chance?'

Marietta lifted her gaze from the pixie to the captain. 'I was not informed they were enchanted!'

He smiled. She couldn't help staring at it, at the dimple that appeared in one cheek, the warm glow in his eyes. With some effort, she realised he was speaking. 'Not to worry; they carry a strong hallucinatory charm but they fade fast. It shall pass in a moment.'

After a troop of acrobatic bears had paused, mid-air, shimmering back out of existence, Marietta's senses flooded back. Although she was certain she'd caught a glimmer of silver hair on a familiar face, just for a second. She whipped round.

A couple of women danced past in matching outfits that were each constructed from a single ribbon, wrapped around them and tied in a strategically placed bow, one gold, one black. They rested their attention on Marietta and the captain. She attempted to calculate how long they had been standing together. And why the captain might have approached her. A little voice caressed her imagination, whispering maybe, *maybe*. She banished it. It was imperative she inquire as to the possibility of his assistance, not languish in his eyes. 'We are interrupting the flow of the ball,' she said, remembering the nutcracker. 'And drawing unwanted attention onto us.'

The captain looked at her. 'What are you suggesting?'

'Dance with me.'

Chapter Thirty-Two

She had not considered he might acquiesce. She had presumed he would decline with some tidy excuse before walking away. She didn't anticipate that he would step forward and take her in his arms. Waltz with her. Moving in rhythm, twirling through the dancers, each time his eyes collided with hers, it burnt.

'I never had the opportunity to thank you for the medicine,' she said.

'It was my pleasure,' he said, his voice deep silk.

She could feel the heat of his palm against her satin-clad back. She wondered if her sugar-dusting would melt. If the captain would snap shut once more if she asked for his assistance. Perhaps she ought not to broach the subject at all. But then she had noticed the way he looked at her when he didn't think she was watching. The way he stared into her eyes, deep enough to see her soul. The way he danced with her. She had spent a sufficient number of years under Madame Belinskaya's tutelage to recognise the emotions demonstrated through dance. And Madame would have approved of the way the captain moved, synchronised with her.

She stepped up en pointe to murmur into his ear. Before her words slid into his awareness, she saw him swallow. His eyes soften. Then her whisper registered, sealing his face back into its mask.

Her stomach twisted. *I need a favour,* she had whispered. Though now she tried not to consider what he had anticipated.

'You already know I am powerless to give you what you need.' He kept his voice low. It slunk into her hair. Hands on his shoulders, she arched back, dipping into a back bend and tossing a saccharine smile back at the king, whom she had noticed observing them. She hoped she would not learn what he had intended by having that nutcracker slipped beneath her pillow. The thought of it made her bones crawl. Like something insidious was creeping along them. She knew she was playing with fire. Yet even if she had not needed the captain's assistance, she would have willingly been scorched for this dance.

'This is quite a different matter; do not fear, I am not asking you to rescue me.'

His gaze flicked down to her lips. 'Then what is it you are asking of me?'

'A mere trifle really; I am in need of some clothes.'

They completed another circuit of the throne room, the music transmuting into something darker, huskier, more intimate. The captain slowed their pace and Marietta stepped closer to him.

'I do believe you possess a dressmaker at your command.' His hands slid down to her waist. Marietta arced her arms up in swanlike flutters, channelling Odile as she executed a short string of fouettés. The captain moved with her, his hands helping to support her weight, the smoky tendrils of her tulle skirt flying up around her legs, his dark chocolate scent encapsulating them both in a moment that Marietta might have dreamt.

She wrenched her focus back to the matter at hand. 'It is not another gown I need but servers' uniforms. Although if you happened to source some spare liveries, I would be happy to accept that; I find it ridiculous that women are not permitted to join the military ranks. In both your world and mine. As if we are less strong.' She lifted her leg up behind her in attitude, her muscles flexing, the captain's hand still fixed on her waist, spinning her slow and sure in a promenade that left them face-to-face. Close enough for her to see the gold and dark brown flecks in his eyes. She twirled around in a bewitchment of tulle, shattering their eye contact as her thoughts warred.

'And how is this not helping you escape?' he murmured.

The captain at her back, Marietta smiled. She turned to face him, resting her hands on his shoulders. 'There is no need for you to concern yourself with the details.'

His jaw tightened. His butterscotch eyes locked onto hers with sugar-melting heat. She commanded herself to move away, look away, but she was immobile under the force of the moment. 'I shall see what I can do,' he said at last.

'Thank you. I shall require three.'

He frowned. 'Three? One alone would be—'

Marietta pressed a hand onto his, silencing him. 'I cannot tell you how greatly I appreciate this.'

The music shifted once more, slow and smooth, the beginning of a new waltz. Marietta glanced away in a bid to dispel her awkwardness; their dance had been a ruse to shroud their conversation in innocence. Yet it had left her a little breathless and adrift, unwilling to admit that she hadn't desired to stop.

The captain held a hand out. 'Would you care for another dance?'

After a beat, she took his hand, unable to resist drifting back into his arms, letting the waltz send them across the throne room as if they were written into the music itself. He guided her expertly, his arms strong and gentle. She rested her cheek against his chest, the dance proving a headier cocktail than the crèmes, lowering her inhibitions. 'I read your diary,' she whispered into his suit.

His arms tightened around her. 'What did you think?'

'Over a hundred years ago, a writer from my world, Voltaire, wrote that "writing is the painting of the voice". When I read your work, I felt that. It lent me a higher understanding of the phrase, reminded me of the beauty words carry.' The captain lifted her chin up, his eyes searching hers. 'Do not forget yourself,' she whispered. 'We are not alone.'

He released her with a start, snapping back into his rank. Mindful she oughtn't continue dancing with him, Marietta made to meander off when he gave her a deliberate look. 'I would advise caution.' He gestured at her bared collarbones, glittering with sugar.

'Are you passing judgement on my attire?'

He cleared his throat roughly. 'Not at all, you present quite the vision tonight. But sugar invites … tasting.'

Marietta turned her attention to the ball. Since the night had thickened, the music as potent an influence as the enchanted cakes and unending streams of crèmes, the ball had descended into debauchery worthy of Bacchus himself. The shadowed periphery was clotted with couples engaged in amorous exchanges. A dress floated down from one of the bubbles to the cheers of a nearby crowd. Several men were wandering about clad in nothing but frosting, in various stages of being licked off. Marietta returned her gaze to the captain, her face flaming. 'I shall bear that in mind,' she said. She danced away and fell into a waltz with a fresh partner.

'Did you manage to win him over with your helpless expression?' Dellara asked once the three women had returned to the suite and performed their ablutions for the night. Dellara reclined in a set of silk pyjamas painted in a rich chocolate shade that gave off the aroma of a delightful little street packed with chocolateries, Pirlipata was clad in a golden camisole and shorts, and Marietta a cream nightdress.

Marietta's fingers stilled, her hair half-plaited. 'I have no such thing as a helpless expression,' she said. 'Do I?' she asked Pirlipata as an afterthought.

'Not in the slightest, you have been gifted with lovely eyes.' She smiled back at Marietta. 'Wide and trusting.'

Dellara's grin sharpened. 'Helpless eyes,' she repeated. 'Ones that beg: turn your eyes on me, captain, swoop me away into your strong, captainly arms—'

Marietta raised her eyebrows. 'Have you quite finished?'

'You're rotting my fun,' Dellara grumbled. Seconds later, she poked the cushion Marietta was resting upon with her scarlet-painted toes. 'Well, are you going to inform us what happened? Or were you too busy dancing in his arms to remember your task?'

'I asked him,' Marietta said, pouring a jug of molten drinking chocolate into three cups and spooning lashings of whipped cream atop the other two women's.

Pirlipata accepted her cup, clasping her hands round its comforting heat. 'Tell us more.'

'I believe he shall attempt to aid us.'

'I can't say I'm surprised.' Dellara's impish smile at once raised Marietta's guard. 'From the odd glimpse I caught of the pair of you, it looked as if you were on the verge of ripping each other's clothes off.'

Marietta dearly wished her cheeks would not inflame at such moments. It seemed they only served to betray her and further Dellara's amusement.

Dellara's smile turned suggestive. 'Don't pretend you're not the slightest bit tempted.'

Pirlipata sipped her chocolate. 'Perhaps there is someone cherished in your life back home?'

'Oh, do tell.' Dellara leant forwards with a gleam of intrigue. 'Does the blushing wanderer have a lover?'

Those long, thin fingers toying with a lock of her hair. Chipped-ice stare raking down her gown. Ballroom doors locked with keys and magic. A nightmare stalking her through cities and worlds, dreams and dances. Marietta closed her eyes against the mounting panic.

A hand on her knee startled her. 'Whatever it is, you can confide in us,' Pirlipata said softly and Dellara nodded, handing Marietta her mug of chocolate.

'The last person I divulged to failed to believe me so I am a little wary to take people into my confidence again,' she said in a low voice, filled with regret that Frederick, who she missed dearly, had brushed her instincts aside at the very moment she'd needed him the most. Then she realised that was not true. She had already confided in Captain Legat.

Dellara's eyes flashed. 'We will.'

Marietta looked at the two women with whom her days unfolded; Pirlipata, a princess whose armour was not a patch on her shining kindness. Who was tender and strong all at once. Dellara, a creature that lesser mortals would do well to fear, yet whose loyalty was as fierce as those sharpened teeth. If they were strong and fierce, what could she bring to the fold? Perhaps she might be brave. She opened her mouth and let her story, her truth, pour forth. The tale of a man that she was to be betrothed to but could never marry. A man that had charmed her until she realised the dark magic he wielded.

And they listened. And they believed her.

'Are you certain you wish to return?' Worry veined Pirlipata's words.

Marietta took a deep breath. 'If I allow him to prevent me from living my life, accomplishing my dreams, then I am not the woman I want to be.'

Dellara clinked her mug against Marietta's with a nod of approval.

'And what of the captain?' she asked a beat later. 'He has feelings for you; do you share those?'

'Do stop interrogating her about the captain.' Pirlipata shook her head at Dellara. Marietta had become familiar enough with the gesture that she now saw the fondness underlying it. 'Besides, we both are well aware that she would not be able to do a thing about it even if she desired to; if King Gelum found out, the consequences would be dire for both of them. That nutcracker was a warning. If the king knew of any romance, his actions would be far darker.'

Marietta drank her chocolate, focusing on its creamy sweetness rather than her wash of bitter regret. She ignored the hunger that whispered in her ear, the fluttering in her stomach as if some tiny winged creature resided there, with hope-bright wings and a silky dress of longing.

'Fine. At least he's aiding us in our secret endeavour. Now, onto other, more pressing matters; how shall we retrieve my wand?' Dellara reclined on her cushion, stretching out and yawning.

'We assumed you already possessed a scheme to liberate it since you knew the details of where it resided.' Pirlipata noticed Dellara's glinting expression and sighed. 'If you required our assistance, you only had to ask.'

'I don't need help. I had merely made the mistake of thinking that since my wand benefitted all of us, we should all work on finding a way to retrieve it as a priority.' Dellara glared at Marietta.

Marietta surveyed her back. Dellara could be trying and each time she assumed she'd reached the point of understanding her, the woman would baffle and infuriate her all over again. 'The only mistake you committed was the time you wasted lounging about in your hand-painted silk pyjamas, cossetted by enchantments, the finest gowns, and silver trays of cakes and drinking chocolate. You have grown indulgent and it is not on my head that you have been too lazy to formulate your own plans in which to achieve your escape.'

As her acerbic attack waned, Marietta did not glance away from Dellara to see whether Pirlipata's face had lost its friendly glow towards her. Neither did she apologise for the strangeness that now hung between her and Dellara, no matter how her stomach twisted and her mind sank, weighted with melancholic regret.

Dellara slowly revealed her teeth in a considering smile. 'Well, well, well, it seems I have underestimated you after all. Who knew the blushing dancer was hiding such a bitterly cold bite.'

'We shall devise a plan between us,' Pirlipata said, shattering the snow globe of a moment and returning them to the matter at hand. 'We three women shall never leave one of us behind, is that understood? In Crackatuck, some believe that our lifepaths are mapped through the veins of rocks. In mountain ranges and rocky hills, you can oft find where your life cosies against another's, your lifepaths entwined forevermore. Such are we. We three escape together, come what may.'

'I agree,' Marietta said.

'Agreed,' Dellara added.

'Then we shall be free before the winter has thawed.' Pirlipata lay back on a cushion, turning her gaze to the invisible star-studded skies. 'What small dreams do you both hold dearest, the ones you envisage doing first? I have been longing to take a solo trip to the Shragran Mountains, in the far west of Crackatuck.'

Marietta reclined on her own cushion. 'What do the mountains hold for you?'

'An abundance of trails to climb, sapphire lakes and the most glorious sunsets you could ever imagine, that set the sky aflame in a decadence of colour.'

'It sounds like a wondrous destination,' Marietta said. 'I should give anything to return to a life where I might dance upon the most revered stages of Europe. I hope to audition for a ballet company again next year so that wish might come true.' Returning to Nottingham felt inconceivable. How could she ever explain where she had spent the past few months? And Drosselmeier would be awaiting her return. No, better not to venture into that dark pit of thoughts.

'I should steal away to the Sugar Alley one morning at an unreasonable hour,' Dellara was saying, her voice dreamier than usual.

'What kind of establishment would you patronise?' Marietta asked, sinking back into her cushion and curling her legs up, the carpet thicker than cloud beneath her.

'All kinds. I used to reside in an apartment in the perfect location; nestled between firs with a view of the great frozen lake from my windows and a short stroll from both the Silk Quarter and Sugar Alley. I dream of the days I'd shut myself inside and spend an entire afternoon cooking, baking and tasting a curated feast, the entire apartment perfumed with the most divine scents. Throw my doors open in the evening to serve a ten-course meal to my friends in my most splendid gown.'

'I had no notion you were such an accomplished cook,' Marietta said.

'There's nothing like a ten-course meal,' Dellara said, still dreamy. 'Sometimes I would make one purely for myself and whatever lover I held at the time. Serve the courses at appointed hours throughout the night.' She grinned at Marietta. 'Life's too short to deprive yourself of a little extravagance.' Her grin morphed into one of wicked delight. 'Though not for me, of course; I'm immortal,' she added.

Marietta was too struck by the casual flippancy with which Dellara had announced her immortality to respond. Before she could formulate any questions, Dellara had lain back and closed her eyes, bidding them both goodnight.

Marietta supposed they'd formulate a plan the following day. Or whenever they happened to rouse themselves; the ball had slunk through the night and blazed into the next day, until she'd lost count of the hours. The constant darkness her head outside the frozen sugar walls added to the disorientation muddying her head. That and the memory of dancing in the captain's arms, the moment when she'd considered the possibility of him lowering his lips to hers and the electricity that had shot through her veins upon realising that she had wanted that. And that she must never let him, for both their sakes. She also dwelled on the bewildering skirmish with Dellara. On the vulnerability that had shot through her prickly exterior, leading Marietta to despise herself for exposing it. And, as they were wont to do at night, fears crept into her head, whispering of a man with ice for eyes and silvered hair. A hunter, his sights set on her.

'You are in deep need of sleep,' Pirlipata said, noticing the tiredness seeping through Marietta. She handed her a soft, thick blanket. 'Curl up under that and let your mind ease up for a spell. My mother always used to tell me that there's no use thinking on a tired head, the worries of the world can wait another day.'

Marietta took the blanket. 'Thank you.' A soft scent that hinted of fresh snowfall unfolded with it. She nestled under it.

'It is laced with an enchantment that will soothe you to sleep,' Pirlipata said. 'A deep, dreamless sleep for it is not the body alone which requires rest.'

Marietta's response lagged, the enchantment creeping into her mind, a light-fingered thief stealing her consciousness. 'I bitterly regret how I spoke to Dellara, lest she think I have spent this time judging her. I do not; I am not in the position to judge anyone.

I have lived my entire life surrounded by riches; who am I to criticise anyone?' she whispered, closing her eyes. 'I have never had friends, sisters, like you both, and I am so very glad of it, but every time I feel close to Dellara, she holds me at arm's length and I cannot understand it. I wished to make her feel the same way. And now she must dislike me more than ever.'

'Do not trouble yourself with such thoughts,' Pirlipata said. 'Dellara has longed to provoke such a reaction in you; it is her way. She is a provocateur. Yet she has never disliked you. Quite the opposite, in fact, but she fears becoming close with the king's "pets". If she had not befriended you then it would have been easier for her to bear your death. Buried beneath her chest beats the warmest heart I have ever had the privilege of knowing. Big enough to bleed for you one day before she confronts you in anger the next, purely from the fear of losing you. There was once a woman she lost, many moontides ago now. She was strong and brave and beautiful. The kind of woman that sets the dawn itself aglow. Her heart was kind and caring and you could not help but love her. Though Dellara loved her most of all.'

'What happened to her?' Marietta asked in a whisper, afraid to know, more afraid not to, battling the insistent tug of sleep long enough to hear Pirlipata speak once more.

'King Gelum murdered Amadea. And a part of Dellara died with her.' Pirlipata's sigh was soft against the night. 'Her words are her armour, Marietta; do try to remember this. Beneath them is a grieving heart.'

Marietta stared up at the ceiling. It was painted in a likeness of the frozen sugar wall, though it lacked its opalescent quality. She missed the stars. She wasn't sure how to respond to Pirlipata's confidence and her thoughts were too slow to shape. When she glanced at Dellara, she saw that the woman's eyelashes were wet. Marietta closed her own eyes. 'I'm sorry,' she whispered.

Sleep came, fast and urgent, the night possessing her as one of its own.

Yet during the night, something roused her from her enchanted slumber. The figure of Drosselmeier was bending over her. She attempted to scream but she was unable, the charm rendering her helpless, her eyelids heavy and closing, closing against her will. When next she forced them open, he was not there. And Marietta couldn't tell if her vision had been real or nothing but a concoction of shadow and imagination shaped into a fear, giving it life and presence.

Chapter Thirty-Three

The weeks blurred together in a sparkling haze of balls, rereading the diary that contained the outpouring of the captain's heart, and the strict confinement that regimented Marietta's days and would have dissolved her sanity had it not been for the twin pillars steadying it: Pirlipata and Dellara. On occasion, Marietta half-believed she was walking through a dream, her days too removed, too gossamer-fragile to hold any meaning, any reality to them. There were no books, no classes or, loath as she may be to attend them, social appointments to keep, and time began to drip from the hours, melting the nights into one pot of darkness. Yet when those nights were at their bleakest, those twin pillars stood firm and unyielding, the two women framing Marietta's life into something which she could tolerate. Each day they discussed another chunk of their uncurling plan. And each night, she devoured the captain's words.

With the string of balls ribboning on throughout Everwood's long, dark winter, their suite was under constant notice. Dressmakers, shoemakers, confectioners all drizzled by at the king's behest, frantic in their devotion to ensure that King Gelum's 'pets' were clad in the finest gowns, the most fashionable accessories, enveloped in the sweetest scents and most bewitching of enchantments. To escape being overheard, the three of them refrained from speaking on the matter of their plan until the opportune moment to steal away presented itself. In the bathing pool, the rush of the peppermint-tinted waterfall foamed over the sound of their voices and there they lingered, until their fingertips puckered and their ideas were spent.

Those moments were fewer and further apart than Marietta would have liked. She did not know how long she had resided within the palace for. Both day and night were cloaked in darkness; and each time she attempted to count, she found she could not remember how many had passed. Night after night, she pirouetted through yet another ball, the throne room a-spin around her, the time hazy, in one sparkling gown after another.

Though her cage was soft and glittering, she refused to allow her sugared imprisonment to rot away her willpower. She would not sit inside it, glazed in meekness and obedience. She would rattle the bars and find her way home. Her days of living on someone else's terms were short-lived. In the meantime, she dwelled on their current predicament: how might they enter the locked chamber concealed beneath the king's throne? Between mulling it over, probing through the possibilities with Dellara and Pirlipata under the gurgle and froth of water, they planned how to play their parts.

And then there were the balls.

First came the Buttercream Ball, where the pâtissiers whipped up rows of petits fours, topped with extravagant swirls of buttercream in vanilla, chocolate, praline, pistachio and glossy frostberry. All the guests wore a frothery of tulle and gauze or sheaths and suits that might have been piped on, and some that were, in buttery pastels and creamy concoctions. The night rippled in scents, torn between sugared vanilla and the darkest of chocolates. It was the occasion on which Marietta had presumed to set eyes on the captain for the first time since their dance, yet hadn't. He was nowhere to be found.

A large envoy of guests from Mistpoint had been escorted to the palace via moose-drawn sleighs, for whom Marietta had been ordered to dance. The women wore grey-blue veils over their hair, silks that moved like river-water. Upon Marietta launching into a springing variation from *Paquita*, the Mistpointian women lowered their veils over their eyes. Dellara had attempted to use the distraction to pilfer the enchanted mechanism from the king's jacket, but his faceless guards had remained too close, watchful due to the Mistpointians' presence. Dellara later informed Marietta that they disproved of King Gelum and the reputation he was garnering over the land.

'Might we form allies with them?' Marietta had asked at once, dismayed when Dellara shook her head, wisps of cirri strewn across her irises.

'It is one thing to despise King Gelum; it is another thing entirely to rise up against him. He might be loathed but he is also feared, and fear is a powerful motivator. It is why the thought of the rebellion chills me; its failure is written in the stars. After the king decimated the royal court preceding him, their gruesome murder has stuck around in everyone's memories, a bloody thorn you can't quite pluck out.'

Then there had been the Ice Ball, when the entirety of the throne room had been coated in a sheen of ice and skating took the place of dancing. Great sculptures of King Gelum, commissioned by himself, had been hewn from frozen blocks. Immense fir trees limned the edges as if the forest had strolled into the throne room for the night. Some guests had resembled woodland sprites, clad in peppermint-green gowns with jewelled antlers crowning their locks. Other guests had taken on the persona of frost fairies, draped in glistening whites, sheer silvers and glacier blues. They'd partaken in crushed ice in little igloo-bowls but Marietta hadn't had a bite, wary of disguised enchantments. She needed to keep her wits. That had been the night she had skidded under the king's unoccupied throne, pleading at how unaccustomed she was to the ice after two faceless guards had immediately wrenched her back out. Yet the bruises she'd endured had been worth it; she'd glimpsed the outline of a round hatch beneath the throne. Enough to verify Dellara's mysterious sources. That had also been the ball when Marietta had caught herself hoping that Captain Legat would see her in her shimmering white gown. She had been disappointed; he had not attended the Ice Ball either.

It had been during the aftermath of that ball, soaking Marietta's bruised knee, that the three women had decided who would be the ones to descend into the secret chamber: Marietta, as the entire scheme had been her prerogative from its conception; and Dellara, as she would entrust not another soul to reclaim her wand. 'I cannot expect you to fathom what it is to me, only that as I fled that dark void of a world, I reached out and tore a piece of it free. A piece that clawed back at me, ensnaring a scrap of my spirit within it. Yet we had nothing but each other and, as like calls to like, I came to rely upon it. Feeding it with my magic, my energy, until it recognised and served only me.'

'Then I shall unleash the distraction for you to locate it,' Pirlipata had said.

Marietta had rested her head back against the pool edge, soaking in the twinkling starlight above. 'What do you suppose the chamber holds?'

'I don't have a flurry of an idea. Though King Gelum is an avid collector, fond of amassing both people and trinkets from other lands, other worlds. I'm sure he retains them all down there,' Dellara said, rinsing her hair.

Pirlipata spread thick, toffee-scented foam onto her arms. 'I am not surprised that a king who is neglecting his own kingdom and allowing it to fall prey to the mineral sickness fails to understand the subtleties of other cultures and only wishes to possess what he could never understand. I do hope we shall be able to best him.'

Marietta lay back in the bubbles, pointing and flexing her toes by rote. 'Of course we shall. We possess more brains and bravery between the three of us than the king does in a single hand.'

And then there had been Marietta's favourite of the balls.

The one in which frost peckers had wandered amidst a ginger-bread town; a perfect replica of Everwood in miniature. The one where truffles and pralines gently floated down the core of the palace like snow, snatched out of the air to be bitten into, chocolate on the tongues of all revellers, turning kisses ever sweeter and darker. The one where Marietta had worn her most beguiling dress yet: a simple white satin bodice that spooled out into a gown fit for a fairy-tale princess, sparkling like a fresh snowflake. When she pirouetted, her dress lit up with an incandescent glow. The one where she'd turned to find the captain looking at her. And he had kept staring at her. And she'd noticed.

The Gingerbread Ball.

Laced with magic, it dripped with wonder and intrigue. Gauze curtains fluttered down, dividing the throne room into smaller, more intimate gossamer-caves. Ones that a server or dancer might waltz through at any moment, rendering each snatched moment between lovers fraught with the delicious anticipation of being caught. Tiny lights studded the floor, as if one was dancing on starlight, and the stream ran in a melted chocolate current. Guests were served empty glasses and cups of crunchy shards of praline, biscotti and plump frostberries to drizzle with the molten core of the palace. Small working gingerbread trains ran alongside it on peppermint tracks, darting faster when someone chased one, craving a nibble, and little islands of marzipan fir trees floated down its current.

Pirlipata, clad in a golden dress embroidered with waltzing gingerbread women, filled a glass with melted chocolate for the king, her conversation with him laced with strategy; attempting to procure a hint on what shape his mysterious mechanism might hold. It led nowhere. Eventually she retired her efforts and danced with Dellara instead.

Marietta approached the captain, her thoughts a-whirling, her gown attracting a nearby whorl of buttercream butterflies with its twinkling lights. She wished to ask where he had been, why he had failed to attend the previous balls. If he was still prepared to supply their disguises. To confide in him how thoughts of his rebellion and possible capture taunted her at night. Sent her nails carving half-moons into her palms with worry. Yet it was none of those notions that tumbled from her lips. It wasn't even a question. 'I have noticed you cannot keep your eyes from me, captain.'

Captain Legat took a pull of his drink, dark and chocolate in a sheer glass. His eyes were buttery bright over the rim, dwelling on Marietta's luminescence and the creamy cascade of butterflies. 'I do believe you are imagining things.' She heard the smile behind his words.

She stepped closer to him. 'Actually, I am certain that you are the one imagining things. After all, I have read your thoughts. I know your mind now.'

The captain's gaze drank her in. 'Is that right?' he murmured.

She wondered if she might rest her hand on his arm, a casual touch, inquire whether he cared to dance. But they had been too conspicuous on the last occasion they had succumbed to dancing and though she craved the touch of his hand on her back, his arm wrapped about her waist, she resisted. 'Where have you been? You promised me certain assistance and that was several weeks ago now.'

He reached for her and twirled them both back, through a ripple of fabric. A fine layer of gauze the sole barrier preventing the rest of the throne room from setting eyes and ears upon their conversation.

Further back, other gossamer hideaways issued sighs and giggles and Marietta grew aware of the small space in which they both stood, her gown a voluminous cloud, pressing against the captain's legs.

'You are all too aware that I never promised such a thing. I said I would look into the matter, and I shall, but events have transpired in the palace, leading me to have set aside the concern.' His words were fast and hushed, his attention locked onto her with urgency.

Marietta regarded him. 'Do explain what you mean by that.' She hoped the cryptic events he referenced weren't regarding developments in Crackatuck. A burst of raucous laughter nearby and revellers flitting through the gauze came as a warning; their privacy was imagined.

'It is not safe to discuss it here,' Captain Legat said, watching the rippling fabric. It shimmered under the light of Marietta's gown, little starbursts that danced over the captain's face and white livery. 'Will you allow me to send for you tomorrow night? Rumours of rebellion have been scattered through the town and the guards will be distracted.'

Marietta ignored the slight dance her stomach performed at his words. It was as if they were waltzing once more and she was close enough to see the faintest scar brushed across his left temple. The reddish tint his hair carried under a certain light. 'You have never sought my permission before.'

'I fear all those occasions I summoned you, had you brought to me, I gave you no say in the matter. I had little choice yet still they haunt me.' His eyes locked with hers. 'I should like to amend this. Though the enchantments do not allow you to leave these frozen walls since the king claimed you, there is a place I would wish to share with you. Things I must tell you. Please, Marietta, meet me.'

Her name poured off his tongue like velvet. Deeply tempting. And perhaps worth the risk of such a rendezvous in order to discover the cryptic events which he had referred to. Or so she told herself. Before she exited their gauzy enclosure, she threw a final look back at him. 'Until tomorrow night.'

Chapter Thirty-Four

As it often transpires when one is anticipating an event, the following day seemed to take an age in dawning. When at last the evening arrived, Marietta had expected the captain to have had her brought to his study. Yet the doors had opened to reveal Fin, who had escorted her a few swirls down, to a winter garden.

A lantern of moonlight silvered a carpet of pristine snow. Snowflake-shaped petals studded bushes in dusky blue and pearl. Fir trees encircled the space, strung with tiny lights bespelled to peal like bells. The ceiling glittered high above in a bewitchery of stars and a large fountain tinkled in the centre. Stone mice danced and hopped over delicate vines entwined around the fountain, reminiscent of the thorny overgrowth Prince Désiré was destined to hack his way through to reach the Princess Aurora. Captain Legat was perched on the edge of the stonework, petals fluttering down onto his shirt and hair like snow. He rose upon sighting her and handed her a long-stemmed flower.

Marietta accepted it. 'How perfectly lovely.' Its blush-pink petals shivered as she ran a fingertip down them. She seated herself on the side of the fountain and, after a brief hesitation, the captain sat beside her. 'The change in location is a welcome surprise,' she said. 'I was beginning to wonder whether I would ever be offered a glimpse into the jewels waiting behind the palace's myriad doors.'

'I'm glad it meets your approval. I often find myself stealing away here, to the winter garden, in search of a peaceful place to sit awhile.'

Marietta closed her eyes, the bell-lights and the melodious fountain sweet and soothing, bathing her senses. 'It is beautiful here. I can feel my pulse slowing, my worries waning.' She caught an echo of the captain's smile upon re-opening her eyes. Precious and fleeting.

'Besides which, an added precaution was in order. The king's suspicions are deepening, paranoia is cutting into his thoughts. I am concerned by reports that he is mounting an investigation into the ranks, ordering his faceless guards to spy on my soldiers. It shall amount to nothing, I am certain of the loyalty in my men, but it is a worrying sign. We cannot afford to incite his attention now, not when I am at a pivotal point in—' He abruptly ceased.

Marietta twirled the flower. 'I would rather you not put your other activities at risk for the sake of aiding me.'

'Now there is a sentence I never thought to hear you say.'

'It would cost us precious time but what is time compared to the lives depending on you? I cannot bring myself to interfere with that, not now, not after what I have witnessed.' She frowned, thinking of the rumours he had alluded to the previous night. 'Should you be here at all if other matters are unfolding tonight?'

Captain Legat rubbed the back of his neck. 'Ah, those matters are but a mere fabrication. I had to ensure the faceless guards were otherwise occupied tonight so I might meet you.'

Marietta looked at him, words failing her.

'And I was wrong in suggesting that you ought not to draw me away. You and the other women are not safe here as I once considered you might be in the short term.' Captain Legat reached down and extracted a bundle from beside his feet. 'Three uniforms. As promised.' He handed it to her.

'Thank you.' She set it down on the fountain. 'I could not help but notice your lack of attendance at the king's balls lately.'

'King Gelum dispatched me from the palace. I was engaged in travelling down the Thieves Road to Mistpoint on some erroneous mission. I suspect it was our dance that prompted it.' His voice lingered on *dance*. Marietta felt a flash of heat. His hand rested beside hers on the edge of the fountain. She nudged her little finger closer until it met warmth.

'He has not interfered in your other plans?' she asked cautiously, noticing the shadows lurking beneath his eyes, the worries that mottled them.

'Not as far as I am aware. Though other difficulties have presented themselves. The king is intending to invade Crackatuck within the next moontide. A show of strength.' He gave a weary rub of his temples. Glanced up at her lack of reaction. 'And it seems as if you already knew that. How?' Marietta did not answer. But Legat wasn't the captain for nothing. 'Dellara,' he said. 'She must have seen the plans in his council room.'

'Why are you informing me of this?' Marietta asked.

'Saving a life, protecting a king is what awarded me the rank of captain. Invading another kingdom, ruling with an iced fist goes against everything I believe in and you know well I wish to hold no part in it.' He rubbed his temple again. She did know. She had read his soul-pain, poured onto paper. And when she danced, he saw her. 'I believed the Crackatian princess ought to be aware of this before you departed.'

'I suppose there is no point in me attempting to persuade you to join us.'

A wry smile, a smile of sadness and what might have been. 'I cannot. I am not alone in leading the rebellion but I could not desert my post. I have to see it to the end, whatever that might be.' He glanced down at the point where their hands met. 'No matter how I may be tempted to leave.'

'I understand.' She knew enough of being confined to see it in another.

He met her eyes for a beat. 'King Gelum possesses more intelligence than you realise, Marietta. I smoothed over some trade agreement for him. Satisfied his ego. But as I mentioned, he is suspicious, with the propensity to make an example of those who would betray him. He is a man with a deep enjoyment of inflicting pain. Your escape would be a cutting betrayal and he would stop at nothing in his attempts to retrieve you. If he were to succeed—' He swallowed.

The scars remaining on Marietta's feet twinged. 'We are well aware of the risks.'

'Are you?' The captain's gaze dropped to her feet for a painful pause. 'What if you were not the one in his grasp but the fairy? Or the princess? Could you watch them suffer? Bear their inevitable drawn-out execution?'

Marietta's imagination conjured Amadea's face, her unknown features foggy and shifting. King Gelum had killed her and a part of Dellara had died with her. Her composure hardened, a brittle veneer over her heart. 'I am not afraid to do whatever it takes. I have never wished for an easy life and when I return I am determined not to languish in another gilded prison.'

He turned to face her. 'You make me wonder about this world you left behind. About who you left behind.'

'In a way, it greatly resembled this one.' Marietta smoothed her dress over her knees. Dellara's reaction to her selecting the scarlet velvet had been satisfying. Her lips were painted in the same shade, her hair curled. Red for the heart-blood of the rebellion. 'My life's path was ordained for me and I was expected to march along to someone else's plan. My future was not at my behest and my own dreams and fears were dismissed.' She thought of the Cartier brooch beneath her pillow, the dreams where a man with a chipped-ice stare followed her, her breath catching as she scanned the dark firs that walled them in, apprehensive of the shadows bunching together, envisioning the hunter forging them as his home.

'There is a celebrated storyteller in Everwood,' the captain said, his response unexpected, ensnaring Marietta's focus. 'His tales always incorporate a variation of the moral that if you do not cherish your dreams, you have forgotten how to live. Dreaming is an intrinsic part of human nature, on par with love and hate and hope.'

'Storytellers are often wise beyond their years. Perhaps all their delving into words and thoughts has gifted them additional lives.'

The captain's hand suddenly covered hers. Marietta turned her palm upwards, a flower seeking the sun. Their fingers interlaced. 'Are you certain you wish to return to this world of yours?' the captain murmured. 'A world where you must fight to be yourself does not seem a suitable place for you. After the rebellion I shall be free. What if I took you somewhere else instead? Somewhere where you might be safe.'

His hands was strong and calloused. Little bites of steel had nicked the flesh here and there, telling a story of the soldier who wielded a sword for the king. Yet that was not the whole tale. She tightened her fingers around his. 'The storyteller you mentioned held the truth. My time here has been transformative, but I cannot dismiss that which I have spent a lifetime wishing for. I know I am strong enough to fight for my dreams now. I am ready to carve a path into a future of my own creation.'

'I admire you for your strength,' the captain said, caressing her hand, tracing the lines bisecting her palm with his thumb. 'I feared this place might break you.'

She shivered at his touch. 'I am not strong, I am a selfish creature that has been spoiled with a life of privilege and every physical comfort I desired. But perhaps I can be brave. And when I do return, for I will return, I shall make a change.'

'And you dare say you are not strong? Change requires a deeper strength than most people shall ever know.'

It began to snow.

'Oh—' Marietta looked up in wonder '—this place is a devilish oxymoron.'

The captain's brow furrowed. 'Whatever do you mean?'

'Each time I consider how much I regret the choices I made that led me here, how I despise being imprisoned, I find something that steals my breath away.' She laughed and lifted her face to the snow, holding her tongue out to catch the tiny snowflakes. They melted in sweet bursts of sugared vanilla.

'I can understand that,' the captain said after a pause.

Marietta smiled at him, feeling snowflakes whispering onto her hair, nestling on her bared shoulders. 'The last time we convened in your study, you were on the brink of telling me something,' she said, a spark of courage liberating her tongue. 'I have often since wondered what it might have been.'

He studied her for a moment. Reached out to brush a snowflake from her cheek. 'It was nothing. Some triviality I can no longer recall.' He offered the snowflake to her, its edges clear-cut as crystal. 'Make a wish. In Everwood, we say that when it melts, your wish shall be granted.'

Marietta accepted it, her fingers grazing his. Their other hands were still linked, his fingers strong around her hand, anchoring her to his golden warmth. She closed her eyes. 'I wish—'

'If you say it aloud, it shall not come true,' the captain whispered. She could hear his smile.

Sometimes it felt as if wishes and dreams coursed through her veins rather than blood. But there remained things that took a greater precedent over her dreams and so she wished for the safety and good health of Pirlipata and Dellara, come what may. On opening her eyes, she tucked the snowflake away in a velvet pocket.

'Fin shall return you to your suite. Those are supposed to be new dancing shoes.' Captain Legat nodded at the bundle beside Marietta. 'Do not let anyone see what it contains and the minute you are alone, hide them. There are spies everywhere.' He extended a hand and pulled Marietta to her feet. She broke their enlaced hands to pick up the bundle. It was chilled and she yearned afresh for his touch. He walked over to the door, incongruous in the lush garden, beneath the flurries of snow. When his fingers touched the handle, he hesitated. 'I do not know when or how you are intending to leave, and it would be better if I were not to learn, but promise me you will be careful?'

'Always.' Marietta moved towards the door, to him. 'And I cannot thank you enough.'

'It was the very least I could do.' Still he lingered, each second the door remained closed another moment that belonged to them. Another moment in which they might pretend that they were but brief acquaintances, stars that brushed against each other in the night.

Marietta held the package tighter. 'I shall be attending the Grand Confectioner's Ball.'

The captain's expression relaxed. 'Then we have a handful of days yet. Though I should inform you; if you were to pick a day to leave the palace, it is in the stars that something shall happen the night of the Grand Confectioner's Ball. It would prove ample ... distraction.'

'I shall take note of that,' Marietta said softly. 'Thank you, captain.'

Legat stepped closer and she felt as if the collision of their stars would set flame to the world. It crackled between them and she wondered why she had denied it for so long. His eyes rested on her scarlet lips in fascination, her eyes falling to his, his white shirt pressed against her red velvet, her face tilted towards his. The winter garden melted away, leaving the two of them in their own world as Marietta felt herself drawn towards the captain, craving the delicious moment where any second his lips would meet hers.

Voices permeated the door.

Legat moved away and yanked it open.

Marietta sighed at the moment that had nearly been.

Fin materialised in the doorway. 'Ah, there you are, captain. The king requests an audience at once to discuss an urgent matter.'

'Of course, I shall attend him now. Fin, do escort the dancer back to her suite,' Legat instructed as they both made their way to the stairs.

Where three faceless guards were awaiting them.

Chapter Thirty-Five

The faceless guards turned as one to consider them, all blank masks and rigid statures. They never failed to coax trepidation from Marietta.

'What is that?' One of the crafters was looking at the package. The faceless guards turned their heads to look, their movements stiff and unyielding.

'They are her dancing shoes,' Legat drawled in a bored tone. 'Forgive me, I had not realised the interest you held in women's footwear.' His expressionless face formed his own mask as he slotted back into the role of captain

Marietta glanced at him. It wasn't him; wasn't the light shining in his eyes, tender smiles and deep, feeling words she had come to cherish. The same way she wasn't herself in the tearooms and ballrooms of high society. Since she had discovered the real Legat underneath his façade, rawer and vulnerable, she wondered at how she had ever considered him distant and impassive. He had never not cared for her situation; he had simply cared too much. She ached for the distance between them now, the kiss that had never been.

One of the faceless guards came closer, looming over Marietta. 'It's a large package for a mere pair of shoes,' he said tonelessly, reaching for it.

'Obviously it contains more than one pair.' She fought back her panic, not allowing her voice to waver as she glared at him. The guard's hands fell to his side but he stayed before her. Beneath the soldiers' livery beat hearts strong and human and capable of fathomless love. She shuddered at what skulked beneath the guards' blank masks. She sensed a coldness to them, obeying the king's orders as automatons. If the captain's suspicions proved correct and the faceless guards were investigating the soldiers then she feared the consequences for them. For him and the dangerous double game he was engaged in, carrying the weight of the rebellion on his shoulders.

'We've been searching the palace for you,' the other crafter said, oozing with suspicion. 'There have been murmurs of rebellious activity within these walls.'

'And now you have found me. Kingsman Fin, return this woman to her suite so that she may prepare what we discussed for the king. I shall deal with this matter.'

Fin jerked to attention, guiding Marietta up the staircase. 'That was close,' he murmured, swiping a hand at the back of his neck. As they continued ascending the stairs, Marietta glanced back to where Legat was standing on the swirl below and opposite them. The crafters were now descending in a golden cage, one of them staring at a small clock face he'd pulled from his collar, the other tapping a foot on the gilded floor. It appeared as if the captain had dismissed the guards, who were now marching onwards and upwards on the spiral. Legat threw a brief look up at Marietta. She wished she was close enough to read it. Instead, she continued with Fin, the spiral whisking them out of sight.

The suite door was unlocked to reveal Pirlipata and Dellara poring over an armoire. The instance Marietta was locked in with them once more, they dismissed their conversation.

'Well?' Dellara demanded.

Pirlipata examined her face. 'Did something happen? You look whiter than a winter's day.'

'Nothing happened, I assure you I am fine,' Marietta said. She pressed a hand to her stomach, forcing it to calm.

'Never mind that now—' Dellara flapped a hand at Pirlipata '—what do you have in there?' She reached for the package.

Marietta relinquished her hold on it. 'We must hide it at once.'

Dellara tore into it, shimmering lilac nails slashing the brown paper open. They all leant forward. A striped red and white fabric lay inside. Dellara's teeth gleamed. 'It looks as if the captain does possess a fondness for you after all,' she said to Marietta, who was trying to regain her composure after her intimate moment with Legat. Even if their encounter had left her longing for him, it was too dangerous a notion to even consider. She could not call the faintest hint of suspicion on herself, not when it could jeopardise everything. A faint clunk froze the three of them into a tapestry.

Someone was unlocking the door.

In a heartbeat, Pirlipata snatched up the parcel and ran with it into the bathing chamber. After she'd whipped through the gauzy drapes, Marietta heard her bank right, into the private section of the bathroom. Dellara shoved Marietta onto a cushion, diving onto the carpet beside her and opening a nearby box of paints to the crimson shade she had slicked on Marietta's lips, retouching them just as the door swung open.

A server marched through, deposited an oversized silver tray on the carpet beside Dellara, who ignored her, and marched back out as Marietta's lips gained a third coating. Dellara tossed the paints aside and called out to Pirlipata in a low voice. 'You can come out now.'

Pirlipata emerged, the opened package still in her hands. 'Where shall we hide it?'

'Is it possible to conceal it within a cushion or one of the chaises longues?' Marietta considered the tight seams of the nearest one.

'We're lacking the necessary tools for that,' Dellara said.

Marietta glanced towards the armoires. 'What about the cape you wore to the buttercream ball? The raspberry-pink shiny one you were so enamoured with?'

'I am not sure I follow,' Pirlipata said, exchanging a curious look with Dellara.

'That night you spilt a snowberry crème on it but it did not stain despite your worry, the fabric repelled it ...' Marietta went to rummage in the armoire. After locating the cape in the glittering rainbow of Dellara's wardrobe, she spread it out on the smooth, lilac stone floor and rolled the uniforms inside, forming a tight seamless bundle which she then stuffed inside a pair of glossy stockings and knotted shut. She strode through the drapes and dropped it into the bathing pool.

Dellara watched it bob on the water. 'Do I care to know?'

Marietta dredged it out a few minutes later. 'Look, it is perfectly dry inside,' she said, marching into the private toilet and leaning against the cistern to slide the lid off.

'Oh.' Pirlipata's confusion evaporated at once. 'How ingenious.'

Dellara's grin revealed her sharpened teeth.

Marietta popped the watertight bundle in and replaced the lid.

They celebrated the successful procuring of their disguises with dinner. Bowls of rich stew, puffs of bread, light and airy as snowballs, and biscotti studded with flakes of nuts and bursts of berry that they dipped into white drinking chocolate.

Marietta lay on the carpet between Pirlipata and Dellara, as they finalised their escape plan. They ran through it once, twice, smoothing out any worries that snagged at the fabric of their resolve. No ball had transpired that night; they had all dressed for comfort in woollen trousers and soft tops as they conversed through the deepening evening.

Marietta glided her fingers through the indulgent carpet pile as the talk shifted to trading stories of books they'd read, people they admired and hopes they held dearest to their hearts. Until a low chanting seeped into her awareness.

Pirlipata straightened. 'No. No, no, no – not again.'

Dellara's eyes clouded into shadows thicker than night.

Pirlipata turned to her. 'I cannot watch another.' Her voice broke. 'Dellara—'

'Hush.' Dellara took her in her arms, stroking her hair. 'You can and you will and I shall be with you the entire time.' Her glance at Marietta was threaded with anxiety.

Marietta was unsure if she wished to know the nature of the horror creeping towards them. Before she could voice this, the door thudded open. Three faceless guards filled the open doorway, their attention fixed on the women, cool and silent.

Marietta stood as Dellara sauntered over to the guards. 'King Gelum forces us to bear witness to his executions,' Pirlipata whispered.

They were escorted down the stairs. The rest of the palace-dwellers were congregating in the throne room. All the hidden cogs that kept everything running smoothly, the chefs and chocolatiers and pâtissiers, along with cleaners and maids, all forced to assemble. They outnumbered even the soldiers. King Gelum sat on his throne surrounded by the Faceless Guards, with the courtiers huddled around the edges of the room. Leaving the centre empty.

Marietta reached for Pirlipata's hand and held it tight, their breaths coming faster and shallower. Dellara stood before them both, though her shorter frame did nothing to obscure either of their views.

'Lev has betrayed me,' King Gelum announced, commanding the palace's attention. Heads snapped to him. Whispers perished unspoken in throats. A soldier was dragged before the throne. Still in his garnet livery, he stood there, spine unyielding, face proud, despite being leached of colour. Nausea skulked in the pit of Marietta's stomach. 'My own soldier,' the king continued, 'caught colluding with the Crackatians, feeding them palace secrets. It seems even my own ranks of soldiers have been stained with the guilt of treason, harbouring a traitor in their midst.'

Marietta's heart thudded harder and she couldn't help seeking out Captain Legat, who stood at the king's side, his taut face betraying the inner tension warring within. So it had begun. He met her eyes across the crowd, concern flashing across his face before he ripped his gaze off her, cutting it back onto the accused soldier, his soldier, begging for his life at their feet.

'I swear my innocence on the stars,' Lev said, his voice low. Strong. 'You've been searching for an excuse to cull our ranks and this upcoming investigation into our honour is merely a farce. A reason to replace us with these inhuman monstrosities.' He jerked his head at the faceless guards securing him in place. 'Be warned, the king does not deserve our service.' He turned to address his fellow soldiers, stood in regimented lines of garnet. 'He's a liar and a coward and he doesn't deserve the throne he cheated and murdered his way onto.'

His proclamation was met with stalwart silence. Averted eyes. Pirlipata squeezed Marietta's hand tighter.

King Gelum's smile was a thin, sadistic sliver of delight. 'For your crimes, you are sentenced to an immediate execution.'

The faceless guards to either side of him began marching him up the stairs. 'Where are they taking him?' Marietta asked Pirlipata under her breath. Perhaps she wouldn't be forced to watch the man's life be ripped away; perhaps they were merely there to witness the sentencing.

'To the highest point of the staircase,' Dellara said, bringing back Marietta's dread tenfold. 'Where sugar and sky meet.'

Higher and higher Lev was escorted up the spiral, until he was but a tiny figure at the tip of the palace. For a moment she was certain she caught a splash of silver wending round the staircase but it vanished before she could blink.

The chanting returned with a vengeance. With a prickle of fear, Marietta realised it was emitted from behind the faceless guards' masks. Deep and toneless. She knew what was coming and ordered herself to look away. In a sound that Marietta knew would never cease to haunt her, she heard the final scream as Lev departed this world.

They all required the enchanted blanket to sleep that night.

'This changes nothing,' Dellara had whispered as they'd spread it over themselves, seeking solace in its scented folds, in each other. 'We cannot live another day with this ever-present violence hanging like a sharpened icicle above our heads. Tomorrow we execute our plan.'

Chapter Thirty-Six

Blanketed in stars and snow flurries of powdered sugar, the Grand Confectioner's Ball defied Marietta's expectations. She paused on the staircase, surveying the throne room. It had been framed in thick, rounded glass, creating a multitude of snow globes with interlinking passages that guests ran through, goblets of ice wine in hand, trailing lovers and silk dresses. Marietta might have been tempted to join them, steal away an intimate moment with the captain, had her nerves not been so thickly knotted. Had Lev's blood not still been visible, frozen into gruesome jewels on the ice.

'And the heist is a-go,' Dellara said, walking down the stairs, flanked by Marietta and Pirlipata. Their gowns were Ivana's pièce de résistance. Matching iridescent satin with full skirts bearing transparent circles, each one of which was bewitched to offer the viewer a different scene. Marietta's depicted tiny dancing princesses, tumbling snowflakes and endless fir forests. Dellara's portrayed miniature chocolateries and patisseries, with cakes the size of fingernails gleaming with frosting. Each one of Pirlipata's set her gown aflame with renditions of a golden sunset.

As she cast her gaze around, Marietta grew unsettled, uneasiness digging into her bones. Snow globes recalled to life Drosselmeier's Christmas gift and the visions it had granted her and Frederick, pilfered from their hearts' wishes. She wondered anew at the silver-haired figure she'd glimpsed, stalking her dreams. Last night she had dreamt of sugarplums and nutcrackers bearing Drosselmeier's icy stare, and awoken to an invisible touch and a haze of confusion. Could Drosselmeier truly be the creator responsible for all of this? She shivered at the thought.

Captain Legat approached Marietta, interrupting her reflections. 'You look enchanting,' he said in a hushed tone, his gaze lingering on her, drinking her in as if he wanted to devour her. It took an effort to dispel the thought of his arms wrapped around her, his lips almost meeting hers. 'I wish I could steal you away and never let you out of my sight.' His fingers twitched at his side. She brushed her hand against his. His pupils dilated. He cleared his throat. 'Perhaps—'

Skirting along the periphery of Marietta's vision, Dellara was nearing the king in small, deliberate steps. It was time.

'I'm afraid you must excuse me,' Marietta said a little breathlessly.

His eyes took in her face. His garnet jacket shone with epaulettes and buttons, his livery too reminiscent of the blood frozen on the ice, the rebellion he was courting such a fate to enact. 'May the stars shine ever brightly on you,' he said before stepping closer and whispering into her ear, 'Be careful, wanderer.'

Marietta danced away from his concern and towards the king. She twirled a finger in his direction, pleading with the fates that the impish smile she dangled from her lips would tempt him out of offence at her audacity. King Gelum's lips thinned upon noticing her. Marietta feigned a pout and pirouetted, raising her eyebrows in a suggestive manner, even as the air thickened in her lungs. The king rose from his throne and strode towards her. Marietta's heart gave an irregular pulse. It was pivotal that King Gelum dance with her. Dellara was relying on her to occupy him so she might purloin the mechanism. If they succeeded in taking it, Pirlipata was awaiting their signal to unleash a great distraction, masking Marietta and Dellara's absence and allowing the two women to descend beneath the throne together.

As the king walked towards her, his ivory cape unfolded in an icy shimmer, bewitched to enact scenes of balls and dancers and mice armed with swords battling little doll kings. Marietta rested a hand on his chest, edging her smile with mischief, a sugar-sweet charm of her own. Her mother may have oft reminded her that she lacked beauty, but the extensive lessons in etiquette bestowed upon her had lent her a catalogue of enchantments that owed no thanks to magic.

Remaining nearby, the captain folded his arms across his chest, watching them. Danyon materialised at his side to speak into his ear. Marietta hadn't seen him about the palace in an age; Claren was a ubiquitous presence, easy to locate in the centre of a comedic exchange or deep in a goblet, but his rigid older brother was much scarcer. Marietta ignored them, disregarding everyone that wasn't the king, locking eyes with him alone and rising up on en pointe for one crisp double pirouette that culminated in eye contact.

She swept back into an arched bend, her arms flowing overhead, forcing the king to step forward to hold her waist, to support her. Recalling how King Gelum had witnessed her and the captain locked in an intimate dance, his jealousy sufficient to have Legat dispatched on a trifling errand, Marietta had bet upon the odds that the king had learnt that move. She had been right. Until the floor slipped away from her pointe shoes as the king took it upon himself to lift her.

Approximating a pas de deux, Marietta raised her pointed toes behind her in an attitude, her arms fluttering in port de bras, holding her muscles taut as they spun, the king's fingers biting into her like frost, the throne room shattering into noise. As King Gelum lowered her back onto her toes, Marietta saw that the crowd was tapping their left feet onto the floor, the connecting snow globes erupting in appreciation. She would have been interested to learn how much of their regard for him was a sparkling veneer pasted over the truth.

'You are aware you were meant to distract the king, not draw the entire throne room's attention onto him, right?' Dellara's voice attacked Marietta the moment she receded to the shadows.

Marietta winced. 'That went vastly differently to how I had intended.'

'You're fortunate that I'm magical in many many ways.' Dellara patted her plunging neckline with a wink.

Marietta averted her eyes from Dellara's cleavage. 'You managed to retrieve it?'

'Someday you and I are going to have a talk about fashion—' Dellara eyed the delicate neckline of Marietta's dress '—especially since you purloined my red velvet so as to rush off and seduce the captain. That was telling. I know there's a daring woman inside all of those ivory nightgowns and demure blushes, screaming to be liberated.'

'Did you retrieve the mechanism?' Marietta repeated through gritted teeth.

Dellara's smile cut wider. 'Of course.'

'Then let us not stand here quibbling over gowns. Time is wasting.' Marietta walked into an adjoining snow globe. The glass distorted their view of the throne room as if they were peering into an antique mirror. Snow nestled in the corners and a snowman guarded the centre, each of his outstretched hands bearing a huge snowflake, upon which were perched white chocolate globes, their hollow centres filled with an edible surprise. Marietta took two and handed one to Dellara. They clinked them together.

'To the end of winter,' Dellara said, biting into it.

'To the Grand Confectioner's Ball,' Marietta said, looking at the praline reindeer hers had revealed.

Dellara's forehead rumpled. 'What's the matter with you? You look as if you've been caught out in an ice storm.' She decapitated her chocolate snowman with relish.

'Nothing. I'm merely anxious for tonight's events to proceed smoothly.' She glanced over her shoulder, the uneaten globe melting in her hand. King Gelum had retired to his throne once more. Pirlipata was nowhere in sight. Claren was surrounded by a gaggle of revellers from Mistpoint in their traditional cerulean trousers and flowing tops, veils folded back over their hair. Captain Legat was still conversing with Danyon, though every now and then, he scanned the throne room. Marietta was certain he was monitoring the premises though she couldn't help a flutter of hope that he was searching for her.

Dellara swallowed the last of her chocolate. 'Ah, I see,' she murmured, her gaze knowing when Marietta turned back to her.

'What do you see now?' Marietta returned her globe to the snowman's tray.

Dellara helped herself to a second. 'You have it bad for our good captain. It's plain you're attracted to him but I hadn't realised how deeply you care for him, too. It's more serious than I had realised.'

Marietta perched on an oversized snowball. 'Nothing could ever come of it. We are almost set to depart this world and he must remain here.' She looked away, patted her hair. Silver twists coiled it into a marzipan-scented swirl. She fought against sinking into the verses she'd memorised of Legat's. Words that transported her deeper into understanding, gave her sustenance, tugged at her emotions. *Look to the stars* ... She knew that the canvas of the night sky would forever remind her of him.

Dellara set her chocolate globe down and studied Marietta. 'Then you have invited him to accompany us?'

Marietta stood. 'I had not intended to. Though where is the sense in hiding my feelings for him on the cusp of leaving?'

'There is never any sense in hiding feelings; they will only embed themselves further in your heart until they're impossible to dig out.' Dellara adjusted the bodice of her dress. 'Speaking of leaving, Pirlipata is late.'

A surge of concern swept like a blizzard through the snow globe. 'Ought we to—'

A great noise broke out. Reverberations shook the glass-bottomed globes, sending flurries of snow dancing. Guards and soldiers surged forwards, hands resting on sword hilts, faceless masks tilted towards the encroaching sound. King Gelum leapt from his throne, shrouded behind a contingent of his guards.

Marietta and Dellara fled through a connecting tunnel and into another snow globe, weaving through the current of guests rushing past. A hand nudged Marietta's. Captain Legat, his hand clenched on his hilt, breathless from his dash across the throne room, abandoning his royal duty for her. 'Do you require my services?' he asked, drawing his Starhunter sword with a glance at the main doors and the faceless guards securing them, ignoring the odd curious look aimed in their direction. His thumb grazed her fingers, a secret touch, a delicious thrill.

'I—' she managed to say before Dellara seized her other hand.

But Captain Legat held tighter to her, sudden comprehension dawning in his eyes. 'If there was a key to another world to be found anywhere in the palace, I'd wager it was hidden among the king's treasures,' he whispered in her ear. She looked at him and he released her hand. Dellara swept her away into the chaos.

The main doors strained behind their barricades and splintered like hoarfrost. When the source of the rumbling became apparent, the guests hesitated, laughter bubbling out of the snow globes. Hundreds of miniature reindeer were pouring into the throne room. Marietta and Dellara broke into a run. The nearest soldiers attempted to corral the reindeer back through the doors as others ventured further into the throne room, finding their way into the snow globe complex, nibbling on cake and skirts without discrimination. Dellara fumbled to hand Marietta a small object as Marietta surged ahead on longer legs and slid beneath the throne. Smoothing her hand down the flat outline of the trap door she had discovered some balls ago, she opened her fingers to reveal a small mechanised mouse sitting in her hand.

Dellara threw herself down under the throne a beat later. 'Why haven't you opened it yet?' She wrenched the mouse from Marietta.

'I am merely waiting for us to be discovered instead,' Marietta snapped back at her, aware that the minute they'd stolen beneath the throne, time had become their enemy. Dellara set the mouse on the trap door, her sugared arms glittering. With a whir and a twitch of its whiskers, the enchanted mechanism within the mouse sparked to life. It ran over the trap door, locating some invisible lock, slotted its tail in and twisted. A collection of low thuds released a section of the floor, springing down to reveal steps descending below the palace.

Chapter Thirty-Seven

They lowered themselves in. Marietta closed the trapdoor behind them, Dellara pocketing the mouse as they turned to assess their surroundings, their breaths crystallising.

The chamber was carved from ice. Silent and thick with secrets. A single staircase had been cut from it, a tight coil that plummeted into the depths of the cliff the palace had been constructed on, encircled by thick frozen walls. Alcoves had been chipped from the ice at regular intervals, displaying a variety of the king's stolen treasures, and the entire chamber was lit with a low blue lighting that felt as if they were trespassing in a jar of boiled sweets.

'We must locate it as a matter of urgency.' Marietta's whisper swirled around the chamber and returned to them. She stepped onto the first ice step. 'It had better not be hidden too deeply; our time frame is too limited for that length of a search. Are you able to sense it in any manner?'

'I feel it calling but we have been separated too long and my power is weaker; akin to searching for a single snowflake in a bank of snow.'

Marietta took another step down. Her weight rushed out from beneath her, the ice staircase a sudden terror. She cried out, reaching for purchase, but her hands slid against ice. Dellara lurched forwards and grasped the material of Marietta's bodice, dragging her back onto her feet and steadying her as she composed herself. 'Thank you,' she said, sitting down to avoid slipping again. The echo of her panic was still being tossed around by the chamber. The eeriness swelled.

A sharp splintering sent her attention skittering back onto Dellara, who had ground the heel of her stiletto into the ice, anchoring herself. 'King Gelum must possess a pair of ice boots in order to walk down here,' she said, passing Marietta. 'Look at the imprints in the ice.' Each step was dotted with perforations.

Searching the alcoves, Dellara voiced aloud a running inventory. Marietta followed her in a seated position that felt rather undignified. 'A tiara, an ancient jewelled set of tails; that's a popular game here in Everwood,' she told Marietta. 'An old book in a language I can't decipher; I'm surprised our king hasn't burnt it. Another tiara, a nutcracker from Crackatuck crafted from a single ruby – they mine rubies there – and some kind of battered hat.' They paused to consider it. 'Stay away from it.' Dellara wrinkled her nose. 'I'm sure it's wrapped in a curse of some sort.'

'Have you encountered anything promising?' Marietta asked a few minutes later. 'What about Pirlipata's armour?' Not a sound filtered down from the throne room above but their distraction would be short lived; sooner or later, the ball would resume. And then nothing would shield them from the king's wrath.

'Yes, I stumbled upon it a while back, I just decided not to mention it and I'm still searching because this ice pit is exactly where I'd love to while away an evening.'

'Why do you feel a need to always be so— Wait, could that be it?' Marietta peered into the slim alcove in front of her. It was situated lower to the stairs, sliced into the wall with slashing diagonal lines which rendered it near-invisible unless you were seated at an awkward position. Inside rested a narrow strip of forest-green lacquered wood, its surface mottled with shadows that undulated like smoke.

Dellara's face appeared beside Marietta's, cheek to cheek. Marietta felt the smile that carved it into delight, reaching out to liberate the wand. 'Oh, how I've missed you,' Dellara crooned to it.

'Brilliant. Now let us make haste. I'm not returning without Pirlipata's armour.'

Dellara closed her eyes. She whispered to her wand. It shuddered and sparked, releasing an iridescent curl of light, a floating moonbeam. It slinked a few stairs down and hovered before a set of crimson armour. 'There,' she said with satisfaction, making her way over. Marietta helped her gently lift it down. This was no suit of armour that Marietta could have envisioned. It looked as if it had been designed by women for women. The metal was thin and light, crafted with thick leather for moveability and in several parts that would ensure full coverage once donned. Marietta ripped her petticoat out from under her dress and carefully wrapped it around the armour, fashioning it into a kind of bag she looped over her shoulder to carry. Dellara rendered it invisible and tucked her wand down her bodice as they ascended.

Her bare arms numb, skin chilled, Marietta was growing aware of the need to return to the softer temperatures that rippled through the palace in one of the many enchantments designed to smooth life into something more pleasurable. She pressed her ear to the oval trapdoor. Deep, resounding silence. The ice had gobbled up any hint of activity above. Huffing out tiny clouds of exertion, Dellara reached Marietta. They shuffled around to allow Dellara, who had produced the mechanical mouse from her bodice like a magician, to insert it into the lock. Marietta waited. And waited.

Dellara's eyes leached of shadows, turning her irises and pupils frost-like. 'There's no lock on this side.'

Chapter Thirty-Eight

Dellara reached into her bodice and pulled her wand out. She offered Marietta a shrug. 'It seems I'm no longer accustomed to carrying it anymore.' She held it in her left hand, her fingers a loose embrace around it.

Marietta glanced down the spiral of ice stairs, imagining eyes freezing into her back. She shivered, unvoiced suspicions storming through her mind. 'Wait,' she said. 'The captain hinted that if there was any place we might find a key with which to cut ourselves an exit from this palace, it would be here. Ought we not to try and find one? If we were able to locate such a key, we would not have to spend an age searching through world after world for a way back to our homes. We could simply leave the palace for Everwood.'

Dellara was studying the trapdoor. 'That's nothing but guesswork. We're fortunate we found both my wand and Pirlipata's armour in such a timeframe. If we were to begin another search now ...' Her eyes swirled into a maw. 'Besides which, it could be a trap.'

Marietta hesitated, her instincts clamouring at her. 'I trust him.' She began to descend.

'Marietta, no!' Dellara hissed at her. Marietta heard her issue a sigh before starting down the ice steps.

Deeper and deeper she went, searching in vain. Down to where the periwinkle-soft glow receded and the cold bit harder, fiercer.

She cast her gaze around until her fingers grew numb and her heart sickened at the treasures King Gelum was hoarding, a sadistic dragon grown fat from the spoils of that which did not belong to him. Bas-reliefs prised from ancient temples, statues far from home, weary with an age of lost hope and sadness, jewels in shapes and colours unknown to Marietta that ached to glimmer and shine under the love of their owner once more. Deeper still, Marietta discovered a fresh horror, terrible and haunting. Bones. 'He collected people in here, too,' she whispered.

'This is futile; we must leave at once, Marietta,' Dellara said. She nodded at the skeleton collapsed on the step below them. 'It does us no good to dwell on such things.'

Marietta looked at her and nodded. Dellara climbed back up the long spiral of stairs, Marietta at her heels, her back beginning to protest under the weight of Pirlipata's armour. Just below the trapdoor, a door had been mounted into the ice. A circular door the colour of frostberries, engraved with snow globes. She paused to consider it.

'Come on!' Dellara called.

Marietta often felt as if the prospect of multiple lands were like gazing at a shelf of snow globes, each one containing an entire world, the snow flurries falling to reveal dreams or nightmares within. She reached out and opened the door. Laughed to herself. Behind it were rows of hooks, and on each one, a key dangled. Golden keys that glittered with a magic of their own. She pocketed one, closed the door and hurried up to Dellara.

At the trapdoor, Dellara was funnelling her dagger-edged focus onto her wand, breathing deeply before snapping her gaze up and whipping the wand towards the trapdoor with fierce intent. Marietta felt the smooth caress of something wild and strange flit past her and their exit opened.

Chaos greeted them. Concealed from view by the throne, they peered out at the scene. Soldiers herded miniature reindeer, some revellers contributing their efforts as if it were just another facet of the immersive ball. Others guarded their frippery, wary of the reindeers' affinity to chew anything in sight. A wall of faceless guards barricaded the staircase, preventing access to the upper levels. Searching the crowd, Marietta unintentionally caught Claren's eye. She froze, a silent plea for him not to betray them on her lips. His face illuminated with mischief as he deposited a miniature reindeer into a makeshift pen, oblivious that another had attached itself to his skewed jacket.

Looking around, he gave Marietta a wink and an exaggerated nod that was decidedly unsubtle. Though she had been gladdened to sight Claren and not his pompous brother, who held more serious career aspirations for which he might have traded them. Or even Fin, who was as sweet natured as he was anxious and whose panic would have signposted their transgressions at once.

'Follow me,' Marietta said over her shoulder, sliding up under the king's throne and darting into the nearest snow globe. Kicking the trapdoor shut behind her, Dellara followed.

'Where in the stars have you been?' Pirlipata hissed at them from behind, giving Marietta a start. The princess rose from a carved ice-seat, the silken folds of her sunset dress gliding to the snow-dusted glass floor. 'You ought to have returned long before now, I—' She fell silent as a passing server scurried past, collecting chocolate globes back onto his tray before they were devoured by reindeer. 'I have been under a snowstorm of worry,' she said once he was out of earshot.

The reindeer had lessened in number since they'd entered the secret chamber. They were being escorted back to their stables in droves as time beat its relentless drum. 'We must make haste,' Marietta told Dellara with urgency.

Pirlipata threw her hands up. 'That is precisely my point.'

'Pass me the mouse.' Marietta held her palm out. 'I shall dance close enough to slip it back into his pocket.'

Dellara gave her a sceptical onceover. Marietta returned the look. 'Fine, fine.' Dellara passed it over. 'But ensure you're not caught in the act,' she added seriously. 'I've grown rather fond of you.'

Marietta hesitated. 'Oh, well, as it happens—'

'*Hurry.*' Dellara ushered her out of the snow globe.

Marietta approached King Gelum. She retained him in her sights, imagining he was one of the stags her father had instructed her to shoot on their country estate. She had refused once it had appeared in her crosshairs, drawn to its regal manner, its intrinsic grace. After Theodore had taken the killing shot himself, she had declined to accompany him on any more such outings.

King Gelum was conversing with Captain Legat. '—situation covered, seems most logical it was a harmless prank. I remain certain it was not an assassination attempt, not the least due to the Mistpointians not possessing sufficient imagination for the likes of this,' Legat was saying. 'You know better than to overestimate the fish-people,' he added in a lighter tone.

Amusement curled around the king's features. It evaporated upon him marking Marietta's presence. She smiled prettily, paying no heed to how the captain's presence toyed with her emotions. He remained at the king's side, standing tall in his impeccable livery, an arm tucked behind his back, the other hand a fingerbreadth from his sword. She felt his eyes on her.

'It would seem the reindeer have been returned to their stables,' she said without waiting to be granted permission to speak. 'I cannot help but notice your guests have become inflicted with restlessness.' King Gelum's eye wandered onto the gossiping, glamorous creatures that filled his halls in an enchantment of gowns, coated in a pall of boredom. Marietta pouted, the expression an unfamiliar configuration of lips and petulance. Legat coughed into a gloved fist. She studiously avoided his gaze. 'And I wish to dance,' she added, stealing closer to the king.

A spark of fury danced over him. The swords on his cape glinted. 'You dare to impose such demands upon your king?' His voice was low, punctured with ice.

Marietta's scarred feet throbbed. 'My apologies, it was a mere invitation.'

He stepped forward, his eyebrows pinching together as she failed to allow him space. His breath was rot-sweet when he spoke into her face. 'I am the king. I am not in need of an invitation. I shall take what I desire, when I desire it and you would do well to remember that.'

Marietta's throat grew too dry to form words. King Gelum considered her with a budding smile.

Dellara materialised at her side. 'I'm certain she intended you no disrespect, Your Majesty,' she said smoothly, pressing Marietta's hand. 'She's merely naïve to our ways.' Her hand left Marietta's, which was now empty. 'Perhaps you might see it in your generous nature to forgive her her impetuosity?' Dellara crept closer to the king and, fast as a snake strike, dropped the mouse back into his pocket, allowing her fingers to linger upon his side as she did so, accompanied by a syrupy smile.

King Gelum looked between them, suspicion gathering like a snow-storm. He removed Dellara's hand, dropping it without ceremony. His other hand dipped into his pocket. Marietta attempted to conjure an air of innocence around herself. She sensed Dellara projecting the same attitude beside her. The captain was expressionless, rigid, refusing to meet Marietta's eye when she stole a glance at him.

King Gelum raised a finger, pointed at both women. 'Do not take me for a fool. Confess your transgressions at once.' Their silence thickened. The king leered at Marietta. 'I have methods for persuading my girls to confide in me.' He stole closer, yanked a lock of her hair free from its curled coiffure. Rubbed it between his fingers. 'Soon I shall taste the sweetness of your secrets when they tumble from your lips as I take you apart, bit by bit.' Marietta closed her eyes, her horror amassing into a beast, strong enough to snap her. The king pulled her hair, making her stumble into his waiting arms, his hands framing her face, forcing her to look upon him, his smile wild and ecstatic. 'You'll look at me when I slice your skin open,' he whispered. 'When I take your bones in my hands.' Over his shoulder, she saw Legat's knuckles whiten on his hilt. Fear iced her veins.

'Guards!' King Gelum snapped his fingers and Marietta saw her fate uncoil in a tableau of masked guards, a sadistic king, her life spilling from her, one blade, one scream at a time. She gave a small shake of her head to Legat, who had paled to snow, revealing several inches of blade from his sword sheath. She refused to condemn his life along with hers.

Pirlipata entered Marietta's peripheral vision, storming towards the king in a swirl of sunsetting silks and slinking golden necklaces. 'King Gelum,' she declared with all the weight of her title.

He looked at her, narrowed his eyes at her imperiousness. 'Were you involved in whatever little conspiracy these two attempted?' His hands tightened on Marietta. 'My guards have informed me that you have formed an affectionate bond. Perhaps it would be preferable to keep you apart henceforth.' His smile was a dark, bloody promise. It chilled Marietta down to the marrow. 'If this one survives our playtime, that is.'

Eyeing the guards readied to seize her once King Gelum relinquished his hold on her, Marietta's nerves lurched. She could not bear being ripped from Pirlipata and Dellara; their strength resided in their unity. Fighting as one to engender their escape. When Marietta was in their midst, the endless night didn't feel as dark, the future as dreamless. They were her starlight, her guiding beacon.

Pirlipata stepped forward and Marietta silently pleaded with her; this was not part of the plan. Marietta and Dellara had chosen to be the ones to descend into the ice chamber so that, if caught, Pirlipata would not share the cost. She was the best of them. 'I have thought on the matter,' Pirlipata continued, disregarding the king's accusations, Marietta's shake of her head, Dellara's hand creeping for her concealed wand. 'And my answer is now affirmative.' Pirlipata's head was as high as if her armour had never been stripped from her. 'I shall accept your hand in marriage.'

Chapter Thirty-Nine

Marietta and Dellara were forgotten at once. King Gelum reached for Pirlipata, holding her hands in his. All the air rushed from Marietta's lungs, deflating her. She had kept hold of the little key to another world to surprise them with. Now that foolhardy notion might cost Pirlipata everything.

Dellara's eyes pooled into glistening, murderous black. 'No.' Her nails cut into her palms, bloodying them. She made to liberate her wand. Marietta snapped into action, making a bid for her hand before she could reveal it, but Dellara swept her aside, already striding for the king, her bloodlust writ upon her face. Then she stumbled. Legat had leapt forward and grasped her satin sash. 'I would advise you reconsider,' he said mildly, before leaning down to whisper at her. '—everything will have been for nothing,' Marietta heard on the tail end of his utterance.

King Gelum escorted Pirlipata to the room behind the throne room. The guards dispersed a little.

Marietta wrung her hands. Captain Legat, having released Dellara, came to her. 'He shall be wanting to discuss matters with her. Console yourself with the thought that no harm shall come to her now. Not now she has acquiesced to his demands,' he said in a lowered voice.

Marietta gave a terse nod, not trusting herself to speak. Dellara had been the last to emerge from those rooms, marked with a flotilla of fresh scars.

Dellara caught her attention. 'Tonight,' she whispered. 'We cannot afford to delay any longer.'

'I'm of the same persuasion,' Marietta said. Provided Pirlipata was returned to their suite. If she was relocated into quarters more suitable for the future queen of Everwood then they should have to liberate her first. Marietta refused to leave Pirlipata behind after she'd surrendered her freedom for them. After the king had laid bare his intentions towards Marietta, her heartbeats were measured. She glanced at Legat. His eyes lingered on her, his concern visible. A bolt of emotion fired through her. Perhaps this would be the final time she saw him.

After being escorted back to their suite by two sets of faceless guards, Marietta sat down, weary beyond her years.

Dellara wore deep tracks into the thick pile of the carpet as she paced from the frozen sugar wall back towards the centre of the suite, again and again. 'I knew this entire scheme was a grave mistake,' she muttered.

Marietta placed the golden key down on a table. 'I found one.' Dellara picked it up and examined it. 'And if I had not thought to surprise you both with it, we would be free already and Pirlipata—' She could not continue.

'Would be freezing in the Endless Forest in a ballgown,' Dellara said. 'As would we. Think not of it again.'

As Dellara's rage grew, so did Marietta's nerves, climbing in intensity until she felt her skin might vibrate off her back with worry. In an effort to keep her darker, bloodier thoughts at bay, Marietta settled for disrobing. The little snow globe scenes snowed and danced as she hung her gown in one of the armoires, exchanging it for a simple cashmere dress in a soft charcoal shade. She unwound the coils from her hair until it spilled down her back in an unrecognisable mess of wild, twisting locks that released snaps of marzipan-scent each time she moved. Pulling on petal-white satin slippers, she wandered over to the sugar wall. Not for the first time, she stared into the blackness beyond its glow. When she'd first arrived in Everwood, it had enticed her. A world of enchantments sparkling beneath a midnight sky. Now, it was an impossible promise.

'She ought to have returned by now.' Dellara came to stand at her side, her creamy voice stripped raw. 'Whyever did we abandon her to that monster? What if she isn't as safe as we presumed she would be?'

'Then we fight for her return.' Marietta pressed her hand, a quick brush, butterfly-wing-soft. Dellara held onto her. They stood there, hands clasped in each other's, the moment delicate as spun sugar.

The lock clicked, and Pirlipata strode through the door and opened her mouth to speak. Before she had tasted the first word, Dellara had crossed the suite and wrapped her in a fierce embrace.

'There is no need to worry on my account; I assure you I'm perfectly fine.' Pirlipata's smile perished the moment it crossed her lips. 'King Gelum has agreed to permit me one final night here as a favour to his future bride.' Her mouth twisted like she'd bitten into something sour. 'I need to forge my exit from this palace; I cannot, and will not, condemn myself to wedding that man.'

Dellara slid her wand out. 'Then let's make haste. I can ready us in a twitch of a moose's tail. And Marietta found a golden key; we can exit the palace from this room now.'

Snow-bright panic hit Marietta. She hadn't had the chance to return Legat's diary, buried in the armoire. To secure one last moment with him, carving out a time and space just for them and them alone. She had known it was imminent and yet still the ferocity of her feelings stunned her. 'I need to see him one last time,' she whispered. 'I need to say goodbye.'

Dellara stared at her. 'Have you rotted your brain? You absolutely cannot meet him, least of all this very moment. Just when everything we — you've — worked tirelessly for is within our grasp, you wish to jeopardise it all for the sake of him?'

Pirlipata looked quizzical. 'Say goodbye to whom?' She touched Marietta's shoulder in concern.

Dellara heaved a colossal sigh. 'Shall I allow you one guess? She's grown attached to the captain.' Dellara raised her eyes as if seeking solace from the stars.

'Marietta, we ought to leave at the soonest opportunity. Is it imperative that you seek out this farewell?' Pirlipata asked.

Marietta wished it wasn't. 'I'm very sorry,' she said, her guilt hot and sticky. 'I am all too aware of what a great inconvenience it would be. Yet if I did not, I know in my soul that I would regret it. It would haunt me. Just a simple farewell, a final moment is all that I ask.'

'Then you must go. We shall change our clothes and prepare before your return. Go and come back at once.' Pirlipata smiled then. 'And may your luck taste sweet.'

'Has sugar-rot laid siege to both your minds?' They looked at Dellara. She held her hands wide. 'We're locked inside this suite. Hence the entire point of our escape. How do you expect Marietta to leave, much less locate the captain?'

Pirlipata's smile deepened with pleasure.

'She has displeased me. I demand that you escort her to your captain and head of the King's Army at once to be rightfully punished.' Pirlipata folded her arms and stared at the faceless guards who had unlocked the door to answer her command.

Expressionless as ever, they didn't seek guidance from each other. The slight tilt to their heads was all that unbalanced the illusion of control.

'Or I shall report you both to King Gelum on account of disobeying your future queen,' she added.

They launched into action. One removed Marietta from the suite, the other locking Pirlipata and Dellara back inside. She caught a final, fleeting glance of their faces, hoped her plan wouldn't collapse in on itself, and allowed herself to be marched up the spiral. The higher they ascended, the smaller the steps grew, the greater the plummet down to the throne room, a distant jewel sparkling fathoms below. Her stomach swirled with vertigo. She had never been taken to this height before. Perhaps they had decided against escorting her to Legat and she was nearing some unknown destination instead. Perhaps they would push her from the tip and she would share Lev's fate.

Door upon door upon door. Some shuddered, bolted closed with iron chains, preventing whatever manner of creature reigned in those worlds from creeping through. Others glittered, the air surrounding them tasting sweeter and wild. Marietta hesitated before one such door, an irresistible urge curling her fingers, tempting her to open it. The guard pushed her, forcing her onwards. A few steps more and the urge suddenly relinquished her from its noxious grasp.

The faceless guard halted without warning, rapped on a small door.

'You may enter,' she heard Legat command with relief strong enough to buckle her knees. It had been a most trying day. And the greatest ordeal remained to be tackled. The guard shoved her inside and shut the door behind her. She heard his boots recede down the stairs, sure in his knowledge that Marietta was due to receive the punishment she deserved and washing his hands of her. She was grateful that the doors in this world were thick and impervious to sound; it seemed eavesdropping was as foreign a concept as beds were.

She turned to a startled Legat. A scarlet stain spread up her neck upon realising she had been led to his private rooms.

Chapter Forty

It was a small room nestled within the curve of the frozen sugar wall, a pale moon-glow blue at this height. To one side resided a thick carpet with large navy cushions mountained atop, a battered notebook and quill beside it. A single garnet chaise perched next to the wall. Steam drifted through an open arch, cut into rock sugar, a small bathing pool visible beyond.

'Marietta?' Legat leapt up from his chaise. 'What are you doing here?' Still in his trousers and boots, his shirt was open, revealing glimpses of his muscular chest.

'I'm leaving,' she said breathlessly. 'I'm leaving tonight. I ought to have gone by now yet something held me back.' Why had she not departed already? This was sheer idiocy. Her laugh was too bright, her hopes tinged with madness. 'I simply could not leave without seeing you one last time.'

The glow of the wall cast a soft illuminance on Legat as he approached her. 'Then this is goodbye.'

'I cannot stay here, you have been all too aware of that from the start,' she whispered as he came to a stop, his hand grazing her arm. 'Staying here would be the end of me.'

'I know.' The golden flecks in his irises burnt brighter as he ran a hand through his hair, dwelling on her. 'The stars have gifted you with such beautiful eyes,' he murmured. 'Blue as the rarest ice, pools I would willingly drown in.'

She bit her lip. His gaze swept down to her mouth and her breath caught. 'I wish you could accompany me. Leave this palace and its cruelty behind. The thought of you remaining, of not knowing what might happen to you, torments me.' Her voice cracked. It was unthinkable to realise that once she had departed Everwood, she would thus relinquish all knowledge of Legat.

He stepped towards her, rested his hands on her arms. 'You must not dwell on such things. I am needed here and you cannot stay. Even if I were to surrender my command of the rebellion, where would I go? Return with you to your world? I could never carve out a life for myself there. And I should never forgive myself if I were the reason you ceased pursuing a life of your own. To see you dance is to witness something truly magical. You dream brighter than anyone I've ever met, Marietta, and it is a thing of beauty. Promise me you will not lose that for anything, anyone across the worlds.' His hands tightened on her arms. Drew her closer to him. 'Promise me.'

'I promise. Someone wise once told me it was in the stars.' She retrieved his diary from her pocket. 'Your words have given me strength when I most needed them.'

His smile warmed her.

'Tell me which you seek when you turn your gaze skywards,' she said softly.

He took his diary back. 'I favour Hethell, the scribe, and her army of writers. So called as nothing contains more power than words. The truth is a sword mightier than any weapon.'

Marietta looked up at him. 'I would share the world with you if I could.'

'And I you.'

His eyes burnt into hers. She stood there, waiting. Each second seemed to last an eternity. He was close enough to reach out and close that chasm between them.

'If the king finds out I've touched you—' His voice husked away into nothing, his words tasting of secret promises, heady and irresistible as chocolate.

'He won't,' Marietta whispered.

The door slammed open.

'Captain, the king requires your presence in—' Claren halted in the doorframe. He looked at Legat and Marietta as if the vision might dissipate the harder he stared at it before regaining his senses and stepping into the room, swiftly closing the door behind himself.

Legat stood to attention, buttoning his shirt in haste. 'Have you so little respect to come bursting in here in such a manner?'

Scarletting, Marietta smoothed her hair, attempting to smooth her fractured composure together.

Claren coughed. Covered it with a fist that failed to hide the twitching corners of his mouth as he retrieved the captain's jacket from behind the desk. 'I believe this is what you're looking for?' he asked wryly. Captain Legat yanked it from his hand with a sharp look. 'I'll escort you back,' Claren told Marietta.

Legat shrugged his jacket on. 'That shall not be necessary,' he said at once.

Claren looked at him. 'How many times have the two of you been seen together? We all heard the palace gossip that reigned for a month after that dance.' He hesitated then. 'I'll give you a moment alone.'

'Fine.' Legat finished fixing his jacket, in full livery once more as he stood before Marietta.

Claren closed the door behind himself.

Legat's eyes lingered on hers. She painted them in her memory;

their butterscotch shade, how they softened when he gazed at her, the flecks of gold in his irises that the light was so fond of toying with. He reached for her hand and held it between his. 'I shall never forget you.'

'Nor I you,' she whispered, looking up at him, her throat thick. 'Goodbye, Captain Legat.'

His thumb stroked a path down her hand, his eyes afire. 'Farewell, my wanderer,' he murmured.

She stood on demi-pointe and pressed her lips against his soft, full mouth. He started and she stepped back, mortified at her own forwardness. 'Forgive me,' she said, 'I was under the impression—'

Legat took her in his arms and kissed her. It resembled nothing of the gentle kisses she had been imagining. It was wild and raw and passionate. Swept her away on a wave of longing as she pressed the length of her body against his, Legat holding her there tightly.

Claren re-entered. 'As much as I hate to hasten you, we have a matter of urgency to attend to, captain.'

Legat tore himself away from Marietta to glance at Claren with a sudden frown. He pushed the door back open. Shouts echoed up the staircase.

A curl of scarlet ribbon drifted down the core of the palace.

Marietta inhaled. 'Is that—'

'We're receiving reports from the town, captain. It appears the ice prison is on the brink of collapse. The red rebellion has galvanised the Everwoodians and they are dismantling it, block by block.'

Marietta followed Legat and Claren onto the staircase. A second scarlet curl fell. It fluttered past Marietta's face from above. When she looked up, the air was littered with falling ribbons.

Legat's smile looked like freedom.

Claren looked uncertain. 'Captain? What are your orders?'

'The truth of the matter is that a king such as Gelum fails to pay attention to the people whom he deems lower than him. Insignificant. Even when they number far greater than the total sum of his soldiers and guards. And that is a fatal mistake,' Legat said. His smile grew.

And what started as a whisper became a roar. *Red for the blood we'll spill in the streets, red for the rebellion.*

Scarlet ribbons snowed down as hordes of people stormed down the staircase. Each server that had been a continuous, demanded, nameless presence, each of the sugarers and pâtissiers and chocolatiers that had devoted hours into crafting the king's whims, each forgotten maid and cleaner. Anyone who had faded into one anonymous background that kept the palace functioning was rushing down the spiral. Clanging pans and brooms and serving trays, they raised their voices, uniting in a deafening chant of revolution.

Legat pulled Marietta out of their path. Claren gripped his sword hilt, his uncertainty growing.

Below, the faceless guards let loose a war cry. The first ranks of palace staff met the guards in a collision that resonated across the ice.

'You must leave, now,' Legat told Marietta. 'Claren, see her safely back to her suite.' He bent to kiss her cheek. 'I presume you have a plan,' he whispered into her ear. 'Do not delay, make your escape at once.'

'But will you—'

Legat's eyes were molten fire, burning a path straight to her heart. 'Do not concern yourself with me; this is what I have been awaiting. Leave while you can and do not look back. And Marietta? It is in the stars that we shall meet again.'

Marietta watched the captain depart with a heavy, aching heart.

Claren escorted Marietta to her suite door. A single faceless guard remained on watch.

'Do take care, Claren,' she said, surprising them both and squeezing his hand. 'Only you can know what is in your heart. Choose wisely.'

'Marietta?' Pirlipata asked softly as the door opened.

Marietta entered to the two women stood before her. 'It has begun. The red rebellion,' she said.

Dellara wore all black. Form-fitting black pin-striped trousers, black bustier and a black military-style jacket. At her side, Pirlipata blazed like a glorious sunset in her crimson armour, broadsword in hand. They were a pair of avenging angels, made carnate.

'Get changed and take what you want, provided you can carry it,' Dellara said. 'We must leave at once.'

Marietta located the ballet dress she had worn on first discovering Everwood. It seemed simpler now, more modest than the extravagant pieces of art she'd become accustomed to. Stranger still, it smelt musty. A reminder of the time she'd spent away from her world. The notion of returning felt odd. Before she could ponder the reason, Dellara appeared at her side, wrinkling her nose at her dress and insisting she wear a vanilla and marzipan-scented petticoat, lustrous with magic, beneath it. Marietta added a velvet cloak for warmth, in deep claret in celebration of the red rebellion. She added a little pointed scarlet hat, reminiscent of a *bonnet de la Liberté*, for luck. Finally, she laced up her ivory satin pointe shoes, battered from the stories they'd danced through.

'Will those suffice for the Endless Forest?' Pirlipata asked.

'Not for long but I wish to leave Everwood as I entered it,' Marietta said.

'Then it is time to make your wish come true.' Dellara held up the golden key.

'One moment.' Pirlipata ripped her golden clothes out of her armoire and knocked on the door. The faceless guard opened it. Before he could react, she tossed the clothes out into the hollow centre of the palace. They floated down in a glittering rain of riches.

'A rightful ending,' Dellara said, watching with Marietta.

'No, a fresh life.' Pirlipata gestured at the hands that reached out to grab the sparkling dresses. 'Each gown shall feed a family for a moontide.'

'Inside.' The faceless guard made to grab Pirlipata. Marietta's heart stuttered. But Pirlipata spun around deftly and unsheathed her broadsword, cleaving him in two. Dellara, hand on wand, halted. Pirlipata's sword had revealed the guard's core of wood and machinery, gleaming metalwork where organs should have rested.

'They were never human,' Marietta said. 'No wonder they possessed such brutish strength.' It brought to mind Drosselmeier's mechanical set of soldiers he had gifted Frederick.

'And unwavering loyalty to King Gelum,' Pirlipata added grimly.

The three women looked down at the wild, bloodthirsty fray. Marietta felt lost; she had neither the necessary magic nor training with which to survive a battle. All those times her father had instructed she study this strategic campaign or that warfare of old, she had never once imagined the resulting carnage that would have ensued. Seeing, hearing and smelling it was a vastly different affair and she wondered how anyone could ever find intelligence in the machinations of bloodshed.

With a crash that echoed to the heavens, the throne room doors slammed open. A wave of Everwoodians clad in scarlet poured in. Robess led the charge, her sword held high. 'To the rebellion!'

Marietta searched for Legat amid the throne room, painted in violence. It was to no avail.

'Come, Marietta,' Pirlipata said. 'It is time.'

Marietta gave her a terse nod. She took a deep breath in an attempt to steady her nerves. This was what she had sought since the king had entrapped her, to claw her way free from him. From this world that Drosselmeier had trapped her within. She yearned to set sight on Frederick and her ballet studio. Besides which, there were things that needed to be said. Other freedoms to chart.

'No longer shall we be caged in ice, beholden to a king's wrath,' Pirlipata said. 'Cut us free, Dellara.'

Dellara reached a hand to Pirlipata who held it, extending her other hand to Marietta. Three women interlinked as one chain.

'This key shall take us wherever we so desire. We must all keep our thoughts on Everwood for the magic to transport us directly into the town,' Dellara warned them, holding the key before her. It was slim and golden with mice tails curling together to form an ornate handle. Dellara pushed it forward into an invisible seam in the air and twisted.

Nothing came to pass. Marietta frowned, her grip slackening. 'Perhaps—'

'Hold on,' Dellara shouted. A faint wind whirled past Marietta's ears, gossamer-fine and seductive, whispering of other lands, other worlds, of all the places she might see and adore.

'Keep your thoughts on Everwood,' Dellara repeated, more urgently.

Marietta filled her head with visions of the picture-perfect little town, shining cosily under dark skies and wrapped in a blanket of snow. Something tugged at her stomach and in the next breath, the three of them were whisked off their feet and into the time-rippling space between worlds.

When they had stopped twisting through the fabric of space and time, Marietta opened her eyes once more.

The crisp scent of snow and fir and frozen sugar welcomed them. Everwood stood in the valley before them, hemmed in by ice cliffs and frozen waterfalls, where starlight dripped from above. The velvet sky swam in endless constellations that Marietta found she could put names to now. Liketh's Lantern, the Great Moose, the Goblin's Smile. She might be a lost girl, far from home, but for the first time in her life, she felt the night air on her face with a sense of deep freedom. Being free of all constraints, societal or physical, was a particularly delicious feeling.

ACT TWO

But Godfather Drosselmeier, with a strange smile, took little Marie onto his lap, and said in a softer tone than he was ever heard to speak in before: 'Ah, dear Marie, more power is given to you than to me, or to the rest of us. You, like Pirlipat, were born a princess, for you reign in a bright and beautiful kingdom. But you will suffer if you take the part of the poor misshapen Nutcracker, for the Mouse King watches for him at every hole and corner.'

——E.T.A. HOFFMANN, THE NUTCRACKER

Chapter Forty-One

Everwood was set a-glittering with celebration.

'Between one event or another, I had almost forgotten what a darling little place this is,' Marietta said, drinking it in.

Dellara slowed the moose to a casual trot. They had purloined a moose-drawn sleigh, abandoned by faceless guards, standing beside the ice-bridge to which the golden key had transported them. Now they were journeying through Everwood in it, knowing it would whisk them away to the Endless Forest faster and in more comfort than if they'd taken the route on foot. First, they would bid farewell to Marietta, then Pirlipata would take it east, home to Crackatuck.

A pair of men with twirled white beards and forest-green pointed hats played a jangling melody on brass instruments. Nearby a group of children were chanting: *The ice prison has fallen!*

'Why, would you look at that.' Pirlipata smiled. 'It seems this rebellion was fated to win back the heart of the kingdom.'

'Queen Altina's star will shine brighter tonight; she will be glad to see peace and goodwill restored in her kingdom,' Dellara said. 'The air is thick with the most powerful magic tonight.' Marietta glanced at her and she added, 'Hope.'

As they made their way through the town, scarlet ribbon-curls littered the marzipan cobblestones. People danced and skated through the streets, clinking together tall goblets of molten chocolate. Vendors sold fairy cakes; tiny cakes crowned with a glittering sugar fairy. Red sparkles shot out from their tiny chocolate wands, dusting everyone with twinkling flecks. Dellara guided the sleigh past gingerbread chalets with sloping roofs and candy-cane buildings with whipped-cream roofs, collecting bits and pieces of the parade of festivities until their sleigh shimmered as brightly as one of Dellara's gowns.

Then the moose tugged them onward and across a smaller snow bridge to the great fir forest beyond. The sleigh runners cut fresh tracks through the pristine snow, sweeping them out further into the forest, the noise of the celebration falling away, leaving them in silence. It was hard to forage for words when they all knew what was to come. Marietta pulled the blanket higher over the three of them, sharing the front bench in the sleigh. The forest air was freezing after they'd been indulged with the warming enchantments swirling about the palace.

The firs grew thicker, crowding together in an effort to blot the starlight. Large lanterns affixed to the sleigh illuminated their way, creating puddles of blackness where their reach ended. Soon it grew difficult to navigate the sleigh through the trees.

'I am not a practised hand at this,' Dellara admitted after a while, bringing the moose to a stop. 'From here we go on foot.' She leapt from the sleigh and set about unharnessing the moose. 'It seems we're not the only ones who have found our freedom tonight,' she murmured to the great, placid animals.

Marietta exited the sleigh with trepidation, recalling the shadows that had stalked her through the forest on her arrival. How they had crept down her throat, constricting her chest corset-tight, disorientating her as if she'd been set upon by malignant spirits attempting to lead her astray. But she was not the same woman she had been then.

Pirlipata kept a hand on her sword hilt as they walked deeper into the forest.

Snow crunching beneath their feet, breaths crystallising, they soon lost sight of the sleigh. Mist slithered between the trunks and Marietta eyed it but the shadows kept their distance. This time, she did not hear the whispers. This time, she heard something else instead.

Dellara stilled. 'What was that?' Her hand vanished beneath her cloak, reappearing with her wand.

Marietta halted, listening to the voices wending through the forest. It sounded as if several persons were headed in their direction. Pirlipata eased her sword from its hilt, holding it before her as they grew closer.

The forest came alive with the sound of marching.

'The king must be making his own exit tonight,' Pirlipata said grimly. 'He must have fled before the rebellion took the palace.'

Dellara pointed her wand before her. 'I shall eliminate him and his guards until there is nothing left for the stars to claim.'

Marietta felt helpless. In such a situation she was a liability. Her nerves swelled as the sound of marching swelled, filling the forest before it eerily vanished. She braced herself for what was to come, Dellara and Pirlipata standing before her as she was the sole woman without a weapon.

Yet it was behind her that King Gelum stepped out of the firs.

Faceless guards began to materialise one by one, vultures clad in livery, appearing between the silent trees. Until the king's entire contingent of guards formed a ring around the three women.

Dellara shoved Marietta aside as King Gelum stared at her. 'To think you believed I had not known of your transgressions.' A film had descended over the king's eyes as if he were surveying them through a thin layer of ice, hard and impervious. As conscience-deprived as his frozen heart.

Marietta's pulse skittered with fear. Suddenly she felt silly for ever believing they could escape the king's clutches, flee his sugar-rotted palace and dance with freedom.

Dellara's eyes were a solid wall of black, one hand clenching her wand as she slowly raised it.

Tension hardened and swords pointed. Faceless guards circled Dellara, their wariness plain to see. She emitted a guttural snarl, reminding them all she was cut from a fiercer world, held a power as ancient as starlight.

'No, I was aware,' the king said. 'You and the captain ought to have known the extent of my reach. It is not just the Crackatians I hold in the palm of my hand.'

Pirlipata drew herself up to her full height, her anger a tangible blaze. 'You shall never hold Crackatuck,' she said, ignoring the guards surrounding her.

King Gelum's smile was warped. Cruel. 'I know, too, of why you acquiesced to wed me. Yet it is of no matter; I shall obtain your vow if I have to carve it from you myself. This shall not be the first rebellion I have quashed. Everwood has never known such a powerful king as I. With all the military might and riches at my disposal, I shall reclaim my kingdom before winter has ended its reign.'

'What riches?' Pirlipata asked. 'Everwood has never suffered such an economic deficit since you murdered your way onto the throne. Toying with the economy, funnelling ever higher taxes into your extravagant affairs. Citizens can no longer afford the imported water from Mistpoint or the ever-rising prices of melting charms and are succumbing to the mineral sickness in droves. Children are dying. Your rule has been a long dark winter but the sun is finally rising. Even your soldiers have deserted you in favour of the rebellion.' She raised her broadsword.

King Gelum suddenly wrenched Marietta away from Dellara and Pirlipata. A blade she hadn't known he'd carried was pressed against her throat. 'I can slit her throat faster than you can draw that wand,' he growled at Dellara. 'Throw it down.' His blade sliced deeper and Marietta stifled a gasp. Blood slid down her neck in a slick path. 'You too, my little princess,' he told Pirlipata.

Pirlipata laid her sword on the forest floor.

'No,' Marietta whispered as she was restrained.

Still Dellara refused to yield. Her eyes a seething tangle of shadows, she held her wand and raised the tip. The point of the king's blade pierced deeper, coaxing another flood of bloody tears from Marietta's throat. Gritting her teeth, she arched her back against the king in an evasion of his knife. He the Von Rothbart to her Odette, their pas de deux a dance of bloodlust.

Dellara relinquished her wand. She was the last to be seized and when she fell to her knees, something deep within Marietta guttered and died.

King Gelum's blade inched deeper. Marietta's last breath withered. She knew he would kill her and she longed to close her eyes against it yet the notion of her last sight being an all-consuming blackness before she slid into the great unknown was one which she could not abide. She kept them open and locked on Dellara and Pirlipata. Watched their anger swell and spill over into helplessness. She stifled a sob.

'That palace belongs to me. Everwood belongs to me. Soon the entirety of Celesta shall be ushered under my rule, too.' King Gelum's voice was tinged with madness, his breath cool on Marietta's ear. He had murdered the last obstacles to his throne in an icy rage. It seemed she was to be next. Her death ushering in a new age of his rule.

Chapter Forty-Two

Pinned against the king at dagger-point, Marietta couldn't draw breath, couldn't contemplate what to do. Panic welled, deep and limitless.

With a crunch of snow, three figures burst from the forest, entering the fray.

Marietta's eyes immediately fell on Legat. She had not thought she would ever see him again. Her heart splintered; was this what he had meant by it being in the stars for them to meet again? For him to witness her death? What unspeakable cruelty that she could not reach out to him, to feel his touch one last time. Flanked by Claren and Fin, he slowed, taking measure of the situation at once.

'Ah, look who has come to join us!' King Gelum's grasp tightened on Marietta. She stifled a wince. 'If you resist surrender, her blood shall be on your hands,' he said.

Legat laid his sword down. His face pale as snow, his eyes trained on Marietta. At the blade on her throat. 'If you do not release her, I vow to spend forevermore hunting you. Until winter has melted away and I am but a speck of light in the skies of a night-time.'

King Gelum's laugh echoed through Marietta. 'It gladdens my heart that you shall witness her death. A fitting end to a traitorous tale.'

Guards seized Legat, forcing him down onto his knees before the king. Claren and Fin were secured alongside him.

Marietta drew the ragged scraps of her courage around her like a shield. This was but a game of chess. A game of wills and control and power. And King Gelum may have been the king but kings were the weakest piece on the board. Nothing more than a figurehead. One that craved power. He had demanded Marietta dance at his command, captured Pirlipata when she'd rejected him and taken Dellara as punishment for demonstrating a power greater than his. King Gelum had murdered, tortured and bribed his path to the palace, utilising fear and pain as tools with which he might command authority. Yet he lacked respect or deference. Marietta looked at the king, who was waiting for her to be shadowed in fear, to break and shatter under his will.

'I know your greatest fear,' she whispered. His grasp on the dagger loosened. Marietta raised her voice. 'Challenge him, Legat.'

Legat met her eyes. The air between them ran thick with a thousand things unsaid. She repeated, 'Challenge him.'

Captain Legat drew his head up high and addressed everyone in the small snowy clearing, his voice filled with his command. 'King Gelum, I challenge you to a duel.'

King Gelum flung Marietta away from him. She gasped, her throat searing as a faceless guard caught her, holding her arms behind her back. The corner of the king's mouth lifted in a facsimile of a smile. 'Has sugar-rot laid siege to your brain? You cannot challenge me to a duel, I am your king.'

Legat surveyed him coolly. 'It had not occurred to me that you might fear accepting. I had believed a king such as yourself would be a most powerful leader. Not hiding behind death threats and executions. Such is the path of a lesser king. A coward at heart.'

King Gelum glared at him. 'I have been trained by the finest, most proficient warriors that this world, among many others, has to offer.

If I so choose to debase myself by engaging in a duel, I assure you that I would not lose.'

Fin's chin was high, the twitch in his fingers concealed behind his back, where only Marietta could see. 'Easy words to claim when we have no way of verifying them.'

Away from the palace, King Gelum's power was weakened. This was the tipping point that might restore Everwood to its former glory. The king's last stand; the rebellion had overthrown his rule and the ice beneath him was faltering. Marietta wanted it to crack.

'You're a coward,' Dellara drawled. 'You know it and we know it. A coward lazing about his throne, hosting balls and indulging himself and stealing women in order to avoid rejection. You may pretend otherwise, hiding behind your dwindling gold and throne and crown, but we see it. We all see it.'

The atmosphere stultified, thickening into a potent cauldron of bated breaths and brewing tension.

The king threw his cloak down on the snow. 'If you so desire a duel then you shall have one. And after I have decimated you, I will take the lives of everyone you've ever cared about, ever loved.' His gaze slid onto Marietta and, his onyx eyes locked on hers, he approached the captain, whispered something into Legat's ear that made the captain's spine stiffen, his pupils dilate, his glance at Marietta thick with fears that stalked the darkest, starless hours of the night.

The faceless guards surrounded King Gelum and his captain.

Legat's sword was returned. The king wielded his own, the Mus family crest of mice engraved in the jewel-studded hilt. Yet Starhunter, Legat's father's sword, shone brighter. Marietta watched from behind the guards, Dellara and Pirlipata at her sides, the three of them still restrained. Claren and Fin bore the same situation further along. Marietta bit the inside of her cheek to steady her nerves and present an assuring face each time Legat glanced at her, drawing strength from her support. After all, this had been her idea.

Slow chanting emanated from behind the smooth masks of the faceless guards, their hidden voices deep and eerie. In a sudden, bone-jarring clash, King Gelum and Legat met. Two Titans at war, their battle echoing across worlds.

King Gelum's footwork was elaborate, embroidering his steps onto the frozen forest floor. Legat's was simple, enabling him to be faster and more direct, stepping through the king's defences time and again. Yet he failed to land a single blow. His sword a metallic blur, everywhere Legat ventured, the king parried. Marietta's encouraging smile froze. It appeared the king hadn't been exaggerating about his skills. On it flew, the pair locked in an endless loop of parrying and striking, fighting to attain the most advantageous position. Slicing and cutting through the sugared air. Several blows came whisper-close to bloodletting. The thin scrape along Legat's forearm, the scratch that had flayed open the king's silk shirt.

The sole noise the continued chanting and crash of blades, the duel skulked on. Pirlipata managed to reach out and grasp Marietta's hand, the guards' restraints relaxing as the duel sucked their attention away from the women.

'Never fear, he shall survive. They call that sword Starhunter for it dispatches those it battles with ease, the stars hunting his opponents to join the farthest, dimmest constellations,' she told Marietta, who squeezed her fingers back, not daring herself to speak.

It was relentless, the king every bit as skilled as Legat. Marietta tracked their movements, maintaining an effort to keep her darkest, heart-shattering thoughts at bay. A few minutes later, she saw it. The King's arm shook. It was beginning to tire under the weight of his sword. King Gelum might have possessed the necessary gold with which to hire the finest tutors in swordsmanship but his hours of fighting were limited to those private lessons. His life of luxury had not equipped him for battle. Marietta turned her attention back to Legat whose arm remained steady, his aim true and his defence strong.

Legat delivered a heavy blow but King Gelum jerked his head just in time and it skimmed the air beside him.

All Legat's focus was trained on the king, his senses honed on anticipating the following move. Which was why he failed to see the boot swiping out at his ankles. It sent him crashing to the ground. Stunned, he failed to roll out of the path of the king's arcing blade. It tore a bright, crimson line down his torso. Marietta clasped a hand to her mouth as Legat gasped and gritted his teeth. It took an effort for him to rise, picking up his sword and ducking out from under the king's attack.

Marietta saw flames. It was clear to all witnessing that Legat would now not emerge victorious. 'We must act,' she said quietly.

Dellara looked across at her. 'You have my agreement.'

Struggling to form a coherent thought, let alone one that might swell and solidify into an idea, Marietta suppressed a cry when Legat was felled for a second time. King Gelum took the opportunity to execute another gouging blow. It elicited a cry of pain from Legat. His sword skidded across the snow into a patch of chanting faceless guards who kicked it back at him. The pommel struck his lacerated chest. His eyes closed for a beat too long. Her brain sticky with panic, her rage coating the forest in a bitter crimson wash, Marietta watched her love being broken before her eyes.

Taking advantage of the guards' distraction, she reached down and untied one of her pointe shoes.

Legat crawled towards his sword, his blood turning the snow

a pale pink. He attempted to stand but his exhaustion felled him. Marietta's fingers tightened around her ballet shoe.

King Gelum's arrogant smile was already edged with triumph as he strolled towards Legat and kicked him in the stomach, flipping him over onto his back. Legat groaned, holding his bleeding side with one hand and searching for his sword with the other. King Gelum's laugh was high, his gaze lingering upon the wounds he'd inflicted. He reached out with his sword and stroked Legat's torn chest with the tip.

Marietta drew her arm back. She threw the ballet shoe with more force than she had ever exerted in her lifetime. Sent it flying, desiring nothing more than to knock the sadistic delight from the king's face, consequences be damned. To allow Legat a brief moment in which to pierce the king's heart and end this infernal duel. Her muscles screaming with effort, the shoe soared through the ring and knocked the king off his pedestal of conceit and onto the floor.

Where he lay, still.

The world hung, a heavy pendulum teetering at the edge.

Dellara launched herself at the faceless guard who had taken possession of her wand and seized it back.

Marietta stared at the king's immobile body, her thoughts a discordant harmony. 'Have I—'

'Fear not, you haven't stained your starname with murder just yet.' Dellara appeared at the king's side. A deliciously wicked smile curved her lips. 'But he's mine now.' She pointed her wand at the king before any of the guards could think to move. His body vanished.

The pendulum swung down. Chaos spilt in its wake.

Pirlipata snatched back her sword. She arced it through the air, dispatching guard after guard to darkness, severing their heads from their bodies and piercing that place where their hearts ought to have resided. Their mechanisms sparked and whirred as they crashed to the floor. Claren and Fin followed suit, as did Dellara, wielding her wand with a vengeance.

Marietta ran to Legat's side.

The sight of his torn and slashed skin filled her with murderous wrath and deep, abiding fear. She ripped her velvet cloak off, pressed it to the worst of his wounds. But his lifeblood trickled through her fingers like sugar.

'Do not worry,' Legat told her, his smile reassuring even as his fate had taken a cruel twist, Atropos reaching out with her shears to clip his thread of life. If it hadn't been for her, he would never have drawn the goddess's eye. 'I would willingly die for the freedom of Everwood. To atone for my past mistakes. For you to find your way home.'

'No,' she whispered. 'Hold on.'

'Look,' he said, his voice withering to a husk. 'We won.'

Marietta looked back as the last of the faceless guards was brought to an end.

Dellara appeared at her side. 'I cannot heal him,' she said gravely as they surveyed Legat's injuries. 'I do not possess that kind of power. It is easy to take a life. Fetching one back from the brink of the night sky requires a greater magic. The stars are hungry once they've tasted a fresh soul. But I can grant him justice.' She stood, holding her wand and surveying the dismembered guards, spread over the snow. Her smile cut wider and King Gelum materialised before them all.

Apoplectic, his face red, his hair wind-worn, the king stormed towards Dellara. Pirlipata, Claren and Fin's swords flew up. Dellara bared her sharpened teeth as she tutted at the king, shaking her wand at him as if he were a misbehaving child. Catching sight of it, he paled and cast an eye about himself.

Shock flitted across his face at the fate his guards had met. Ousted by raw terror as he turned back to Dellara. 'Spare me, I beg of you,' he whispered, slipping on a guard's lost cog and falling to his knees with a whimper.

Dellara slowly rolled her sleeves up, revealing the torture he had inflicted on her moontide after moontide. The king backed away, sliding across his fallen army's broken mechanisms. 'No no no no, have mercy. Please.'

Dellara tilted her head to one side, considering his plea. She caressed her wand. 'I shall grant you mercy,' she said at last. King Gelum relaxed. 'The mercy of a swift death,' she added.

Registering her words, his head jerked up, panic setting in as he opened his mouth to either protest or scream. Which, couldn't be determined. Before he uttered either, Dellara's wand came tearing down and King Gelum was cleaved in two.

The forest rang with silence.

Claren and Pirlipata rushed to Marietta's side to help staunch Legat's wounds. His blood stained the snow. It rattled Marietta's heart.

Fin cleared his throat. 'I know this is not the time but I feel I must remind you that King Gelum altered the laws to allow for his murder of King Elter and Queen Altina.'

Pirlipata looked up. 'Altered them in which way?'

'As it happens, the individual who deposes the ruler is free to seize their crown, throne and kingdom,' Fin said.

One by one, their eyes fell on Dellara.

Her pointed teeth glittered. 'I do believe you mean queendom.'

Chapter Forty-Three

A soft flicker of blue ran over Marietta's face. Pale as the frozen blue heart of a glacier. It flitted away to be replaced with shards of emerald green. She looked up. Lights were dancing across the sky, turning the forest into a cave of glimmering starlight. It tasted like magic, wild and strange and heady.

'The Star Lights,' Dellara said, her victory falling away to wonderment as she looked up. 'Queen Altina is shining brighter than ever tonight. It must have been her that sent them our way.'

'She knows we won her land back,' Pirlipata said, laying a hand on Dellara's arm.

Both turned to Marietta. 'Legend has it the Star Lights are sent in times of war by the kings and queens that watch down on us. It is said that the last time the Star Lights swept over the skies, they healed an entire army in gratitude,' Dellara said.

Legat groaned in Marietta's arms and she looked down, her hope fragile and glitter-bright. She peeled back her cloak to check his wound. Fresh skin had blossomed over his lacerations, the skin knitting back together once more.

He opened his eyes. 'You were hurt,' he said, reaching a hand out to her sliced throat. His voice was husky, his eyes sliding in and out of focus.

She smiled, her heart a staccato beat at seeing him, hearing him, tangible and solid and alive. 'You're one to talk.'

Claren exhaled. 'You gave us a fright there, captain.' At his side, Fin exchanged a smile with Marietta.

Legat's eyes lost their glassy finish and focused on Marietta. The magic that swept wild and wondrously through the forest was healing him. Above, the playful lights danced in all their rich soul-singing colours. Marietta watched them with Legat, having never thought she might attain the chance to glimpse the Northern Lights for herself since they only deigned to appear in the coldest, farthest reaches of her world. Her world. She must be close to her door now. To the end of her story in Everwood.

'Come back to me,' Legat said softly, his fingers encircling her hand, his steady warmth anchoring her. 'The future belongs to us once more.'

Yet even as the words departed his lips, Marietta tasted the impossibility they contained. 'One in which we shall not be together.'

Legat's smile was born of sadness. She stifled his next words with her lips meeting his. Sweet and soft with a thousand regrets, she longed to lock the moment away in a snow globe where she might relive it again and again. 'For a while there I feared you might never kiss me again,' she said after.

He looked deep into her eyes. 'Wherever I go, wherever this life may take me, I shall find you again, you may be certain of that. It is in the stars that we shall meet again.'

✿

Pirlipata was the first to leave.

Claren and Fin were dispatched to fetch sleighs. While they waited, Legat handed over a purloined correspondence of King Gelum's – which detailed intelligence of Crackatuck collecting its troops, its anger at their abducted princess and King Gelum's looming invasion sword-sharp and on the precipice of marching up the Thieves Road towards Everwood. It was imperative she rode fast to smooth the situation down.

'They must have received my note,' Pirlipata had said, her smile bright as her armour. 'They had missed me after all.' When Claren and Fin returned with two sleighs, she took one. Then turned to Dellara. 'Are you certain you do not require my assistance?' she asked, taking up the reins.

'There is much to do but I have spoken with Legat and I shall appoint Robess as my counsel and advisor. I shall be fine,' she said firmly.

Pirlipata's answering smile shredded Marietta's poise. 'I never considered otherwise,' Pirlipata told the new queen. 'After I have addressed the situation in Crackatuck, I shall return. Then we might work together to set up a new order between our lands.' She turned to Marietta, who was attempting to compose herself. Pirlipata's eyes rimmed with tears of her own. 'Meeting you brought fresh happiness into my life. These past moontides I have come to treasure you as one of my closest friends. I shall never forget you, Marietta.'

Marietta leant over the sleigh to embrace her. 'Neither will I, Pirlipata. You are so very dear to me and have been the sunlight in a long winter.'

They watched her leave, pulling out into the eternal night, returning home at last.

Dellara was the next to leave, escorted by Claren and Fin. Marietta stood beside her sleigh. Dellara's smile was that of a proud parent. 'Who might have known that when King Gelum claimed a dancer for his newest pet, she'd bring his entire palace crashing down.'

Marietta smiled. 'And I can think of no finer queen.'

'And I shall never need an heir, being immortal, which solves that little conundrum,' Dellara said, her delight plain on her face. 'Though once all is done and told, I should be most interested in adopting a Mistpointian way of ruling.'

'They elect their rulers, do they not?' Marietta asked. 'I should not have thought you would care to relinquish your crown.'

Dellara's delight deepened. 'I never claimed I would. If I recall rightly, you once explained to me at length the system you possess in your kingdom. Perhaps I shall emulate that.'

Marietta laughed. Then Dellara looked at her, serious once more, and her throat tightened, knowing that this was it, their farewell, the last words they would ever exchange. She clasped Marietta's hands. 'Be safe and strong. Never dull your sparkle for anyone else, flame fiercely into your own glittering future. We are not so unlike, you and I. We're angry girls with hearts made of glass.'

Marietta smiled over the shine of threatening tears. 'It is not like you to so freely admit a weakness.'

Dellara's grin reappeared, bloodier than before. 'Who said anything about it being a weakness? Nothing can cut like glass.'

Marietta choked out a laugh.

The shadows in Dellara's grey eyes drifted like smoke. 'Now you had better leave. It's time to go and flay your demons.'

Fin took the reins, smiled at Marietta. Claren saluted her. When Dellara — Queen Dellara — rested a hand on Marietta's shoulder, a brief, tender touch, Marietta pulled her towards her and embraced her. Then, with a snap of the reins, Fin sent the moose charging back towards the palace with their new queen, where her own glittering future awaited her.

Leaving Marietta and Legat alone in the forest.

Once, Marietta had considered the Endless Forest filled with horrors, twisting shadows and dark whispers. Now, gazing at Legat, the Star Lights gently rippling away, revealing a midnight sky rich with stars, it felt a magical winter wonderland.

Before Legat could speak, Marietta kissed him. She pulled him towards her, suddenly needing his arms around her. But a hidden tree root tripped her and she tumbled back into the snow. Legat stood for a moment, surveying her from above, his lips reddened from her kiss as she'd desperately eked out their inevitable farewell, his hair tousled from her fingers. His shirt ripped and stained from where she'd almost lost him. Her heart beat faster at the sight of him. He slowly, deliberately cast off his jacket and laid it down on the snow. Marietta brushed her cloak off and sat there, surrounded by forest and moonlight and the man she wanted. She reached for him and he went to her, kissing her with urgency, their limbs entwined, his muscles flexed as he held himself above her, her hands slipping inside his torn shirt, gliding down his bare back, marvelling at the new skin that had mended him.

He smiled, reached out to frame her face in his hands, tenderly rubbing her lip with his thumb before kissing her. His lips soft and gentle, his hands sliding to her neck, Marietta lost herself in him, time melting away in a syrup-sweet current. She sighed and grazed his back with her nails as their rhythm grew more urgent. Hungrier. He groaned and found his way beneath her dress, exploring her with his mouth, teasing her with his tongue until she cried out for more and his hands sank lower. 'No matter what becomes of us I shall never stop being the luckiest man alive for having had you wander into my life,' he said, his voice rough as he lowered his head, his lips grazing hers in a breathless kiss that sent her spinning.

She unbuttoned his trousers, wanting more, needing more, and wrapped her hand around him until he kissed her harder and flipped them around. She traced his face in her hands, memorising it until she knew it would fill her dreams forevermore. 'I want you,' she whispered, watching his throat bob up and down, his eyes darken at her words.

'Are you certain?'

She nodded, biting her lip. He leant forwards and kissed her sweetly, lifting her atop him, slow and soft and tender until they were pressed together, moving as one. Marietta buried her cries in his shoulder as he filled his hands with her, coaxing her to fresh heights until she was soaring, as incandescent as a meteor shower.

After, she lay in his arms, Legat's touch trailing along her back as they looked up at the starry sky together.

As the night deepened, Marietta couldn't bear the thought of leaving Legat's side. Lying there with his arms wrapped around her, her heart warm at the time they'd spent together, she felt she could never grow cold.

Until he whispered, 'Come, we must return you to your world.'

The fir trees were shadowed, the snow coating their branches gleaming in starlight. Marietta felt as if she and Legat were the sole two occupants in this world of snow and stars. As they walked through the forest, she glanced up at him to find him already gazing down at her. His smile was a beam of moonlight. It tugged at something deep within her.

Though they maintained a careful watch, Marietta had to admit she had never glanced back upon her arrival and so had not the faintest notion what they were searching for.

'Doors might resemble anything,' Legat said after a while. 'And I have heard tell of a thousand worlds, a hundred other lands a mere door away. Yet I have never heard the slightest mention of a world such as the one you hark from. It seems far vaster than anything I know.'

'What are you attempting to tell me?' Marietta asked quietly. She hoped it would take all night to locate her door just so she might carve out those extra hours with Legat. Her theory that it ought to be easier to bid him farewell this way was proving refutable.

'That if this Drosselmeier is as powerful as you say, then it is entirely possible that he created this portal solely for you. It may not endure once you have crossed it once more. And your world may not possess another door back to Everwood.'

'I know.'

A short while later, they found it.

A vintage armoire stood half-buried in snow. Surrounded by firs with delicate snowflakes pooling in the engraved roses that graced the pale cream wood.

Legat lifted Marietta, wrapping his arms around her as she memorised each touch, every kiss, each word he spoke, knowing that she would never forget them as long as she lived. Never forget him. Even when she had aged beyond recognition, gazing up at a different sky, a different world of constellations mapped out there, she would think of Legat.

'This is the hardest thing I have ever had to do.' Marietta leant her forehead against Legat's.

'And I.' Legat held her close, kissed her deeply. His lips tasted of chocolate and snow, salted from her tears. His too, she realised, as his butterscotch eyes burnt into hers. 'And I shall never stop thinking of you,' he said. 'No matter how many kings and queens come and go, how many stars join the skies, my heart shall be yours forevermore.'

She kissed him in response. Bit his lip to hear his soft growl, their kisses raw and wild, salt-flecked and laced with sweet sweet agony.

'I shall disregard your warning for I know within my soul that one day I shall return to you,' she said as he cupped her face, watching her mouth. 'I have witnessed magic once in my world; now that I know it exists I shall find a way. Locate a door and come back to you. I promise.'

'I do not wish for you to spend the rest of your days thinking of me. Go out there and chase your ambitions, Marietta,' Legat said huskily. 'Do not condemn yourself to a half-lived life. Live your life with all the richness of your dreams. Find someone to love. Though when you do care to remember me—' He withdrew a hand from his jacket. His fingers uncurled to reveal a small mouse, carved from ice. 'Perhaps you might keep this close. The ice is enchanted to never melt.'

'I will find you.' She smiled through her tears, slipping the mouse into her pocket. 'We have already said goodbye before; what is one more world between us? After all, you said it was in the stars that we meet again.'

He rested his forehead against hers. 'Then there is something you ought to know,' he whispered. 'If you should ever need it to find me once more, my starname is Vivoch. Each time I look up at the stars, I shall fill my thoughts with you.'

She kissed him hard. 'I love you, Legat,' she said.

Then she turned and ran through the door before she might hear him tell her not to come back, hear him say goodbye.

Chapter Forty-Four

The darkness felt thick and sticky, as if Everwood wasn't quite ready to relinquish its hold on her. Marietta passed between layers of worlds and magic she couldn't begin to fathom. It weighed her down, muddied her head. A faint chiming sounded in the distance and she stumbled towards it, the crunch of snow beneath her threadbare pointe shoes thinning as the chiming grew louder. Nearer.

The grandfather clock.

One final crunch and she felt the unmistakeable shift from snow-laden fir forest to wooden boards, exchanging the scent of snow, pine needles and sugar for wood and well-oiled mechanisms. A low light skulked round the edges of a rectangular panel ahead. Marietta pushed it open. She staggered out onto the elaborate set that Drosselmeier had constructed in the Stelle ballroom.

The grandfather clock was chiming midnight.

As the final chimes sounded, Marietta watched the clock seal itself shut. When she tried to open it once more, her fingers glided over the varnished wood; the panel no longer existed. She took a deep breath and turned to her own world.

The set was a distant memory. On occasions when her thoughts had turned to home during those months locked in the frozen sugar palace, she had conjured images of it decked out in all its festive glory. An exact replica of the last time she'd set eyes upon it. Yet now she was standing here it was odd that it hadn't changed. Perhaps her parents had busied themselves with other matters. Or Frederick may have insisted on it; he was the most sentimental of the lot of them. Down to the snow globe with its tiny enchanted visions that she'd left perched on the stage, everything was identical. Except her. Her hair was a wild tangled creature, scattered with pine needles, her dress was still torn from her entry to Everwood and her pointe shoes were tattered. All marked her with the twist her life had taken, down to the scars she wore on her skin like a story.

She walked slowly across the stage. Picked up the snow globe and shook it. The flurries settled round a snowy fir forest with a tiny sleigh wandering through the trees. When she squinted, she discerned it was pulled by moose and carried a sole occupant.

The grandfather clock measured out the final chimes of the midnight hour.

An awareness prickled at Marietta in the silence that came rushing in. Snow globe still in hand, she whirled round.

Drosselmeier stood at the corner of the stage, leaning against a column, observing her. He was clad in the same suit which he had worn on Christmas Eve and in a crack of ice it all came back to her like a blizzard. His hands on her. Entrapping her within the ballroom. Ensuring she fled into a strange, cruel, wonderful world of magic and pain. Sending her into that world to toy with her, bend her mind to his, manipulate her until she shattered like a bauble. Yet she had not.

'It is still Christmas Eve here,' he said.

'And you are the Grand Confectioner,' she replied, finally voicing the suspicion that had haunted her for some time.

He inclined his head, holding out his arms like a show master. 'You made for irresistible entertainment.'

Marietta's world shuddered around her, the walls of her life turned fragile and pliable. She forced her heart to slam its doors shut, to resist asking the most precious question that danced upon the tip of her tongue. Instead she asked, 'How did you come to possess such power? From whence did it originate and for what purpose did you send me into another world? I can only imagine you desired to punish me. Prove that I might be under your control.'

Drosselmeier's smile chilled his pale-blue eyes. 'Magic is without reason. Though I am greatly delighted to hear your acknowledgement of my power. That ought to ensure what is to come will proceed more smoothly.'

Marietta tamped her swelling emotions down. Iced her voice with calmness. 'You dispatched me into a prison. I might have been killed or spent an eternity rotting away for your own amusement.'

'And yet you were not.'

'Whatever you believe is to come, whatever insidious purpose you might be planning to wield your power for, I assure you that I shall hold no part in it.'

Drosselmeier's lips carved into a thin smile. Something elusive darted over his face. Marietta had glimpsed it before on occasion and wondered at it but this time she placed it. It was magic. It crackled in the air around him, strong and heady and potent. Once, she had not been able to recognise it; yet after a spell in Everwood, she had become well acquainted with all manner of enchantments. She took a step back. She had been naïve enough to believe that being in a magicless world would have ensured they were on more of an equal level. Yet his magic seemed stronger than ever. 'What are you?' she breathed.

'I am but a man.'

She shook her head as he walked slowly towards her, relishing her reaction, examining her portance for a flutter of fear. 'No ordinary man could have the abilities that you possess.'

A strange light gleamed in his eyes. 'Ah, yet I have never claimed to be an ordinary man. I tend to find ordinary things rather dull, do you not agree?' He reached her then, with her back pressed against the castle set. He stretched out a hand towards her.

She slapped it away. 'From whence does your power originate?' She wished she could save even a mere crumb of his magic for the future. A future where she might seek out Legat once more.

Drosselmeier surveyed her with cold amusement. 'Oh, *meine kleine Tänzerin*,' he murmured, 'attempting to prise her way into my secrets. Do you think me that foolish to share them with you?'

Marietta said nothing.

He leant closer. 'My power is ranked *with the gods of old and the sons of Finn, with the queens that reigned in the olden fables.*'

Marietta sighed. She rather missed the directness of the Everwoodians. Here, the mere act of holding a conversation with another seemed fraught with pretension. 'I find your constant espousing of your own merit and quoting poems to be most tiresome. Yet it is of little consequence now. Your magic might be as deep as a starlit sky and I still should not accept your betrothal.'

The smile slid from his face.

'Nothing holds more value for me than my own freedom.' Marietta evaded his arm and walked off the stage.

A ripple of thick fabric sounded behind her. Marietta glanced back, wary at once. Drosselmeier had opened the red velvet curtains on the stage. He stood between them, his form shadowed. 'You are not a woman that might find satisfaction in dresses, jewels or furs. Not since you have had a taste of magic. The very blood in your veins shall clamour for it. Only I possess the means with which to grant you a life of enchantment.'

Marietta looked away. 'I have had quite enough of your magic.' She continued walking down the ballroom until she reached the doors. Her heart beat in irregular rhythms as she grasped the handle, daring to hope they might be unlocked. She needed to seize an opportune moment in which to secure a weapon. Arm herself against Drosselmeier's advancements, against the magic he would wield against her, attempting to bend her to his will. She needed a blade.

'What of your darling captain?' Drosselmeier called after her.

Slowly, Marietta turned. His gaze rubbed against her skin. Spoke of ownership. It discomfited her.

'Would you prefer your rather touching farewell to be a true parting?'

The knowledge that he had been watching her at her most raw, intimate moments sent her thoughts pirouetting. Witnessing her and Legat's slow descent into something more, something deeper. 'Your elaborate manipulation took a misstep, did it not?' She voiced her creeping realisation. 'You desired to exert your power over me. Manipulate me for your own entertainment, my punishment for daring to decline your proposal.' Her laugh was bitter and gleeful at once. 'The last thing you had expected was for me to fall in love with another. A love which you would then be forced to witness.'

Drosselmeier's face might have been carved from ice for the lack of reaction he gave. The smallest twitch in the corner of his mouth betrayed his fury. A single finger tapping against his arm. The rigidity of his spine.

'I shall never be yours.' Marietta's whisper twisted with spite. 'Yet I gave all of myself to him.'

Drosselmeier stormed down from the stage. Marietta opened one of the doors but with a click of Drosselmeier's fingers, it ripped from her grasp and slammed shut, sealing her inside the ballroom once more. She let forth a scream of rage as she pulled at it but it was to no avail.

Drosselmeier tore the snow globe from her hand. 'Actually I do believe you shall be. For if you do not become mine—' He shook the snow globe slowly, his gaze resting on Marietta as the snow settled. It revealed Legat, sitting in a sleigh in the midst of the forest. 'Well, I shall make a true soldier out of your precious captain.' He held a hand above the snow globe and, with a choked cry, Marietta watched Legat forced to his feet, his body turning rigid. His face adopted a strange cadence, his expression stiffening, taking on a resemblance of the nutcracker she had found beneath her pillow in Everwood.

'No,' Marietta whispered.

'A remarkable little charm,' Drosselmeier continued, 'and a nut-cracker is rather useful this time of year, is it not?' His smile was a wicked show of triumph.

Marietta lifted a foot forward. Pointed her toes. And snapped her leg up, shattering the snow globe with a single grand battement. She had not skills in steel and blade yet she possessed a great strength all of her own. In a tinkling of glass, the snow globe lost its magic and Drosselmeier's grasp on his failed. The miniature Legat shook off Drosselmeier's spell, his butterscotch eyes staring into the distance as if he could glimpse Marietta through the bounds of reality for a beat. She watched until the vision of him melted away.

Marietta glanced at Drosselmeier. His face had paled to the cold fury of an ice storm. Sparks raged between his fingertips. He opened his mouth to speak, to unleash some untold horror upon her.

In a flash of fear, Marietta spun past him and grasped a cande-labra from the nearest table.

Drosselmeier began muttering; unintelligible words pitched too low for comprehension.

Marietta's fingers tightened round the bronze candelabra, prepared to battle. A growing coldness against her leg tugged her attention down. When she slid a hand into her pocket, her fingers brushed ice. And paper.

Before Drosselmeier could draw another breath, Marietta swung the candelabra at his head. He evaded her with ease. As she had intended. She whipped her leg back in an attitude derrière Madame Belinskaya would have applauded. High enough for the box of her pointe shoe to crack into Drosselmeier's head. He staggered back, his magic flickering.

With shaking fingers, Marietta pulled out the small twist of paper the market woman had bestowed upon her when she'd first entered Everwood, tore it open and poured the entire contents on Drosselmeier.

The magic clouded out and Marietta stepped back. Drosselmeier had not yet regained his senses; his gaze was unfocused. He attempted to speak but coughed instead, having inhaled part of the cloud. The rest nestled against his skin.

Her heart shuddering beneath her bodice, Marietta watched the moment he became aware of his fate. Drosselmeier's fury swelled, his anger a visceral beast devouring his composure. He reached out but she danced away. Then Drosselmeier started to shrink. Marietta found herself unable to glance away. With a scream of rage, Drosselmeier shrank to the size of a child, then a baby. Marietta dropped the candelabra, frozen in morbid fascination. And still he continued to shrink until he was as small as the mice that had flitted over King Gelum's brocaded suits. Then, a thimble. A thimble-sized man, a real-life approximation of Tom Thumb, gesturing at her and shouting in tiny, high-pitched squeaks she failed to understand.

Yet this was no fairy tale.

Marietta looked down. 'I dance only for myself,' she told him.

Staring up at her, his chipped-ice glare still distinguishable in his miniature stature, Drosselmeier raised his hands. Tiny sparks of magic fluttered between them.

Yet he was still shrinking. Down and down until he was the size of sugar granules. Then, particles of dust.

Marietta leant down and blew. Watched as the man crafted from magic and nightmares simply floated away.

Chapter Forty-Five

When she reached her bedroom, she shut the door behind her and sank onto the floor. The wood was hard and scented with familiar polish. Her room was smaller than she'd remembered, as if it had inhaled some of the shrinking magic, too. It had been Christmas Eve for the entirety of her time in Everwood. Other than Drosselmeier, not a soul possessed a hint of an idea that she had been worlds away. And no one would believe the tales she could spin. It was a peculiar kind of isolation.

The pain of missing Legat was fierce, a branding she wore upon her heart. Yet had any of it truly been real or had they all been mere marionettes in Drosselmeier's puppet theatre? She wished she had a tangible memento to remind her it had all happened, been real. The good and bad, painful and delicious. To prevent the entire experience from melting like snow in the first wash of spring. She withdrew the ice mouse from her pocket with a pang. Oh, how she wished Legat had crafted it from stone or sugar.

She closed her eyes and took a steadying breath.

Something warm wriggled in her hands. Marietta's eyes flew open. A real mouse was peering back at her. With snow-white fur and a sugarplum-pink nose. She laughed. 'It seems Everwood had one last sigh of magic.' She named him Marzipan for the streets of that enchanting town and the night she had danced with Legat when her hair had been spun with marzipan. Ever since, the scent had wended its way into her dreams, filling them with the memory of his touch.

She had sunk to the depths of fear and despair and emerged victorious, imbued with a courage she had been capable of all along and fortified by her wits. There was one final plan yet to enact.

Pulling together wisps of ideas and spinning them into her own kind of magic, Marietta eased her pointe shoes off and hung up her dress. The petticoat beneath was the elaborate confection Dellara had insisted upon. It was ivory and enchantments dripped off it in puffs of vanilla and marzipan, the spangled icicles losing their sparkle and trickling to the hemline. Marietta folded it in tissue paper in an attempt to retain the last, lingering snap of magic in a world that couldn't sustain it. Instead she pulled on a simple nightdress then laid her head down upon her silk pillow to sleep the night away in her own bed.

The following morning, on Christmas Day, Marietta rose late, pulled on a robe, and wandered along the corridor to her drawing room, sleep still tickling her mind with wild fancies and shadowed figures. As she awaited her brother, she sifted through a small stack of envelopes, no doubt delivered by her lady's maid, Sally, during their Christmas celebrations. Yesterday, she amended to herself, fumbling to order time. Letters from her correspondences, Christmas cards and, residing at the very bottom of the stack, an envelope stamped with the return address of the Nottingham Ballet Company.

Marietta opened it with trembling hands.

Dear Miss Stelle,
We are delighted to confirm your acceptance ...

Marietta scanned the lines and closed her eyes. Held the paper tightly to her chest. She had fallen out of her turn during the audition, victim to Drosselmeier's magic. Yet she recalled how the judges' eyes had seemed glazed over, their attention scattered. They must not have seen it after all.

'Merry Christmas, old girl. Now I do realise you are playing the principal role in *The Sleeping Beauty* but I truly had not expected you to commit yourself this heartily to it. Were you intending to sleep the day away in its entirety?'

Marietta laughed and embraced her brother. 'It is good to see you, Frederick.'

'Steady on, what's all this?' he asked and she knew that if she glanced up at him that instant, his brow would be furrowed, pleased but befuddled at her show of affection.

Marietta relinquished her hold on him. 'Nothing but the sentimentalities of the season.'

'That was quite some night. Though I noticed you disappeared before midnight; where did you vanish to?' Frederick raised his eyebrows. 'I would have accompanied you, you know.'

Oh, the things she longed to confide in him. Of a world of enchantments and exquisite creations that set your imagination aflame. Where you might find yourself and follow your star. The sisterhood and first love she had left there. Instead she struggled back into her societal poise like an old dress, over-starched and poorly fitting, and offered him a smile. 'I felt the most incessant urge to rehearse for today.'

'Well, you quite deprived me of the chance to gift you this.' He handed her a small box with a satin bow affixed on top.

She opened it to discover a gold ballet slipper on a glistening chain, delicate in its size and detailed down to the diamond bow on its laces. 'Why, it is beautiful. Thank you, Frederick.' She fastened it round her neck and pressed it to herself.

'I am glad you admire it. I wanted you to always possess a reminder of that which you love,' he said.

Marietta hesitated. 'Freddie, I've been accepted to the Company.' She showed him the letter.

'Oh, Ets—' He took it. Read it twice through. 'I was unaware you had even auditioned.' He handed her it back.

'I shall not hear a word against it; my mind is quite made up, you know.'

He gave her an evaluating look. 'Yes, I do believe it is. I am proud of you, you know that. Though I had wanted an easier path for you.'

'Sometimes the easy path is harder than one might ever imagine,' Marietta said softly. 'Was that why you decided to follow in Father's footsteps?'

Frederick seated himself on the wingback chair nearest where Marietta sat, at the little writing desk. 'Is that what you have thought of me? That I decided against fighting for what I wanted?'

'I confess I did not know what to think, Freddie. We speak of everything; why have we never spoken on this?'

Frederick rubbed a hand over his forehead. 'I fight every day, Ets. After a time, it simply grows wearisome. I can never hope to be with Geoffrey in the way in which he may be with his betrothed. It pains me to think of it, much less voice that pain.'

Marietta reached out, rested a hand on his shoulder. 'I wish the world was different for you. Perhaps one day it might be.'

'Perhaps. Until then, he is who I fight for. I paint every day and I shall continue to do so. Once I have my own house, Father cannot control where I direct my energies and I see no reason why I should not pursue my love of the arts alongside a successful career.' He offered Marietta a wry smile. 'I do enjoy the finer things in life; I should hate to relinquish my champagne and silks when I need not. I do believe the tortured artist's soul is romanticised, not a necessity for creating great art.'

Marietta felt her eyes glisten, her heart brighten like a crisp winter's day, when everything is lighter, cloudless. 'I am gladdened to hear your plans.' Frederick would paint, Legat would write and she would dance. 'As I hope you are for mine.' The world shone fiercer and Marietta blinked away her budding tears. 'For I cannot lose my brother.'

Frederick was suddenly at her feet. 'And you never shall,' he said firmly, clasping her hand. 'Though I worry for you, my loyalty remains, as ever, yours. Besides, you shall need someone to visit and supply you with some small luxuries.' He wrinkled his nose. 'I cannot imagine your new accommodations will be quite what you are accustomed to.'

Marietta's laugh took her by surprise. 'Oh, Frederick, you cannot imagine how your support has gladdened my heart.'

Marietta hummed to herself as she made her way back to her bedroom to dress for the day. A song infused with a magic more potent than anything Everwood had to offer. Hope.

Sally dressed Marietta in her corset, its rigid, unyielding shape unfamiliar after what seemed like months of forgoing one, and a dark-green taffeta with an overlay of French lace and jet beadwork. She pinned a spring of holly into her hair to mark the festive occasion and slung midnight beads over her dress. Marietta tucked her new golden necklace inside her bodice and looked into her cheval mirror, wondering if she appeared as altered as she felt. Frederick hadn't noticed the irrevocable changes that had been wrought on her yet he never had been gifted with observance. She smoothed down her dress and thought of Pirlipata. Marietta hoped the princess possessed a wardrobe of gowns in a rainbow of brilliant, glittering shades, not one of them gold.

Her daydreaming was interrupted by the announcement of breakfast.

Ever a formal affair in the Stelle household, Marietta walked downstairs to see her parents for the first time since she'd been swept away into Drosselmeier's dark and delicious magic. The house bore its familiar scent of tea, hothouse roses and the trailing smoke of her father's tobacco. The lack of sugared air was noticeable. Maids and valets scurried around in starched uniforms. Evergreen wreaths complemented Marietta's gown and the Christmas tree was as she'd remembered it; commandeering the drawing room in its robe of tapered candles, strung with ribbons, baubles and sugarplums. A clockwork mouse wore tracks around the Persian carpet, each perambulation slower than the last as its mechanism faded. It darkened Marietta's mood as she recalled the faceless guards that had been another invention of Drosselmeier's, in a world where his machinations ran far crueller and colder than anyone would know. She banished the thought at once and strolled on to the dining room. Everything felt duller and smaller as though she was peering into a cracked looking glass that distorted her own recollections of how things had been.

During breakfast, Marietta's attention kept drifting over to the windows, observing the pale English sun in its cloudy basin.

'Merry Christmas, darling Marietta,' Ida said upon her arrival, in a manner that touched Marietta. Perhaps her mother sensed that something had altered. 'I do so adore the festive season,' Ida continued, seating herself at the table and admiring the wreaths of ivy and holly festooned round the candles. Her attention slid across to Marietta. 'Though I do not doubt that the arrival of the new year shall bring about other occasions to celebrate.'

Disappointment clouded Marietta. She said nothing.

'Indubitably so,' Theodore chimed in from the head of the table, gesturing for his coffee to be poured. A valet scurried forth. 'Though I had an appointment earlier this morn to discuss matters further with Drosselmeier. I had thought our good doctor was keen to be wed at once, yet—'

Ida shot him a look of alarm. 'Why Theodore, you must temper his enthusiasm. I shall require sufficient time to organise a proper society wedding. It must be superlative in all regards.'

Frederick glanced at Marietta, his concern fading into quiet puzzlement when she smiled into her Sèvres coffee cup. She paid no heed to her parents' discussion as she added an extra lump of sugar to her cup with silver tongs, relishing her long-awaited taste of coffee.

'Must you interrupt me so?' Theodore met Ida's eyes in a clash of steel and willpower. He cleared his throat as Frederick frowned at him. 'As I was saying, I had believed him keen yet was most disgruntled to find him absent.'

'Perhaps he had forgotten? It is Christmas, after all,' Frederick said.

'That's the curious thing. I spoke with his butler and it transpires that he did not see Drosselmeier this morning. Neither did anyone witness his homecoming last night. It appears the man has quite vanished,' Theodore said.

After taking one final sip of her coffee, Marietta set her cup down. 'As it happens, I believe I was the last to speak with Drosselmeier. I am afraid he left most displeased. Perhaps he has disappeared to lick his wounds.' Her hands did not tremble as she recalled how he had dusted away to nothing last night. After all, it had been the consequences of his own actions that had led to his death. Marietta refused to allow guilt to stain her heart. Nor did she invite speculation that she might be blamed if his disappearance were to be investigated; for who would believe in such a thing as magic?

Ida stared at Marietta.

Theodore stood up. 'Do you mean to inform me that you refused his hand?'

'I did. And I do not hold any regrets on the matter. Mother, I told you that I should not be able to accept Drosselmeier's offer, that I could not marry the man. You ought to have taken it seriously,' Marietta said. She could not now tell them of his advances against her, even if she wished. Though no one could find her guilty of any crime, she desired to avoid the suspicion it would invite upon her.

'Oh, Marietta, of all the reckless acts—'

'I do not believe it reckless to stay true to one's intentions,' Marietta told her mother.

'Your decision, your attitude, displeases me,' Theodore said quietly, in a tone that once would have inspired fear in Marietta. Now, it merely rankled.

'That is no longer my concern,' she said. 'Now if you will excuse me, I must ready myself for this evening's performance.'

Chapter Forty-Six

Backstage that evening, Marietta sought Harriet and Victoria out. 'Have you received news from the Company?' she asked.

Harriet nodded. 'We have both been accepted.'

Victoria wrinkled her nose. 'Though I shall most definitely not be accepting their offer of residency. I doubt the contents of my wardrobe should fit within those ghastly tiny rooms.'

'So speaks a woman with the luxury of declining such an offer,' Harriet scoffed.

Marietta smiled, smoothing her dress down. The palest lilac with rose-pink sequins encrusted on the bodice, it sparkled like pink champagne. Frothing chiffon capped her shoulders and a dainty silver tiara marked her for the role of Aurora.

'What of you? How was your audition?' Harriet directed her shrewd gaze onto Marietta.

'It was fine.'

Victoria's frown creased her powder. 'And what of your results?' Her whisper was loud, prompting Harriet to gesture at the velvet curtains. Behind, a ballroom's worth of people were gathering, finding their seats as the ballet dancers in the prologue silently took up their positions. Marietta, Harriet and Victoria were in the wings, awaiting their introduction in the first act.

'And in the new year, I shall be moving into one of those ghastly tiny rooms.' Marietta laughed.

Harriet raised her eyebrows. 'Is that so?'

Victoria let out a theatrical gasp. 'Oh, Marietta, you are renouncing your fortune for your dancing? How *romantic*.'

'There's nothing romantic about a lack of money,' Harriet said. 'Honestly, Victoria. But Marietta—' she beamed '—that is wonderful news. Do let us know if there is anything we might do to ease your transition.'

Marietta's smile was warm honey, sweet happiness. 'I was wondering if we three might reconvene for afternoon tea at your convenience. I have been in a mood of contemplation these past days and there is much I should like to share.'

Victoria exchanged a look with Harriet. 'How curious. We would enjoy that but mightn't you give us a clue?'

'If we are all to dance together with the Company, I thought it might be nice for us to become more acquainted with each other,' Marietta said, a little awkwardly. At first, Dellara and Pirlipata's companionship had brightened her days yet by the end of her time in Everwood, they had become much more. A sisterhood. Marietta would not spend her time in the Company mourning their presence but would honour them by forging new friendships. She had learnt much about sharing herself with others and had no desire to devolve to her lone, closed state of being. Life held many challenges in store for her yet but she did not have to face them alone.

'It would be our pleasure,' Harriet said and Marietta's warm honey-smile spread, setting her spirits a-glow.

The music started. The curtains drew back, revealing Drosselmeier's glittering set to the audience, who gasped and clapped upon witnessing its moving mechanisms. Marietta, Victoria and

Harriet proceeded to watch their peers dance out the prologue. It was interposed with mimed storytelling that unravelled the scene of Aurora's christening and the fairy-tale gifts bestowed upon her. Marietta's smile turned wistful; she would have longed to glimpse Dellara's face on learning what constituted a fairy in this world. She was far more likely to sympathise with Carabosse.

Their turn arrived.

Marietta burst onto the stage, her steps playful and light, interspersed with pas de chats; quick, leg-flicking jumps, the carefree glee of a young princess at her birthday party written into the choreography. Her limbs like liquid poetry and starlight. Dancing soothed Marietta's aching loneliness, her yearning for Legat, Pirlipata, Dellara. Of another world she could no longer access. She had taken time to examine the grandfather clock earlier and it was sealed shut. Until, and if, she happened upon another door, she was confined to this world alone.

Ribboning across the stage in a string of piqué turns, her arms fluttering, she reached out to embrace the night. Shifting into chaînés; faster, tighter turns, Marietta kept spinning, her love of dance consuming her, secure in the knowledge that she had made the right decision.

Harp strings, sweetly plucked, signalled the beginning strains of the Rose Adagio.

Marietta concealed her deep breaths beneath a smile as she approached the fur-cloaked figures of the queen and king, filling her lungs before the challenging variation. The one that had defeated her, sent her falling in the midst of her audition. Yet Drosselmeier could never set eyes on her again; she herself had ensured that. She had been her own knight in armour, scaling the heights of her tower and setting herself free from Drosselmeier's dark mechanisms at play.

She laid her hand on each of her suitors as she maintained her en pointe position on a single leg, allowing each of the four to promenade her. She never once allowed her balance to lapse, nor her other foot touch the floor, not until she stepped away from the suitors and reached up for that high, unsupported arabesque en pointe, soaring into the stars. She held it as the ballroom dissolved into applause.

Marietta soaked in the moment before immersing herself back in the ballet and dancing the Christmas night away.

As the ballet reached its finale, the moment Marietta had been nervously awaiting arrived. With Harriet to one side of her, Victoria on the other, the rest of the dancers falling in around them, they curtsied as one in a révérence, to a storm of applause.

Marietta searched out her family. Theodore was frowning at the vacant seat beside him as if he expected Drosselmeier to suddenly materialise. Frederick was aiming his Sanderson camera at her as Geoffrey clapped heartily. Ida was fussing with the centrepiece. Marietta waited for Madame Belinskaya and the orchestra to each claim their share of applause before she stepped forward. The ballroom hushed, expectant of an encore.

'I would like to extend my deepest gratitude to you all for attending our Christmas performance of *The Sleeping Beauty* tonight,' she said, taking care to include several of their more esteemed guests in her gaze. 'Your patronage was most appreciated. And if you would care to view my upcoming performance, I am delighted to announce that it shall take place at the Theatre Royal, where I am to dance as a new member of the corps.'

A second wave of applause sounded. This one was accompanied by whispers and flitting looks at Theodore and Ida Stelle, rigid in their seats.

In a swoop of heavy velvet brushing against the floor, the curtains closed.

'And that concludes our final dance with the studio,' Victoria said, her face flushed, décolletage gleaming with sweat.

'I presume Madame Belinskaya wishes to speak with you,' Harriet told Marietta, the tell-tale thud of her cane making its way across the boards. She clasped her hand briefly. 'We shall speak further this week. I look forward to it.'

'As do I.' Marietta inclined her head and turned to their ballet mistress.

'Well, *devushka*, it seems you have chosen to honour what it means to dance ballet.' Madame Belinskaya leant closer in a swirl of pistachio-green chiffon and the scent of Jicky. 'Now your education in ballet can truly begin.'

'I shall miss your classes dearly,' Marietta said.

'No. Those classes shall be with you always.' Madame Belinskaya prodded Marietta with her cane. 'In there.' Her face powder cracked as she broke into a semblance of a smile. 'I look forward to seeing what greatness you shall gift the stage. Now, I do believe your family desires to speak with you.' Her forehead creased. 'They are awaiting you outside the ballroom. Take heart and do not waver from your path.'

Chapter Forty-Seven

Marietta exited the ballroom. The guests were deep in their saucers of champagne and otherwise occupied as she walked by in a whisper of tulle and chiffon. Couples were flocking to dance and the orchestra were busying themselves with playing a jaunty Christmas tune that was far simpler than Tchaikovsky's rigorous compositions.

She halted outside the library door. It was closed. Through it, she heard her parents discussing her in hushed tones.

'Are you leaving tonight?' She started and turned round.

Frederick was leaning against the wainscoting, watching her. She hesitated, then nodded.

'Go upstairs. Gather your things and speak to them on your way out. It will be better this way, give them less opportunity in which to act against your plans.' He walked over to her. 'I'll stall them while you pack.'

'Thank you,' she whispered.

After Marietta changed into a woollen travel dress and her warmest coat and gloves, she packed a brown leather case in a hurry. She couldn't resist adding a few of her finest gowns after she'd packed the case with her simpler dresses and warmest clothes which would be better suited to her new life. A couple of her most time-weathered books, ballet slippers. A box of her favoured pistachio macarons, a small pleasure for her first night alone. Aware that time was melting away, she swept the contents of her dressing table into her vanity case with one hand and looked around, her heart measuring the final beats of her life in this rose-patterned room. She slid out the top drawer of her bedside table. Marzipan stood on his hind legs and looked up at her, twitching his nose. A reminder of Legat in soft fur and quivering whiskers. 'Now to find a home for you,' Marietta murmured, scooping him up and setting him down in a silk-lined hatbox. She stabbed breathing holes into its lid with a forgotten hatpin and picked up her cases. With a final glance around, she folded her acceptance letter into her pocket. She had planned on departing the Stelle townhouse regardless of its contents, on renting a small room from the funds she'd garnered from selling her Cartier brooch. Yet now she had lodgings already secured for her. That letter was a dream shaped in ink and paper. A glimpse into the future she'd returned for. One that filled her heart with hope and music. She took a deep breath and walked downstairs.

'Exactly where do you suppose you are going?' her father said, awaiting Marietta at the bottom of the staircase.

Ida appeared at his side. She blanched upon catching sight of the cases, a slender hand coming to rest on her glittering neckline. 'Marietta, this is not the answer. Come, accompany me to the drawing room where we might discuss matters in a more befitting way.'

'I am afraid my mind is set on the matter. I am taking my leave,' Marietta said.

Frederick hurried into view. He instantly took measure of the situation. 'Let her go; you know well how tenacious she is.' He winked at Marietta and Ida whirled around.

'Frederick!'

'I am afraid, Mother, that there is no resolution available. We have a fundamental difference of opinion and I doubt this can be reconciled.'

Theodore began to speak. Marietta quelled him with a single pointed look. 'And Father, I have publicly announced my intentions and if I do not follow through then people shall take notice. I have also taken the care to write several letters to allies who will hold you accountable if you resist my departure.'

'I shall not stand in your way but if you so choose to leave then know this: you may not return. Neither shall you see one penny of your inheritance.'

Ida had to sit down. She looked pale at this turn of events.

Marietta's smile was slow. 'I shall hold you to that.' She stepped down and around him. Past Frederick, who pressed her hand as she went by, out to the foyer, where a footman scrambled to open the door for her, his eyes wide.

She walked out into the night, cutting a lone figure in the deserted streets of Nottingham. Windows were aglow with festive vignettes of families celebrating together. Marietta kept walking through the slumbering city and towards her new lodgings. Towards the future she had sacrificed everything for and which beckoned her with a glittering promise.

A tiny flake of snow fell onto her face. She paused and glanced up. Endless snowflakes were tumbling towards her; the very first snowfall of the year. A white Christmas.

Marietta laughed and spun in a circle, tilting her face up, snow collecting in her eyelashes and hair. The stars were invisible under a white sky yet she knew they were smiling down on her. She vowed to them, to Legat, that she would never stop dreaming.

She decided thereupon that in the tradition of Everwood, she would select a starname for herself.

Rêverie.

Acknowledgements

This book has long been a book of my heart but it wouldn't exist at all without my magical agent, Thérèse Coen, who utterly refused to give up on it. I'm forever grateful for everything you've done for me.

I owe an entire frozen sugar palace of thanks to my wonderful editor Katie Seaman, who has championed *Midnight* from the start and expertly worked her magic on it until it glittered. I can think of no-one else I'd rather have danced this *pas de deux* with; Team Unicorn!

Thank you to the amazing team at HQ Stories for welcoming me and making the most enchanting home for *Midnight*, complete with oodles of support and the shiniest proofs! Special thanks to Katrina Smedley (soul-collector) and Lucy Richardson for setting everyone a-flurry and being generally brilliant. Huge thanks to Charlotte Phillips for the cover of dreams. Thank you to Fliss Porter, Harriet Williams, Darren Shoffren and Angela Thomson for all their sales magic.

To Stephanie Garber, Sarah Morgan, Alex Bell, Sophie Anderson, Nydia Hetherington, Heidi Swain, Veronica Henry and Beth Cartwright, who were the first to read and blurb *Midnight*, thank you for your kindness and support.

For Lauren Cassidy (@fictiontea), Gavin Hetherington (How

to Train your Gavin) and Dan Bassett (@dantheman1504), I owe a whole Land of Sweets for your early championing of this book.

Thank you to Jenny and The Dance Studios for inspiring me with years of ballet classes.

To Amy McCaw for constantly cheering me on and being a generally lovely jewel of a friend.

For Vic James, LD Lapinski, and the Swaggers for all being truly excellent writing friends, deserving of a hundred special Mia hot chocolates!

To my wonderful friends: Christine Spoors, Alex McGahan, Sarah Hackmann/Mother of Ferns, thank you for always being there for me. For my Shakespearean Sisters, I couldn't do without you. And to Jonathan Norman, thanks for being the best ice-skating partner-in-crime.

Many thanks to everyone in my family that's cheered me on and celebrated my successes with me, especially my mum, who has always believed in the fairies at the bottom of the garden.

For Michael Brothwood, my husband, no matter how many kings and queens come and go, how many stars join the skies, my heart shall be yours forevermore.

Finally, to everyone that's picked up a copy of this book; my deepest thanks. I do hope you enjoyed the enchantments of Everwood.

ONE PLACE. MANY STORIES

Bold, innovative and
empowering publishing.

FOLLOW US ON:

@HQStories